KU-711-581

DEATH OF A
RIVER GUIDE

by

Richard Flanagan

ATLANTIC BOOKS
LONDON

First published in Australia in 1994 by McPhee Gribble

This edition published in Great Britain in 2004 by Atlantic Books,
an imprint of Grove Atlantic Limited.

Copyright © Richard Flanagan, 1994

The moral right of Richard Flanagan to be identified as the author of this work has been
asserted in accordance with the Copyright, Designs and Patents Act of 1988.

All rights reserved. No part of this publication may be reproduced, stored in a retrieval
system, or transmitted in any form or by any means, electronic, mechanical,
photocopying, recording, or otherwise, without the prior permission of both the
copyright owner and the above publisher of this book.

10 9 8 7 6 5 4 3 2 1

ISBN 1 84354 219 6

Printed in Great Britain by
Mackays of Chatham plc, Chatham, Kent

Atlantic Books
An imprint of Grove Atlantic Ltd
Ormond House
26–27 Boswell Street
London WC1N 3JZ

DEATH OF A RIVER GUIDE

Richard Flanagan was born in Tasmania in 1961. *Death of a River Guide* is his first novel and won the Australian Fiction Award 1996. His second novel, the multi-award winning *The Sound of One Hand Clapping* was one of the biggest-selling novels in Australian history. His most recent novel, *Gould's Book of Fish* received international acclaim and won the Commonwealth Writers Prize 2002.

International reviews of *Death of a River Guide*:

'Richard Flanagan's first novel could well become a classic, doing for Tasmania what Gabriel Garc'a Márquez did for Colombia or William Faulkner for Mississippi.' *Mercury*

'A powerful novel, its narrative movement skilfully negotiating narrative rapids and eddies of memory... A compelling celebration of river and landscape' *Age*

'The flow of language brilliantly simulates Tasmania's mighty Franklin river... A powerful and exciting odyssey that can fairly claim to be an epic' *Weekend Australian*

'A striking novelistic debut about life and history reeling before a man's eyes as he drowns in the Franklin. A sort of Tasmanian magical realism.' *Sunday Age*

'There is a great sense of humanity about this book, a concern for the spirit as well as for the trials of physical existence... Uplifting and immensely rewarding.' *Australian Book Review*

'*Death of a River Guide* makes good on a truly soaring ambition and flirts with literary greatness... An indelible vision of how surely the history of a land plays its part in shaping the interior landscape of the human beings who occupy it.' *Chicago Tribune*

'Beautiful and lyrical' *Washington Post Book World*

'Haunting and ambitious... realistic and biting... Aljaz's ancestral secrets – miscegenation, convicts in the family, and a legacy of violence – are, of course, the 'secrets' of Tasmanian history.' *New York Times Book Review*

'A novel of consummate artistry and towering humanity... An enormous, intricate, intimate tapestry not only of the wilderness, but also of a family, an expansive tribal community.' *Baltimore Sun*

'*Death of a River Guide* is the birth of a daring talent. The mythos here is wholly Australian, but Flanagan uses rafting as effectively as Hemingway used bull fighting to explore the existential struggle to act nobly in the face of death.' *Christian Science Monitor*

'A triumphant tour de force... A novel that succeeds brilliantly in its audacious design and offers the smart reader complex and memorable rewards.' *Raleigh News & Observer*

to Majda
my rock my love

Acknowledgements

I would like to thank Debbie Cox, who taught me that writing is a craft, both serious and strangely powerful. Sophie Cunningham for believing in me as a writer. Meredith Rose for marking the copy with a creative grace. Patrick Hall for an inspired cover illustration. Tom Errey, Peter Hay, Margaret Scott and Greg Lehmann and the others who gave of their time to comment upon various drafts. Darryl Gerrity, who loves people, perhaps too much. My family, large and lustrous.

To Arts Tasmania who gave me a grant that allowed me to finish the book, I am grateful. But to my fellow doormen at the council, Leon Wright and Mick Lonergan, who caught me scribbling the beginnings of this novel in the burghers' time and looked the other way, I am indebted.

Who Present, Past & Future sees
Whose ears have heard,
The Holy Word,
That walk'd among the ancient trees.

William Blake

That is at bottom the only courage that is demanded of us: to have courage for the most strange, the most singular and the most inexplicable that we may encounter. That mankind has in this sense been cowardly has done life endless harm; the experiences that are called 'visions', the whole so-called 'spirit-world', death, all those things that are so closely akin to us, have by daily parrying been so crowded out by life that the senses with which we could have grasped them are atrophied. To say nothing of God.

Rainer Maria Rilke

— One —

As I was born the umbilical cord tangled around my neck and I came into the world both arms flailing, unable to scream and thereby take in the air necessary to begin life outside of the womb, being garrotted by the very thing that had until that time succoured me and given me life.

Such a sight you never clapped eyes upon!

And not only because I was being half strangled. For I was born in the caul, that translucent egg in which I had grown within the womb. Long before my damp rusty head was crowned between my mother's heaving flesh as I was painfully pushed out into this world, the caul should have ruptured. But I miraculously emerged from my mother still enclosed in that elastic globe of life, arriving in the world not dissimilarly to how I am now to depart it. I swam within a milky blue sac of amniotic fluid, my limbs jerking awkwardly, pushing with futile gestures at the membranes, my head obscured outside the sac by the wreath of umbilical cord. I made strange, desperate movements as if condemned always to see life through a thin mucousy film, separated from the rest of the world and the rest of my life by the things that had until then protected me. It was and is a curious sight, my birth.

I didn't know then, of course, that I was about to be exiled from my imperfect circle, itself just exiled from its own enclosing circle, Mama's womb, the walls of which suddenly, less than a day before, began moving most violently and extremely. If I had been forewarned of all the troubles that were so soon to befall me I would have stayed put. Not that it would have made any difference. The walls pulsed and pushed solely with the purpose of expelling me from a world about which I felt nothing but good, and against which I had done nothing bad, unless my continued and vital growth from a few cells to a complete person can be construed as some aggressive action.

The roof and floor of my world worked ceaselessly from that time onward, the power of each movement more powerful than the previous, like a tidal wave gathering size as it skips over each new reef. To such a violent determination I, of course, could not do other than acquiesce, allowing myself to be battered up against the narrow walls of the birth canal, my head squashed this way and that. And why this indignity? I had loved that world, its serene pulsing darkness, its warm sweet waters, loved the way I could effortlessly roll this way and that. Who brought light to my world? Who brought doubt to my actions that were once innocent of reason or consequence? Who? Who started me on this journey I never asked to begin? Who?

And why did I acquiesce?

But how do I now know this? I can't know it. I must be fantasising.

And yet . . . and yet . . .

The midwife quickly and expertly unravelled the cord, then pushed her thumb into the caul as if she were Little Jack Horner searching for the plum and, ripping her thumb upwards toward my head, burst the bag open. A small deluge of fluid fell upon the dusty floorboards of that small room in Trieste and made them as slippery as life. A scream followed. And laughter.

Mama kept the membranes. Later she dried them, for the caul that a baby is born in is considered to be of the greatest luck, fate's guarantee that neither the baby born within the caul nor the possessor of the membranes will ever drown. She was going to keep them to give me when I was an adult, but in my first winter I fell badly ill with pneumonia and she sold the membranes to a sailor so that she could buy me some fruit. The sailor had the membranes sewn into his jacket, or at least that was what he told Mama he planned to do with them.

After my birth that night all those years ago, the midwife – who was known by the magnificent name of Maria Magdalena Svevo but whose true name, which she hated, was Ettie Schmitz – switched off the harsh electric light and opened the shutters, now that there were no screams of the agony of a woman giving birth to fall upon the ears of those in the street outside. The pleasant autumn night air and the stench of the Adriatic flowed in, that peculiarly close European smell of millennia of war and sadness and survival, and this smell battled with the open bloody smell of birth that scented that little bare room, with its draped blanket for a door and its crumbling plaster walls and its solitary silverfish-sanded picture of the Madonna touching a bleeding heart with the outstretched fingers of her right hand. Ah, those fingers! So perfectly long and soft and silky. So unlike Maria Magdalena Svevo's short battered pinkies.

Maria Magdalena Svevo got down upon her knees and with those rough worker's hands and a rag began scrubbing off what blood and birth fluids had not yet seeped into the floorboards, the stains of which, she mused, were an archive of human life, a record written in fading blotches of blood and wine and sperm and urine and faeces of the progress of life from birth to youth to love to disease to death. As Maria Magdalena Svevo scrubbed, my mother watched her large round back rock back and forth, a half moon silvered by the light of the full moon that filled the room of my birth with its peaceful illumination.

How do I know such things? Maria Magdalena Svevo, who had untangled the cord from my neck, laughing, and who had continued to laugh about it every time she saw me ever after, told me only a little about my birth, so it cannot be from her. And Mama told me almost nothing. She didn't even bother to tell me that I was born in Trieste until I was ten – after we heard the news that Maria Magdalena Svevo had nearly died there in somewhat comic circumstances upon a return trip to her home. Two drunk students had accidentally ridden their moped into her at the market. It was generally considered to have been typical of her strength and stubbornness that whereas the two students died within twenty-four hours, the octogenarian Maria, after spending three months in hospital, returned to Australia in better health than she had left it. But then, as my father Harry often said, she always took more than she was given.

When Mama paid her the standard fee for assisting in my birth, she felt underpaid and on the way out swiped a bottle of prized whiskey – my mother's only bottle of whiskey, which she had gained in consequence of a night of lust with my father. That, and her unwanted son, me, was all she had at that point obtained from my father, who was then serving time in a nearby prison. My mother frequently lamented she would have been much better served if Maria Magdalena Svevo had taken me and left her the whiskey. Maria Magdalena Svevo laughed at that too.

'You Cosinis are all the bloody same,' she would say. 'You get given the gift of life and what happens? You want to throw it away! Your mother wants to give you away, and you were so unwilling to come into the world that you tried to strangle yourself the moment you saw daylight at the end of the canal. Huh!' And with that she would resume smoking her cigar, a vice she shared with my mother, from whom she was not above nicking the occasional smoke.

'She is only lessening her own life and prolonging mine,' Mama would say of such petty thefts, 'and for the fact of having to spend less of my life in her company I am truly grateful.'

Which was less than honest, for in all truth they revelled in each other's company but were loathe to admit it. When Maria Magdalena Svevo did buy her own cigars, which was but rarely, she bought an obscure Austrian brand that came packaged in a cardboard box embossed with the double-headed eagle. 'The last flicker of the empire,' she would laugh as she took the final delicious fruity draught of smoke from the butt end of the cigar before stubbing it out. Her favourite subject of conversation was the pleasure of the last cigar. 'How many people never know that pleasure of the final smoke? Cigars, cigarettes, the principle is the same. Tell me, how many, Aljaz?' She always made my name sound soft and beautiful. Sometimes I even fancied she took some pleasure from feeling my name gravel up her rutted and tarred throat to slowly billow from her bloated lips in clouds of smoke. 'Ali-ush, Ali-ush, Ali-ush,' she would incant like a nursery rhyme to no one in particular, and I would look up and smile and sometimes she would see me, smile back, and resume her monologue on smoking.

'Then on their deathbed they smoke first one, then another, then another, never knowing which is the last smoke before death, and being therefore unable to savour that last fragrant moment of taste.' She would point her huge cigar at me, waving it like a conductor's baton, to make her point. 'And that is why, Aljaz Cosini, you must make it a point to give up smoking at least once a year — for then it is an annual pleasure to be looked forward to and long remembered after. Like taking the waters.' She would tap the double-headed eagle cigar box, wink at me knowingly, and laugh. 'Like empires renouncing wars.' I understood almost nothing she said, but it all seemed to remain with me, embossed on my brain like the double-headed eagle on that cardboard box, vivid, meaningful, if one could only understand what such things meant.

Maria Magdalena Svevo had innumerable stories about her last cigars. Some she spoke of fondly as great and memorable moments of romance or tragedy, others as times of small pleasures taken easily, remembered lightly. There were the melancholic last cigars, such as the one she smoked on the day she left Trieste to go and live in Australia, sitting on the balcony of the *pension* of her despised son-in-law Enrico Mruele, looking at the sun rise one last time over her beloved home town. She would recount most movingly how her tears dropped onto her hand and ran from there onto the cigar, adding a bitter briny after-bite to her last taste of smoke. There was the amusing last cigar she had when she and Mama got jobs at the jam factory on the Hobart wharves, putting labels on the jam tins. The butt went into a tin of pineapple and melon jam. Maria Magdalena Svevo was a woman for whom quality was everything and she very much loved the Australian phrase 'Sydney or the bush', which summed up much of what she thought about life. Why had she put the butt in a tin of jam that would be opened by some poor housewife in the new and hyperventilating Australian suburbia? 'Sydney or the bush,' she would reply, burnishing the phrase with dark smoke as she spoke. 'The jam they made was shit. People ought not be so foolish as to buy it. Either make good jam or don't eat it at all. That last cigar was my warning to the good Australian people upon this matter.' She would draw her right hand into a fist and throw a few jabs with the cigar jammed in between her fingers, a smouldering knuckle duster, to dramatise her final point. 'Good jam (*jab*) or no jam. (*jab*) But never that shit. (*jab*) Sydney or the bush.'

There were the tragic last cigars, such as the one she smoked at Mama's funeral, the ash of which she flicked into the grave as the priest intoned, 'Ashes to ashes, dust to dust.' This is a last cigar to which I can personally bear witness. The priest halted and his eyes rose in disgust. Everyone stopped looking into the grave and looked around at Maria Magdalena Svevo. She wore a black dress and a black hat with a sweeping brim in a style that may have been fashionable in Trieste in the 1930s. Certainly in Hobart, Tasmania, in 1968, it was not fashionable. On anyone other that Maria Magdalena Svevo it may well have looked ludicrous. On her it looked grand. From under that sweeping brim, her half-shaded eyes – those large dark brown eyes set so deep in wrinkles they looked like the half-soaked muscatel sultanas with which Mama used to make *stritzel* – with these extraordinary eyes, into which you felt if you dived you might never again surface, she fixed the priest with one of her most fiercesome stares. For a short fat woman, Maria Magdalena Svevo could look ferocious. She had, at such moments, what can only be called presence. In her sing-songy Triestino accent she said in a most commanding voice '"Vanity of vanities, saith the preacher. All *is* vanity."' And with that, flicked the stub out of her hand. '"One generation passeth away, and another generation cometh: but the *earth* abideth forever."' The glowing stub rose and fell in the most marvellous arc before all our assembled eyes, a smouldering spiral of smoke descending into the grave. When our collective gaze rose back up from the grave, it was to see Maria Magdalena Svevo's high heels (that she had bought especially for the occasion) swivel and Maria Magdalena Svevo stride off.

Ah, Maria Magdalena Svevo, would that you were here now, as I lie drowning, here of all places, on the Franklin River, looking up through aerated water at the slit in the rocks, above which I can make out daylight. It is not very far away, that daylight, and I would, if you were here, tell you how much I want to reach it. Sydney or the bush. Life or death. There are no other choices.

It makes me laugh to think that after all your smoking it is me rather than you who will die of lung failure. My lungs no longer feel like gigantic balloons burning up with a fierce fire. Well, that is not entirely correct, they still feel that way, but it no longer worries me; indeed, my mind has become entirely separate from the pain and is drifting in strange jerky motions like the air bubbles I can see above me, darting first this way, then, as if seized by some powerful magnetic current, tumbling the opposite way. Like those bubbles, my thoughts seem to have no specific direction, as much as I try to fix them on one point and move them along the path it indicates. The fire in my lungs I observe like a campfire in the receding distance, and my mind passes on to matters of much more immediate import, matters which, if they are still incomplete, if I remain unable to follow through, I still at least see with a clarity that I never possessed at the time they took place.

And then, before I can think it, I know.

I have been granted visions.

Suddenly it is clear what is happening to me.

I, Aljaz Cosini, river guide, have been granted visions.

And immediately I am unbelieving. I say to myself, This is not possible, I have entered the realm of the fabulous, of hallucinations, for there is no way that anybody stuck drowning could experience such things. But contradicting my rational mind is a knowledge that I was never previously aware of possessing. And the rational mind can only reason against that knowledge: that the spirit of the sleeping and the dying in the rainforest roam everywhere, see everything; that we know a great deal more about ourselves than we ever normally care to admit, except at the great moments of truth in our life, in love and hate, at birth and death. Beyond these moments our life seems as if it is one great voyage away from the truths we all encompass, our past and our future, what we were and what we will return to being. And in that journey away our rational mind is our guide, our mentor. But no longer. The rational mind is not persuaded by the knowledge – my knowledge – that everything I am seeing is true, that everything I see has happened. No matter. They may not be the facts of newspapers, but they are truths nevertheless. One generation passeth away, and another generation cometh. But what connects the two? What remains? What abideth in the earth forever?

I have been granted visions – grand, great, wild, sweeping visions. My mind rattles with them as they are born to me.

And I must share them, or their magic will become as a burden.

— Two —

Let me say that I am not surprised by this vision business. Not in the slightest. As far as I know, it runs in the family. Harry was forever having visions, mostly at the end of each week of hard drinking of cider and cheap riesling with Slimy Ted, his old crayfishing skipper. At his weekly barbeque, to which fewer and fewer of us came because of his increasingly erratic and drunken behaviour, Harry would address a whole range of animals who, apart from a few stray cats and mangy dogs, no one else could see, but whom Harry claimed greatly enjoyed the event and with whom, on occasion, he claimed blood relation. Cousin Dan Bevan, whom some members of the family claimed to be mad but who nevertheless was undeniably family, who could cure warts just by looking at them and who bit the tops off whiskey bottles before downing their contents in a few gulps, also saw things, although he saw them not only at the end of a bottle but also in the shape of warts. He saw all sorts of things, both bad and good, and around the Forth district in which he lived, his reading of local warts and carbuncles was treated with some seriousness. On Mama's side, her mother had the third eye and read fortunes in the dregs of turkish coffee and by this method foretold that worms would crawl out of Mama's stomach, which was more or less what happened. Of my fate my *staramama* was much vaguer: she only saw a bird wheeling in the sky.

So let me say that I am not surprised by this vision thing. But I am not sure if any of it adds up to much. I mean, what use to me is a vision of a bloody bird? Does that help me to work out whether I am fated to live or not and, therefore, whether I ought be struggling to survive or not? No, I can tell you it doesn't. A vision should give you some answers, shouldn't it? But all I see are more questions. It's not right, I tell you, it's crook and it's wrong. But I am not surprised by that either. Life has only ever been a constant puzzlement to me, so why should I expect death to suddenly make a whole lot of sense?

Let me also say that I am not even surprised to be here drowning. I knew it could only end badly when Pig's Breath first rang and offered me the job. Even the Cockroach knew it would end badly. Why did I take the job anyway? *Madonna santa*, as Maria Magdalena Svevo was inclined to say in moments of ill temper. *Madonna santa*. The hard ones upfront. How can I answer that? Things have never really gone right for me. As they say, it's all written in the book above so why should I give a bugger why I took the job that led to this when I can blame anything? I was gone for a long time before this little number came up. Let me tell you. I mean, where do I begin? The family? The church whose walls wept blood? The school that taught people to run backwards? My father who used to hold big barbeques for ghosts and people who had never even been? The baby and all that bad bloody business? The bedspread with the tear stain that wouldn't wash out? Couta Ho's crazy code flags? That bastard Pig's Breath? That idiot Gaia Head? I get a bad feeling in my guts just thinking about it all normally, but at the moment there are so many other pains crowding around my body I just don't care. Nothing ever really seemed that important to me, not since Jemma's death. People worry about how their hair looks, or what other people think of the colour they've painted their house, or, as I was once asked by a woman, what size doily to put on her washing machine. But you will understand me when I say that if you are drowning none of these things seems overly important. And I am drowning. I don't care whether your hair is done or not done, whether your house is painted or not, or whether you even have a house or a washing machine to place a doily upon. Granted I ought to. I'll give you that, but then I've always been easygoing. Lazy, some might say, but I wouldn't agree. Or maybe I would. All that they say about me being lazy, about being a drifter, about having no future, about not knowing what I want out of life, maybe it is all true.

Maybe I was always drowning.

The only difference now is that I no longer have to put up with all those bastards crowding me, making me want to leave, to run, to piss off out of there as the saying goes. I could even get used to where I am now, enveloped in rushing white water, if it didn't plain hurt so much. Where do I begin? Maybe with what I am seeing at this moment. Because it makes me feel funny, what I am seeing. Because I have never seen such things, least not in the way I am seeing them now. It's like a movie, right? Except that I have this one vision and it stays there while all these other things happen around it. And right at this moment, this is how it presents itself.

First. A smell. Of flood – of earth eroding, of peat washing away, of rainforest heavy with rain. More precisely – for though lazy, I have always admired precision – more precisely: the energetic stench of decay. Then. A sound. The roar, the tumult of sounds of a river breaking its normal banks, crashing through the low-lying shrubbery, forming large rapids where none existed before; of sheets of rain driving like blows of an axe into the guts of the gorge.

Then, breaking forth from a bizarre low angle, a ray of light shining up the gorge illuminating a world otherwise cast in darkness by the black rain clouds above. The water reflects a white brilliance. From where I am watching, the mass of glistening white is momentarily blinding. It takes some time for my eyes to adjust to this whiteness and recognise the river. The Franklin River. A world pure and whole and complete unto itself. Neither rubber condoms nor rubber tyres nor tin cans nor dioxins nor bent rusting chrome reminders of the cars they once graced nor any of the other detritus of our world seem to abide here. This is an alien world. This is the river. Rising in the Cheyne Range. Falling down Mt Gell. Writhing like a snake in the wild lands at the base of the huge massif of Frenchmans Cap. Writing its past and prophesying its future in massive gorges slicing through mountains and cliffs so undercut they call them verandahs, and in eroded boulders and beautiful gilded eggs of river stone, and in beaches of river gravel that shift year to year, flood to flood, and in that gravel that once was rounded river rock that once was eroded boulder that once was undercut cliff that once was mountain and which

14

will be again. And then I see them. At the top of the whiteness two red rafts, each bearing people, each person craning their eyes earnestly over the rapid, down which they are now to fall.

— Aljaz —

In front of that white brilliance, there is a rock. A huge, sloping rock the size of several houses, flanked on one side by a sheer cliff and upon the other by a waterfall. And nine or so people and two red rafts pulled up on that rock. But I can't make out the people's faces. They are hard to clearly see in the pattern of the myrtle leaves that dance in the swirling water before my eyes. The people are gathered where the boulder edges the waterfall, and they are staring at an arm that rises ghostlike out of the waterfall only a few metres from where they stand.

Like a spotlight in a theatre, the low ray of sunlight illuminates the arm, further emphasising its ethereal nature. The people on the rock observe in fascinated horror the way the fingers of the hand open out into the ray of light as if in question, stretch as far as it is possible for such extremities to stretch, and the fingers shiver and as they do so the hand pivots around the wrist, roaming its small and tightly circumscribed sunlit world, searching for some hope it might grasp. At the point where this mesmerising moving limb rises, the waterfall has not begun its absolute drop, which is a metre or two further downstream. Here the fall is a maelstrom of wild, confused falling water. And jammed between submerged rocks, stuck underneath that furious water, is a man to whom this arm belongs.

Me. Aljaz Cosini, river guide.

More precisely: the spotlit arm is my arm.

My head, jammed between the rocks, can no doubt be made out from the large boulder above. No doubt. The blue of my guide's helmet and the planes of my face visible to those looking down through these few centimetres. (How many? Seven or eight or nine? What does it avail? I'm a bee's dick away from those people and that beautiful air they breathe and I can't reach it or them, or them me.) But my body, snagged in the rock, wedged into the black water below, would be visible to no eyes. To those staring down, desperate and impotent, I probably look like John the Baptist when his head was brought to Herod on a plate. Funny thought, that. Funny that even funny thoughts can happen when you are dying. Maybe the humour is part of the horror.

And then it strikes me: the site of my death, albeit in a small and humble way, will become a tourist monument. And this idea – this *revelation* – amuses me. Here in my agony I'm about to be enshrined as part of the joke. I suppose I *have* become part of the bloody joke. This idea is too much for me. I burst out laughing. And as my laughter empties into ever smaller bubbles and rushes away to join the other bubbles in the current, I involuntarily try to breathe in. Water rushes into my mouth and courses down my throat.

I feel faint.

I feel as if I am dissolving.

And when that sensation washes through me, it washes me away. Not my body, no, but *me*, takes me elsewhere, to another time, another river. No, the same river, but so gentle, so kind, so warm, as to make it seem an entity from another world. And now I recognise it – this

16

place where we enter the river and start our trip. The Collingwood River Bridge. It must be six, no, five, five and a half days ago; it was then, and there. There, it is me, standing at the edge of the river. When I look back at myself all that time ago I see only a stranger. But it *is* me. I can pick the gawky hooked nose, with its eaglebeak-like profile, and the body – yes, the body – there is a giveaway if ever there was one. My god, will you just get a goosey gander of *that*! It is my body, I can see that now, short, stumpy, but I don't feel the revulsion to it now that I felt then. Then, I hated its combination of scrawniness and flab – wherever a guide should have muscle I had more loose flesh the colour of dripping. But looking at it now it seems more than perfectly adequate for the purposes of living. It can walk on both its legs with an admittedly awkward and somewhat comic lope, more like a baboon than a person, but walk nevertheless those legs do. And the arms are fine for picking things up and putting them down and all the other armlike functions they must perform. As for the face, well it breathes without effort.

Without effort!

To think that a man who breathes *without effort* would have as his major concern whether or not the customers who have paid to come on this trip will think the less of him because of a slightly chubby waistline. It is amusing. I ought laugh.

Most interesting is that none of this nervous vanity is apparent. Nor his customary shyness. He seems relaxed and confident, his dishevelled appearance generating confidence in his customers, who marvel at his nonchalant approach. As for the piss-flambeaued face – well, I think it a not uninteresting face. It lacks, it is true, the boyishness of his fellow river guide. It is a desolate visage, all sallow angles and stubbled, strangely high cheekbones looking as though they have been cable-logged of most of the vital signs of life and further eroded by the passage of time, and, like a clearfelled mountainside, not without a perverse attraction. An eroded black-bedrock wasteland of a face, relieved in its monotony only by the large nose that sits like an abandoned mining tower over the desolation it inhabits. So splendidly large I am compelled to wonder if the face has been bred only for this feature, while the rest of its aspects have been allowed to degenerate. Why is there something fascinating in that face? Maybe it's because in its early traces of broken purple lines, in its dirty teeth, in its lank red hair, in its darkness, there is something suggestive of experience and suffering. Perhaps even knowledge.

Perhaps.

And those eyes burning, a jagged blue. Like the blue heart of the guttering yellow flame of an oxyacetylene torch as the gas is being switched off. Red haired, dark skinned, blue eyed, big nosed. Strange. And unsettling. Vulnerability and doomed pride and very large nostrils.

I watch in fascination as this Aljaz Cosini squats down, puts his hands in the creek, lays his body near parallel with the ground, then slowly lowers himself, taking the weight upon his arms as though he is beginning a push-up. His head disappears into the river. Beneath the water's surface Aljaz opens his eyes and looks at the shiny brown and gold river pebbles beneath him. The light falls through the water as it does through the air, in shafts created by openings in the all-encompassing rainforest, falling upon the rocks beneath to give the entire river its red-gold glow. As he looks he opens his mouth and takes a draught of river water into his mouth and lets it feel its cool way down his throat. I watch him think that no water tastes as good as water drunk like this. I watch him wonder what it would feel like to be part of the river. As his thin red hair floats back and forth like kelp in the slow current of the shallows, I watch him think that perhaps it would feel like this. Then think, or perhaps it wouldn't feel like anything at all. Then think perhaps this is what he likes best about being down the Franklin, the ditch, as the guides call it. The way the mountains and the rivers and the rainforest care nothing for him. They feel him to be neither part of them nor separate from them, neither want him to be there nor want him to go, neither love nor hate him, neither envy nor disparage his efforts, see him neither as good nor bad. They have no more opinion of him than of a fallen stick or an entire river. He feels naked, without need, without desire. He feels enclosed by the walls of the mountains and the rainforest. He feels, for the first time in such a long time, good. Perhaps this is what death is, he thinks. A peace at the heart of an emptiness.

Shush, shush, shush. The large shiny red pontoons of the raft they will use to navigate the river begin to inflate as the doctor from Adelaide with the expensive purple polar-fleece jacket and the white legs like an emu pushes the foot pump up and down.

Shush, shush, shush. I watch myself encouraging him in his labours and revelling in my insincerity. 'Great job, Rickie, great job. That's the way.' It's not the way, but Aljaz knows it is better that someone else does some of the work than he do it all, even if they do it badly. 'Stick with it, Rickie.' I watch Rickie give a purposeful smile, watch him feel wanted and needed and appreciated.

19

'To finally be here at the Franklin River,' *shush, shush, shush*, 'you don't know how much it means,' says Rickie. *Shush, shush, shush*.

'A stiff back, bad food, and weak bowels, that's what it means,' says Aljaz, and I see that this Aljaz is something of a comedian, that he sees his role as much one of entertaining as of guiding. I see that his customary shyness finds a cover in theatrical exaggeration.

I watch as this Aljaz slowly looks up from the river at the bush that forms around its banks and I watch him smile. I know what he is thinking at this precise moment: he is happy to be back at last upon the river, back upon the lousy leech-ridden ditch. Around him, the myrtles and sassafras and native laurels and leatherwoods mass in walls of seemingly impenetrable rainforest, and in front of him flows the tea-coloured water of the river, daily bronzing and gilding the river rock a little further.

I know he is smiling at the punters, who, despite their protestations to the contrary, despite their assertions that this is the most beautiful country, are already feeling a growing unease with this weird alien environment that seems so alike yet so dissimilar to the wilderness calendars that adorn their lounge-rooms and offices. It smells strongly of an acrid, fecund earth, and its temperate humidity weighs upon them like a straitjacket of the senses. Wherever they turn there is no escape: always more rainforest, and more of it irreducible to a camera shot. No plasterboard walls or coffee tables are to be found to act as borders, to reduce this land to its rightful role of decoration. Not that they don't try, and almost always at the start of a trip there is at least one customer who shoots off a roll or two of film in nervous excitement. But for Aljaz, this place that they feel to be moving behind them, causing them to sometimes give an anxious look over their shoulder, for Aljaz this place is home.

'What a one we got here,' whispers his fellow guide, the Cockroach, pointing at the large accountant from Melbourne. 'He looks a real goose.'

'Like an emu,' I hear Aljaz say.

'Like a . . .' says the Cockroach, and I can see him searching for the appropriate animal with which to compare the gauche and arrogant accountant, 'like a fucken . . .' But the precise analogy eludes him. 'What's his name anyway?' whispers the Cockroach.

'Derek,' Aljaz replies, then further pondering upon Derek's form, says, 'praying mantis.'

'Yeah,' says Cockroach, then, 'no', says the Cockroach. 'No. Almost, but no.' The Cockroach thinks again, then says, 'Like a locust, that's what he's like, a fucken locust.' And the analogy is entirely correct.

Derek looks like some strange creature that is far too big to be a human, his large pupils at once oddly sensitive and entirely inhuman, capable of suggesting both an emptiness and a certain greed. His nervous hands are rarely from his mouth, to feed it food or cigarettes, and below that bulky body those ludicrous stick legs clad in luminous striped-green thermal underwear.

Aljaz turns and heads up a side track, where in early summer they put bees to harvest the nectar of the leatherwood trees that dapple the rainforest rivers with their white flowers as if it were a wedding and their petals confetti. He feels good. Even his guts, for the first time in such a long time, even his guts don't feel knotted and aching and lurching themselves in readiness for another diarrhoeic discharge. I watch Aljaz change into his rafting gear, dressing in an unhurried fashion, enjoying once

21

more putting on the various bits and pieces. First the bathers, then the long-john neoprene wetsuit with its vivid fluoro-green slashes. Aljaz likes the feel of the wetsuit around his body. It lends him an illusion of strength and purpose. Next layer: the thermal tops, then the bright white and blue nylon outer jacket they call a cag, and finally the lifejacket, bright purple and replete with sheath-knife upon one shoulder, whistle and brightly coloured anodised aluminium carabiners and prussic loops upon the other. Ah, the old carabiners. The customers ask their guides why they wear them on their bodies, and in a condescending tone the guides explain their high and serious purpose; how it is that the carabiner might save all if they become caught in the middle of a flooded river and the guides have to set up pulley and rope systems to get to shore. But the truth is they look dramatic, they lend the necessary sense of danger that instils both fear and respect among the punters – fear of what is to come, respect for the guides on whom they must now depend. It is a visual lesson that talks of life and its smallness. The guides wear the carabiners everywhere, like Mexican revolutionaries with bandoliers, bit players in an extravagant theatre of death. It is all part of the joke. Around his waist Aljaz wraps his flip line, three and a half metres of rainbow-coloured climbers' tape, buckled with yet another carabiner. Upon the side of the flip line he crabs a throw bag. And upon his head goes the crash helmet. Like some luminous and savage tropical insect he returns to his customers.

As they ferry the gear down to the river Aljaz notices that Sheena, the dental asistant, takes and gives things only with her left arm. Her right arm seems to move not at all, seems to hang there like a hinged stick. 'Excuse me,' asks Aljaz, 'but have you hurt your arm?'

'No. No, it's fine.'

Aljaz looks at the arm. He is not persuaded.

'It's withered.' Sheena says nothing. 'Your arm.'

'So what?'

'This is a very physical trip, Sheena. You have to paddle a raft for ten days, carry heavy loads . . .'

'I am strong.'

'I am not saying you ain't.' Aljaz halts. What is there to say? She is there. It is his job to get her down the river. Somehow.

'Look,' says Sheena, but before she can go on Aljaz interrupts, saying what he has to say.

'It's fine. Don't worry. You'll have a great trip. Just let me know if ever things seem a bit hard.'

Afterwards he goes over to the Cockroach, who is tying gear frames into the rafts, and tells him the story.

'He's not supposed to take people who don't meet the necessary physical requirements,' says the Cockroach, referring to Pig's Breath.

'Fit enough to sign the cheque. That's Pig's Breath's sole physical requirement.'

They look down at the river's edge where Sheena is working, ferrying gear with her left arm from the trailer to the raft. There is about her something so determined that it makes Aljaz mad.

'Why the hell did she decide to come on the trip? She ought to have had the sense . . .' He shakes his head.

'I had a polio victim once,' says the Cockroach. And laughs. 'Nice bloke, actually.'

'I'll take her in my boat,' says Aljaz without enthusiasm. 'I suppose she's my responsibility.'

They finish tying the gear frames into the middle of

the inflated rafts and begin to load up. I watch as Aljaz stands in the boat and calls for the gear in its correct order. First the big black plastic barrels full of food, each weighing in excess of sixty kilograms. It takes two punters to carry a barrel, but a guide must be able to carry one by himself. Aljaz grabs a barrel and feels its immense weight and wonders how he will ever be able to lift it. I can see that Aljaz is badly out of condition. But such things are simply matters of will. The customers believe they are weak and in this instance must act prudently. Aljaz, to the contrary, must look strong and fearless, whatever he knows himself to be, however weak and frightened he might feel inside. It is a charade that is necessary to sustain the whole trip. It is the antidote to fear that spreads like a contagion if it is admitted by a guide. There is a sad lesson in this: people must believe, even, if it must be so, in a lie. Without belief all is lost. And yet, like all blind faiths that seem to go so much against the evidence of reality, they in turn foster their own truths. As long as no fear is acknowledged, great things are possible and the punters are capable of feats of endurance and courage of which they never believed themselves capable. And so Aljaz lifts the barrel onto his shoulder, swings it around and gently deposits it in the cradle formed by the gear-frame netting. Beneath the load I can see his face smiling and laughing at the absurdity of it all.

The beginning of the trip takes on something of a carnival atmosphere. A bottle of cheap rum is produced and passed around. All have a swig, some giggling at their boldness, others affecting a nonchalant air, pretending it is something they do regularly in their daily lives as accountant or nurse or merchant banker or public servant.

The bottle comes to the Cockroach. He has already had a joint with Nino the busdriver in the dusty solitude of the empty microbus and is half stoned. The Cockroach drains the bottle, gives a yelp, and grabs Sheena and begins dancing with her on the river rocks. He lifts her up in the air and sweeps her through the air, carrying her into the river, in which he gently lets her down. She staggers to her feet and with her good arm slaps the Cockroach on the face. The Cockroach hasn't anticipated such a response and falls backward.

Aljaz goes back to loading the rafts. On go the waterproof personal gearbags, brightly coloured in blues and greens and reds. On go the additional bags with tents and tarps and cooking equipment. On goes the hard vegetable bag, allowed to swill around at the bottom of the gear frame. On go the ammunition boxes full of first-aid kits and repair kits and punters' cameras. On go the ropes and spare carabiners and carabiner pulleys and rescue throw-bags and bailing buckets, all clipped on at various points to the frame. On goes everything ten people need to survive for ten days in the wilderness.

I can see that Aljaz likes the beginning of the trip – it gives him certainty, it brings order to the chaos of his thoughts. It gives him tangible fears, real fears. Will the food stay dry for ten days? Will the customers get through safely? Will none burn themselves? Or drown? That is always a great, Aljaz's greatest, abiding fear. That he will lose a customer on the ditch. It is so easy, it happens so *smoothly*. Violent death can come with a deceptive grace; so quick, so effortless, so silent, that it is not immediately apparent what has taken place. People turn around thinking that the person is perhaps standing behind their back about to surprise them, whereas they are not playing an elaborate joke, they are dead. Simply dead. A revealing phrase in itself – death is not the complex matter life is. At least not for the dead.

'I once saw a woman who had drowned in the Zambezi,' says the Cockroach. He is back out of the river, wet, still smiling, and is standing next to me in the raft, helping to buckle the netting down over the gear. 'She was with another company, not ours, and she had fallen in and got tangled up with the rescue rope. By the time we turned up they had fished her out, but it was too late. She was already blue and they were giving her CPR. But they knew she was gone, you could tell the way they went through the CPR routine so calmly and efficiently, like they were preparing the corpse for embalming rather than trying to keep her alive. This punter on my raft turns around and says, as if he's just seen a fish jump, he says, ''She just drowned, is that what it is?'' A stupid bald Pom he was. Of course she *just* drowned, her lungs *just* filled with water, I felt like shouting at him.'

But Aljaz hardly hears this story. His mind is elsewhere and I am with it. He is thinking how without the trip his thoughts take on a darkness he cannot overcome. Upon the ditch he can meet his fears, name them – Nasty Notch, the Great Ravine, the Churn, Thunderush, the Cauldron, the Pig Trough – and having met them, bid goodbye to them all. Without the trip his thoughts are beyond his control, and wander toward a divide that he can never see, the presence of which chills him to the bone. At such times he feels the workings of his mind hang by a few slender threads, and if they break he will be unable to do anything, unable even to get up in the morning, unable to do the simplest of things that people take for granted. Unable to say hello without bursting

26

into tears, unable to talk to people without feeling his bowels being gripped by the most terrible fear, unable to meet with friends without experiencing the most horrifying sense of vertigo, that he might suddenly tumble and fall into the abyss.

'Then suddenly,' continues the Cockroach, 'suddenly, some spasm of her muscles made her spew up all this water and they got their hopes back up for a minute. But it was too late. I knew that. Even the bald Pom knew that. She was a goner.'

Now I can see that Couta Ho had understood all this, that long, long ago when she said it would take time to heal but that time could never entirely fill in the hole, that she had said it not because she knew nothing better to say, but because she was right. For a long time I had been sick, and she had found me once and tried to stay with me, still as the moon. And I, like some errant satellite, had drifted away to return only when it was too late. Far, far too late.

— the first day —

I watch the river trip proceed in front of me. On the first day the river was so low they had to drag their rafts most of the seven kilometres down the Collingwood River, to the place where it ran into the Franklin. At such a low level, the Franklin at the junction was also little more than a dry creek bed studded with occasional rock pools. The first day was hard in every way for Aljaz. Physically it was a torment, because the punters had neither the wit nor the inclination to lift and drag the two rafts, each of which weighed hundreds of kilograms, so it was he and the Cockroach who had to do most of the labour. His body was unequal to the hard work. His soft hands burnt from where he pulled the nylon deck lines. His back knifed pain when he lifted the pontoons. They camped at the Collingwood's junction with the Franklin, in the rainforest above a small shingle bank. The night was so clear they slept without tents and Aljaz knew that tomorrow, with no rain, the river would only be lower, their bodies stiff and bruised and their work even harder.

That evening they sat round the fire drinking billy tea and Bundaberg rum and watching the moon, waxing to near fullness, rise high enough for its light to silver the river valley. Their weary bodies felt bathed in mercury. The fire and the banks of rising rainforest were mirrored in the monochrome river as a dancing daguerreotype. They traded stories back and forth, the guides of river lore, of feats great and ridiculous, of floods that awoke them with a roar in the middle of the night, the river banking up around their tent before washing it and most of their equipment away, to deposit it at some point downriver atop a cliff, along with uprooted trees and dead snakes and devils. Of droughts in which the river was so low the rafts had to be dragged along the dry bed for four and five days before enough water could be had to float them. The punters' stories tended to be smaller and sadder. There was Rex from Brisbane, who three months before had taken a large redundancy to leave his position with Telecom and now was totally lost. 'I am only thirty-five,' he repeated, 'only thirty-five. What am I to do?'

'Keep travelling,' advised Derek. 'With money you can see or do whatever you want. Every spare cent since the divorce I put into travel. What an age it is!'

No one else much knew what Rex ought do, except

for Rickie, who said he had a very good broker with whom he could put Rex in touch come the end of the trip. Sheena suggested maybe Rex didn't really have that much to worry about, but the others were more sympathetic.

There was Lou's story of working as a crime reporter on the old *Sun* and being sent to interview a crim who had a contract out on him. The crim lived in a squalid bedsit in Fitzroy and only went out twice a day, once to shop at a Vietnamese store up the road, the other to eat tea at a Syrian café. 'Why don't you run?' Lou had asked him. 'Why don't you just do a bunk and go to Darwin or Dubbo or somewhere they won't find you?' The crim sat on his bed the entire time and seemed gentle and pleasant. He agreed it would be the sensible thing to do, but life, he suggested, wasn't always such a simple thing. 'This is my home,' he said. 'I live here,' he said. 'And I'll die here.' So he did. Two days later they came while he was lying in bed and, as Lou put it, vitamised his head with shot.

At the time Lou told that story I had been poking around in a barrrel trying to find another bottle of Bundy and the tale had largely passed me by. But now I think it an interesting story: a man who could evade death chooses against good advice to meet with it on his own terms. Is this an act of cowardice or courage? Of stupidity or wisdom? Of ignorance or enlightenment? I don't know the answer. I wish I did, because it would help me resolve what I am to do, whether I should continue to struggle, or just give in now. This battle of mine, all these strange thoughts and these bizarre visions, why should I hang on to any of them, what does any of it matter if my ultimate fate is only to be carried away by this river as waterborne peat?

But at the point where I most need time to reflect and think, my thoughts are overtaken by my vision. I watch the small solitary camp sleep beneath the vast southern sky, enshrouded in rainforest. Flowing above them and over the valley, the quicksilver river of the night. Aljaz felt the bright moonlight lap at the edge of his sleeping bag. Then, as the moon rose further, the light washed over him, his body a stone too heavy to move in the flowing water of the night. He felt the running shadows caress his body in fluid stripes. He grew lighter and lighter, and heard his body wonder how long before it floated away into the night. In his meandering dreams Couta Ho was upon a beach waving a flag toward him and he was in a boat far out to sea, unable to see and hence decipher the fluttering code.

— the second day —

I watch the moon reach its zenith then slowly fall into the darkness of the pre-dawn hour. I watch the beginning of the morning of the second day, when the river world takes on new colours. And I watch myself awaken.

Aljaz knuckled the sockets of his eyes. He ran his hands down over the roughening skin of his cheeks to join together at his chin as if in prayer of thanks, shaping the flesh into the face that he would wear through that day. He looked across at the tents. No punters up. Across at the fire site Cockroach was up and rebuilding the fire from the evening's coals. Aljaz divested himself of his sleeping bag, stood up and walked down the short, steep track to the riverbank. He pissed on some rocks near the shore, sleepily observing how the steam rising from his urine matched and then merged with the steam rising from the wet black logs of river-fingering fallen trees. He walked upriver fifty metres to where he had set three dead lines the evening before. The first had been snagged by some unknown river creature in a log jam downriver, the second had been snapped, and the third had a two-foot eel writhing like a wild sea snake at its end. Aljaz collected the various pieces of catgut and carried the eel, lashing back and forth, by the line that bore down through its primeval mouth and throat into the remote regions of its gut. There the hook had been irretrievably lodged and there its barbed presence was an uplifting horror for the pitiful creature. At the fire Aljaz with his free hand used a stick to clear a place in the coals, into which he gently laid the eel. The eel twisted and slid as if it were, in its final agony, miming its own swimming movement, for it did not and could not move beyond the hot ashes. As its slimy skin began to smoulder and its flesh to roast and its life juices to simmer, the creature relaxed to a slow movement almost sensual until it began to stiffen then moved no more. Aljaz carefully scooped the eel's charred form out of the fire and ran a knife along its sooty back, splitting the charcoal skin and neatly peeling it away from the sweet steaming white flesh. Upon the rainforest floor he and the Cockroach ate, though none of the punters took up their offer to join them.

Instead they ate porridge, which Derek cooked and which Derek burnt. Two hours later Derek managed to fall out of the Cockroach's raft in a small rapid and become ensnared on a dead tree limb in the middle of the river. Unable to paddle their rafts back to where Derek was stuck, Aljaz and the Cockroach swam down and Aljaz cut Derek's life jacket to free him. The Cockroach helped him swim down the rapid to the riverbank. There the relieved punters beamed and laughed, even Derek. They hugged him and he hugged them, and it was almost as if they were celebrating his fall as a great achievement. The punters looked at Aljaz and the Cockroach with some awe, and both guides knew that now, because of their rescue of Derek, their authority was complete, that anything they said or suggested would be done, taken as gospel, and it frightened Aljaz, this blind belief, like it always frightened him.

'If only they knew the truth about us,' he whispered to the Cockroach.

'They've got to believe in something,' said the Cockroach, 'even if it is only us.' He turned around with a broad smile and slapped Derek on the back and said loudly so that all could hear, 'We're your ticket out of this slimy hole, aren't we Derek?' Derek nodded his agreement.

'You won't let us down?' asked Derek, whose fear remained.

'Only if you burn the porridge again,' said the Cockroach, his smile unmoving.

The second day was hot and the guides sat motionless at the back of the rafts, making imperceptible paddling movements to steer, even their restless eyes stilled behind the reptilian black pupils of their RayBans. They sat unmoving in the glare of the sun, goannas absorbing energy from the surrounding elements, waiting for the moment to strike.

About midday the river, its volume subtly increased by the water of numerous minuscule tributaries, began to deepen enough for them to paddle for stretches of up to a kilometre before having to get out and drag the rafts again. The water lapped at the sides of their rafts as they made their way downriver, the punters sitting sideways, one at each corner of the raft, dipping and pulling their single-bladed paddles through the water. Aljaz rocked back and forth in rhythm with the slow surge of the boat. He thought that perhaps they were not such a bad crew after all, for it was only the second day and already they were beginning to paddle in time. He sat in the middle of the rear pontoon that formed the back wall of the raft, his paddle trailing in the water, acting as a rudder. Aljaz let his body sway and his mind wander as the four punters pulled in long, slow, rhythmic strokes. The day was warm, the sun having finished its slow climb down into the valley to the river. Aljaz took off his cag and thermal, and put on his life jacket and helmet. 'What's that tree up there?' asked Rickie, pointing up at a bank of dense rainforest.

'*Erica ragifola*,' said Aljaz, quoting the name of a plant he had seen in a nursery Couta had taken him to once.

'*Erica ragifola*,' repeated Marco.

They passed snakes swimming, unravelling ripples in warm flat pools. They passed platypuses that floated like sticks as the rafts approached, then sank like stones at the sound of a punter's exclamation, leaving only a few fatty bubbles on the water's surface. They startled a flock of swifts from a cliff face and saw a giant lobster sitting on a log at the river's edge, glistening iridescent greens and purples and blues in the sunlight, and even the punters did not have an immediate response to its proud perfection.

They paddled on. Now there was enough water to paddle, Aljaz taught them how to paddle properly. He took time with Sheena, showing her how to twist her torso so that the power of the stroke came from her body rather than from her arms. She learnt quickly, locking her arms into the stroke, using them only to transfer the power of her body. They paddled on. Sheena sat at the front of the raft and she told the story of her withered arm. Of how she had had radiation treatment for moles in Switzerland in the 1950s. Of how the radiation cured the moles but destroyed the arm, so that it never developed properly. Of how the radiation had rendered her unable to conceive children. Derek said he had no children because he was yet to meet the right woman to mother his offspring and asked Aljaz if he had any kids. 'No,' said Aljaz, his face unmoving. 'Guess we're all in the same boat then,' said Derek laughing. 'Guess so,' said Aljaz, though neither he nor anyone else laughed with Derek. Withered and dead, thought Aljaz, in different ways, in different places, all of us withered and dead. Sheena told her story lightly, in the sun, almost gaily. She smiled as she told the story. They paddled on.

They came upon three people on mossy boulders next to a creek that fed its clear wrinkling water into the Franklin, two men and one woman and they seemed to be drunk or stoned or perhaps both; the woman, wearing only a pair of ageing Adidas tracksuit pants, playing strange discordant notes on a nose-flute while the two men danced with movements that were in accordance neither with the music nor, as they had it in later conversation, with the rhythms of the earth. They stood in one spot, heads dropped, and waved their arms in slow exaggerated gestures. One man had dreadlocks dyed red, the other was entirely bald save for some slogans tattooed into his forehead, the most dominant of which read 'This Head Kills Fascists'. Aljaz swept his raft into the bank near this strange trio and went to talk to them because he liked to know all who were upon the river, liked to hear the latest river news and exchange tidings from the outside world. The trio had no news, only multiple opinions on the state of mother earth, the fundamental evil and destructive nature of all humanity, and the great and total beauty of the river. They had been on the river for eight days already and had in that time only managed to traverse the distance that Aljaz's party had travelled in a quarter of that time. Aljaz's party were the first people they had seen since departing the Collingwood River bridge, but they were little interested in anything outside of the dance and the music of the nose-flute. Both men appeared to strongly desire the woman, who seemed to have little interest in either, concerned only with attaining some state of supra-natural harmony with cosmic forces that she alone seemed capable of divining. The trio's supply of food was already low and Aljaz left them with some fresh sweet potato and cabbage, though, as he later said to the Cockroach, he didn't know why he bothered. The woman abused him for even carrying sweet potato, which she said was a bad food, being too high in aggressive energy. In spite of this psychological objection, she accepted the vegetables. They had two old yellow rubber rafts in a bad state of disrepair, and they had named one Gaia Seeker, the other Fagus Finder, presumably a corruption of the Latin name for myrtle, *nothofagus cunninghamii*. Aljaz cast a careful eye over their gear as he spoke with them: dowel and plywood paddles, no helmets, kapok life jackets that looked as if they had been excavated from a pre-war Manly ferry. 'What were Gaia Head and his two cobbers like?' asked the Cockroach afterwards.

Aljaz cast one last look back upriver where the two forms of the men could still be made out weaving their deranged dance through the whitey wood and riverine scrub. What was there to say? He said nothing.

The Cockroach said, 'Any stories?'

'No,' said Aljaz. 'They had no stories.'

In the afternoon of the second day they stopped for a break at the side of a rapid where a kayaker had drowned the year before. Like other sites on the river where people had drowned it had become something of a highlight for tourists. Aljaz looked into the slot in which the kayaker had become wedged. With the river so low, the slot was not a part of the rapid as it was at higher levels, but simply an exposed mass of warm rock undercut by erosion. Within these undercuts were sieves of sticks and logs through which a trickle of water gently splashed. When the kayaker drowned there would have been nothing gentle about the sieve. He would have been tumbled into it by the force of the river, as if he were a leaf being hosed off a pavement, and his body would have slammed into the slot and jammed there. Face pressed up against the sticks, his shoe or life jacket snagged upon a branch, powerless to free himself, he would have remained for some days, his face slowly turning from florid red to the soft white of wet dead flesh, pinned by the onward rush of the water until such time as the river ebbed enough for his body to be found and retrieved.

The ammo boxes unsnapped and half a dozen Nikons and Canons were unleashed upon the wet rocks in the mid-distance, to capture upon film the place that once ensnared a human underwater until he breathed no more. They stood in a semicircle around Aljaz. Where *exactly* did he drown? they asked. *How* exactly did he drown?

Neither Aljaz nor the Cockroach were comfortable with the questions. Both had rafted enough to know that some day it could be one of them, or, worse, one of their punters. 'He opened his mouth and filled it with water,' answered Aljaz. And smiled. The punters looked askance at each other, then looked away in embarrassment and stopped asking questions.

From the bank Aljaz and the Cockroach continued to watch the punters examine and document the site. 'I wonder if the tourist industry pays his family a commission,' said the Cockroach. 'Fighting against the water to live is one thing. But fighting against becoming a tourist monument – that would be impossible.'

'Like Queensland,' said Aljaz.

The guides gazed upon the death site, unknowable, inscrutable behind the blackness of their sunglasses, behind the whiteness of their zinc-creamed lips and cheeks and noses. Like greasepainted clowns whose whole act was at once a denial and a celebration. The Cockroach smiled. 'If they can do that to an entire state, one bloke doesn't stand a chance.'

Aljaz turned around. 'No wonder the poor bastard gave up the ghost.' And laughed. He felt a liking for the Cockroach. The punters, like mosquitoes, returned. Their guides' smiles vanished and their white lips returned to an autistic straightness.

'Incredible,' said Marco.

'Bloody interesting,' said Derek.

It was as if the kayaker's life had been pointless and his drowning only meaningful as a photo opportunity for the tourists who would follow. As if the beauty of the place was born with his death.

Madonna santa! Could that be me? Could that be me?

I watch Aljaz pretend not to hear. I watch him raise his eyes to the sky and stare through darkened lenses at the thin clouds that drift into the narrow space permitted them by the mountain ranges that flank Irenabyss Gorge.

Thinking: *Rain is coming.*

— Three —

Of course, although I can see all these things in my visions, including myself in days gone by, nobody in my visions can see me. I am simply invisible, like I have been invisible for such a long time in my life. The world changed, rolled on, the weekend papers and women's magazines and TV talk shows and the talk radio full of what was now the fashion and what wasn't, of who was changing things and who had power and who was in the process of losing power. The movers and the shakers. But I was never part of that. Though I was in constant flight, something about me was essentially still. The world rolled on but without me on it. I watched in disbelief. All of it. Its wars and its famines and its children selling themselves off Fitzroy Street and its old women beggars being hustled away by security guards from the shopping plazas, so that the old women too could enjoy this wonderful state of invisibility. The world had no place for me and I saw it in all its ludicrous, crazed ways but it did not see me, and I would have to say there was a strange freedom in this. Nor did the world see all the bad things and the evil things and the wrong things, nor those who suffered accordingly. I am not saying I objected or even cared. I just felt a slight sense of slippage in the world and it made me laugh, which seems to me more preferable than crying. So my invisibility at events is nothing new, nor even anything unique. It is only being able to transcend time that now gives my invisible spectating the curious power of a vision.

These visions come to me in all manner of curious ways. I can no longer be entirely sure whether my eyes are open or closed, but it does seem that I am looking at a sweep of bubbles rising up from God knows where, and sometimes one bubble grows and grows until it has taken on the form of a face, and that face is the beginning of the vision. At other times the faces simply appear from nowhere and are vast, huge apparitions and I seem to be able to see all the gorge below me, but all the gorge is filled with the immensity of that face as it begins to talk. Whether they come as bubbles or manifest themselves as vast entities, the faces are more often than not curiously distorted at the beginning, as if shrouded by the passing of time. They do not depart from me in the same manner. Sometimes they dissolve into new images, while at other times I slowly, dimly become aware that I have not thought or felt or seen anything for a period of time that may only be a few seconds or may be an infinity.

My strange torment blurs the whiteness of the rapid before me into vast emptiness, and sings the emptiness full of a new colour: blue.

An immensity of blue. Sky-blue. A fleck, a piece of fly shit at the centre of this vast emptiness. A fleck of fly shit upon a sheet of blue glistening satin. Moving. And there, me, moving with it.

With what?

A boat.

A small boat. A small wooden clinkered boat known as a punt, lovingly built of planks of Huon pine impervious to the worm and to rot, seven a side steamed into perfect shape and trenailed and caulked into position by old Gus Doherty – no finer piners' punt builder there be on all the west coast of Tasmania, one pound sterling per foot of punt for his craftsmanship and this boat fifteen of the king's finest for old Gus, beamy as buggery for heavy loads and square sterned and square bowed for riding the rapids, laden with hessian bags of chaff and flour, onions and spuds, wooden crates of jam and butter and sugar. A dog asleep on top of the mound of sacks. An axe and a crosscut saw at the bottom of the boat. A man rowing the punt, his mind as empty and as vast and as still as the inland sea called Macquarie Harbour that he is rowing his punt across, heading it toward the wild rivers, the rainforested rivers, where his axe and saw will work in rhythm in the damp and the humid closeness and the heavy sweet smells of the peat-created wet earth, among the myrtles, craggy and towering and bearded with hanging festoons of lichens, cracked and scabbed with fluorescent orange fungi, among the scented leatherwoods, among the pungent lime-green sassafras whose aromatic leaves make women want men (or so men who want women say), among the crazed pandannis, emaciated elongated trunks betopped with pineapple heads of thrusting leaves, among the celery top pine and the lemon-tasting whitey wood and the spiralling native laurels; there his axe and saw will work in rhythm in the damp and the humid closeness and the heavy sweet smells of the peat-created wet earth, to fell the waxy whiteness, the wet-cheese coloured, the prized, the Huon pine.

More precisely: I am observing my father as a young man heading off to work.

— Harry, 1946 —

After a time, a long time, he came to the river mouth, and after a further time the mouth disappeared and the inland sea behind it disappeared as the man, the name of whom was Harry Lewis, continued to row. The Gordon ran deep and black beneath him. Deep and black and cold. Harry Lewis looked at the low hills, rainforest-rumped, humps like hunchbacks heading away from the river. The water was dead-flat calm. Not a breeze. The cold in the river was the last of the snow melt from the big freeze the week before. Though the cold rose up from the water through the Huon pine planks of the punt's flooring, Harry wore only a blue singlet and his denim trousers, his body hot and sweating from the exertion of rowing his punt twenty miles already that day. He had started out early and the sun still lay on his back, as he headed further up the river, further away from civilisation, if that was the right name for Strahan. Harry's eyes looked to the west, but his arms placed the oars at the beginning of the stroke east. East to west, east to west to east, that was the direction of the oars, as they pulled Harry and the punt further into that vast wild land known only by its geographical description: the South West. He was heading into the rainforested wilderness, up the mighty Gordon River, up its tributary the Franklin River, up the Franklin's tributary the Jane River, following the paths these serpentine watercourses cut through the green carpeted temperate jungle into the land once called Transylvania, now shown on the government sketch map Harry carries in an oilskin satchel as an empty wilderness designated only as 'Little Known About This Country' but which was well enough known to Harry and his workmates.

Some good pine to be had up there, thought Harry.

In the ongoing pain of his body I feel Harry's hurts and sadnesses dissolve into small concerns, dwarfed by the red-hot poker that burnt into the back of his neck, the ripple of soreness that ran across his breast each pull of the oars, the ache in his arse. The river was beginning to run faster. Harry took the punt to the edge of the river and rowed up the slower water at its edges, just far enough out from the banks to avoid the Huon pines and native laurels that blanketed the bank. He liked looking up close at the big trees, at the myrtles leaning at all angles, huge majestic trees with big iridescent fungi growing off them.

Harry always hated the first hour of rowing, when his body rebelled against the demands being made of it. But after a while it warmed up and then there was something enjoyable about the journey. Imperceptibly the pain transformed into a rhythmic ache that demanded the steady caress of the action of rowing. Each pull of the oars hurt, but Harry's body revelled in the strength that came with the ache. He could feel each muscle, every sinew in his arms and upper body when the pull began, and harnessing them all together, stretching and tightening them simultaneously, he was able to achieve power in his stroke and the smoothest and easiest of movements to accompany that strength. His mind emptied of thought and worry, and as his body took control of the punt, taking it this way and that to best and most easily get up the fast flowing river, his mind drifted into the hills far away, up the wild King River valley, past the ruins of Teepookana, past the ruins of Crotty, up into the town of Linda and beyond to the mining town of Queenstown with its strange, bald hills – a desert valley that had once been full of rainforest, now denuded of all vegetation by the dense plumes of sulphurous smoke which emanated from the copper mine's smelters and which, rich in heavy metals, heavy in evil riches, caressed the downwind hills and mountains in an embrace of death. His mind watched the suppurating rivers that ran in garish pus-green and bloodied rills down those sad hills when the rains came (which was near enough to all the time) then wandered back into Queenstown itself and into the Empire Hotel and Gwennie's eyes, those eyes that had led him out into the back of the pub where she let him touch her breast then asked him fivepence for the pleasure; into those dark empty pupils that said nothing and hid everything; beyond their vast universe back to the Strahan wharf, where, as he had set out in the mist of that morning, a seal lay dying on the nearby rocks. It was said that the souls of the drowned came to rest in the bodies of seals, and once Auntie Ellie would have been down making the seal comfortable, worried lest it be Jimmy Rankin, who had been washed off a boat at Hells Gate, or lest it be Ron or Jack Howard, who had drowned the previous year at Granville Harbour going in too close for their cray rings in a gale, their cray boat picked up by a giant wave and dropped like a toy on a rock. His mind wandered up along the Eagle Creek track that ran from the Gordon River across the flank of the Elliot Range and down into the Franklin valley, and the large shingle bank there with its red- and brown-coloured rounded river rocks, which gave the bed, when the sun shone through the tea-stained water running over it, a beautiful red-gold colour.

The punt arcs around the corner, Harry's breath as regular and hard as the stroke of the oars, the rasp in the rowlock and the rasp in his throat one and the same pain and purpose. His eyes drift like the white leatherwood blossom that dapples the Gordon's steel-grey waters, focused on nothing, seeing everything. Seeing the low shard of smoke distantly rising up, then drifting languidly downriver. Smoke. Campfire. He looks up the river now, his eyes searching, and he sees what he knows: the dilapidated jetty that runs and falls down below Sir John Falls. He sees two, no three, men coming down to the bank and waving. Smeggsy, Old Jack and Old Bo, Bo the king of the piners. Harry rows up to the jetty and he stands up to moor the boat, his young limbs long and lean, still not yet fully muscled, unwinding like a rope coil, rising, reaching, climbing out. They exchange greetings and swigs from Harry's rum bottle. Harry tells them how he is heading up to the Jane to work with Norry Heddle. 'That far-keen Jane,' says Old Jack, rolling a cigarette, shaking his lowered stubbly head, labouring the two syllables of his favourite word, 'far-keen mean up that second gorge.' Harry knows the story, has heard it a hundred times. 'Cut pine up there for Josh Newton, must be thirteen years gone now, and most me logs still stuck up the gorge in them there far-keen waterfalls.'

Harry stays the night. They make a fire outside, even though the night is starlit and cold. 'Bo don't like it inside,' says Smeggsy. Old Bo sits close to the edge of the fire. The leaves in the myrtle trees move gently in the warm air draughting up from the flames. Nobody talks much. 'Them Yankee cowboy movies,' says Smeggsy after a time, 'they always yak around the fire like they got so much to say. I don't know what they got to talk about so much. Ain't nothing to talk about up here. Ain't nothing but silence up here.' Old Bo stares into the flames, playing with the coals with a stick. Harry taps Old Bo on the shoulder to get him to move aside so he can put the billy on for another cup of tea. Old Bo turns around and looks at him with a terrible fear in his firelit eyes. He looks at Harry, then curls up in a ball and rolls away from the fire yowling like a dog.

'Pay no heed,' says Old Jack. 'He ain't been right since he come back from them Jap prisoner-of-war camps after the war.'

'When it's too much for him,' says Smeggsy, 'he disappears for days and you hear stories months later that some prospectors have seen him up around the Frenchmans or up at Lake Pedder or down round Liberty Point way. All round the bloody south west. Gawd knows where he goes.' Smeggsy throws the leaves from a long-finished cup of tea onto the fire and stands up. 'Just into that bloody rainforest and he's off.' Old Bo lies like a foetus at the edge of the fire circle, whimpering like a dog, as if he expects someone to kick him. When the billy boils Smeggsy offers him a cup of tea with one hand and puts his other around the shaking old man.

'The old jim-jams,' says Smeggsy to Old Bo. 'That's all it is, mate, the old jim-jams.'

I watch as the next day Harry makes good time up the Gordon River. He rows for half a day without seeing a soul. Up past the Gordon's junction with the Franklin and then up the Franklin itself. Up past Pyramid Island he rows, and the river grows shallower and slower. Up past Verandah Cliffs, where as high up as he looks he sees fresh driftwood deposited by the recent flood. Near the top of the serrated limestone cliff face, a large long log of pine sits precariously balanced in a hole in the cliff, threaded through there by the river in flood like a piece of cotton through the eye of a needle. Harry laughs in wonder and keeps on rowing. Up to the Big Fall, around which he carries his gear and drags his punt.

The day turns to drizzle and Harry pulls an oilskin over the bags and puts a woollen flannel on over his singlet. Beyond the Devil's Hole he comes to another shingle rapid, flowing fast and ripply over the rocks. He takes the punt close into the riverbank and rows up the side eddy as far as he can, then jumps out with the bow rope. He walks up the river's edge, knee deep in rushing water. He walks twenty yards or so beyond the rapid, turns and walks into the middle of the shallows. He gets a firm footing facing downriver and begins to pull the rope in. He plays the line a little, letting the boat get in the middle of the current, where it is least likely to be flipped or to snag on one of the logs that litter the edge. And with a slow rhythm, like a strange ritualistic dance, he begins to haul the boat up the rapid, putting one arm right out then twisting his torso slowly, powerfully around, until that arm is at his waist and the other is fully extended on the rope, ready to pull the next length. I watch with respect as he skips the punt up the rapid's choppy waves.

Something makes Harry look up. There, a hundred yards downriver, high up a precariously leaning myrtle stag, a sea eagle stares back. Harry stops hauling, his body frozen in position, one arm fully extended, one arm at the end of the cycle. The sea eagle. Auntie Ellie was big on sea eagles. She told Harry they were the family's animal and that the family had to be kind to them, that the souls of Harry's ancestors came back into this world as sea eagles.

Suddenly the sea eagle falls from the tree. Halfway down to the river, the fall turns into a glide, and the glide is straight toward, straight at, Harry. And just when the bird seems to Harry as if it is about to snatch his face in its claws, it swoops up and climbs a cone of hot air, spiralling ever further upwards, each circle larger than the preceding one, without apparent effort, its wings outstretched and only the slightest tremor of feathers and body to correct the angle of ascent. Harry notices that two of the flight feathers on its left wing are missing.

And now, though he can no longer see it, Harry knows its eyes bear down on him.

— Harry as a child —

My vision is lost with the sea eagle in the white clouds. I scan them so intensely that the world below is lost to me, and the cloud begins to take on the shape of a snow-covered country. For a short time I am unsure where I am, but then I know I am seeing the road from Paradise, on the way to Beulah and Lower Beulah, normally long and lush and green but this night, this snowy midwinter's night, the road is white and impassable. This night of the birth of Harry Lewis. And because of the blizzard the doctor cannot be fetched to bring Harry into the world.

My vision, as if seeking refuge, passes from this cold white outside world into a rude wooden house that stands alone in the snow-hushed bush. There Harry's mother Rose pants and screams the agonies of birth in a tiny kitchen, the warmest of the three rooms that comprise her home. At the end of the kitchen the fire burns and crackles with fury, sparks lifting into the chimney from the piled up gum logs. Her husband, Boy Lewis, as he was known until his dying day, helps her through the birth himself, and when she has delivered the afterbirth he lays the two small bodies upon her chest, the dead boy baby and the living boy baby. Rose lies on a blanket on the split paling floor and listens to the sleety wind rustling the branches of the huge stringybark gums outside, and she thinks it the saddest sound in the whole world.

Rose names the dead baby Albert and the living baby Harold. The next morning, early, even before the blue mountains near them have become properly defined in the cold wash of first light, I see Boy Lewis bury the large placenta, like some giant lamb's fry, he thinks; walk ten yards and bury his cold blue son beneath one of the silver- and salmon-trunked stringybarks. He covers the hole and stands there for a time, not wondering. Then he kneels. They had not expected two babies. The doctor had suspected nothing. So, he thinks, he should not feel what he feels. But they had had two, and one was already gone. Boy Lewis rises unsteadily to his feet, turns, and slowly walks back home.

Each winter thereafter, no matter how cold, no matter how much snow, the stringybark gum would burst into immense flower. After a time the tree became something of a local landmark, then after a further time the unique unseasonal flowerings came to be expected and hence commonplace and went largely unremarked upon, save for beekeepers who fought each other for the right to put a hive beneath the flowering gum of Paradise, which produced honey sweeter and more succulent than any other known.

The gum of Paradise lay in the shadow of the Gog Range in which Boy Lewis had a wallaby snaring run. Boy also had a run with his brother George near No Where Else, but then he and George had a falling out and, besides, it was too far to walk, least that's what Boy told Harry. When snaring, Boy could be away for months on end and in that time he lived high up in the snow country, in a hut of King Billy pine he had made himself.

So I watch and continue to watch Harry Lewis as he grows up, watch how even to Harry as a small child his mother's body seems small and frail, his mother who had been sick for as long as Harry could remember. Her body seems unequal to what she has to do with it, the endless, relentlessly hard physical labour of housework, the bringing of children into this world, the sewing and ironing she takes in to try to make ends meet. I watch Harry recoil when Rose on the rare occasion finds time to tenderly stroke her son, for her rough, callused hands grate upon his soft boy skin and he is repelled by them, and all his life he will feel ashamed of having not wanted the touch of those beautiful worn hands. During her last years her body smelt close and sickly, and even after her weekly bath – for Rose was a woman who prided herself on her cleanliness – Harry was struck by how the smell remained. No matter how much she scrubbed the smell away, it would be replaced by more of the same – stale, rancid and repugnant. Harry would always remember his mother as old, even ancient, though when he was ten she was only thirty-five. Her thin face was harsh, harrowed. The flesh, rather than rolling in curves to form a round whole, was strained into planes that made her look, at least to Harry, vaguely Oriental. When Rose was angry, which was often, Harry ran out of the house into the bush, but he never felt scared. Only when she stopped her incessant work out of weariness and sat down on the old russet-coloured armchair in the parlour, her shallow green eyes focused upon nothing, her fingers absently pick-picking out the threads of horsehair through the holes in the arms, did he glimpse a despair so total that it terrified him. There was an old photograph that sat upon the mantelpiece, which showed Harry's mother when she was a young girl. The card, yellowed, acid-blotched and silverfish-chewed, had curled so much that it was now almost impossible to stand it up properly. The photograph seemed only to want to lie down and curl in upon itself, and the gentlest of draughts would knock it over. Across the back, in a bold round hand, was written, 'Rose agd 8 y.o.' Written in brown ink that had dried and faded like blood spilt long ago. She looked beautiful, soft, happy. Harry would sometimes get this photograph down, run his fingers over it and whisper some of his secrets to its sepia image, and wonder what it was that connected this happy child with his unhappy mother, and what it was that had separated them.

Harry, born in the moist shadow of the Gog Range in the north of the island, could never summon the same feelings toward the dry Richmond country of the south that his mother, whose birthplace it was, could. For Rose, Richmond was, as she was fond of saying, a place where people knew their place and where, she said, her family was much respected because her mother was a woman of some culture, who could read most beautifully and mov-ingly from the Scriptures and who even was a friend of musicians. Not only that, but her grandfather Ned Quade had once been mayor of the mainland town of Parramatta. Around Paradise, on the other hand, people were alto-gether coarser and some even talked openly of their convict forebears in the mean little wooden huts that they called homes, set in paddocks stubbled with tree stumps too big to pull out until they had rotted for years or decades. Such talk narked Rose, who rarely missed an opportunity of reminding the locals how her family, even if poor, was nevertheless descended from stout free settler stock. 'People have to make of themselves something better than they be,' she was fond of saying, 'so why on earth do they put themselves down by reminding others of their sinful origins?'

Rose believed there was nothing so shameful as having convict blood, and in her family she was not alone in this opinion. Rose was proud of her family, who, as she often remarked, had been people of some standing around Richmond. Occasionally one of her many brothers or sisters would come to stay with her and Boy up at Paradise. The men were soft creatures who brought sherry and proffered tailor-made cigarettes from tin cases that had their initials inscribed in the top right-hand corner in italics. They had jobs in Hobart as clerks and teachers. They had snobbery as a dog has fleas. It wasn't offensive. It was simply part of them. Albert, the eldest, was a priest. Boy liked Rose's brother Olsten the best, the one they all called Ruth. Rose said Ruth was a musician, which was true, but like much that Rose said about her family, it was a half-truth, as Boy discovered from Jack Roach, a fellow snarer, who had met Ruth at Boy and Rose's home. 'Musician my arse,' Jack said to Boy, 'that brother-in-law of yours tinkles the ivories in the Blue House in Hobart. The night I went there he was so pissed that one of Ma Dwyer's girls had to lean up against him to stop him falling off his stool while he played.' Even Ruth was not immune from the family weakness. He would sip sherry and talk of how the grand families were going on this or that estate, how the O'Connors had not had a good year at Benham, how the Burburys were set to expand, and so on and so on, expounding endlessly in a familiar fashion about a world that had nothing but contempt for a man who played piano nightly in a brothel on Hobart's wharves.

I tell you, it's far from an easy thing for a drowning bloke to watch the wretched truths of his family unfold. Because for me to watch all this is the same thing as telling it to you, as if I were simultaneously filmmaker, projectionist and audience, and I am not sure if it's really the right thing to do to divulge the family truths in this manner, even to myself in this watery hole. Loyalty is boasted of as both a Lewis and Cosini family trait, in between the whispered tattle-tale. Maybe I'm a miserable bastard even watching such things, for instantaneously what I see is what I know, and what I know you know, and what I see is that Rose's sisters were, like Rose, vivacious redheads, and, like Rose, I see that they had a streak of hardness that became more obvious as the sheen of fun that had been their youth tarnished. Boy learnt to respect them, but he could never find it in him to like them. They became more and more dogmatic in their religion as they grew older. Like Rose they craved respectability, which they equated with education and a peculiar accent that much amused Boy. Over tea – an elegant if somewhat forced and awkward ritual that inevitably took place in the parlour – they would purse their lips, pushing their top lip forward in a V shape, and in endless failed attempts seek to inflate their flat vowels by speaking a half-octave higher than they would in conversation in the kitchen. But their words sank to the floor and remained there, draped across the parlour like so

53

many uninflated balloons. Their conversation was about priests they had known and about bishops they had never met, but mostly it was about Richmond and the people they had grown up with there. Some they spoke of with great affection, and some, such as the Proctors, the local bakers, with great hate. This was unusual, for although the Quades were good haters, they also were obsessed with etiquette and believed that while it was permissible to whisper poisonous asides, it was a rudeness to openly condemn anybody. But of the Proctors – and particularly their eldest son and now the town baker, Eric, referred to only as Doughy Proctor – they were openly venomous. This perplexed Boy until Ruth, one night after two bottles of sherry and a few whiskies, told Boy how, as children, the Quades would come in from the farm on their dray to Richmond for church on Sundays, and Doughy Proctor would walk in the dust behind the dray as it slowly wheeled into the main street, with a gaggle of kids behind him, all of them chanting, 'Convicts! Convicts! Convicts!' And how their mother would just look straight ahead, as if the thin lines of her bonnet defined her world.

'Why would they carry on like that?' asked Boy when Ruth divulged this piece of information.

'Well,' said Ruth, 'what greater insult could you hurl at a proud free settler family?'

Sometimes of a night Harry would hear his mother crying in her sleep and wonder what bad dreams she had that would make her feel so.

Though Rose talked of her mother and her father a great deal, the truth was that unlike Ruth, who was ten years older, she remembered little of them, for her mother Jessie Quade had died of consumption when Rose was three. Rose's father George decided he didn't want to be burdened with having to look after Rose and her three older brothers, Eddie, Albert, and Ruth, and two older sisters, Celia and Flora. So it was that Jessie's sister Eileen and her husband, known only as Tronce, who had no children, took Jessie's children and raised them as if they were their own. George disappeared to the mainland for four years and returned married to a young woman called Lil Winter. Two years went by and George and Lil discovered that they were a barren couple. Unable to have children of their own, they began calling upon Eileen and Tronce. George took to being with the kids as if he were their father, which, as everybody knew, he was in the flesh but not in the soul. After some months he announced to Eileen and Tronce that he was taking Rose back. He wasn't interested in the boys or the older sisters though, not that he said that to Eileen and Tronce. 'We'll see how Lil goes with Rose, and if that works out then we'll take the rest back,' he told Eileen. It nearly broke Eileen's heart, for she had grown fond of all the children and particularly fond of Rose. And she knew that George would never come back for the other children. He and Lil Winter just wanted a pretty little daughter. Rose sat next to George on the trap as the horse plodded all the long distance from Richmond back up to Bellerive crying all the way.

'What you sobbing about?' asked George. 'Ya going home, don't ya know?' And as he put his arm around her George smiled, for she was indeed a pretty child.

When George brought her through the door Lil smiled too. 'She is beautiful. Why George, she has got your eyes too!' Rose knew only too well and sobbed all the louder. Having his daughter back didn't stop George drinking too much and he and Lil began to fight something terrible, so bad that in the end they decided to leave Tasmania, which they blamed for all that made them unhappy.

'We'll disappear and ain't nobody'll ever know what became of us and the child,' said George, 'and won't that just nark Eileen and Tronce.' They booked a ticket on the boat to Sydney, and it was on the evening before the boat was due to go that Uncle Tronce turned up and demanded Rose back. Eileen, who was from the spiritual side of the family, had strange powers. The index finger of her right hand came out in warts and she sensed something bad was about to befall Rose. She told Tronce that he must go and bring her back. George wasn't happy about it, but then he was drunk and Tronce was bigger, and in the ensuing fist fight George was laid out. Lil screamed and screamed, but beyond throwing a vase at Tronce and missing him, did nothing. Rose sobbed all the way back to Richmond as she sat next to Uncle Tronce on his trap. She stopped sobbing when they didn't stop at Richmond but kept heading east. She stopped feeling upset and started feeling mystified as the trap made its slow way along the old rutted coach road toward Port Arthur. Tronce took the dray down through the wild, thickly wooded Forestier Peninsula, and when Rose turned around and looked behind she saw that the huge trees seemed to close in, swallowing up the narrow track behind them and the moon and stars above them. Tronce continued all the way down to Eaglehawk Neck, the slash of land connecting the Tasmanian mainland to Tasman Peninsula. There, in the long early morning shadows thrown by a huge and ancient almond tree, stood the old officers' quarters, a dilapidated half-wood, half-brick building that was the last remnant of the once infamous dog line – a chain of poorly fed wild dogs that had stretched across the width of the Neck, their job to rip apart any convict escaping from the vast penal settlement at Port Arthur – and in this sparse military barracks turned into a humble home, Rose was hidden by the Costello family, long-time friends of Tronce.

At Richmond Eileen prayed and prayed that no harm would befall Rose, and even sent money to holy places in France so that they too would pray on Rose's behalf. George came down to see Eileen and Tronce and threatened and blustered, but got nowhere, so he went into Hobart and hired a lawyer to find Rose and get her back. At the Neck Rose cried from fear of that eerie place. Of a night the boom of the waves crashing in on the wild ocean beach that lay below mixed with the screams – like that of a woman being strangled – of the Tasmanian devils as they came into the vegetable garden and ate the cabbage and rhubarb. The Neck was not a place in which Rose felt it was possible to be happy. She cried day in, day out and wet her pants for the first time since she was a wean, and then cried all the more from the shame and the fear of it all.

One day, playing near the sand dunes a few hundred yards from the vegetable garden, Rose found a strange piece of bone, too big to be a sheep and unlike any cattle bone she had ever seen. The children took it home and Mr Costello took the bone to the police constable at Nubeena. At first it was thought that the bone belonged to an unfortunate convict who had perished attempting escape decades earlier. But when they came to excavate the sand dune, they discovered not one but many skeletons, all in the same position, with the knees pulled up underneath the chin. Scientists came down from the Hobart museum and concluded that it was an Aboriginal burial ground. Rose's nightmares found a recurrent form in the shape of the sand dune skeletons unfolding and standing up and then chasing her all the way back to Lil and George's in Hobart. As she ran they screamed, and their scream was that of the Tasmanian devils in the dark.

The case of who should have possession of Rose was only days away from being heard when Eileen's prayers seemed to finally have some effect and George's lawyer was found with his brains blown out. It was said to be suicide. Even Tronce was impressed, and to the end of his days said that you should never push Eileen too far because she could pray so powerful she could kill you. Soon after there was a scandal when Lil ran off with a horse trainer to Kalgoorlie in Western Australia. George didn't have the money to pursue the matter any further, drank even more, and some months later he too left Tasmania, bound, he said, for Sydney. Not that Rose was aware of any of this down at the Neck. Nobody thought it fit or proper to fill her in on such goings on. Even with George gone, Tronce and Eileen kept Rose hidden at the Neck for another year before they dared bring her home. So until the day that Tronce returned with his dray, she continued going to the small school on the far side of the Neck, playing on the vast, empty white beach with the few other kids who lived local, and listening to the ocean ebbing and rising, wondering if her own life had any more reason to it than the gentle rise and sudden crash of the ocean waves, wondering if it was her destiny to spend the rest of her life at the Neck, far from her brothers and sisters.

Harry never met Tronce, who died some years before Harry was born. His memories of Eileen were of a tiny sparrowlike woman with a large, bright pink nose, off which hung peels of skin, the parchment-yellow colour of toenails. These memories arose from Rose's yearly holiday in Richmond with Eileen, which came to an end with Eileen's death in Harry's sixth year. Eileen's house was dark and smelt of carbolic soap and stale bread, for Eileen, who had grown hard and mean in the manner of the women of her family, ate little. She had also grown, if anything, even more religious in her old age, and for most of those holidays Harry remembered being upon his knees chanting the rosary with other old biddies Eileen gathered in to help her beseech the Lord above for forgiveness.

Eileen's funeral was a grand affair in the Hobart cathedral. Half of Richmond seemed to be there. As the Scriptures were being read it began to rain so heavily that the sound of the rain on the roof above, amplified in the cavernous space of the cathedral's interior, drowned out the reader. Harry looked up at the ceiling and noticed something moving at the top of the walls. Droplets of crimson fluid. Harry reached up and tugged Rose's coat arm. 'The walls, Mum,' he whispered, 'the walls are bleeding.' Rose looked down at Harry, rather than up at the walls, but even as she scolded him, others who had overheard Harry looked up and saw the walls now bleeding in thick heavy runs and droplets. Even the priests, dressed in their finest mufti, looked up and abandoned their normal solemnity and started to point and chatter to one another. As the storm above grew in ferocity, as thunder roared and rain crashed upon the roof in sheets, the bleeding became more pronounced, until the walls appeared to be haemorrhaging. Wherever the congregation of mourners chose to look there was blood. Occasional droplets fell onto the burning candles in the brass stand that sat up against the wall to the right of the altar. Blood began to run onto the Stations of the Cross. It dripped over the figure of Our Blessed Lady, giving to the Virgin Mother a ghoulish aspect as a rill of blood ran round her cheek to her mouth, from where it dribbled down onto her open palm.

But the most miraculous sight was that of the large crucifix behind the altar. At first a small amount of blood had merely – and, it had seemed, solemnly and respectfully – run onto Our Saviour's nailed right hand, whence it gently fell to the floor, the effect melancholic and in keeping with the sublime and transformed suffering portrayed in the sculpture. But then, as the storm grew wilder, the blood spilled over His head and flooded over His body, until the crucifix seemed awash with blood. As it ran all over the body of Our Lord upon the cross, the blood gave to the previously inert figure a most immediate and horrifying sense of physical agony. Sobs of shock and fear ran through the mourners and a few scurried along the aisles and left, too frightened to stay. But most remained, transfixed by the spectacle, their fear outweighed by their wonder. And when at last the rain stopped and the bleeding subsided to occasional drops and the priest held out his arms and said, 'Let us pray,' most believed they had witnessed a miracle in keeping with Rose's Old Testament religion. Those who later heard that the blood was actually the result of incomplete restoration work on the roof were not inclined to believe it. The story of roof repairmen, immediately prior to an unexpected storm, abandoning wet red paint to run in the rain through unplugged gaps in the roof had little chance against a miracle. While one story was repeated and grew in the telling from a small seed to a large tree of tales, until half the town swore that they had been at the funeral and had seen the Lord bleed, the other story went astray, languished and soon was heard no more, for none wanted to know it.

There were two unforeseen consequences of Eileen's spectacular funeral. One was that the cathedral became something of a local pilgrimage point, and some miracles were ascribed to its special powers. The church authorities were uneasy about its new status, but were unable to publicly say a great deal against it. The other was that Eileen, in her death, was elevated to the position of something of a local saint, which was an exaggeration of her virtues, for she was on occasion bad tempered and vicious, and invariably hard and mean. But whereas in life she had by nature been contrary and always contradicted anyone and everyone, in death she was silent upon the virtues attributed to her, and so the stories of her goodness and charity grew. These amused Boy, who remembered how parsimonious she had been with food and how silly she could be when frightened.

When the bushfires had ringed Richmond in that year of fires, 1934, she had gathered as many local children as she could find inside her home and solemnly told them that the end of the world was nigh. Outside, the day was ferociously hot and gale-force winds whipped small sparks into raging infernos in the tinder-dry bush and pasture. As the fires burnt over an ever greater area of land, the sky filled with ash and the town fell under a pall of smoke so dense that, were it not for shafts of late-afternoon light shining underneath the heavy dark voids of ash, it would have seemed as if it were night. Inside the house Eileen shut all the doors and windows, and in the stifling stillness made the children take turns reading from Revelations

61

about the end of the earth. Harry, who was on holiday with Eileen, had been rounded up from the street outside along with the MacGuires, some of the Greens and Juno Proctor. Harry wasn't so sure it was as bad as Eileen was making out, and, curious to know what was going on outside the darkened parlour, out in the cracking winds under the ash-black sky and amidst the heavy smell of smoke, said he would just go out and make sure the earth was ending, because if it were, he didn't want to miss it for quids. And before Eileen could scruff him, Harry and Juno Proctor were up and out the back door.

Rose died giving birth to Daisy when Harry was ten. Her death came as a surprise to no one except Harry, who had accepted as normal and healthy what was rather the evidence of a person not long for this earth.

Before the funeral the men sat around the coffin in the parlour and drank beer while the women sat out in the kitchen and drank tea. Neither the women nor the men talked that much, because Rose's life had not been a long one full of incident and anecdote, had not been a life that in death made people realise how much they shared in common. Rose's early death made people think, and what it made them think about brought nobody much happiness. It reminded them that they were poor people whose lives were largely ones of hard drudgery, that the incessant work took its toll and could take people away before their time. It reminded them that their lives could be as thin as the gruel made up of kangaroo tails and spuds that they some-times fed their children. There was not even that rich, desperate melancholia about the occasion that might accompany the death of an old local celebrity – a melancholia as thick as the clotted cream on the sponge cakes that sat heavy upon the lace-dressed sideboard in the parlour.

After a time the men made their farewells to Boy and his family. The women cleaned up and put the children in bed, then they too left, until there were only Boy and Ruth sitting in the parlour. Ruth pulled out a tin hip-flask, a sister piece, Boy observed, to his cigarette case, complete with Ruth's italicised initials engraved in one corner. He poured half the hip-flask's whiskey into his empty beer glass and half into Boy's empty beer glass. Boy sipped at the whiskey. Ruth didn't. Ruth ran the nail of his right thumb along his upper front teeth. Then he spoke.

'You think I am the only one of Rose's family here because the rest of them are snubbing the funeral. Because they think Rose married below her station.'

Boy looked up at Ruth. 'No,' said Boy.

'You'd have a right to think it,' said Ruth.

'No,' said Boy. 'I don't think it. It's a long way, Richmond to here, and they've got their work and their families. I understand that.'

'They could have come,' said Ruth. 'If they had wanted to. But they're snobs. You know that, Boy. You don't need me to tell you. But you have got to understand.'

Boy looked at Ruth and saw he hadn't touched the whiskey in his beer glass. He saw that Ruth was looking at him, not at the beer glass and not at the floor, and he guessed that he could perhaps speak his mind. Boy spoke without rancour, without even bitterness. But with a certain deep sadness that now Rose had gone the wrong he felt would never be righted. Boy spoke slowly. 'What do you mean, I've got to understand? Ain't nothing to understand. They think I am shit. Well, they're right. I am shit. I snare in winter and I work on the threshing machines in summer and in between jobs I poach to feed the family. I ain't proud but I ain't ashamed.'

Ruth looked at Boy uncomfortable in his old cheap navy suit cut in the fashion popular before the Great War, at the wide black band around his right sleeve; looked at the way his big flat fingers played with his beer glass, at the thin black hair parted in the middle.

'You have to understand,' said Ruth, 'why we are snobs.'

'Well, I understand *that*,' said Boy. 'Some people are cranky and some are bone idle and some are snobs. That's just how it is.'

'Maybe,' said Ruth. 'Maybe not.' He paused and leant forward in the overstuffed armchair with the horsehair falling out of the holes in the arms. 'Look. Did Rose ever talk to you about family? Our family?'

'Yeah. All the time. Never stopped about what you were doing and how well you were all going.'

'But did she ever talk about old Grandad Quade?'

'No, not really. A lot about old woman Quade. But not much about him, no.'

'He was a convict.'

'Who?'

'Ned Quade. Rose's grandfather.'

Madonna santa!

I can see that Boy was shocked and not shocked. And no wonder – so am I. Nobody ever told me this either, and yet, I, like Boy, feel as if I always knew but never suspected a thing, never ever thought but always knew such momentous shame hung over the family.

Boy's lips started to move, then stopped. Boy then mumbled a word or two, all the time the furrows in his face dancing up and down as if he were doing some long involved piece of mental arithmetic, adding up so many different things that he had never before recognised as being part of a single grand equation. Realising that he had not said anything proper in reply, Boy grew a little embarrassed and made a small joke to buy a bit more time thinking. He lifted his beer glass and said, 'Thank God you poured me a whiskey,' smiled weakly, gulped down some of the whiskey, then finished the glass off with a second, more determined, swallow. And then he was back adding up all the strange evasions, the conceits, the curious pride, the black shames that had been his wife's nature and his despair, and he arrived at the same solution that Ruth had offered. He checked and rechecked the evidence in his mind, but the addition was its own truth, allowing no other solution. Ruth continued to watch. Boy's face finally stopped twitching and moved upwards to look once again at Ruth.

'Why the hell . . .?' said Boy, but his voice trailed off, because he did know why the hell, because he did know what it must have meant to her, because he did know how it must have been terrible for her to continually lie to herself and to everyone else, but worse to turn and look at the unspeakable, unnameable shadow, and to give it a name and give tongue to that name in conversation with others. 'Why the hell didn't . . .?' said Boy, but for a second time his voice trailed away, because he knew fully why, even before Ruth told him.

'Why would she want you to know? Ain't no good anybody knowing you got convict blood. Who's going to respect you? There ain't nobody respects a crawler's kith and kin. And respect is everything. Without respect a man is no better than a dog. Who's going to give you a decent job if you've got the *taint*?' The final word came out of Ruth's throat with a peculiar harshness, as if the word itself carried chains and could be summoned up only with some effort from his guts, as if it flagellated his throat and tongue on its journey to his lips. Ruth sipped his beer glass of whiskey to ease the pain the word gave his mouth.

'It might not matter much snaring up in the highlands,' he continued. 'But it matters everywhere else. And what sort of future your children got if word gets out they got the taint? They're as good as filth. There's no future with that sort of past.'

Now, I've never been much interested in history. What's past is past, that's been my motto. Get on with now. All this business Ruth is dredging up should be dead and long gone. But it's not. The past isn't ever over, otherwise why would I be starting to get that pain back in my guts just watching Ruth and Boy? And if the past doesn't matter, why was Boy getting so angry?

I can see that now he knows the lie, he hates the way it came between him and Rose, the way it always kept them separate despite his love, the way it always made her despise as dirt the one she loved above all others, and inevitably left him unhappy when he was with her. But the angrier he gets, the less any of it makes any sense, and though he knows the answer he asks the question.

'Then why the hell is the family such a pack of bloody snobs if they're only the whelps of an old crawler?' Boy asked Ruth.

'Because they *are* the whelps and the whelps of whelps of an old crawler. Because to get somewhere we had to make up a new world to replace their old world, because there was no hope for any of us in that old world. That's what old Eileen taught us, and she was right. And if part of that new world means being a bit superior and putting on the plum – well, so be it. I admire the family for making something of itself out of nothing. Cos having nothing and wanting something meant pretending to have everything.'

Ruth paused. He had played piano for some difficult crowds at Ma Dwyer's and he had learnt the value of the pregnant pause. Boy looked up at Ruth, expecting him to say more, then looked away when no more came, then looked back and said, 'But you can't go around denying your own blood.'

'Why not? Look, the whole country does it. We pretend we're gentry and we're not. And you think it's bad. But do you ever wonder why they renamed Van Diemen's Land Tasmania? They wanted everyone to forget, that's why. And everyone wanted to forget with them. Whether they were convict or policeman, none of them thought it was worth remembering.' Ruth was an educated man. He had, after all, finished high school. And Rose had often told Boy how, if he had not followed his path in music, he would almost certainly have become a school teacher, so clever was Ruth. He was a great reader and owned over fifty books, all of which he kept locked in a big battered green trunk in his bedroom. Boy found it hard to say anything that came close to matching the cleverness of what Ruth was saying. But without being able to analyse and reply on equal terms to Ruth, he felt – as he sometimes felt when he saw a piece of timber and, without using a level, without even raising it to his eye, felt so strongly that he *knew* – that something in Ruth's logic was warped.

And the next morning when Ruth arose late and said that he had drunk so much that he could remember nothing of the night before, then Boy knew that what he knew was right.

A river can grant you visions in an act at once generous and despicable, but even a river like the Franklin in full flood cannot explain everything. It cannot show me where, for example, after Rose's death, Harry's three older sisters were sent into domestic service in Launceston, cannot even show me what their faces were like, and that is a cause for sadness for which the river seems to try and compensate by showing where his baby sister Daisy was sent, the town of Strahan, a small port on the remote and wild west coast of the island, to there live with Boy's mother, her grandmother, known in spite of her many and varying blood relations only as Auntie Ellie. Nor can the river's waters reveal to me why Boy was at such a loss what to do with Harry, or why, when the snaring season opened, he felt impelled to take Harry with him, but I can only assume that he too must have had some vision, some premonition of his own mortality.

The river does show me that the father and his son spent two weeks packing their gear and food into the remote hut. They walked through the last of the farmland, the boggy, marginal paddocks of the soldier settlers whose hope sagged even more than their post-and-rail fences. The meadows gave way to button-grass plains and scrub, then, as they slowly climbed, to a wonder world of pencil pine and King Billy pine forests, wide and open, interspersed with lawns of undamaged moss, the occasional deciduous beech copse orange in its final autumn show. Harry had never been to the hut before, and was surprised when he first had it pointed out to him by Boy. They stood at the head of a thickly forested valley, and down below them in a small and pleasant grass clearing sat a hut built of split timber and roofed with wooden shingles, the whole long silvered in the rain and sun, each plank finely etched with tiny tendrils and tufts of dry moss. To the left of the hut was a more roughly built shed, which Boy explained was for storing the skins.

Harry learnt to lay the thin twisted brass-wire snares out along the wallaby runs. He set them so that they dangled just above the track, near invisible. When a wallaby or possum came scurrying along their customary track it would run straight into the snare. The wire loop would slip around the animal's neck and, released from its peg in the ground, spring into the air, tightening as the desperate animal struggled and thrashed to be free. 'It but bothers them little,' said Boy to Harry, but Harry was never quite so sure. The small shit that hung out of their arses and the dried blood line down the side of their mouths said otherwise. But Boy was not one for killing anything unnecessarily, and all his family were as soft as warm dripping when it came to killing things that didn't need killing. Boy's brother George would lay a piece of wet bark down the side of the logs burning in the fire to allow the ants to escape, and only shot just what was needed for his pot. Harry learnt to kill quickly and cleanly. He learnt to cook wallaby stew, to not cook the delicate meat for too long lest it became dry and papery to the tongue, learnt to cook his father's favourite meal, roo patties, and he learnt to make bread in a fire. He learnt also to love his father, who until that time had been a distant figure, often away for months at a time snaring, or working on the huge threshing machines that went from farm to farm up the coast, returning to sleep, drink, and fight with Rose, sometimes hitting her when he had drunk too much. At such times Rose would cry, though it was evident even to Harry that she cried as much out of sadness as physical pain. When she held her children to her belly and Harry's head pulsed in and out with the sob of her body, Harry

69

knew, though he would not have been able to say it, that she wished for something better between her and Boy, and that she knew it would never happen.

In the hut and out on the snaring runs Harry found Boy neither distant nor violent, but quiet and happy and warm and open to his son. He pointed out the ways of the animals and the birds and plants and smiled more than Harry could ever remember him smiling. One morning Harry asked Boy why he had never brought Rose up to the hut. The question seemed obvious to Harry, for if they had lived in the hut, he thought, then their lives would have perhaps been happier. 'What would your mother be wanting to live here for?' said Boy, perplexed by the question. Harry never raised the matter again.

Of an evening Harry would make the roo patties and watch the red firelight flutter upon his father's small compact body as he tacked the latest batch of skins around the inside of the fireplace to dry. Harry would watch the fireglow briefly illuminate in old-gold puddles the grey flannel his father wore upon his upper body, long and loose, flapping down to his worn brown breeches. The glow would sometimes throw his father's face into total darkness, then highlight in turn a part of the wooden wall behind, so that Harry would imagine his father merging into the soft brown and grey hues so completely that he became one of the hut's upright King Billy pine posts. Sometimes Harry would be sent out to the drying shed where the skins were stored to fetch more wood, and though he would go obediently he would be filled with fear by the leaping, cavorting shadows thrown by the dull greasy yellow light of the kerosene lantern that swung from his outstretched arm.

Those shadows, those greasy, slippery shadows, they

dance before me now like some cabaret of lost souls of slaughtered animals performing a burlesque in Hell, and amidst the moist snouts of possums and wallabies I can see one more soul depart its human body. But then, of course, nothing was so immediately or obviously apparent, particularly for Harry. Watching him now, I can see Harry did not know when Boy died. Harry did not know for four days that his father had been squashed lifeless under a rotten myrtle limb, fallen down in the wind and his father unlucky enough to be standing beneath it. Harry lay in bed all the first day, sick and sweating from a fever, seeing in his hallucinations strange things form themselves out of the rough split rafters, animals cavorting and square-ended dinghies rowing through the air. Boy had told him to stay put for the day on account of his sickness and not bother with any work. 'Cept maybe keeping the fire going and getting the roo patties ready for tea.' Harry lay there till late afternoon, then he built the fire up good and blazing. He went out to the drying shed and picked the oldest of three wallaby carcasses hanging in the drying chimney there. The carcass was black from the smoke. Harry cut a leg off the carcass and took it inside where he boned and minced the meat. He then boiled and squashed some potatoes into the meat, adding some bacon and diced onion, then, despite his nausea, rolled the mixture into ten balls, which he squashed flat. He set them in the pan with some dripping, but didn't put them on the fire, waiting for the signal of the noise of his father returning. After it had been dark for some time Harry's unease turned to a terrible cold fear, and he fought the fear down by pulling the blankets over his shoulders and face and retreating into the strange strong sleep of the sick.

When he awoke everything was black, the fire long out. He looked at the bunk below him, but no form covered the stretched hessian sugar sacks that served as a mattress. His father had not returned. Try as he might, sleep would not come to Harry. Outside he heard the soft swish of snow falling and the occasional scream of a devil, loud and piercing. Finally he got up, lit the kerosene lantern, and sat in its weak puddle of light till morning came. Only then did he return to his bed. That night he built the fire up again, but this time he had filled the hut with wood during the day so that he would not have to venture out into the drying shed in the dark. Shortly before nightfall he stood at the doorway and called his father's name, but there came no reply. He called again and again, called until he was hoarse, then went inside, but did not cry for fear his father would at that moment of weakness walk in and find him blubbering. He sat the pan with the roo patties next to the fire once again, ready to go on the fire at the sound of footsteps. There were no footsteps that night or the following night. There was a lot of snow. There was a lot of cold wind. Harry burnt the kerosene lantern through the second night and through most of the third night, until there was so little kerosene left that he had to put it out so that there would be some to use when Boy returned. On the morning of the fourth day Harry's fever passed and was replaced by the serene weakness of those who have not eaten for so long that their bodies no longer recognise the sensation of hunger. Though he felt no desire beyond that of wishing to endure till his father returned, he recognised that he must eat. He cooked the ten roo patties he had prepared four days before, ate them all with a growing urgency, then prepared and cooked and ate another ten. Then he knew he must go search for his father.

He boiled some potatoes to take with him and put them in a sugar bag. He put on his father's bluey coat, which his father had left the day he had last been at the hut, for that, unlike now, had been a warm and pleasant day. He strung the sugar bag around his body with a piece of old thin hemp. He stood up, walked over to the fireplace, hitched up the thick black flaps of the bluey coat that hung heavy as a woollen blanket down to his knees, opened the buttons of his fly, and pissed on the dying fire. A small cloud of ammoniac ash and steam rose from the fireplace, as if a miniature bomb had struck. Harry did up his fly, let the coat flaps fall back, turned, and walked out of the hut.

He found his father an hour and a half later, up one of his runs, a great branch on top of him, his body a stiff snow-white form. It did not anger Harry that the carrion-eating devils had eaten half his father's face and parts of his hands and arms. That was how it was. It was the same law that allowed them to snare wallabies with the slag of blood about their mouths. But like he felt for the wallabies he felt for his father. He felt shock. The way that in death the pink bone of his father's skull looked so similar to the pink bone of the wallaby carcasses. Shocked at the way living things can be killed, and how there is no coming back from death. He went back to the hut and returned with a rope, an axe and a spade. He chopped the branch into sections that he could drag away with his rope, then nearby found a small, straggly stringybark gum, Boy's favourite tree, close to which he dug a hole through the snow and into the hard, stony earth below for his father's body. This labour took most of the rest of the day. By the end of it he was very weak again. Harry placed his father's body in the grave, covered the savaged side of the face with small branches of beech, looked at the half that remained and tried to remember his father. But Harry could recall nothing, and he felt ashamed that the only thought in his mind was how the sprigs of beech betopping Boy's coarsely hued and textured woollen clothing made his father look more like a tree than ever. Albeit a fallen, broken tree. Harry filled the grave up with dirt, at first slow but then quicker and quicker, because as his body worked he felt his soul fill with an anger. Why had his dad done this? Harry's anger became a fury and the fury propelled mounds of earth violently into the grave, until there was no respect or grief but only something that verged on hate. Why had Boy stood under this tree? Why had he allowed this branch to fell him, when all that while Harry was waiting at the hut for him in his sick bed? Why had Boy forgotten him? Left him? Betrayed him? Not that Harry said any of these things or anything at all. Not that Harry even had words for what he thought. But Harry felt it and he felt it as a flame that consumed his body. Then the grave was full and complete with a mound. And Harry's fury dissipated into the cold early evening air as quickly and completely as his mist-breath. He felt as if nothing remained within him, not love, not hate, not even a desire to move. He turned for home and had taken at best six steps when something impelled him to swing around and look one last time at the grave. What he saw was miraculous. The stringybark was unfolding into massive lemon-coloured blossom, six weeks of summer compressed into as many minutes of winter.

Harry returned home in the dark. This time the

darkness did not frighten him. Nothing seemed to touch him. He felt as if he were his father's ghost.

He went straight to bed without even lighting a fire. The next morning he ground up more of the roo meat, cooked sixteen roo patties, ate four, and packed the rest in a possum skin in his sugar bag. He boiled a dozen potatoes and put them in with the patties. He filled up the rest of the sugar bag with matches, a billy, some tea and sugar and a blanket. Then he went out to the drying shed and carefully tied three dozen wallaby skins onto the back of his pack with hemp string, wrapping the lot in Boy's oilskin coat. To not carry them out would, he knew, be a waste of a trip. There were hundreds of skins remaining and it would take a number of trips to get them all out, but Harry knew that by taking what skins he could, no one could accuse him of being a bludger and shirking his duties. He knew he ought go and clear his snares of the latest catch, but he did not desire to see any more death. Instead he struck out north west, back to the land of people and farms and towns.

Harry had been walking for a day and a half when he met up with his uncles George and Basil. Before Harry even spoke, they seemed to know what had happened. They looked at him in a way different than he had ever been looked at before. They looked at him as if he were no longer a child but an adult. Harry looked up at the two men. George short and, as was Boy, built like a brick shithouse. Basil as thin and sinewy and tough as a piece of reused fencing wire, and on occasion as brittle. The one whom Harry would end up resembling. Basil went round the back of Harry and took the pack off his shoulders. 'Get the load off your feet, Nugget,' said George, Nugget being the name the family had taken to calling him on account of his complexion, so dark that Basil, who (and perhaps for this very reason) was every bit as dark as Harry, once said Harry looked as if someone had rubbed his face with Nugget boot polish.

They all sat down. The long man with the sinewy arms and wide shoulders on a fallen log, thereby accentuating his height; the squat, powerful man with his back to the log, thereby accentuating his shortness, and opposite them the dark boy-man with the face that spoke of nothing and suggested everything. Basil rifled around in the right pocket of his pants and pulled out a battered tin, from which he took a pack of cigarette papers and some tobacco. Placing the tin between his legs, Basil moistened the edge of three cigarette papers and stuck the three papers to his chapped lower lip, so that they dangled like washed nappies from a clothesline, then used his flat index finger, the tip of which was missing from some long-ago chopping accident, to roll the tobacco leaves into three sticks in his left palm. He placed each stick into a paper and rolled it into a cigarette. When he was finished, Basil placed the three cigarettes in the left side of his mouth, lit all three with one vesta struck off his boot, and passed one to Harry and another to George. They sat there, enjoying the brief flare at the end of the smoke as they inhaled and the sensation of the savoury wet sweet smoke filling their mouths and tumbling down their throats and out of their noses, not looking at each other, all looking straight ahead or straight down till George, in his low voice both melodious and gravelly, finally spoke.

Saying: 'And Boy?'

Harry turned and looked at George, and knew what he must say and how he must say it, like a man, and he was at once grateful for being allowed the space between his feelings and his tongue that this response allowed: 'A tree,' said Harry. He stopped.

After a time George said, 'Yep,' as though he had just lost some money at the horses and was philosophical about the loss. George looked down at the rollie he held between his thumb and forefinger, the smouldering end shielded within the cavern of his curled hand, and, his voice now a halting whisper, said, 'Ye-ep,' as though it were two words, two of the saddest words he knew.

Harry knew he had to say something more.

'A rotten branch of bloody myrtle,' he blurted. Now he was a man, now that he had the respect of his uncles as their equal, he immediately wanted back the woman ways allowed a boy-child, wanted to hug George's belly and cry and cry. But that was not possible. So instead he focused his eyes on the coal-red tip of his rollie, inhaled to make it flame, and then closed his eyes as the smoke unravelled in fern coils in his mouth. He thought he saw his mother coming toward him, a very powerful feeling it was, and she said, 'I love you,' and then was gone. Harry opened his eyes and spoke in a slow and quiet voice.

Saying: 'Six days ago.'

— Four —

I could, of course, be mad. That is a possibility. That is also a form of hope. If insane, this entire horror is nothing more than a delusion, a malfunction of nerve endings and electrochemical impulses. If sane, I am in true agony. In hell. If sane, I am dying. And being humiliated by memory at the same time. For I am none too happy with what this moving weight of water, this river is showing me. When I was a kid I wished for a set of x-ray specs like they had in the cartoons, that showed you the bird cooking in the cat's mind while the cat croons sweetly to the bird, that showed the crook with moneybags for a heart who is telling the sweet old rich lady how much he likes her terrible cooking. I used to watch them with Milton, on the street outside Burgess's electrical store where they had a grand display of televisions working in the front window, and everyone who didn't have one of these new wonders — which was most of Hobart for a long time — stood in the rain and the heat and the traffic fumes, laughing and pointing and saying it was only a fad. Now my wish has come true and I wish it hadn't. These visions are my x-ray specs – with them I see not the surface reality but what really took place, stripped of all its confusing superficial detail. Except what I see now exposed isn't a cat or a comic crook. It is me. And I am not pleased about that, about the way the river is shoving my mind and heart about, pushing my body, forcing open parts that I thought closed forever.

Because I could be mad, but I know I am not. And I know I can't stop seeing what I am seeing, what took place back then – the bedroom filled with tears, which then spilt over into the small kitchen and the dingy bathroom and from there filled the bedrooms and the loungeroom, so many tears that we swam in them and began to drown in them. At which point I opened the door and the dam burst and out roared a river of tears, and being washed away with that river was me, to be taken in its turbulent waters in a crazy serpentine course through the next thirteeen years of my life all over this vast continent.

A river of tears.

Upon its banks, on a small beach of river sand, I spy Aljaz sleeping as the forest takes its forms and shapes for the day in the earliest of dawn's dim light. Wet and pungent comes the smell of the damp black earth to my nostrils; of the forest dying, to be reborn as fecund rot and fungi, small and waxy, large and luminous; to be reborn as moss and myrtle seedlings, minuscule and myriad; as Huon pine sprigs, forcing their way through the crumbling damp decay, forked and knowing as a water diviner's stick; as the celery top saplings, looking as if a market gardener had planted them there; as the small hardwater ferns and old scrubbing-brush-topped pan-danni. Here, ensconced within the river's waters I see it all, feel it all, sense everything that once was part of my recent life. It's as if I am now lying there on the ground beside Aljaz on that morning so distant it seems impossible it was only three days ago. As if I too am beginning to drink the richness, of that early morning into my body and soul. Aljaz sits up and sees that his sleeping mat and bag lie within the white sand perimeter of riverbank dried and kept dry by the campfire that lies at the hub of the circle, now reduced to a fine hot dust and a few pieces of charcoal. A kangaroo rat scavenging vegetable scraps at the fire's edge bounds away the moment it senses Aljaz's woken presence. Aljaz rolls over onto his stomach and looks at the black wet earth beyond the circle, at the mist above and around, and runs his fingers through the white river sand, dry and warm. He deftly kicks his sleeping bag off and naked walks to the site of the fire, upon which he place a few sticks as thin as string and upon which he then blows gently through pursed lips until a lick of flame begins that morning.

— the third day —

That day, the third of their journey, they paddled their rafts on and their paddling took them further into remote country, more days away from any vestige of modern people. Took them past huge rocks that arose from the water like monsters, past sandbanks bearing traces of strange animal prints, took them through the sound of wind moving manferns in the most beautiful of motions, like sea anemones on the ocean floor. Not that the punters saw this or much else for that matter, for they only saw what they knew and they knew none of it, and recognised little, and most of that was the world they carried within their crab-backed rafts – their tents and dry camp clothes and coffee pots and routines and rules for ordering the crowding chaos that loomed over them and threatened them and which Aljaz felt as a caress. They felt consumed by the river, felt that they had allowed it to chew them up in its early gorges and were now being digested in its endlessly winding entrails that cut back and forth in crazed meanderings through vast unpeopled mountain ranges. And it frightened them, these people from far away cities whose only measure was man; it terrified them, this world in which the only measure was things that man had not made, the rocks and the mountains and the rain and the sun and the trees and the earth. The river brought them all these feelings, and of a night it brought worse: the most terrible blackness, the most abrupt and ceaseless noises of rushing water and wind in leaves and nocturnal animals moving. There were of course the stars, but their infinite space was no solace, only evidence of a further encircling world in which it was possible to be lost and never found and never heard.

Some of the punters went quiet. Others began to talk more and more. They took photographs of streams that looked like wilderness calendars, and rocks they fancied looked like a human face or a man-made form – a boat, a machine, a house. On balance, Aljaz preferred the quiet ones.

A cold zephyr raced past them, hurriedly announcing the cold front it preceded, and then like some youthful scurrying envoy of war was gone again, too soon for the punters to readily apprehend its message, long enough for Aljaz to stop feeling relaxed.

They paddled on. Then two kayakers in boats of bright

yellow and luminous blue were upon them and they said that their names were Jim and Fin and that they had left the Collingwood Bridge only the day before. Their kayaks were much faster than the plodding rafts and the kayakers were skilful and nimble in their handling of their craft. They played on the rapids like water creatures, darting back and forth as if they were freshwater porpoises. They talked a little to the punters and said that they were pushing on through Deception Gorge that very same day because the long-range weather forecast was for a huge low coming in from the west and they wanted to be well clear of the gorge before the bad weather really struck. They appeared a little drunk and every so often one would pull a bottle of port out of their kayaks and have a swig and then pass it to his companion. And then they were gone, vanished into the river beyond. The rafters paddled on.

As they floated past Rafters Race and left Fincham Gorge and entered the long stretch of river known as the middle Franklin, the rainforest gave way to a more scrubby type of bush that had grown in consequence of repeated firing, all tall gums and silver wattles. Aljaz was no longer sure exactly where he was. A little past where the Walls of Jericho rose up white and striking on a close mountain tier, Aljaz sensed that the punters were unhappy. It was cold and drizzling, yet despite the rain that had arrived soon after lunch the river had not risen an inch. With the river so low their progress remained slow, there being little or no water running over boulders and logs, and the rafts constantly ran aground. Then the guides would have to jump out chest-deep into the river beside the rock or log, grab hold of the deck lines that ran around the pontoons, and reef the raft this way or that, getting all the punters to sit on one side so that their weight worked with the guides' hurting, aching arms to free the raft up and get it moving again. It seemed the worst of both worlds, this paddling a shallow creekbed of a river while the rain fell upon them, heavy and mocking. After three days of hard work the punters were exhausted and wanted to know how far it was to that night's campsite. But for the moment Aljaz did not know where he was. After a further hour's paddling they had not arrived, and it was about then that he realised they had missed the campsite altogether. His eyes had searched the riverbank intensely, hoping that through the sweeps and drifts of rain the telltale little pebble bank with a log sticking out above would be obvious against the backdrop of dense dank greenness. But he had somehow missed it. Perhaps the log had washed away in a winter flood during his absence of so many years.

The punters were even more unhappy when Aljaz told them they would have to paddle for another hour to reach the next campsite, called Hawkins and Dean. He would rather have used the campsite in between, known as Camp Arcade, but there had been reports of it being infested with wasps that summer, so no one was using it.

Another hour of dreary paddling in the growing gloom of late afternoon. The punters' resentment faded into a dull determination to simply get to the campsite. Aljaz scanned the riverbank, hoping against hope that he wouldn't miss this one as well. Suddenly he leant back and reverse-swept his paddle to swing his raft towards the riverbank. He yelled to the Cockroach's raft, pointing at the bank. They landed, tethered the rafts, and Aljaz and the Cockroach went off to explore the site while the punters waited for their verdict. The guides climbed up the steep bank and disappeared into the rainforest. The

Cockroach knew that something was wrong. There was no path up to the campsite, and the campsite, apart from a level platform of sand ten metres up from the river, was difficult to recognise.

'Shit a brick,' said the Cockroach. 'No one's camped here for years.' It was true. In only a few short years the rainforest had reclaimed the tent sites. A hardwater fern grew up through a small patch of charred earth that Aljaz recognised as a firesite. Blackwoods and celery top pines and myrtle seedlings and freshwater ferns crowded what were once cleared areas. Here and there trees had fallen across the sites levelled for tents and new growth rose up from the fallen trunks staggering toward the distant sun.

Aljaz shrugged his shoulders. 'There's nothing between here and the gorge,' he said. 'We're stuck with it.' The Cockroach was annoyed at Aljaz's choice, and Aljaz sensed his annoyance and it only accentuated his own feeling of encroaching depression. For his memory of the river was being destroyed by the natural world of the river itself.

They went back down to the punters and told them, inadequate as the campsite was, they were staying there the night.

'And tomorrow?' asked Sheena.

'Tomorrow?' said Aljaz. 'Tomorrow's a breeze. Tomorrow we are set up for a good run into the big one – Deception Gorge.' Aljaz paused. He looked at the punters and thought he ought say something positive to make amends for the poor site they were about to spend the night in. 'Look,' he said, 'I know it's been hard. But the good side of a low level is that Deception Gorge can be got through easily. At high water it becomes difficult. Dangerous.' He made a casual gesture with his hand indicating the low level of the river. He gave a theatrical smile. He said, 'But we don't have to worry about that.'

With her good arm Sheena had been twirling her paddle back and forth in the water as Aljaz spoke. She looked up when he'd finished. She said, 'What if the river rises?'

I watch the sheets of rain blur the exhausted, depressed punters into small blobs of colour speckling the big red blobs of rafts; the weary, angry guides more recognisable standing in the shelter of the rainforest. One, the Cockroach, looking downwards and shaking his head, the other, Aljaz, looking not at Sheena but at the dark sky, fearful and not wishing to say so. And then Aljaz does something entirely unexpected: he begins to dance a crazed jig, a berserk cross between a polka and a bush dance, all legs at wild angles and shrieks and yahoos, presenting himself as a fool to the punters below. One by one, the punters begin to smile, and when Aljaz unexpectedly takes a flying leap out of the rainforest and hurtles himself into the bleak cold river they burst out laughing aloud, their depression exorcised in mirth.

— young Aljaz —

The tableau freezes at the moment Aljaz ought arise back out of the river spluttering. I realise that unlike then I am not now going to resurface, maybe never again open my big wet gob and gobble up huge gulps of beautiful air. Perhaps up there on the rock above they still half expect to hear a shriek and turn around to see me dance

85

a soggy polka before them, as if it were all only part of a joke that ought not be taken seriously. It is an old trick, this playing the fool for the customers to divert their attention from their genuine worries. Or not even a trick, but a recognition that the whole thing, the entire trip, is so contrived, so idiotic, that an idiotic act is the only adequate response to the circumstances. I would like to say, looking back on my childhood, that I consciously resolved to always present myself as an idiot to a world I found idiotic, that from the moment Maria Magadalena Svevo sliced my umbilical cord with her green-handled kitchen knife I had already come to the conclusion that this world was one not worthy of trafficking with.

But it wouldn't be true. It is true that as a child I found the company of Milton, an adult idiot with an early Beatles haircut that predated the early Beatles by some years, far more congenial than that of either purportedly normal children or purportedly sensible adults. Milton had a big nose, an even more aquiline number than my own snoz, and he looked somewhere between a battered, crazed John Lennon and an enlightened Mo out of *The Three Stooges*. Milton and I would sit around the Hobart bus depot hanging out together, watching the busy shoes and legs of busy people go busily back and forth to destinations that seemed to us without purpose or reason. Milton would catch slaters and ants and spiders and we would place them in the gutters next to which clankered up the big diesel buses. We would watch the insects' funny hasty movements, going first this way and then that, there being no reason for any direction because a filthy big bus would suddenly career over the top of the insects, ending their pointless harrying journey forever. And then Milton would laugh his crazed half-horse half-snort laugh, then sometimes he would cry until I could find him some more insects to watch.

There were grand, wild stories explaining Milton's idiocy. That he was fathered by Edward VIII while on a secret mission to Australia during World War II. That he was descended from a family whose line began with a flagellator who had been cursed. That the government had used his mother for secret tests while she was pregnant during the war. But the truth behind my idiocy was more prosaic. I was deaf, unable to talk because I was unable to hear much beyond the deep vibrations of the bus engines and Milton's laugh.

But these thoughts are getting ahead of my vision: of a small boy with a mop of wild red hair standing alone in the middle of a bitumen playground, which, along with the state school he attends, lies beneath the level of the highway that runs past the school's northern border. The boy is small for his age, smaller than the children who play around him, who play hide and go seek, who play chasings, who play British bulldog and kick the footy. While the other children's eyes are fixed upon each other, his eyes stare at the sky. And I know what that child is feeling, not because that child is me, Aljaz, but because I am watching not only the movements of the boy Aljaz's body now, but the movements of his heart and soul.

The boy Aljaz feels himself new. He feels his world around him to be alien. Sometimes he closes his eyes and then reopens them quickly and all the playground looks to be made of angles that make no sense. I say his world, but he feels nothing in it to be his. Everything belongs to everybody but him. The world has not shaped itself around him yet, nor he around this strange place lit by the cavernous sky with the china-blue light. He looks at the clouds in that sky, watches them wander past himself and where he is rooted by his body. He thinks that perhaps it might be possible to learn to fly like the comic characters. He thinks it might be just a matter of will and magic, like learning to walk and learning to talk, both events which he remembers clearly. Of the two, talking had been the harder. No one had understood him. He would say sweet things, beautiful things, funny things. People would look at him quizzically and then with pity. He didn't want pity. He wanted conversation. He wanted to be understood. After a time his knowledge of words grew greater and greater. He now listened to the way in which words were used, the way one word could carry so many different meanings, how every word could be a tree full of fruit. But when he asked questions he was answered only with a quizzical shake of the head. Harry and Sonja worried that their son was simple.

'Perhaps it was inevitable that he would be damaged goods,' Harry said one day, saying it in front of Aljaz, thinking their simple son would not understand. *Damaged goods.* Aljaz had grown angry with the way no one understood his words and would burst into terrible rages, screaming and thrashing around the floor. Sonja took him to the doctor, who discovered that he was not simple but deaf, his idiot's speech the consequence of hearing words only as shadows of sounds, as vibrations through the skull. According to the doctor the deafness was the result of an improperly treated pneumonia at an early age. The child was not so deaf as to be unable to comprehend, but deaf enough that his speech was severely impaired. Aljaz's ears were operated upon. The operations were successful and his speech improved.

I see the boy, now older, still smaller than his fellow

schoolmates. And I can hear what the schoolmates are saying to the small boy. They are calling him wop and dago and greaser and Jewboy. He is hurt, but none of it hurts like the hurt of the time when he discovers that everyone in the class has been invited to Phil Hodge's tenth birthday party. Except him. Forty-one girls and boys. 'But not you, Cosini,' says Phil's younger brother Terry. 'We don't have wogs,' says Phil's younger brother Terry, smiling. 'Especially not snotty red-headed wogs.'

The small boy quickly learns that he must fight back, no matter what the odds. No matter that he will day after day lose and come back into class after lunch with torn shirt and bleeding scratches. For he knows that when the circle forms around him and they start to spit on him, when they start to shove and the shoves turn to blows, that he must strike back. Even when they have him down on the hot black bitumen of the playground and a few hold him while others kick, even then he knows that he must keep flailing with whatever limb they have forgotten to pin or that he can momentarily wrest from their grasp, must keep on fighting because they can only win if he gives up. Day after day the circle hits him, punches him, kicks him, spits on him and chants, 'Grease and oil change! Grease and oil change!' Rubs steaming golden chips' white potato pulp in his bright red hair and chants, 'Blondie! Blondie!' And he never gives up, and he never cries in front of the circle, not even when the teacher after lunch complains about the smell of his hair, and upon examining his head orders him to the sick bay to wash it immediately, shaking her head and saying under her breath, 'Those migrants' hygiene . . .' Not even then, when his face burns with the pain of the total and utter humiliation of his pitiful plight, does he cry or give in.

Nor, curiously, does he assert the fact that half of him is Tasmanian. Because he is proud, because he believes that people ought accept him for what he is, without him having to invoke half of his parentage in order to deny the other half. He simply refuses to accept their estimation of him as being less than them. He is joined in this refusal by one other child, Adie Haynes. Adie, like Aljaz, is an outsider. He is quiet around the other kids, who call him Coon. Adie doesn't look that black. He is about as dark as Aljaz. 'But we're blackfellas, see,' he tells Aljaz. 'I dunno why that makes me different. But it does.' And he, like Aljaz, seems to be in a state of permanent war with all the other school-kids. In Grade Four Adie leaves school because his family is heading back north. Aljaz plays with Adie the day Adie's family pack up and load an ancient Austin with their possessions, and he laughs when Adie puts on his snorkel and goggles for the journey in a back seat crowded with five other children so that he won't have to smell their farts. 'See you, brother,' says Adie and turns and disappears into the mêlée of the back seat, to resurface behind the parcel-shelf like a skindiver in a submersible bell, a smile evident even through the scratched dirty glass of the window and snorkel mouthpiece.

Looking back upon it now my childhood seems to have been a series of farewells. Saying goodbye to relatives going to live and work on the mainland where people were said to be happy and believed that tomorrow would be even better than today, saying goodbye to my aunts off to be interred in cemeteries. It all begins with saying goodbye to Adie that day and watching him wave furiously out of that rear window, his face obscured by a pair of goggles, and it all ends with saying goodbye to Couta Ho and leaving myself many years later.

The day Adie left I was so upset Harry decided to take me for a drive. Harry's drives were without purpose: more precisely, they were circular journeys which the path of the new main roads and highways seemed only to frustrate. Every tree stump, every ageing gum tree sitting alone in a paddock, every derelict wooden hut – looking half pissed, leaning like Slimy Ted at angles that seemed to defy gravity, supported only by blackberry vines and an almost human tenacity – every vista that looked away from the road, seemed to be cause for another of Harry's interminable stops. We would all empty out of the battered Holden EK stationwagon – we being Maria Magadalena Svevo, Sonja, almost always a couple of cousins, of whom I have an unending supply – mess about in the roadside cutting, then head off into the bush with Harry beginning stories like this:

'Never had the story straight from Uncle George, but I do know that Auntie Cec always maintained . . .'

Or like this:

'Well, it was here that your Uncle Reg was had up for poaching with Bert Smithers and Reg and Bert both played stupid in court, playing up Reg's harelip and Bert's cleft palate so bad that the magistrate declared them imbeciles who could not be held responsible for their actions and let them off and after . . .'

Or like this:

'Beyond them paddocks there, back where the Ben begins to rise up there, that's where the cave that Neville Thurley and your grandfather lived in for two winters while they were snaring possums early in the Depression . . .'

The stories went on and on. Harry's was a landscape comprehensible not in terms of beauty but in the subterranean meanings of his stories. The new roads were not made for such journeys, but, as Harry put it, were simply straight lines to get you from A to B as quickly as possible, which was, he maintained, the way only fools travelled. The old roads built along the routes of carriageways, that more often than not were cleared widenings of old Aboriginal pathways, were the roads Harry seemed to like best. But he also made do with the highways, stopping the car at the oddest points to get out and chat about such places as the site where Father Noone – he of the magical powers – had frozen an adulterer to the spot. The man had, as Harry would say, been fooling around, and Father Noone had been speaking with his wife inside the now long-vanished hut of a house and had stepped outside to remonstrate with the faithless husband, who awaited Father Noone bearing evil intentions and an axe above his head. Just as the husband went to cleave Father Noone's head apart like a melon, Father Noone uttered his immortal words: 'You will stay such until ere the sun sets.' So the poor man did, frozen to the spot, arms and axe immobile above his head, until night fell. And to this day there remains a piece of barren ground where the luckless adulterer so stood. At this moment in his story Harry would point downwards and sure enough, there it would be, the piece of barren earth. Year after year we returned, listened to the same story, and at its conclusion looked earthward and nothing ever grew there.

Just when you thought you had heard them all there was a new story, but of course that always led back to old ones, which you seemed to learn not through desire or determination but through sheer repetition. Sometimes Harry would talk of his days upon the rivers, and the stories grew bigger and Harry more animated in their telling and these stories in particular entranced the young Aljaz.

Of course there were no roads to the Franklin and the Gordon rivers and it was almost impossible to get to such remote country, but when Aljaz was seven Harry took him along on a trip to Strahan and from there by steamer across Macquarie Harbour to the lower reaches of the Gordon River. There Smeggsy and two others were camped, reworking some of the old pine stands upon the Gordon's bottom reaches. Harry and Aljaz stayed with the piners for two days and nights in the humid rainforest, living at the edge of the great steel-black waters of the river. The piners drank strong tea sweetened with immense amounts of sugar or condensed milk and talked of how there was no money left in the game, of how they were the last pining gang on the rivers; talked of how it was all changing, of how not only the river people but the rivers themselves were doomed, to be dammed forever under vast new hydro-electric schemes and already there was bush work to be had cutting exploration tracks for the Hydro-electric Commission's surveyors and geologists and hydrologists. They talked of Old Bo and swapped innumerable stories of his many feats, including his last and possibly his greatest, certainly his most celebrated, when he and Smeggsy had rowed Harry from the Franklin through to Strahan in twenty-four hours, only for Old Bo to die of a heart attack just as their punt rounded the point and Strahan came into view. And as we too returned to Strahan aboard the steam tug, a long raft of Huon pine logs caterpillaring behind in the choppy waters, Harry told a story about every point and every cove and every island.

Stories, stories, stories. A world and a land and even a river full of the damn slippery things.

After Adie went away I can see that at primary school Aljaz makes a point of succeeding. And I can see it does him no good. The teachers find him too trying and too challenging. 'He's smart all right,' Aljaz overhears one teacher tell another, 'but it's a quirky smartness. Undisciplined. More rat cunning than intelligence. If you know what I mean.' Young Aljaz doesn't. I can see the boy doesn't understand the immediate meaning of these words, but that he gets the message nevertheless. To the teachers he is a smartarse. At high school he makes a point of failing at everything. But only after he has made a point of showing the teachers that he is smart. Only after he writes a good story. Or does all his maths quickly and correctly under the eye of the teacher. Why? wonder his teachers. Here within the river it is hard to see exactly why, but even through the thousands of litres of water rushing over me one thing is abundantly clear: by failing Aljaz begins to fit in with people. I watch him quickly come to the conclusion that success brings only contempt, whilst there is a camaraderie amongst the ranks of the fallen. The high school is new, set up for the vast housing commission suburb nearby that is rapidly filling to overflowing with young desperate families. The children of these families by and large expect life to give them nothing. They expect to be failed. By and large they expect to be unemployed, to be pushed around, to know only despair. So the honourable way to survive in the school is to make a cult, an artform, of failure. And if you are good yet insist upon failure, then so much the better. There are the heroic failures such as Slattery, who wins his place in the school running team with ease, and is a favourite to win the 400 metres at the Tasmanian high school championships. At the championships Slattery wins his heat in the fastest qualifying time. In the final, at the 300-metre mark he is ten metres clear of his nearest rival. He suddenly halts and starts running backwards through the pack of runners behind him, emerging triumphant at the wrong end of the race waving his long arms in triumph to the crowd of the school's supporters. The teachers are outraged and perplexed as to why the children cheer and laugh until the tears run down their cheeks. But only the children understand that to win is for Slattery to participate in a lie that everyone in life has a chance of winning if they try hard enough. By losing so spectacularly, by turning his loss into a triumph, he has turned their collective fate into a celebration and a challenge to the teachers, who could not begin to comprehend what it all meant. They ask Slattery why, but Slattery can not put words to his actions, any more than the children can explain why, at that moment when his long legs began to move backwards into the mêlée behind him, they felt such a sense of euphoria. They only know that for one moment in their entire school lives they had posed a question about the injustice of their destiny, and the adults had not only not known the answer, they had been too ignorant to understand the question. But none of it can be put into words. And nobody tries.

The small boy is not a heroic failure like Slattery. He is one of the many quiet failures the school gladly rids itself of at the end of his final year.

Young Aljaz, now out of school and without work, looks at the photo of Harry and Auntie Ellie that sits on the mantelpiece. It doesn't mean much to him. None of his family or his forebears means that much to him, and he takes a certain pride in how little he knows about them. Such photos sit in dark recesses in dark dusty rooms. And Aljaz was never one for being about inside, poking around in this and that. Inside is where Harry now spends most of his time, more often than not drinking in the company of Slimy Ted, who, after he had his cray-fishing boat impounded by the authorities for poaching, more or less stopped working. Aljaz was one for getting out and doing, and it didn't matter much for a time whether the doing was good or bad, just so long as it seemed to pulse with the thick bloodbeat of life. Until the doing became the undoing of Aljaz, and the police came with their blueys, their blue-papered summonses, and Aljaz had to go to court again and again for being drunk and disorderly and drunk and incapable, once for drink driving, and once, though it really had nothing to do with him because he was only hanging onto the girl's handbag, possession of marijuana. And then the judge said that if it didn't stop, next time it would be jail, and Harry looked up from the game of crib he had going with Slimy Ted in the kitchen, put down his beer glass, took the cigarette out of his mouth, and said it had to stop and that the doing had to find other forms.

The doing became football, for which Aljaz had always shown some aptitude, but which his school's philosophy of losing had prevented him from ever shining at. He started training with the South Hobart reserves and by mid-season was regularly getting games with their senior side as a rover. With the senior games came regular money, and this meant considerably more to Aljaz than all the talk of the club, which others used to gabble about. The fans loved Aljaz, the way his long mane of flowing red hair would suddenly appear out of nowhere to be alone leaping into the sky, and they called him the Red Panther and the Great Cosini and Ali Baba. The newspaper dubbed him Fellini Cosini because of his cinematic marks, and opposing teams' fans took to chanting, 'Eight and a half, eight and a half.'

I observe that I was happy then, in the fashion of those who know that happiness is as transitory as the clouds. My mind stops seeing and returns to thinking, my thoughts like persistent pigdogs who have run their prey to ground, refusing to let go, demanding that I answer their insistent question.

Why did I take the job?

From my present point of view, the perspective of the drowning man, drowning in consequence of having taken the job, this question is not without importance. My decision to take the job, to put myself on the train of events that would lead to my present fatal predicament, must be one that betrays what is self-destructive about me. Or at least what is flawed. Why did I take the job? Well, Pig's Breath rang, and what was I to say?

After so many years I had finally returned home. I was so glad to be back. But my happiness soon turned to dismay. Wherever I went I heard the same refrain: so-and-so has crossed the water to the mainland to get work. There were no jobs, but then, as friends pointed out when I became downcast about the subject, there never had been. The island had been depressed for a century and a half. I had been back for a few weeks and not a sniff of work, but then what the hell did I expect? I was a sick man too. Not badly sick, not life-endingly sick, but sick all the same. I seemed to have acquired a permanent form of mild dysentry and my belly felt soft and watery near enough to all the time. I got bad headaches, my hair came out in tufts so bad I had to get it cut back short as buggery; it then went all spiky and I looked like some crazy red razorbacked pig. Truth be known I felt rotten, felt so bad I'd find myself crying for no explicable reason, found myself weeping just watching news of some disaster on the TV or hearing a mother shouting at a kid on the street. I needed something real bad, but I didn't know where or what or who it was. So Pig's Breath rang, and what was I to say?

Why did I take the job?

Everyone knew how much I disliked raft guiding. It was one of my inexhaustible conversation topics. I seemed never to tire, particularly when in the company of other river guides, of telling all who would listen what an appalling job it was and how glad I was at long last to be out of it. I didn't say that I had once loved it. I did say that the pay was terrible and getting worse, the conditions those of nineteenth-century navvies, the customers — referred to derisively by everyone in the trade as punters — fools or oafs or both. Raft guiding was all right if you were young and had nothing better to do, I was fond of saying, but it was no job for anybody over twenty-five.

And I was thirty-six.

And yet, when Pig's Breath rang, before I had time to say a word, I felt the old excitement come back.

I wanted to do one last trip.

And, I suppose, it has to be admitted, there was the matter of Couta Ho. Without meaning to I walked around to her place on my first day back home, but I couldn't bring myself to go inside.

I see her now at that party, all of twenty-three, standing close to Aljaz, he three years younger, throughout the evening that they first met, all those years ago. Each time he went into the kitchen to get another drink, he was aware of her eyes following him. He had never been desired in this way, so overtly and so sexually. It frightened him. He had dreamt of such things and fantasised about such things, but when confronted with the reality he felt an unease so great that he thought nothing good could come of it. He asked Ronnie if he wanted to go, now that the party was beginning to die away. 'Go? Why? There's still beer to be drunk.' He jabbed a thumb over his shoulder in the direction of the lounge-room. 'And I think someone's got you booked for the evening.' Aljaz felt a terrible embarrassment. He knew how to cope with girls giving him the flick – at that he was expert – but a girl chasing him, well, that was unnerving. He went back out to the party and joined a circle of people on the opposite side of the room to where Couta Ho was talking to some friends of Aljaz's. He had only been there a moment and she was back at his side. She was smoking furiously, though she only rarely smoked, talking ten to the dozen, and Aljaz, to hide his nervousness, joined her. He did tricks with smoke coming out of his nostrils to make her laugh, and as she relaxed, so did he. And when he leant down – for she was smaller than he – to show her another trick and took the cigarette out of his mouth, he felt her lips upon his. He felt his lips respond and then open, and felt her tongue leap into his mouth like some smoky damp fish. He felt himself falling and momentarily staggered as he readjusted his weight to take hers, then in response to her same gesture, put his arm around her and he felt her flatten into his body.

In the end it was four-thirty in the morning and there were only five other people left, two of whom had flaked in the kitchen, one of whom, Ronnie, was still awake but only just so, swigging the dregs from a bottle of brandi-vino as he lay in the bathtub humming an Abba song, while the remaining two were coupling fully clothed on the carpet, dry humping at the edge of the lounge-room, occasionally rolling in their drunken, languorous passion into a half-empty bottle and spilling beer or cider over themselves. Neither seemed to notice, or if they did, showed no outward signs of caring. Aljaz's head ached and he was totally confused as to whether he ought stay or go. He and Couta Ho had been passionately embracing on the lounge suite for what seemed an infinity and Aljaz was unsure as to what the next stage was, and recognising that he had neither the experience nor the energy to make a decision, announced that he'd better take off home. Couta Ho, and not for the last time, shook her head, took his hand, and led him into her bedroom.

He had not known it would be like this. He had expected that somehow he would initiate and lead, make the big and vital decisions. And now knowing that this was not expected of him, that she wanted him and his body urgently and would lead him through the mystery of what remained of the night, he felt a curious relief. When he joined her in the bed, and when he felt her naked body next to his, when he smelt the ocean rising up from her thighs and when she guided his hand down-wards to feather through that ocean's wonders, then he found himself possessed of a tenderness so exquisite and gentle that he felt afraid she was unlocking parts of his soul that had until then been hidden even from him. Aljaz marvelled at how his body, a few moments previous loose and without purpose, now entwined so powerfully and fiercely with that of Couta's, marvelled so much that he no longer saw her body or felt his own, but thought that they had been transformed into two strands of some strangely animated steel cable, a writhing tautness, that was at once still and moving, twisting, enwrapping and springing off the other's sinuous strength. It was a battle and it was a dance, and where she led he followed with such a provocative purpose that he found his body responding to her desires and not his. He no longer thought of nor cared for himself, but was lost in her pleasure and he was grateful. She simply wanted him to *be*, not to do. She began to sigh, and each sigh he felt as a rush of hot petals tumbling over his body and he felt a great rising emptiness, which overwhelmed him so completely that afterwards he found himself shivering with an unnameable anxiety.

Couta Ho lived alone in the old family home. She seemed to have an infinite number of brothers and sisters who, although they shared the same father, had a number of different mothers and therefore different homes. As his name suggested, old man Ho had Chinese blood in him, but his Oriental heritage seemed to have largely passed him by, culturally and physically. He was, as he was wont to say, as Chinese as a Chiko Roll. He was of a small and powerful build, and did have large brown eyes that Couta inherited from him. But his thin blond hair which, along with his eyes, he believed made him irresistible to women, was a consequence of pasts other than that of China.

And now I am being washed into the Ho family past. Without wishing it, I should add, for frankly I have no desire to see any of it – but this newly acquired capacity of mine to witness the past means that the stories of the dead weigh like a nightmare on my still-living brain. I try

101

to stop it. I try to make my mind see something else, but it's no good, for there's the original Sun Ho, patriarch of the Ho clan, and he's being busily belted up by a dozen drunk English and Irish prospectors on a Victorian gold-field. No. *No.* I really don't want to know about it. *Oh no!* Here's his son Willie in a chair-making sweatshop in Melbourne in 1885 trying to organise the Chinese Workers Union, and here's the local furniture-union steward (a white man, of course) telling him they don't want slant-eyed opium fiends, for a slope must be a bad union man by the fact of his Oriental nature. And here's Willie some years later at the north-east Tasmanian town of Garibaldi, where, apart from being stoned by an irate mob of unemployed from the nearby town of Derby and losing the sight of one eye in consequence, he suffered but rarely from racism. In his youth Willie read Dietzgin and Henry Hyndman's tracts on the coming proletarian revolution. In his old age in Garibaldi he had a grocery shop and helped run the local josshouse, in which he regularly prayed, asking his gods that men might love their fellow beings.

Willie Ho's grandson Reg did love all his fellow beings, particularly those who were women. Most particularly, women other than his wife. Quick-witted and lively, and constantly falling in love and making vows to one woman at night while breaking them with another during the day. As a consequence of her father's numerous infidelities, Couta Ho's parents had split when she was four years of age, but not before Reg (who had been, as his father before him, a fisherman) gave Couta her nickname. It was in honour of the wormy baracouta from which he made most of what had to pass for a living, and in celebration of her catching worms from the dog next door, in whose kennel she would spend much of her day. The nickname stuck so thoroughly that even Couta had to sometimes think twice when she went to write her Christian name of Kylie down on some official form. After the marriage bust-up Reg Ho had gone to live and fish in Darwin, where he had ended up remarrying a Tiwi Islander. For a few years afterwards, Couta had gone to Darwin to stay with her father for holidays, but then in her mid-teens that too came to an end. Couta stayed in Hobart with her mother and her father's mother, old Mrs Ho, who never spoke again to her son following the marriage breakup. On evenings when old Mrs Ho had bad dreams about her ancestors visiting in her sleep, Couta Ho would sleep with her. When Couta Ho was sixteen her mother and grandmother were killed in a car accident, their car being cleaned up by a train on a level crossing when the warning lights failed to work.

As the months went by Couta Ho talked a lot about her past. 'I hated the bastard for doing that to Mum,' she said. 'I got all the photos I had of him and I cut them up into little pieces. And the photos that had us and him in them, I just cut him out of.' She paused. Aljaz looked up and down her body, at the smoothness of her face, at the down beside her ears, at her eyes, which are unusually large and whose pupils are a deep brown. She looked at him with those eyes and he knew at once that she trusted him entirely and completely, and it frightened him, because he knew he was not equal to that trust and that there would come a time when he would inevitably disappoint her. She looked at him with those large eyes and he felt guilty, though about what he did not know. He had to look away.

For the first time Aljaz talked about his mother's death.

He told Couta Ho how one night he had found Sonja sitting on the floor of her bedroom weeping with pain. Sonja had told Aljaz she was dying, that although the doctors said it was only gallstones she knew different. She told him she loved him, that the world was out of kilter, that she loved him, that she loved him. She held his head into her chest and wept and wept the more and he felt her tears wet his hair and some even splash on his face. In his stomach, for the first time, he felt the fear arise, the terrible terrible fear that was never to depart. She lost more and more weight, till in the end she was a shrivelled up shell weighing only six and a half stone. When in the hospital they cut her open to remove the gallstones they found three huge hydatid cysts. They successfully removed two but the third burst and the dreaded hydatid seeds dispersed into her body to complete their fatal mission. She died within half an hour, still on the operating table. Harry stopped talking and laughing and for a time even stopped working on his barbeque. His drinking grew steadier, or worse, I suppose you would say, says Aljaz to Couta Ho, his mouth a sort of smile.

'He'd be off most nights at the pub, or round at Slimy Ted's drinking and playing crib, and when he was at home he just sat around quiet as can be, smoking at the kitchen table, drinking, saying nothing, looking at nothing. Sometimes, not often, he'd say, "How's school goin then, Ali?" And I'd say, "Not great," and he'd just kinda look down and shake his head just a fraction and say, "Well, 'spose that's how she goes," like he kind of expected it anyway. "Yeah, well. That's how she goes," and he'd take a big drag on his cigarette like we were in this thing together and neither of us could beat it. Which I suppose was pretty much how it was. Mama had held it all together, made sense of all the hard times cos we were going somewhere and we were going there together, as a family. But we weren't a family any more. Dad and I weren't making the journey any more. We were a sad old drunk man and a boy who was getting into more and more trouble, and the more trouble he got in the more people just expected him to be in trouble.'

'Things kind of fell apart at school after that,' says Aljaz. 'One day, a teacher scruffs hold of me and he tells me off and he says, "The problem with you, Cosini, is that you don't take school seriously." And I said, "Yes yes, sir," but what I wanted to say was that I couldn't take anything seriously any more.' And he looks around at Couta Ho who looks at him. 'Not after what happened to Mama. But I didn't.'

And finally he says, 'You're the first thing I have taken seriously since Mama died.'

Aljaz liked Couta's thick black hair, liked the way she tied it behind her head in a ponytail, liked the way she moved, the way she smelt. He liked the jewelry she wore, big and flamboyant, gypsy rings in her ears, plentiful bangles and chains. He liked the smoothness of her olive skin, he liked her youth and he liked her old outlook on some matters. He liked watching her sleep at night, her heart-shaped face illuminated by the light that filtered in from the street lamp outside, and he wondered if there was anything in the entire world as peaceful or as beautiful as the sight. He liked her so much that for a long time he wondered if there was anything about her he didn't like. Within five days of their first meeting Aljaz had moved into the Ho family home, and there he was to remain living with Couta for the next three years.

Throughout that time – which was, looking back now through these refracting waters, the best time in my life – Couta Ho was a source of constant wonderment to Aljaz. She had as full a sense of self as anyone he ever knew. For Aljaz, who had so little sense of who or what he was that for a long time he wondered if he might not be mildly autistic, this was a marvel. Couta Ho lived fully and completely in her world, celebrated its small moments with love and wonder. He continued telling her jokes and stories and after a month began to fret. She asked what was the matter and he felt compelled to answer honestly and say that he had run out of all the jokes and stories he had ever heard and no longer knew what to say to her. At which she also laughed and he relaxed considerably and took to not bothering to say anything much at all unless it seemed absolutely necessary. He liked the way she seemed to know things about life that he believed to be beyond his ken and which allowed him to continue to be a child in much of his thinking, as if her experience was enough to sustain them both, which of course, I can see now, it was not. She was stronger, she was surer, and he felt like a shallow creek whose babbling waters had just run into the silent current of a big river, moving swiftly and powerfully, though to where, he knew not. He was humbled, and he disliked it, and he disliked her for making him feel this way, while at the same time he was forced to recognise that he needed her more than he had ever suspected.

They would sometimes go to Roaring Beach, abandoned save for a few solitary surfers, and on Couta Ho's insistence swim in its dangerous rips and ride the wild waves that formed on the beach's steep bank. And though it frightened him, Aljaz found his fear overwhelmed by a feeling of enchantment as he watched her emerge laughing from that treacherous surf. There was something so desolate in her that it was akin to a magnificence, and he was filled with awe at her wildness.

Aljaz's life took on a discernible pattern. He played professional football in winter and worked as a river guide on the Franklin River in summer, taking parties of tourists down Australia's 'famous last wild river' as it was billed, a job he had originally got through a mate in South Hobart. The job filled in an otherwise empty season, and filled in something else besides – a sense of who he was and what he was and where he was, and though he said it was all about money and having a laugh, it wasn't entirely that. Sometimes the work down the river was wet and miserable with crews of selfish shitheads who saw the guides as nothing more than sherpas. But sometimes it was warm, with the river running high, though not too high, with big rapids not too big, the customers decent, and the nights long and full of talk. And there was, of course, life with Couta, sometimes difficult and often bizarre, for Couta, as Aljaz was to discover, had a few bizarre edges to her character.

The weekend before Reggie Ho had walked out on his marriage he had given Couta a wooden apple case full of old marine code flags, used for signalling between boats at sea. To each flag Reggie had attached a dowel. He and Couta played with them in the backyard, signalling messages to one another from opposite ends of the garden. Long after Reggie had gone, Couta learnt the flags' meanings off by heart from a booklet she found at the bottom of the apple case. Over the years the old box of flags became her most prized possession, though why she took to using them in her lovemaking with Aljaz, I am unsure.

All I know is that on the second night they slept together she took to semaphoring her desires.

How did she use them? Well, I see a great deal, and much of it of a very intimate nature. Suffice to say that Couta used the flags to signal her passions to Aljaz and that Aljaz learnt the flags' meanings from the silverfish-chewed booklet. It is difficult to convey in a few words the erotic charge carried by a horizontal blue- and white-striped flag (meaning: I have a diver down, keep well clear at low speed), or a blue flag divided by a horizontal white stripe (meaning: I am on fire), the lascivious intent signalled by a flag divided by crossed diagonal lines into black, yellow, blue and red quarters (meaning: I require a tug), or the carnal satisfaction implicit in a white square in the middle of a blue background (meaning: my nets have come fast upon an obstruction). Difficult. And even more difficult to describe how they were used, because I am of nature a private person. Sometimes Aljaz would object that there was no code flag to adequately express his physical sensations. 'Such,' Couta Ho would reply, 'are the limitations of language.'

Couta Ho had grace, a quality I much admired as I had none of it. Even when she sat naked in bed, staring through and beyond the wall, she remained possessed of it, and she knew this to be her redeeming strength in a tortuous lifetime unravelling the mystery of her past. Perhaps expected one day to finally sight the code flag that at last answered it all. Perhaps expected to see a face and torso shaping out of the plaster and then emerge limb by limb until a body, powdered white, had separated from the wall and it would be her father and he would hold that code flag, would lower it, would take her hand and lead her back into the wall and together they might walk the final distance between here and that space on the horizon that lies between the sky and the sea, their colours finally merging in a brief azure gloaming.

For a young man it was an easy life and would have remained so, had not in their third year together two events, one tragic, one trivial, conspired to destroy all that they had. The trivial event was football. In his third year with Couta Aljaz made the cardinal error of getting serious about his football and wishing to play for the national league. That was a mistake because, good as he was, he was simply too short for the national club scouts ever to be interested. When this became clear to Aljaz his interest in the game waned and for a time he contemplated throwing it in altogether. But it had become a way of life, and for someone without work, it offered the society and routine and money of a job. Because it was a job and one with which he had become bored, the offer of a professional contract with a Darwin club was an appealing prospect save for the fact Couta Ho did not want to leave Hobart because she had fallen pregnant with Jemma.

Then, sometime between the hours of 5 am and 8 am on the first Tuesday of May, Jemma, our perfect baby, our beloved Jem-Jem, my child my beautiful beautiful child, all of two months, died in her cot. And though the thought and the memory will not go away I have frozen that memory like Father Noone froze the hapless adulterer, and there remains in my soul a barren patch of ground in which nothing will grow. About Jemma there is nothing else to recall. I can say that now, because I retain no memory of her save for the salient facts of her death, the great fact of her life.

Of course, Jemma's death changed everything. Couta

Ho had no capacity for self-delusion: a tragedy was, for her, exactly that, a terrible burden beyond words, the experience of which she understood would be bordered by the encroachments of passing time, but the pain of which would always endure. Couta Ho knew this to be something she had to bear alone because, much as she loved Aljaz, it was beyond his imagination, because his imagination could only encompass the present and her tragedy was one that needed the passing of time to be revealed. She knew the vast dimensions of what they had suffered, even if she did not understand it. He, on the other hand, claimed to understand the tragedy, tried to reduce it to something small, and thought it could be left in its time. For Aljaz saw Jemma's death as an obstacle to be got around, and once passed, to be left behind.

These vague thoughts of mine are spreading out like the jetsam that washes past my wet flesh. More precisely: how did Aljaz try to shrink the tragedy? By pretending it was Couta's alone. Watching all this unfold for a second time, it is this macabre refusal to acknowledge his own involvement in the death that is so sad. More precisely: his sadness shortcircuits itself by being unable to recognise its own existence. Aljaz said little; in fact he said less and less. What he did say were disconnected things like, 'Life must go on,' or, 'I'm just glad we had her for two months.' Things that made no sense to Couta, but which Aljaz seemed to gain some comfort from; things he kept on repeating as if they were some incantation that, if uttered enough, would ward off the darkness. Sometimes he tried to express his sympathy for her, to give her a cuddle or kiss he believed to be affectionate. Which she resented. 'I'm just trying to be tender,' he protested.

She exploded. 'That's not what tender is. Tender is

having respect, and you have no respect for anybody. Not even yourself. Maybe that's what the problem is.'

She cried for a month and was inconsolable for a further six months, and when Aljaz one day berated her for not picking herself up and getting on with her life she looked at him and, with a sudden hardness that he had never heard in her voice, said, 'You don't understand. Do you?' And then, still looking at him, her bitterness turned to pity and she said, in a softer voice that scared Aljaz more than her hard voice, 'You poor thing. Even if you wanted to, you couldn't understand.' Which was true and he knew it.

Couta Ho continued speaking. 'I thought maybe one day we could belong. Like people with families do, having their own time and their own place and growing old and crotchety and full of love in them. And other folks might even laugh at them just because they belonged there so powerfully and fitted that time and place so well that anywhere else they'd look plain silly. But they would belong there. Do you know what I mean?'

After this conversation a great silence grew up between Aljaz and Couta, so great that in the end Aljaz could bear it no longer. There was now a sadness at the heart of Couta Ho, and the sadness grew till it overwhelmed them both. When they made love she averted her face, and though her body would often (though not always) respond, her mind was always elsewhere, and rarely did she permit him to kiss her on the lips. At the end of their lovemaking he would feel as if he had wronged her terribly and he would apologise and feel a great shame, though about precisely what, he was unable to put words to. He was polite, asked her if perhaps it would be better if they dispensed with lovemaking altogether, and she said no, that she did not mind. But there was sadness at the heart of it and it pained him to see how his caresses seemed to burn her skin, each one a new wound upon an old scar. They both knew it to be destroying them, and they both knew they were unable to influence their fate, that they had been relegated to the role of spectators at the tragedy of their own unhappiness.

One evening, about eight months after Jemma, as they were washing up the evening's dishes, he turned to her. 'Couta. I've been thinking. And I think it might be best if I go.' Couta Ho smiled wanly, as though he had said nothing more significant than that he was about to go to the corner store to buy some milk.

'Fine,' she said. 'Fine.' And smiled a second time, as though it all amounted to nothing. And when Aljaz realised that he felt no anger at her response, only a remote, abstract curiosity, then he knew it was finished. They continued to wash up and Aljaz did an unusually thorough job of cleaning the kitchen. They went to bed and lay side by side. He held her hand but she took it away from him and crossed it over her chest. When he awoke the next morning Couta Ho was already up. He spent some time in the bedroom, sorting through his clothes, deciding what to take and what to throw away. He left a little before midday, kissing Couta Ho demurely, almost absently on the lips at the front gate as if he were off to a day's work.

Aljaz went as far away as he could go. He went and took the footballing job in Darwin. Each summer for the next three years he returned to Tasmania during the tourist season to work as a river guide on the Franklin. Then at the age of twenty-six he threw in footballing in Darwin and guiding in Tasmania and drifted off around the east coast of the mainland, working here and there at whatever was going, driving harvesting machines on farms, serving in bottle shops, labouring on building sites. For ten years he did not return to Tasmania.

Until this day.

And there I see him: at the end of a river of tears, standing in a dry riverbed of stone, his gaze rising from the rockpools of memory, looking up at the front of her house that had once been his home also, wondering what she remembered of those times, wondering, Will I or won't I knock?

Wondering also: But would she want to see me?

And then turning away and clambering back up that harsh, dry riverbed of boulders.

— Five —

'An idea can be a dangerous thing. Hell, everybody knows that,' Maria Magdalena Svevo used to say. 'It's a century of ideas eating the people who reared and fed them.' She's right, an idea can be a dangerous thing. Even before I got jammed down this dam plughole with half a river running over the top of me, I knew that. As much as I can, I steer clear of ideas, of believing in anything. It is simply too dangerous and I am in any case always afraid. I mean, I didn't even allow myself to believe in my own grief at Jemma's death. Because that's an idea. Right? Grief is just an idea. Of course it's bad when someone dies, but the fact is they have died and are gone and that's it. Full stop. What do I feel about Jemma's death? people used always ask. And I told them truthfully, I feel nothing. Nothing. But a desire can be a dangerous thing too. That's what I didn't know. And my desire was buried so deep within me that when Pig's Breath rang I didn't even realise that he had me worked out better than I had myself worked out.

Even on the phone it was easy to hear that Pig's Breath

was evasive. Even then I could tell that he had no desire to be offering me employment. Not that he mentioned that at first. I could tell that he had no desire to talk to me. But I could also tell that he had no choice. So I reckoned things must be rather bad for Pig's Breath, that he needed me, and that even though I needed him, there was no way I was going to let Pig's Breath know how desperate I was for work.

'Heard you were back in town, so I thought I'd give you a ring and we'd get together and see how life's been treating you,' said Pig's Breath. And so I went to meet with him in his office. That morning my health seemed to go from its normally bad state to one close to a fever, my body perhaps experiencing a physical premonition of the fate that meeting would inextricably bind me to.

I can see Aljaz now, sitting on the other side of Pig's Breath's dishevelled desk, trying to look relaxed because this time Aljaz thinks he has got Pig's Breath nailed. Aljaz has braced himself for this interview, determined upon being hard with Pig's Breath, rather than being quiet and deferential as he more normally is in such situations. He has had a couple of steadying rums at a pub on the way, and he feels their flame not as something warming but as something unbelievably cold, glaciating his throat and innards. For all his determination Aljaz is shivering, not only because of the rum, but because he feels nauseous and cold, because Aljaz wants to go down the river but is frightened of going down the river, because he wants to confront Pig's Breath and tell him what he really feels about him, but is frightened of Pig's Breath attacking him back. Aljaz's feet begin tap-tapping the floor in nervous anticipation and his hands start shaking so much that he has to put them in his pockets. 'That's kind of you,

Howard,' I see Aljaz saying before he takes refuge in flattery. 'Well, you've done all right for yourself, Howard. Operations manager of Wilderness Experiences now.' And Aljaz waves an expansive, empty, only slightly shaking hand around Pig's Breath's mess of an office.

'It's a long way from being a river bum,' says Pig's Breath. I watch Aljaz agree. It *is* a long way, for a dickwit. Pig's Breath was always stupid enough to think that operations manager of a small branch of a national outdoor tourism company was making the big time.

As I watch Aljaz and Pig's Breath confront each other over his crowded, messy desk, faxes, accounts and letters papering over wetsuit boots, petrol stoves, and tins of hypalon glue, I am shocked at how obvious is Aljaz's contempt for Pig's Breath, although, there, at the time, I think I am doing a great job of disguising it beneath banal pleasantries. Pig's Breath is, as he always has been, bearded and tousle-haired, though his geniality has degenerated into an irritating obsequiousness, his stocky build into fat. He is a wombat of a man, always shuffling away if approached directly. So there he sits across the desk from Aljaz, a mound of smug and bristly body odours so overwhelming that it turns my water-bloated belly even now. He relates a few stale anecodotes, enquires as to Aljaz's recent activities, flatters him when he tells a few stories.

'You're a crazy Cosini,' says Pig's Breath finally. Then he comes to the point. 'Ali, we've got a problem here, and I was wondering if you could help us, being an old mate.'

'Sure, Howard, I'll do what I can, but, well, my life's pretty busy right at the moment.'

'Ali, I won't beat about the bush. We've got a twelve-day Franklin River trip going out on Wednesday and we haven't got a lead guide. I was wondering if you'd be interested.'

'I don't do that sort of thing any more.' There is then a silence that goes on for too long and Aljaz feels obliged to say something more, anything. 'I used to. But I don't any more.' It is a stupid thing to say and Aljaz regrets it immediately.

'I know *that*,' says Pig's Breath, who is obviously a little surprised at Aljaz. 'We worked together – remember?'

I watch Aljaz's face flush with panic. He has a momentary blank and can think of nothing, while he hears himself saying out of some automatic part of his brain, 'Yes, yes, of course I remember.' But what does Aljaz remember? All he sees is a puffy baby's shin and a yellow woollen bootie and he does not want to see it, he does not. He feels his bowels go weak and watery. 'Excuse me,' says Aljaz, 'but where's the er . . . ?' Pig's Breath points out beyond a side door. In the toilet Aljaz, after relieving himself, throws water on his face and clenches and unclenches his hands in a vain attempt to stop their ever worsening shaking. When he returns to Pig's Breath he manages to haul himself away from the dangerous abyss of the past back into the present by clinging tenaciously to the purpose of the conversation.

'Who's the other guide?' he asks.

'New blood. Jason Krezwa. Know him?'

'No.'

'They call him the Cockroach. Big, but agile. They say he can carry two loaded barrels down portages leaping from rock to rock, never loses his balance.'

'Like a cockroach?'

'No, they just call him that because he's ugly. But he's a good guide. A lot better than you.' Pig's Breath has scored his first point, and I can see now that this is the pivot upon which the meeting turns Pig's Breath's way. I know Aljaz is rocked, his momentum lost. Having nothing smart to say, his body shaking with his unnameable fear, his guts again rumbling, he leans back in his chair and says nothing, waiting for the appropriate moment to step in and subtly humiliate Pig's Breath. Except it doesn't happen. Pig's Breath continues. 'He's experienced. Two seasons on the Tully, a season on the Zambezi, another on the Colorado. He's just never run the Franklin. So I need a head guide that can show him.'

Here I see Aljaz manage to pull himself together enough to say, 'Head guide wages, of course.'

Pig's Breath stops and sucks his breath in between his teeth. 'No. We don't have head guide wages. We have Wilderness Experience rating wages. Single D through to triple A. Triple A guides get $109 a day.'

'So I get $109 a day.'

'No. To be a triple A Wilderness Experience guide you need to have worked for us continuously for five years plus attended all our in-house training courses.'

'Which the guide pays for, of course.'

'Well, that's head office policy. There's not a lot I can do about it. In any case, it's not unreasonable that people pay for their own training. Look Ali, I know it seems a bit rough, but that's how it is. I've spoken to them in Sydney and they've agreed to give you a special one-off single A rating in recognition of your past experience.'

'What's a single A worth?'

'Eighty-seven dollars a day.'

At this point Aljaz's outrage temporarily overwhelms

his nervousness. 'Jesus, Howard! We earnt more than that ten years ago doing the same job. And we didn't have to put up with this sort of shit.'

'I know. I know it's rough. I've complained, believe me, I've argued with them. But what can I do? They're the rates, it's the company's conditions. I mean, I just don't have that sort of power.'

'Who does? I'll talk to them. Fucking $87 a day. You got to be joking.'

'I know. I know it's — it's wrong. But look, Ali, I went out on a limb to get you this job. Believe me, they weren't happy about having you. You were a good guide, but you had a certain reputation . . .'

'Reputation?'

Pig's Breath had had no reputation when we guided together on the river all that time ago, except for cocking things up. He had been a bad boatman and rude to his customers, on one occasion refusing to talk to anyone for two days while we were on the river. But I did, as Pig's Breath put it, have a reputation. For running the big ones, the rapids no one else would run, and making it through; for threading lines so fine no one else thought it possible, and for never wrapping my raft on rocks or looping or flipping or losing punters. I could turn the most useless pack of punters into a team that could make a raft dance down a rapid. You should have seen what I could do with a raft on a rapid — dangerous things, wild mad things, but always beautiful to watch and even more beautiful to be part of. You might think there's not much to getting a raft of people down a rapid, but you watch a bad boatman then watch a good one work that water. The bad one just gets washed every place it's bad and dangerous and his raft is buffeted and tipped and sometimes flipped and looped. The bad boatman is frantic as can be trying to heave that big bastard of a raft back, and the punters are swimming from arsehole to buggery. But the good boatman has time on the river, time in the rapid, and he waits for just that moment when his raft's pontoon smacks into a stopper or a wave, and at that moment when it is almost too late and his raft is almost set to capsize he snakes his body about and twists his paddle so that his purpose and the river's become one and he takes the raft where it ought to go. A great thing, a beautiful thing to see. Like ballet on water.

'Yes, that's the word,' Pig's Breath continues. 'Reputation. And I said, I promise this time there'll be no trouble. I gave my word to them, Ali. *My* word. And they said, All right, you can hire him, but only as a double B.'

'Double B?' Aljaz hears himself saying.

Anyhow, that's all over and done with and what does it matter anyway, whether I was good or bad? I am not inclined to boasting, but not everyone can be a good boatman. The good boatman has to know himself, he has to know his punters and he has to know the river, he has to be able to read the water, how and why it moves, know what the particular forms of water – plumes, rooster tails, tongues, pressure waves – mean, what they tell about the nature and power of the rapid. He has to know why a rapid that is safe as houses at one level is as deadly as a tiger snake at another level. He has to smell and hear and love the river to know what the smells and sounds mean. I had the knowledge. And I had a name on the Franklin. I had a body that burnt and it astounded even me who inhabited it. I had a body that did what I wanted it to do, that was taut and hard and jumped and leapt and had time, that knew how to wait for just the

120

right moment to act and then to seize that moment for all it was worth and make something magic happen. It was a terrific thing, that body, and the memory of it is enough to make me smile a little even while I'm here drowning.

But I was a poor guide. A good boatman, a wild man, a man of legend and hearsay, a man of reputation, yes, lordy-o, yes. But a poor guide. For now I can see that my concerns, my ways of seeing and knowing, were not those of my customers, were not even what might be of interest to my customers – were not facts, details, names of geological substrata and plants and animals, but feelings and intuitions that this tree, this *dacrydium franklinii* was not the same as that *dacrydium franklinii*, that the same Linnaen specification did not denote the same spirit. That height was not the most important attribute of a tree or what had to be scaled in order to clearly see something. My poor punters. They came from other worlds, and mine did not open for them to come inside, not because I did not wish it, but because it was a world that would frighten them too much and they knew it far more than me. And so it went, trip after trip, a few good, a few indifferent, many bad like some extended Hitler Jugend outing, joy through ignorance, and once one fellow river guide called Needles had burst out singing 'Deutschland Über Alles' and we had pissed ourselves laughing and the punters never got the joke, thank Christ, how could they?

Anyhow, what does it matter now? Only the memory, and that's a fragile thing. A name, be it a good or a bad name, washes away quicker than the peat that gathers in the potholes in the river rock, there to briefly swirl for an hour or two before disappearing, to be ground into the mass fecund nothingness of river loam.

121

'Double B,' says Pig's Breath, '$52 a day. And I said, No, no that is an insult. He's my friend, he's hard up and he can guide and no one knows the river better.' He exhales theatrically. 'Ali, I got you $87 and I can tell you I really went out on a limb to get that much.'

'Eighty-seven dollars a day?' I can see now that I was trying to sound outraged and look outraged. We both knew it was outrageous. But now I can see what Pig's Breath is seeing: a sick man who has aged far more than Pig's Breath thought possible, a sick ageing man who needs work and any money real bad, even the crummy money he's offering, and who needs something other than work as well. Sometimes I'd get to thinking that this sickness of mine – my bad guts, my shaking, my aching head, the prickly odour that oozed out of my clammy skin – that maybe it came out of my soul and not my body. Of course who can say where bad health comes from. Who can? But that stench was something I couldn't exorcise with drugs or rest or other tonics for the body. I needed something aimed at the soul. But I didn't know that. And Pig's Breath did.

I can see that Pig's Breath knows Aljaz well enough to see that Aljaz desperately wants to visit the Franklin River country, that there is a need in him, which Pig's Breath does not have, to go back there, and that this is his only way of doing it. And while Aljaz sits there trying to look as if he is chewing over numbers, Pig's Breath can tell that what he is in fact doing is smelling the river, hearing it run, watching the rain mists rise from its valleys, drinking its tea-coloured waters from his cupped hands. It is so obvious that Pig's Breath knows Aljaz thinks him a fool, and that Pig's Breath, not being a fool, is able to use this knowledge to his advantage. He says nothing about Aljaz's desire to go back to the

Franklin. He says something entirely different.

'I'm sorry. You can always refuse.'

I can see Aljaz looking and giving the small laugh of a man who knows he has been trapped. 'I don't have a lot of choice.'

Pig's Breath drums his fingers and says nothing.

'When did you say the trip goes out?'

'Wednesday morning.'

'Wednesday. So I've only got today and tomorrow to buy food, prepare and pack all the gear?'

'Yes,' says Pig's Breath, who suddenly leans forward over his cluttered desk in a movement almost aggressive. 'But you look as if you're not interested.'

Aljaz feels suddenly tired. His guts start cramping up again. He is beaten. He knows it.

'No,' says Aljaz. 'I'll take the job.'

'You're a crazy Cosini,' laughs Pig's Breath.

Overnight a westerly change blows in and people awaken to the smell and sight of water falling to the hot earth and then rising as soon as it hits as steam. The sky is black, but beneath the languid curling dark clouds the low sun shines hot and hard. Hobart sways as if mesmerised by the battle between the two fronts, the hot harsh northerly and the cold dark westerly. The elements combined throw a weight upon the city so that it can move but slowly. Aljaz wakes early and breakfasts on apricots that he had simmered in sugar and water the night before. He meets the Cockroach at Pig's Breath storeroom for the second and final day of packing gear for the trip. It is tedious, frustrating work. The storeroom is a mess because Pig's Breath refuses to pay for a storeman and things have been simply thrown in at the end of each trip, uncleaned, unsorted, uncared for. The Cockroach, who has had no breakfast, eats two tins of smoked mussels which he finds beneath a mouldy tent and almost immediately falls ill. He vomits in a supermarket car park when they later go to buy more food for the trip. Somehow they manage to sort and pack all the gear and food, and mid-afternoon they head out for a drink.

In the dark bar there is little noise. All is hushed, save for the low crackling of the caller on the radio giving the results of the fifth from Moorabin. Aljaz and the Cockroach Krezwa sit on stools leaning up against the bar of the New Melbourne, an old pub facing an uncertain future, soon to be either demolished or renovated as a backpackers' hostel. The publican, once hearty and strong enough to do his own bouncing, is these days a broken man who sits behind the bar pouring for the few who still patronise his palace of vanquished, yellowed dreams.

As a refuge from the hurly-burly of the city, the New Melbourne's time is done. But for a month or more perhaps, people such as the Cockroach and Aljaz can still sit down within its plywood-panelled walls and drink and talk in quiet. In the corner sits an old man, much like the old men in the corners of bars everywhere, whose future is as uncertain as that of the pub in which he has drunk the now unfashionably small six-ounce beers for the last twenty years. As the old man pulls the beer up to his lips in a jerky movement, his head stutters around to see who else is in the bar, in the manner of a chook in a henhouse checking out who has come to steal its eggs. The Cockroach asks for two more beers. The Cockroach is big and he is ugly. He is also young, perhaps twenty-four at the most. He has the body of an athlete and a face that looks like it has been trodden upon. He is all river guide, all Teva sandals and polar-fleece garments, suitably baubled and slightly filthy to impart the impression of experience, bangles made of brightly coloured knotted cord, silver earring with a scimitar hanging off it, weak eyes and strong hands, long laugh and slow voice. The buck teeth are a discordant element, but they have the effect of rendering his unfortunate face happy and cheerful.

The Cockroach seems to accept that Aljaz is to be the head guide without rancour, for which I can see I was clearly grateful, for it must have been obvious to him how out of condition I was, and, once upon the water, how long it was since I had rafted. Perhaps it is this gratitude that makes Aljaz more talkative than normal. The Cockroach talks about whitewater rafting methods Aljaz has never heard of. Aljaz decides to come clean with the Cockroach.

'To be honest, I'm totally out of touch,' says Aljaz. 'I'm long past it.' He looks up at the Cockroach. 'I only got the job because they have to have someone who knows the river and there was no one else available. That's all.'

The Cockroach shrugs his shoulders. It doesn't worry him. 'I'm just keen to get down there to have a look,' he says. They talk slowly, quietly, for although they are unknown to each other, they know that for the next twelve days they are condemned to live and work closely together. I notice now how the Cockroach is staring at Aljaz as if trying to put two and two together, and I know what the Cockroach Krezwa is thinking. He is reminded of a tempestuous affair he had the previous summer with an art school student who had a postcard of each of her

125

two artist heroes stickytaped on the bedhead above her pillow. In moments of passion the Cockroach had occasion to focus upon these pictures while his body was transported elsewhere. The Cockroach Krezwa is thinking how Aljaz looks (with the exception of his very large aquiline nose, which is magnificently and uniquely his own) like a slightly podgy cross between the two great artists featured on those postcards: Vincent Van Gogh and Frida Kahlo. As if the pictures of the two famous painters had bizarrely merged to form this one obscure river guide – the Dutchman's intense, driven features and prickly red hair combining with a dash of the Mexican's swarthy visage and proud refusal to accept her fall from physical grace to make Aljaz Cosini. A little mad, a little possessed, sure only of the certainty of his terrible destiny. Strange. And unsettling. The Cockroach wonders what this Aljaz would paint were he an artist. Probably a very large mess, he concludes. The Cockroach's thoughts stray back to more earthy memories of what occurred beneath the postcards and from these I am thankfully spared. Strange that I never saw such obvious and famous likenesses glare back at me from the mirror. I am not entirely sure when I started to look that way; presumably it can only be recently, because I'd always fancied myself better looking and more easygoing than that driven, demented face I now see.

The Cockroach senses that Aljaz is troubled, but he does not ask Aljaz what his troubles are. He wonders whether Aljaz is seeing a woman. He feels how something in Aljaz is like a broken spring that does not drive anything but only pricks things. The Cockroach decides to make a joke.

'Bound to be an accountant called bloody Barry,' he

says, staring at his index finger drawing lines on the condensation on his beer glass. 'Always is. Fair dinkum, I did six trips in a row on the Tully and on each trip there was an accountant called Barry.'

They laugh. The barman passes two more beers across the bar. 'Yeah,' says Aljaz quietly, 'always plenty of Barrys.'

'And doctors called Richard,' says the Cockroach. 'I had two in the same boat once.'

'And dentists called Dennis,' says Aljaz.

'From Bankstown,' says the Cockroach. 'Always dentists called Dennis *from* Bankstown.' The Cockroach grows more animated. 'And don't forget the nurses,' he says. 'You never get *a* nurse. Never. Always, always two nurses.'

'And you don't ask any of them what they did last week. Because that's talking about work and they hate that.'

'Christ, no. You say, So *hey*, Barry, where did you get to last holiday? And he likes that, because in his heart of hearts he only wants to pretend to you and everyone else that he is something other than the boring bastard he is. In his holidays he can pretend to be something he's not. And so Barry wanks on about skiing in Austria or trekking in Tibet or ballooning in Bhutan, and all I can think is pity the poor underpaid bastards that had to wetnurse you through all that, because, Christ knows, if you were left to your own devices you'd kill yourself in an hour.'

The radio gives out the results of the tote on Randwick and announces that they are two minutes away from a start at Flemington. The Cockroach tells a story about himself in the mistaken hope that Aljaz might do the same.

'I went out with this girl once, while I was working

up on the Tully it was, and it turned out she had worked as a pro. And she was saying how it's just the same if you're a pro, like you never let on to the punters – *they* even call them punters, can you believe it? – you never let on what you are really thinking. And you can't help disliking them even when you want to like them, because if they weren't wankers they wouldn't be paying for it in the first place, they'd be off doing it themselves, not having to pay people to do it for them. They want to fuck your mind, that's what she said, and that's the part you don't let them buy. Because they can go, but you've got to stay and do it again and again and you can't go. Anyway, I am talking shit, I know it. But it was like we had something in common, she being a pro and me being a river guide. I liked her, you know. Liked her a real lot.' He smiles and drains his beer. 'When people asked us what we did, we'd always say we worked in the tourist industry.' He holds a finger up to the barman, who nods and picks two fresh glasses out of the tray beneath the bar. 'Which I suppose was the truth of it.' He stops looking straight ahead and turns and looks at Aljaz.

'We're all punters,' says Aljaz giving a little smile. 'At the end of the day, all of us.'

'What's the trip like anyway?' asks the Cockroach.

'A joke,' says Aljaz.

When Aljaz had begun river guiding this was the cardinal rule among all guides: don't ever take it seriously. Treat it as a joke, Gibber, the first guide he worked with, had told him, and Gibber was right, it was one big joke that went on for nearly a fortnight, a joke whose essence was that only the guides ever understood what was funny. The big joke was made up of innumerable smaller jokes played upon the punters. Rules

128

were one part of the joke. There were rules all the way down the river. There were rules for eating and sleeping and even for shitting, which had to be done in a plastic bag (which would be carried out at the end of the trip) at a point distant from the campsite, always selected by the guides, who would sometimes, solely for their own amusement, set it at the end of a precarious and long trail along cliff edges. The punters loved the certainty, order and rhythm that the rules brought to the world of river and rainforest, which to them seemed so uncertain, chaotic, and discordant. Beyond that, and the amusement they afforded the guides, the rules were largely useless. Once Aljaz had grown sick of forever issuing edicts covering every aspect of daily life, from how they ate to where they slept, and he had told a group of punters that they could work it out for themselves as they went down the river. The punters rightly blamed him for what ended up being a lousy trip.

He knew things were changing, that for many of the new guides the ditch wasn't a joke at all and the only jokes they knew were the ones they had committed to memory to retell in the raft or around the campfire for the punters to laugh at. And when Aljaz had tried to explain all this to a young guide who had been preparing for a day's rafting trip in Pig's Breath's storeroom, when he had tried to explain that the whole thing was a joke, the young guide had not understood. No it's not, he had said, it's serious. But that's the point of the joke, thought Aljaz, but he did not bother to say it. Those who refused to recognise the joke became part of it.

The Cockroach smiled. 'They're all jokes, mate,' he said. 'Otherwise we'd take 'em seriously. Otherwise it'd be so fucking serious you'd die from the seriousness of it all.'

True, thought Aljaz, true. So true it pings. Jokes are what separate them from us and all their shit about being in harmony with the wilderness. Jokes destroyed all their systems for understanding, for knowing this land, and made it once more strange and unknowable, irreducible to human ideas. Jokes, Aljaz further thought, are all we have to dissolve the lies that come between us and the earth we walk upon. 'They're all jokes,' said the Cockroach, 'every fucking river I've ever fucking rafted.'

They drank another two beers in silence. But the Cockroach knew what Aljaz failed to see about himself: that for Aljaz the joke wasn't funny any more. The art of being a good river guide was looking after your customers while remaining indifferent to them. Sometimes, though loath to admit it, the Cockroach even ended up liking some of his punters. But Aljaz seemed to hate them, and that made the Cockroach uneasy. Most of all, he seemed to hate himself. The Cockroach swivelled around on his barstool and looked at the swarthy, nuggety redhead gone slightly to fat sitting there next to him. The Cockroach thought Aljaz, with his large, slightly crooked nose, looked a little like a broken-down boxer. The Cockroach had worked before with river bums who were sour, but Aljaz was more than sour. The Cockroach had a nose for fear and he could smell it on Aljaz. But fear of what? The Cockroach began to wonder how this trip with such a driven man would end. After a time, he decided that it could only be badly.

There wasn't an accountant called Barry. There weren't two nurses. There were two accountants, one from Melbourne called Derek, and one from Brisbane called

Marco. There was a doctor, but he was clearly under some misapprehension as to his position. He wore an earring and insisted on being called Rickie. 'It amounts to the same thing,' the Cockroach whispered, as they met the punters for the first time at the trip briefing in Pig's Breath's dingy office. There was Sheena, who was a dental assistant. There was a thirty-year-old farmer called Otis from outback South Australia. There was a journalist called Lou. There were some others, but Aljaz couldn't remember their names. He was not interested and he was a little drunk from the two hours spent drinking with the Cockroach in the New Melbourne.

It was the first meeting between guides and punters that Aljaz loathed more than any other. It depressed him, and coming as it did after two days of frantic work rushing around town, buying a fortnight's food for ten people, then stripping it of its packaging and waterproofing it by wrapping each piece separately in three layers of plastic bags, then carefully packing them into large black plastic barrels. After two days scouring the chaos that was Pig's Breath's storeroom for knives and woks and billies and petrol cookers that worked and tents that didn't leak and paddles that weren't bent and pumps that had pressure and first-aid kits that were not wet and repair kits that were not empty, after all this hectic, crazed, frustrating work, they had to meet the punters and impart to them an air of serene organisation and calm control, while all around them was blind panic. And as always, the punters looked so pathetic, so hopeless, so dependent upon the quiet leadership of their guides. The Cockroach took refuge in seeking to be efficient.

'Now,' he said, 'who's going to be needing to hire a wetsuit?'

The pork satays that Aljaz had prepared for the evening of the third day had gone rancid in the heat. Aljaz delved down into a large barrel, pulling out bag after carefully packed bag of food, until he at last found a piece of silverside that smelt only a little bad. He washed the lump of meat in the river, then boiled it for an hour, after which he diced it into cubes and tossed it into the wok on the fire along with some canned tomatoes, kidney beans and a more than generous serve of chilli powder.

'Ekala,' said Aljaz in reply to Derek's questions as to what they were eating for tea. 'Traditional Brazilian dish. Aged silverside is the closest approximation available to smoked llama meat.' Derek looked on with interest and Rickie said that he would have to visit a Brazilian restaurant when he returned to Adelaide.

After they had eaten the meal out of their plastic bowls the Cockroach told them the stories about Tasmania that they wanted to hear. About the grandfather who slept with his daughters until his son chained him up, beat him every morning until he was mad, then used him as a watchdog. About the son who carried his dead mother in a sugar bag to the nearest town to register her death and, finding her too heavy, stopped at the wayside and did what he did with all the roos he killed and carried, gutted the corpse and then proceeded on. The punters greeted the stories with nervous laughter and nods and shakes of the head, meant to convey bewilderment at such horror but which was rather them affirming that Tasmania was as they had always conceived it in their ignorance, a grotesque Gothic horrorland — as if they knew the stories already, which really they already did. The Cockroach tells the stories for effect, not because he believes them but because he knows they are what the punters want, and his job is to satisfy their needs. Aljaz says nothing. Other nights on other trips he has told the same stories. They ought be honoured by their repetition and by their currency. But they are not and Aljaz dislikes them, dislikes telling them. What is there to say? It is too hard to say something different, to tell a new story that no one has told and to which he doesn't know the response of either the punters or himself. Those stories are too hard. They come from something too close.

I can hear a sobbing, a soft sobbing in the darkness, a swish of fabric. Thank God it's not Jemma but a tent on the Franklin. Aljaz is looking inside the tent, his torch light beaming upon the expansive sitting form of Otis, whose farmboy's body moves gently up and down with his weeping. Outside in the darkness the rain softly thrums the tent's taut nylon.

'Otis,' said Aljaz, 'what's the matter, mate?'

'Nothing,' said Otis.

'Otis,' said Aljaz, 'this is the third night you have eaten no tea. Tell me what the matter is.' Otis looked up, his big freckled white face tear-glazed, stretched like uncooked shortcrust pastry over a meat pie. 'Has someone being giving you the shits, Otis?'

'I ain't never eaten that sort of tucker,' said Otis.

'What you talking about?' asked Aljaz.

'All them curries and poppadots.'

'*Dams*,' said Aljaz, 'poppa*dams*.'

'Eh, yeah. Them. All them and them modern rice things as well that you and the Cockroach cook up in the wok,' said Otis, then paused, his humiliation great. He swallowed. 'Well, I ain't never seen such food and I can't eat it.' Aljaz smiled, and would have laughed if he had not been concerned about upsetting Otis even more. With some sense of finality Otis said, 'I tried and I just can't and I feel a bloody fool ever coming.'

'There's no shame in it, Otis,' said Aljaz.

'Mum'd cook us roasts and three veg and chops and three veg, and jam roly-polies and apple crumble and beef soups and steaks and three veg and all that stuff, and I ain't never eaten this modern city tucker and I just can't get it down. I tried but I can't.' Otis burst out sobbing again.

'I'll fix you something decent,' said Aljaz.

'I tried gittin it down but it just wouldn't get past my throat,' said Otis between sobs. 'I tried but I can't and I just feel so stupid.'

'There's no shame in it,' said Aljaz and turned, dropped the tent flap and was gone.

He searched two barrels with the light of his head torch till he found the food he was after. He fried up four eggs and eight tinned sausages, and boiled five pinkeye potatoes and a canned self-saucing chocolate pudding and brought it all to Otis's tent arrayed on a large enamel plate and plastic bowl.

'I'm grateful,' said Otis.

Ten minutes later Aljaz spied Otis leaving his tent with an empty plate and bowl. Otis saw Aljaz standing alone by the fire and came over. 'Now, that's what I call a proper feed,' he said with a broad smile. Otis and Aljaz fell to talking. Otis told him stories about growing up on a remote South Australian farm, two days drive from the nearest town, confessed to Aljaz how he had a daughter to an Aboriginal woman. 'You're the first person I ever told that,' he said. 'You got kids?'

'No,' said Aljaz looking into the fire.

Aljaz lay down on his air mattress. Too tired to get into his sleeping bag, he just threw it over himself. The rain had ceased some hours earlier and he and the Cockroach could not be bothered pitching their fly, had simply placed their air mattresses on the small platform of river sand a few metres below what remained of the the main campsite. His body felt leaden, the effort to raise or move one limb enormous. Were it not for his bones, he thought the whole mass might simply dribble away like molten lead into the depressions and recesses of the earth. He slept the sleep of lead: dark, heavy, immobile, malleable and, ultimately, molten. Aljaz dissolved in his sleep, and I with him.

– Ned Quade, 1832 –

Slowly people appear around me, faces of people I have never met but about whom I know everything. A curious thing, I'll admit. And an annoying thing. I've always tried to keep myself to myself, as the saying goes, and here I am besieged by people clamouring for their stories to be heard and seen and felt. *Piss off!* I screw up my face and shut my eyes and scream a second time. *Piss off!* But it does no good. My bad humour is to no avail. The vision won't depart and my throat just feels as if it is burning.

There is the face of the stone man, Ned Quade, small, round, and scarred all over by the pox, so that he looks much older than he is. How do I know it is Ned Quade? How the hell do I know? I just know. I don't want to know, but there it is. I mean, Harry once told me how his great-grandfather, Ned Quade, had been the mayor of

Parramatta. But this Ned Quade is not dressed as a mayor. He is dressed in the coarse piss-yellow and black woollen uniform of a convict, and there are chains around his ankles. And I know what this Ned Quade is thinking. He is thinking of what a convict woman called Joanna Heaney had told him: of how some hundreds of miles to the north west of Parramatta there is a great river which, if one could make a craft and travel upon it, leads to a huge estuary, on the other side of which is the land of China. And in the middle of this huge estuary, suspended halfway between Australia and China, is an island upon which a large stockaded town has been built by a free and happy people, bolters and their kin to the last, all those who had escaped from the chains of the System and never returned. Joanna, she who spoke in tongues and saw things that others had only heard as rumour, had seen the island in a vision. It was, she said, a land where all were welcome save for His Majesty's soldiers; a crowded land with bustling streets, a lack of priests, social arrangements where man and woman lay together without the approval of any church but with the sanction of their love and hence God, farms and workshops owned not by distant fat men but by the people who cracked open the rich river-flat soil with the plough and who forged the iron into the plough, a land where there was schooling for all children paid for by levy from all. Joanna called the town the New Jerusalem and said it was led by a single woman known only as Mother Lucky.

And I see Ned escape from his gang working upon a remote reach of the Gordon River, rolling logs in waist-deep water, he and eight others whom he persuades to go with him. They strike their overseer from behind, garrotte him with their chains until he goes floppy, and, after breaking their chains with their picks but still burdened by their steel ankle-collars, they hold the overseer's head under the Gordon's water for a good five minutes, then leave his limp body to slowly spin in the river's side eddy. They hobble on foot heading north east, using a crude compass one convict has made out of lodestone and a stolen fob-watch case. After two days' travelling, three decide to abandon their walk toward the New Jerusalem and return instead to the shores of Macquarie Harbour, there to take their chances robbing convict gangs of their supplies. Ned and the five others press on. Of their number, only Ned Quade and Aaron Hersey believe in Joanna Heaney's vision of a New Jerusalem. Liam Breen, Jack Jenkins and Paddy Galvin plan to join the banditti that run the country surrounding Hobart Town almost with impunity, terrorising Babylon. Will Dorset travels with them without destination, only with the relief of no longer being in the hell of Macquarie Harbour. The harsh brightness of the sun wanes to a slowly encroaching greyness, the scrub they are bashing through gives way to an alpine moor, all russet browns. Then the men's faces begin to dim and disappear altogether as I return to the darkness of my paralysed body, left only with questions and doubts.

— the third night —

Aljaz was woken by the *hop hop* of raindrops landing on his sleeping bag. The sound hauled his mind up from the great depths where his dreaming took place and brought him enough to his senses to realise he had to get out of his sleeping bag. The gentle rhythm of the drops was being swamped by the sound of a heavy downpour smashing on the rainforest canopy, pressing its intent upon the myrtles and the sassafrases, then permeating downwards, entering the forest branch by branch, leaf by leaf, until every branch and every leaf could be heard to move by the power of the rain. Until the rain was cascading down on the forest floor and all the billions of raindrops and all the millions of leaves moving had become one deafening sound and one overwhelming purpose.

Aljaz and the Cockroach, who by now had also woken, quickly stuffed their sleeping bags into their waterproof gearbags, donned anoraks and worked quickly to pitch a light brown nylon fly above their sleeping site, their head torches darting cones of light describing white lines of rain wherever they moved. Outside of these cones the world was entirely black. Twice after pitching the fly the rain, which now fell in torrents, began to form in ominous pools in the fly and they had to steepen its pitch. They hadn't bothered bringing a tent for themselves, although the punters always slept in tents. Guides never slept with the punters in the tents, and they always slept at a slight distance.

Aljaz and the Cockroach went and checked the punters' tents to make sure they were pitched properly and then they scrambled down the bank, their naked legs feeling the cold wet caresses of the hardwater ferns and tea-tree. Aljaz wondered why paths always seemed so much longer in the dark. They manhandled the rafts up from the river onto higher ground where they tied them to trees, then gathered all the life jackets, helmets, and paddles left lying dangerously close to the river's edge and brought them up to the safer, higher ground of the campsite. The rain continued to pour, but the river hadn't risen. They stayed awake for half an hour, playing cards by candlelight under the fly.

'Bastard,' said the Cockroach unexpectedly. He flicked a finger across his forearm upon which sat a bloated leech.

'Watch this,' said Aljaz. He crawled out of his sleeping bag, went over to where the black food barrels were, and returned with a box of matches and the salt container. He made a ring of salt on the ground, the size of a five-cent piece. 'Now watch.' He lit a match, let it burn, blew the flame out, then placed the red hot tip on the leech. As the match tip seered its back the leech arched up in pain. It fell off the Cockroach's forearm onto the ground. Aljaz picked the leech up with a piece of bark and placed it within the circle of salt. Every time the leech tried to move, its body touched the salt circle and the salt was absorbed into its body. The leech began to writhe and bleed the Cockroach's blood. 'See how it suffers,' said Aljaz. 'Wherever it moves, however it moves, it only absorbs more salt and suffers more.'

'You're twisted, Cosini,' said the Cockroach.

'How come you became a river bum?' Aljaz asked.

'I had a job in Cairns working on airconditioning at a new resort – I'm a plumber by trade – and thought, To hell with it, I don't want to be like the other old farts on the site knowing nothing else but plumbing at sixty. So I got a job working on the Tully River, four years ago now.'

'You ever think about going back to plumbing?' asked Aljaz.

'Sometimes. But guiding sort of gets in your blood after a while. It's a way of life, really. Partying and women and always the river the next day. Making you feel like you going somewhere. Even when you're not.' The Cockroach turned and looked at Aljaz, who continued to study the death agonies of the leech. 'Sometimes though, I think how I'd just like one woman and one job in one place. Settle down like. You ever feel that?'

How could he explain what he felt? How could he explain that beyond his family nothing had seemed important and yet he had turned his back upon his family. How could he describe being pursued by a terrible fear he could never name that sat behind him like a shadow, how as if in a dream he could never turn and face that shadow and name its truth. How the fear sometimes grew so vast that he thought it might crush him, and how he felt as if he could no longer hold it all together, that even getting up in the morning and saying hello to people and smiling and laughing had gone beyond his powers. And he had drunk and drunk and smoked bags of dope until he felt so bad from his overindulgence that that pain temporarily eclipsed the pain of his shadow. At which point he would lay off the bottle and the dope, in the hope that the shadow would have gone. But it would only reemerge stronger, as if it had fed off his madness and wanted more, demanded more. And then he would deny the pain with work in some new job, work till his body burnt with physical aches and pains, and sheer exhaustion gave him the blessing of sleep, the deep sweet sleep of those who labour, where even when the mind has sunk into its farthest recesses there is still a surface consciousness of the pain of the body. And the body seems unbearably heavy and sinks like a necklace of stones into the mattress, and any movement is avoided because the effort of moving those fatigued limbs even once more is too great. But then after some weeks the shadow would reemerge in his dreams, and he would suddenly sit bolt upright in bed, eyes wide open, feeling so terribly afraid. He would try to find a woman to take away the darkness and occasionally, though not often, he found one, but instead of him crying to her, he inevitably made her cry in front of him, as if her suffering assured him that his suffering wasn't a solitary insanity but the keystone of a humanity he desperately wanted to share in, and the more women he had, the worse he treated them and the more they cried and the sooner they left him. And then he knew it was time to move on and the whole thing started to replay itself, this circle of hell.

It had become easier not belonging; he had learnt to cope with that, had made a life out of it, drifting, made a virtue of having no roots by never allowing himself to hang around one spot too long. He felt himself a nobody, an invisible nothing, told himself that was the beginning and end of it. But it wasn't and he knew it. He didn't want to know about it, but it had always known about him and it had shaped him, and though he could deny it there was no way it could deny him. It just seemed to be more food for the shadow, and Aljaz hated it and hated himself even more. And how could he tell the Cockroach any of it?

'No, I don't,' said Aljaz.

'You're lucky,' said the Cockroach. 'Maybe you're the sort of bloke who gets a woman when he wants one, then moves on when he doesn't want her. But me, I dunno, I can't do that any more, you know what I mean?' said the Cockroach. Aljaz said nothing. He pushed the leech back into the salt ring with a twig. The Cockroach continued. 'I don't know anything any more. Not what I

141

want or what I'm gonna do, nothing. If I could find one woman who wanted to sleep with me through the night – sleep, I'm saying, nothing else – I'd love her till I die. Know what I mean?'

'No,' said Aljaz.

'You're so twisted,' laughed the Cockroach. 'You know that? Really twisted.' But he looked at the writhing leech and not at Aljaz.

By then it was 4 am. They left the leech to its agony and went back down one final time to check the river level.

The river flowed west quietly. But Aljaz could hear its waters beginning to lick the edges of the bank, its appetite heightening.

The river was beginning to rise.

And with it me.

Beginning to float.

– Six –

This night of rising water I see a bedspread. Very clearly. It looks like this: pure white, elegant in its prewar fashion, the size of a double bed, and at its centre a large faint yellow stain. The whole, in spite of or perhaps because of this aged blemish, elaborate and beautiful in its design and texture and feel. But there is no double bed. There is a single bed and the bedspread is folded to fit upon it. I look more closely at the stain till it has assumed the proportion of a large estuary. And floating up that estuary a ship, ambling up the broad reaches of the lower Derwent River.

An old rustbucket of a steamer contracted in that year 1957 to bring wogs from Europe to Australia. And upon its deck, is an ashen-faced Sonja, wearing a long coat, clutching a three-year-old child to her hip: me. And the child is smiling and laughing his weird, gurgling giggle. Because the idiot child recognises his other home, that is to his mother a strange country.

— Sonja and Harry —

When she first saw it from the ship, Sonja fell to weeping.

'What is this place that you have brought me to?' she asked of Harry. The town, with its wooden buildings that teetered and sloped at all angles in consequence of their age and a lack of care and money, with its huge purple mountain that rose behind its offspring like a crabby matriarch ready to strike out at anybody who badmouthed her child, this town looked like a nightmare. None of the town made any sense to Sonja. It was painted in the drab colours favoured by the English, and the sky was black with clouds that threatened to rain but didn't. Yet, as their ship shimmied up the Derwent River, the town glowed a rainbow of colours in the winter light of late afternoon. The town looked crabbed and cramped, hemmed in by olive-coloured forests on all sides bar that of the sky-blue river that defined its front, yet it seemed open to something that Sonja had closed her mind to many years before. The town was obviously not old, only a hundred or so years, yet in the streets they walked down from the ship Sonja could smell something much older, the smell of the receding tide, the smell of salt and drying kelp. This world that seemed like it ought be full of people was largely empty. Through a stillness so vast that it seemed an ocean, the wind cracked and swept from every angle as they walked the quiet, empty streets.

'What is this place?' Sonja asked again.

'What do you reckon it is?' said Harry, somewhat annoyed at what he felt to be a pointless and silly question. 'It's Hobart.'

They saw a man arguing with a telegraph pole, and a woman pleading with him not to make a fool of himself.

'Piss off,' said the man, 'this is private.'

They saw a woman sitting in a gutter with pigeons, laughing as they fed from her hands. They saw a drunk fisherman stagger out of a pub with half a broken beer bottle in his face.

'I went searching for the pink-lipped abalone and found this instead,' he said to Sonja and Harry, then staggered away, weeping not from pain but out of an infinite sadness.

Sonja grew harder with the years that then passed. She was wont to recall her time in the Radovlica chain factory as a young woman. 'You know what they made? Chains – not dog chains or little necklace chains, but those huge heavy things that ships use. And our job was to lift and stack them.' She would at this point normally pause and reflect upon her time in the chain factory, to the memory of which she remained inextricably shackled, then look back up with her pupils reflecting rusty steel, saying, 'And I never want to carry chains again.' In this regard – that of material betterment – Harry was to prove an ongoing disappointment, never being able to rise out of the class he had been born into and, worse still, seemingly content to sink further into it. Nevertheless, Sonja's relentless industry and astonishingly focused purpose meant that they did get a home and they did in a few short years manage to pay it off, and they did manage to be if not affluent, well then, neither struggling. And they did manage to share a dream. Of a large family.

But after me, there were no more children. Why? I don't know. Certainly not for want of trying, because I can now see a whole sequence of ever more desperate couplings of Harry and Sonja taking place before my eyes. She blamed it on the drink and was inclined in her more perverse moments to see his lack of a thumb as a portent of a more fundamental incompleteness that she ought to have heeded. They went to the doctor, who sent them on to a specialist, an aspiring young man called Mr McNell, who assured them that it was almost certainly Sonja's fallopian tubes and that this could be easily remedied. Sonja was hospitalised and endured an excruciating procedure in which air was pumped through her tubes to clear out supposed obstructions. This was repeated at monthly intervals for a year and at the end pronounced a success by Mr McNell, who told them that there was now no scientific reason why the couple could not have children. Now the nature of their couplings changed from desperate desire to a huge sadness. For Sonja felt her body to be a husk, its purpose stolen from her, and her husband's attention a futile mockery of the consequences that ought to have flowed from such passion. Now she lay beneath him and did not move and did not milk his testicles with her hand. She lay beneath him and closed her eyes and saw herself back in the chain factory.

Harry and Sonja's marriage was not, then, a great success. No, I'll rephrase that. Harry and Sonja's marriage was as unpredictable as this river. It could be terrible. They would stand screaming at one another and Sonja would sometimes lay into poor old Harry with her fists, and he would hold her out at arm's length, preventing her landing a blow while she flailed her fists and berated him with every Slovenian curse peculiar, not to that nation, but to Italy. 'Slovenians,' she would remind him, 'are too polite to invent their own swear words. That's why we use the Italians' instead.' Not that Harry was always successful in avoiding her fists: sometimes she managed to strike him. Over the years he grew quieter and drank more, and tried to avoid antagonising her, which was harder than avoiding her wild punches, because there was much about Harry that irritated Sonja immensely and it would sometimes take only a careless sentence to send her off again. Over the years, her early passion spent, she grew physically distant with Harry, went limp in his hugs and stiff if he came up from behind and kissed her on her neck. She particularly despised him kissing her on the mouth. Her lips would remain frozen and her face unmoving and she would say, 'Finished now?' Or, 'Can I get back to what I was doing now you're happy?' She found him shabby, dishevelled, and ill-kempt. He found her cold, removed and uninterested in him. Over the years she changed from a young, somewhat wayward and even wild woman who wanted to leave her past behind to one that increasingly wallowed in a past that never existed. She dressed ever more conservatively, took up going to church, and kept the house looking like a museum of rundown and recycled Mitteleuropa. She became an old European mama. But for all that and all that, it was not a bad marriage. Sonja loved Harry with a passion, albeit an ever curioser one, and he in turn loved his lady of the clove dust, as he sometimes whispered to her as they lay in bed. And for all her coldness, there were times in that bed when she revelled in being with Harry. I am a witness to their lovemaking much against my will, for it is not the way I wish to see my parents. I am, as I have said, a private person and this intrusion upon their privacy seems somewhat unfair. What is evident from what I see is that while Harry knew he loved her, even if he would never understand her, Sonja knew she understood Harry and wondered therefore if he was worth loving.

Long after, as Harry was dying, he thought about the day he and Sonja had arrived in Hobart, thought of the love he had once had for Sonja, the love that had seemed so strong, that had seemed so eternal. Where had it gone? As he lay there with the drips spiralling around his cancer-bloated belly he remembered Sonja and what they had and what they had lost. Why do such things so often prove so transitory? In the end he thought that he hated Sonja. But then, in the methylated-spirit afterscent of the ward, the smell of the flesh of her back as he lay curled up behind her came back to him and the smell of clove dust came back to him and the sound of her voice came back to him one last time.

O I am missing you.

How much he had loved her.

O I am missing you.

– Ned Quade, 1832 –

Two faces. Among the many bubbles, two faces – one scarred with the pox, the round head almost shaven so that its red hairs appear as jagged points over the scalp, like so many rusty needles.

My hair! My red hair!

Ned Quade, the stone man.

Why this curious name? Because upon the triangle where he is flogged for possessing a wad of tobacco, or, once, for singing a song, he betrays no pain. On his first flogging of a hundred lashes I hear the flagellator, a one-time baker called Proctor, say as he unties Ned Quade's white wrists at the end of the punishment, 'You are of stone.' And his back is transformed by the relentless slash of the cat-o'-nine-tails into blood-flecked alabaster. Because in his heart he is innocent and he will not betray his innocence with a single cry of suffering. For that would be an admission that punishment had been felt and was therefore somehow just.

The second face is thin and long, with a scar above the left eye that twists that eye away from the nose, giving the face a distorted appearance. It is topped with medium-length brown hair that is dirty and matted. Aaron Hersey. Dissenting weaver from Spitalfields. One-time Muggletonian, later of the Ancient Deists of Hoxton, he talks of dreams and of having communion with the dead, and regularly sees angels with burning wings and smells the ash of their passing. The angels are beautiful, save for their breath, which he finds most putrid.

The two men sit in a corner of a chilly, fetid stone dormitory, on the floor of which some hundreds of other convicts lie, some moaning in agony, some giggling in madness, some shouting curses in their sleep, some pissing through the gaps in the floorboards upon the Aborigines rounded up from the surrounding wild lands and imprisoned on the floor below. Chill draughts blow through the open slits that serve for windows. From outside, the sound of the gale-whipped waters of Macquarie Harbour slapping the shore of the small island which is their prison. Sarah Island. The Devil's Island of the British Empire, the endpoint of the vast convict system, the remotest island of the remotest island of the remotest continent. From the blacks incarcerated below, from the throats and mouths of the proud people of the Needwonne and Tarkine, come screams and weeping and terrible coughs and wheezing. They believe the building to be possessed of evil spirits. Some are terrified and some propose escape, and some are dying of influenza and colds and horror, and all believe that devils run around the room and spear them in the chest with evil. From outside, the splatter and surge of the rain carrying off the last of the topsoil from the island that has been totally deforested by the convicts' slave labour.

Tomorrow Ned Quade and Aaron Hersey are to be part of the gang that is to row up the Gordon River and relieve the Huon pine-cutting gang that has been stationed there for the past two weeks. It is from there that they intend to effect their escape. Ned Quade dictates a note for his wife, who is incarcerated in the Hobart Female Factory, to Aaron Hersey, dissenting weaver from Spital-fields and fellow plotter, who learnt to read and write in various churches.

'How will it be got to her?' asks Aaron.

'Solly. In the commissariat. He owes me. He'll smuggle it out on the next ship bound for Hobart Town.' Ned Quade looks around to make sure that none of the other convicts in the barracks are taking any undue interest in their whispered conversation. 'How should it begin?' Ned Quade asks Aaron Hersey.

'However you'd like it to begin,' replies Aaron. 'My task is only to capture your words on the paper and speed them to her mind.'

Ned looks at his feet and thinks awhile, then looks up sheepishly at Aaron and says, 'What if you write "My beloved Eliza"?'

'That is what you want?' asks Aaron. Ned says nothing, but nods.

Aaron Hersey writes with a stolen stub of pencil on a sheet of paper that both men hide with the positioning of their bodies. Aaron Hersey writes what he would write if he were to write to a queen. Aaron Hersey writes:

My Esteemed and Most Noble Madame Elijah —

His confidence in the process now boosted by the sight of his words being transformed into a flourishing script upon the paper, Ned Quade continues. 'Tell her,' he says, 'tell her how we are bound for the stockaded town many, many hundreds of miles to the north of Parramatta where all are free and no one is bonded, and that having arrived there and secured work and lodgings, that I will send word and someone to bring her and our children out of bondage into the glorious light of liberty.'

Aaron Hersey writes what he can. Aaron Hersey writes:

Well say You in th. New Jerusalem.

As the flourishes and swirls and loops continue to grow in their grand parade upon the page Ned begins to sense the power that words might have, their subversive possibilities, their seductive strength. 'Write her,' he says, 'that I love her, and only that love has kept me alive till now, God knows there is so little else to nourish a man's soul in this Hades.'

Aaron Hersey writes what he knows to write as a conclusion. Aaron Hersey writes:

Your loving And humble Servant etc etc in Eyes of The lord Ned Kwade His Mark

And below this message Ned Quade scrawls the outline of a Celtic cross, a cross enclosed within a circle.

Madonna santa! Just as I want to stay and watch what now happens the cross and the circle begin to dance and swirl before my eyes, begin to form spiralling chains with other white swirls of foam, and then, there, standing above the river's swirling currents, looking down into the river, I see Aljaz.

— the fourth day —

In the early morning light, grey and soft and spreading, Aljaz watches the water rise. He stands a little beyond the river's edge upon a large protruding log, and to the Cockroach glancing down from the campsite above he looks uninterested. But his eyes are everywhere, reading the immediacy of the quickly surfacing, quickly disappearing whirlpools, reading the swirling white patterns of foam washing down from newly formed rapids upriver, hearing the river's new sounds, seeking to understand what the shushing of the branches of low-lying tea-tree as they throb under the rising, shoving waters foretells. The river seems to be urging the plants and him to come with them downriver, to join the smooth fast madness of a river in rising flood. The tea-trees bend but don't yield, forever grow with a permanent downriver lean in recognition of the power of the flooded river, but never move from their original position. They grow year in year out, these stunted plants, perhaps a century old, only a metre or so in height, their hunched form bearing physical witness to a hundred floods and a hundred droughts. In the detail of a piece of rushing water Aljaz reads the changing visage of the entire river, hears the terrible soul history of his country, and he is frightened.

He goes back to the campfire and squats down. The others look at him, knowing that he and only he can divine the river and its moods. Aljaz ignores the gaze and looks into the coals of the fire, but he sees only the foam and mist rising from the waterfall at the Churn, feels not the warmth of the flames but the clench of his guts as they push the raft into the big rapid below Thunderush and hope to God that they make it through safely. No one speaks. All wait. Aljaz takes a piece of wood from the heap and goes to make firm a precariously balancing billy. But before he is able to fix it, the Cockroach has kicked a log from the outer of the fire into its centre and deftly repositioned the billy for Aljaz. Then, as he levels the billy, the Cockroach looks around to Aljaz and speaks.

'What you reckon, Ali?'

Aljaz stands up and brushes his trousers. 'A good day for cooking,' says Aljaz, 'that's what I reckon.' And he goes over to a barrel and takes out some flour. 'Reckon we might start with pancakes, that's what I reckon.' Some of the punters are relieved, their own fear arising not from a knowledge of the river, but an intuitive foreboding born of their awareness of their guides' growing unease. Some read this unease as an opportunity to display their own bravado.

'I thought that was what the trip was all about,' says Rickie the doctor. 'A few thrills.' He says it slightly uneasily. The Cockroach looks at Rickie.

'Feel free to take a raft and go,' says the Cockroach. 'I might hang back for a pancake myself.' A few of the group laugh.

Rickie thinks the guides are not going because they think their customers will be scared. 'I am not scared,' he says. He says it hesitantly.

Aljaz looks up from the margarine melting in the frypan. 'I am,' he says, but then immediately regrets saying it in front of them all.

'I'll go a pancake,' says Otis with a smile. 'Mum'd cook a truckload of 'em every Sunday lunch.'

They spend all the day in their dripping wet rainforest camp. The men stay in their tents and their sleeping bags as if they existed only to live in them. The women do what the men are always too tired or too uninterested or too caught up in a conversation about sport or politics to be bothered doing. They work. They peel vegetables. They collect firewood. They fetch water from the river up the steep and awkward bank to the campsite. They wash dishes. They help the guides organise the camp, unpacking and packing barrels. Repairing equipment. The men reserve their energies for some future conjectural act of courage. The women's courage is of a type that endures this day of rain. Meanwhile the men get depressed. The men feel some embarrassment that women are on the same trip and doing things that really only men ought be doing. The guides prefer it. Nothing, for a river guide, is worse than an all-male trip. They are boring and lazy and inclined to foolhardiness. They are considerable work to look after. They are generally not in the same class for company. Aljaz likes sitting down with the women around the fire. The Cockroach organises them into a massed Welsh miners' choir and makes them sing old Tom Jones songs, to which he seems to know all the words. They sing 'Delilah' and they sing 'The Green Green Grass Of Home' and they sing 'Me And Mrs Jones' and they sing them all badly, says the Cockroach, who claims to be of Welsh extraction.

After lunch the Cockroach and Aljaz unpack and pitch the spare tent, and then try to catch up on some sleep inside it. About mid-afternoon they awaken, unzip the flyscreen and look outside the vestibule. The camp is dark, what little light there is having trouble penetrating the rainforest. Out on the river, which looks lit up in comparison, the rain falls heavily in sheets. But in their dark camp, beneath the dense, interwoven canopy of myrtles and blackwoods and Huon pines, the rain falls lightly, a mizzle interspersed with an occasional drip from a branch. Two punters – Marco, in a bright red Goretex anorak, and Derek, in a damp black japara – stand under the large blue polytarp which is pitched as a fly, under which cooking can take place out of the rain. Derek and Marco talk in low tones.

'They're bored,' says the Cockroach.

'Get out the monopoly set,' says Aljaz and they laugh.

'Fucking punters,' says the Cockroach.

Dappling the blue polytarp are green and brown myrtle leaves, fallen with the rain. A pool of water has collected in the middle. Marco pushes a paddle up under the pool, sending water rushing down into an open food barrel, drenching the food inside.

'Fucking idiots,' says the Cockroach.

– Sonja and Harry –

Couta Ho called on Maria Magdalena Svevo to hear the latest news about Harry. The talk was of old times, of Aljaz, whom neither had seen for many years, and of Sonja, whom Couta Ho had never met. Maria Magdalena Svevo told Couta Ho the story of how Sonja met Harry in Trieste in 1954. She began the story in a dramatic fashion.

'On either side of the border, troops were massing. Tito demanded the Slovenian town that the Slovenians called Trst and the Italians called Trieste be returned to Yugoslavia. The Allies refused. For a short time all the tensions of the Cold War built up in a painful boil on the arse of the Adriatic.' Here her tone returned to the everyday. 'And who should be selling Japanese sewing machines door to door but Harry Lewis. No one was buying. Post-war Trieste was still finding it hard enough to get money to buy polenta, much less a shonky machine from Asia that promised a lot, cost more, but looked inadequate to its ambitions and was pushed by a foreigner with a strange accent and missing his right thumb.

'Sonja was working in the café in which Harry, at the end of his second fruitless week of salesmanship, stopped for a coffee. Harry liked the expresso, so unfamiliar and strange to him. For a time he wasn't aware that it was even coffee, but thought it some exotic foreign beverage.

'Sonja was intrigued by the dark stranger who carried a sewing machine under his arm, who looked as if he came from the south of Italy, yet walked differently from the peasants streaming up to the north for work. His movements were slow, as if space and time meant something different than it did to everyone around him, something somehow open and bigger.

'When he came up to the counter to pay, he reached in his pocket and then his face flushed. "Not enough money," he said in halting Italian. Sonja looked in his dull eyes, but she noticed that they had already fallen to the rack of cakes below.

'His cheeks were pinched. Sonja knew that hunger had not only a look but a strong odour. Sonja remembered how her mother and her sisters had stunk of hunger during the war. Harry didn't stink but he did smell pretty bad. She reached into her pocket and slid some money

156

across the glass counter to Harry's hand. Their fingers touched. Harry looked up into Sonja's face, perplexed, worried. Sonja smiled, and then laughed. "Which cake, sir?" she asked.

'Harry ordered four, then, upon examining the money, decided against rashness and ordered two, keeping some change in reserve. He paid for the coffee and the cakes, thanked Sonja profusely and promised to repay her as soon as possible.

'Sonja became embarrassed, what with the other customers and staff now looking up. She took the correct change out of Harry's palm and began serving a group of loud GIs. When she next looked up, Harry had gone.

'Katharina, the manageress, was one of three hundred thousand Italians who had abandoned their homes and villages and memories in Fiume, Istria, and Dalmatia to live in old capitalist Italy, rather than the new socialist Yugoslavia. She had a traditional and hearty contempt for Slovenians that was reinforced by the knowledge that they now lived in her old family home, and this contempt rose like fresh gnocchi in boiling water whenever her temper flared, which was frequently. She stage-whispered to another waitress in Italian, "Stupid *vlacuga* – as if she'll ever see him again," giving particular emphasis to the Slovenian word for whore.

'Days passed, then a week, then another week. The manageress made jokes about how she should keep all Sonja's pay, and use it to give coffee and cakes to every dopey half-starved southern Italian who wandered in. Late one afternoon Harry returned. He no longer wore the old threadbare coat. He no longer carried a sewing machine and he no longer smelt of hunger.

'He walked up to the counter and, in front of the

manageress, opened up a wallet bulging with money and gave Sonja a thousand lira. She refused the money but accepted the carnations he had brought. The manageress watched with interest. Harry ordered an expresso and two cakes and when he came to pay, passed an envelope along with the correct change to Sonja.

'In the envelope were two 500-lira notes, a dried edelweiss, and a note written in bad Italian asking her if she would meet him some evening. He would be in the café at the railway station between seven and nine each evening for the next week.

'When Sonja read the note by the yellow light of the electric bulb in the grimy toilet of her café, she was not to know that Harry went to the railway café not only for warmth but also because it was an ideal place from which to conduct his new business activities.

'Not wishing to appear hasty in her interest, Sonja waited four days before deigning to visit the railway station café. At her work she mixed up orders, gave out the wrong change and generally found it difficult to concentrate. The manageress abused her and said it was only because of the manageress's good heart that she kept Sonja on, stupid and useless Slovene that she was, whereas both Sonja and the manageress knew that Sonja was there because no Italian would work for as low a wage as a Slovene without papers would.

'On the fourth day Sonja lit the brass petrol stove that her mother had found among the gear of a dead German soldier, put a dented aluminium mug on top and proceeded to melt a cake of soap. When the soap became molten she beat an egg into it using the fork with which she ate and cooked. With the mixture still warm and frothy, she took the dented aluminium mug off the stove.

She placed the mug on the floor in the centre of her room, next to a jug of water and an enamel dish that had red roses painted on its side and a blue-edged rim. She knelt in front of the dish and there, with the soap-and-egg mixture and the water, she washed her wiry hair then rinsed it with cider vinegar she had stolen from the café. She filled the basin a second time and washed her body with a coarse pumice stone, then looked at her flesh glowing red from the scouring and the cold. She paused before dressing, and went over to the broken mirror that leant against the plywood wardrobe in the corner.

'She looked at her reflection with interest, ran her hands round the glory of her pot belly, strong and round, defined on the sides by her hips, and from below by her pubic hair. She looked at her breasts with their still-girlish nipples, and ran her hands from her breasts down to the small of her back where she rested them, then turned her hands outwards so that her knuckles pressed inwards and her elbows stuck out. She threw her chin back and laughed at what she saw.

'Il Duce stared back at her from the glass in the guise of a naked woman.

' "The Slovenian people must realise that they have a destiny only in so far as and for as long as they merge their identity with that of the great Italian people," she said, imitating the bombastic tones of Mussolini. Then, taking a step back, she lifted her right hand off her buttock and used it to placate an imaginary Roman crowd. "Until they have learnt this fundamental lesson of history, until they understand this fundamental lesson of history, they cannot complain if, because of their own arrogance, they suffer," she continued. Her left hand rose from her other buttock to join her right hand in quelling the tumultuous applause that greeted this profound announcement. "And until then, and not before then, stupid *vlacugi* must realise that strange men offered kindness will simply take it and never return."

'A knock at the bedroom door. It is Maria Magadalena Svevo with the dress she has borrowed from a friend and just ironed for Sonja.

' "A man that would lead you to go to so much trouble over yourself can only lead to trouble," she admonished Sonja. But before she left she sprinkled the inside of the top and the waist of the dress with ground cloves. And cackled, "Fruit is best eaten seasoned." Never again would Harry be able to eat apple strudel without feeling the most terrible desire.

'The dress was made of cotton and printed with a floral design. It had two broad shoulder straps, was gathered at the waist, and fell to mid-calf. Sonja tried it on and her small, muscular body slipped easily into the scented fabric. She looked at herself again in the mirror and wiped the brown clove dust off her face with a towel. The dress was a size too big, but standing in front of the mirror, Sonja felt good in it.

'At the railway café she saw Harry engaged in deep conversation with another, considerably older, man with a large moustache and heavy black bristles. She knew him from the past. She became nervous and decided to leave, but just as she went to depart, Harry spied her and jumped up from his table with a large grin.

' "Hello," he said, then faltered, because he still did not know her name. His eyes fell but he quickly recovered, saying, "Harry Lewis. I am so glad you came." His grin returned.

' "Hello," she said. "My name is Sonja Cosini."

'The man with black pig bristles stared at Sonja's breasts and his nostrils twitched. He looked worried. Then he made excuses that he must leave, saying in a somewhat forced manner that he would meet Harry tomorrow at the post office, placing particular emphasis on the final two words. After he had left, both Sonja and Harry relaxed.

' "Business associate," said Harry, just in case she should think he may have been a friend.

' "Sewing machines?" asked Sonja.

' "No," laughed Harry, lighting two cigarettes in his mouth and passing one to her. "Well, yes," he added. For the first time she noticed that he had no thumb on his right hand. Then he said, "Not exactly sewing machines." And again he grinned. "Actually, I am trying to give them up. Trieste seems as good a place to do it as anywhere."

' "Sewing machines?"

'Harry laughed. "Yeah. Them too."

'For a while neither spoke. Then Sonja went to say something just as Harry began to speak. Both stopped, then nervously laughed.

' "I am not Italian," Sonja said.

' "Nor am I." Harry drew in smoke.

' "That much was obvious," said Sonja and she smiled again, nervously, affectionately. "Almost as obvious as your new job."

'Harry pulled the cigarette out of his mouth, his smile gone, and looked at her intently. "Is it that obvious?"

' "My father worked as a smuggler between Austria and Yugoslavia before the war. So I know. But it's a lot more dangerous now. Now they shoot to kill."

'Harry said nothing.

' "What are you taking over?" she pressed him.

'Harry looked furtively around, then leaned forward and whispered in her ear.

'Sonja burst out laughing. "Sewing machines!"

'Harry looked somewhat aggrieved. "Nobody but nobody has got sewing machines in Yugoslavia. They're worth a fortune. Drago – that man who was here before – he has the contacts in the Party." He raised a finger and waggled it at her. "We sell only to the top – generals, high-ranking Party officials – and they pay in American dollars." He put the cigarette back in his mouth and leaned back. "It's very safe."

'Sonja looked at him and just shook her head, and wished she didn't feel the desire for him that she did.'

Maria Magadalena Svevo stopped for a moment. Couta Ho raised an objection. 'The problem with these stories is that they presume there are one or two moments in your life that define what you are for the rest of it. Life's not like that.'

Maria took the cigar out of her mouth, smacked the grey salmon flesh of her tongue around her lips to moisten them, and said, 'What if it were?'

'It's not. My life doesn't feel that way anyhow. It feels just the opposite – rushed. Always having to decide this or that. Countless decisions.'

Maria watched the languid rise of the smoke from her near-dead cigar toward the ceiling. 'What if it is? As I get older and older I think perhaps there is a great truth in such stories. I used to be quite confused about such things. Now I think that maybe the confusion is what we use to not hear the silence. To not see the emptiness.' Maria Magadalena Svevo paused, but Couta Ho said nothing. Maria Magadalena Svevo decided to tell another story.

'I knew a young girl once and she fell in love with a young man, a nice young man, from her village. She must have been ... well, at least eighteen. And she fell pregnant. And the young man, because he was a good man, said he would do the right thing, as they say, and marry her. And she refused him. They sat together in her bedroom for two days, crying. She said she would not marry him because of the baby, because the baby was the wrong reason to get married. And because he was a good man he countered that he loved her and that he believed in the idea of their marriage. They could not agree on what was to be done, and because they did love one another with all their hearts they ended up crying at their own tragedy. They cried so much that their tears stained the bedspread upon which they sat. Her family listened to the couple crying and wondered what would happen. When they finally came out of the bedroom it was for her to announce that they would not be getting married and that she was going on a short holiday to the nearest town. At the town she had an abortion – by what means I don't know, because this was a very long time ago, when such things were done in secret. On her return journey home her cart ran off the road into a tree and she was killed. After her death there was a funeral, and a respectful time after the funeral they cleaned out her room in preparation for a boarder. There was not much there, because they were a poor family. The tear-stained bedspread they took off the bed and washed, but the tear stain would not wash out. Try as they might they could not wash the tear stain away. They bleached the bedspread several times, and in the first few years following her death washed it frequently, but none of it made the slightest difference. The tear stain remained. I suppose it troubled them in the end, this bedspread, for they gave it to the young man who had been her lover.'

'And then what happened?' asked Couta Ho. 'To the young man, I mean?'

'Oh. Nothing. Nothing at all really. He married, many years later. Not a happy marriage, nor an unhappy one. His wife bore him four daughters. And when the eldest turned nineteen he gave her the bedspread and told her this story.'

'And then?'

'Then nothing.' Maria pulled a cigar out of the double-headed eagle box and tapped the double-headed eagle on one of its two beaks with the cigar end.

'*Es ist passiert*,' she said ruefully. Her head was bowed, and just for a moment, though only for a moment, Couta Ho thought the craggy old voice quavered. 'It just happened like that, that's what the old Austrians used say. *Es ist passiert*.' She stopped again, as if her thoughts were interrupting her speech. Then, as abruptly as she had halted, she recommenced talking. 'Now the daughter sleeps under that bedspread every night, and as she falls asleep she looks at that stain and wonders about the strangeness of life and what she would be, if anything, if her father's lover had not made that fateful decision.'

Maria looked at her cigar for some time, as if minutely examining it for flaws. Then she lighted it, inhaled and, holding her breath, spoke in a husky voice. 'Would you like to see it?' she asked Couta Ho. She swallowed spittle. Then exhaled a dragon breath of smoke.

The smoke fills my vision. When it finally clears I see the punters gathered round the fire site and Rickie the doctor making a few desultory efforts to get the fire going. It is a dismal affair, for after so much rain even the wood under the fly is wet. The fire in consequence spits and hisses and steams and smokes as a thin slink of flame slides in and out of the wet sticks, as if searching for one that will burn. It is breakfast. The morning comes slowly, the light weak and oppressive, the black clouds, though no longer emptying torrential rain, still there, making the bluey-black sky look as though an ink bottle has fallen upon it.

The Cockroach looks at the menu, a typed sheet in a clear plastic envelope, to see what they are meant to be eating on day five. The Cockroach doesn't bother with the fire, but instead cranks up two petrol stoves and puts a billy of water on each; one for coffee, one for porridge. As the stoves busily rumble with the rapid pulsation of the petrol vaporising I can see Aljaz walking down out of the rainforest and onto the riverbank. I watch him stretch and yawn; his body, dry and warm from a night's rest in his sleeping bag, now at odds with the cold and damp.

He checks the stick he put in the bank as a water gauge the evening before. The river's edge ebbs and rises in minuscule waves and he spends some time watching, making sure that his reading is correct. The river is up perhaps ten centimetres on its level of the previous evening. Compared to the five metres it rose over the previous day, it is a marginal increase. Aljaz goes and fetches the Cockroach. They both go back down to the river and look at the gauge. They wonder whether they should try and go through the gorge or stay put. They look at the clouds and try and guess what the weather will do. If they stay put for a second day they will fall further behind schedule. The lost time is not impossible to make up by any means, but it will be hard to rendezvous with the seaplane at the pickup point on the Gordon River. But if the river continues to rise then the gorge will become far too dangerous and they must simply wait, no matter how frustrating it is for the punters, who are already thoroughly sick of seeing their precious vacation days drift away with the rushing flood waters.

'Should we wait one more day?' asks the Cockroach. Aljaz looks around, surprised that the Cockroach shares his thoughts. The Cockroach laughs his easygoing laugh, his buck teeth protruding. 'Ah, well. The gods will punish us if we don't wait long enough,' he says. It is a joke and his buck teeth protrude again. The Cockroach notices something. He leans down, squints, and then points at the gauge stick. The river has started to drop, albeit slightly. And at the very moment of the Cockroach's discovery, a single shaft of light cuts through the gloom and illuminates the two river guides as if it were a spotlight. They look up toward the heavens and see that the clouds have parted and some blue sky has appeared. Their decision seems to have been made for them by an ethereal force. 'Into the gorge on a falling river,' laughs the Cockroach. The two river guides turn and start heading back up into their rainforest camp. 'The angels have ordered us,' says the Cockroach.

When they get back they find that the porridge has burnt. Derek the accountant apologises. 'I stirred her twice,' he says by way of inadequate explanation, 'but I wanted to pack up my sleeping bag.' The Cockroach rolls his eyes, tells Derek he's a moron, and says that he'll make the coffee. He makes it extra strong and black, and the grounds fill Aljaz's mouth. As he sips from his chipped green enamel mug, Aljaz squats on the ground. His guts rumble as the thick black coffee mixes with the fears in the pit of his stomach. His bowels feel unusually heavy. The punters gather round the two river guides like animals around a corpse. They sense that a decision has been made, but no one asks. They murmur in low tones to each other about their digestion or their night's sleep and the little tricks they have deployed to make sure they rest better.

'I roll up my clothes and put them in my sleeping bag cover and make a pillow of them,' says Sheena.

'I dig a little hole for my hip,' says Rickie.

'I sleep in my wet socks and they dry in my sleeping bag from my body heat,' says Derek.

'I light up me farts and that keeps me warm of a night,' says Otis. The others look around at the big boy-man. Watch his face slowly turn up into a smile. 'Itsa a joke.' Aljaz smiles. The Cockroach laughs. The others follow.

Aljaz stands up and stretches, rubs his hands over his stubbly cheeks, pulls his Fitzroy beanie off and runs a hand through his thin greasy hair, then pulls the beanie back on. When the laughter dies down, he speaks. 'If I could just have everyone's attention for a minute.' The low murmuring dies away. 'Normally we don't set off into the gorge at this sort of level. But as you can feel, the air is warmer than it was yesterday and the rain has stopped. That warm air means the weather has changed round to northerly. That means it should be clear skies for at least the next few days. The river has started to fall and I think with this sort of good weather it will fall real quick through the day.'

Aljaz looks around at the punters, takes one last swig from his enamel mug, then throws the remnant coffee grounds on the fire. 'The Cockroach and I feel that we would be safe going through the gorge and that maybe we ought give it a crack today. If we do decide to go, we'll only be going as far as the Coruscades today, where we camp at the top of the second major portage. Tomorrow we would go through the rest of the gorge.' Aljaz's statement is greeted with a general murmur of approval. The punters are as sick of waiting around in their tents as Aljaz and the Cockroach.

'So we're going or what?' asks Marco.

'We're going,' says the Cockroach. 'Into Deception.'

— Harry —

I watch Aljaz go to say something but I can't hear what it is. I see Sheena shake her head. I see Rickie begin to move off toward the thunderbox but then he too is lost to my sight as the whole scene fades away. My mind is in any case already elsewhere. I am wondering not about what will happen to them on the river, for I know all too well what fate awaits them. But it's what I don't know that I wish to see. And I want to know how the hell Harry came to be in Trieste in 1954. I mean, it was so out of character for him. After returning to Tasmania with Sonja and me all those years ago he never left the island again, as though Tasmania were a world total and full in itself. Which for him it possibly was. And he never ceased to find wonders within it, new and marvellous for both him and everyone he shared them with. Even as his drink-ing slowly dulled his mind and dimmed his spirit, as though his body were a lamp and his soul the diminishing fuel, even as his heart guttered in the torrent of drink daily falling upon it, he still found time to express wonder, be it at his bizarre barbeques, or be it in his occasional forays into the bush, fishing and hunting.

I remember the way he used smile. How he would bow his head slightly, as if a little embarrassed. How the corners of his mouth would curl slightly upwards. I remember these things now in the hope of exercising some control over this capricious river of visions, in the hope that it might show me why my father ended up in Trieste. The river, as ever, does not explain. But it does show me some things I never knew.

A vision at first most mysterious comes to me.

The crossroads. Night-time. Sky black. A man in rain-darkened trousers and an ancient black bluey coat. Once his father's bluey coat. Now worn and old. And, in the incessant rain, wet and cold. It wasn't meant to turn out like this, I can see him thinking as he pulls the steaming damp collar of the bluey up around his face. It shouldn't have ended like this. Black lapels pulled hard against wet cheeks, ruddy with chill through the small white clouds of his breath that envelop his face.

Whose cheeks? I look harder, closer into the river, scan its fleeing waters intently. And finally I recognise them.

Harry's cheeks. Harry's face, empty of anything save his ongoing belief in fate determining everything and him having no control. Too many deaths and none expected. Him meant for the mincer and surviving and Old Bo not. Auntie Ellie not. Daisy not. Boy not. Rose not. Him meant for the mincer and surviving. But a thumbless man is a man unable to chop and saw and he has to leave his beloved rivers and head wherever work might be had. He travels up to Queenstown from Strahan that morning on the ore train's return run, hoping to pull some work suitable for a one-thumbed man in a pub or bank or store well before evening. But all the employers either publicly said they were right for men, or, thought Harry, were wrong in their private suspicions that a lone-thumbed man was not to be trusted.

Wind blowing hard, howling in the lonesome telegraph wires wet with rain and humming with the desire of people to somehow touch one another, no matter how far away. No matter, thinks Harry. He trudges out of town to the gravel crossroads, hopeful of thumbing a lift with his left hand to the next mining town up the coast, Rosebery, where a cousin tends bar in the bottom pub and might be prevailed upon for an evening's accommodation on his floor and some introductions to places of work in the morning.

He watches the few cars all chug past him without stopping. He had hoped to be in Rosebery in time for tea. And now it is late and he is wet and cold and hungry. In the end a truck heading in the opposite direction stops, an ancient old Dodge driven by a fisherman, name of Reggie Ho, whose boat is stuck in at Strahan because of a big blow-up in the Indian Ocean. Reggie Ho has been drinking and tonight he is going all the way through to Hobart, though not to see his family, who lives there, but to see a girlfriend. Hobart. Eight long hours heading east over the wild unsealed road that snakes its way around mountain passes and along the top of ravines to the other side of the island. Hobart. The big smoke. The opposite direction to where Harry wishes to travel. It's not where

Harry is going or has ever thought of going. No matter. Even though until that moment he has never thought of going anywhere near the city, Harry accepts the lift because that is his fate, that's how the dice have fallen. Reggie Ho drives the truck hard down that treacherous lonely windy gravelly track and Harry sits and slides in the cold wet seat, shielding himself from the rain that drips into the cabin as best he can.

They arrive in Hobart clammy-cold well past midnight and Reggie Ho takes Harry to Ma Dwyer's Blue House for a warming drink. There, amidst the steaming wharfies and smoking fishermen and smouldering cops and fuming politicians and numerous bored women who work there, he sights a familiar figure playing the Wertheimer piano. Half drunk or entirely drunk, it's hard to tell, but he's still dapper in his Bidencopes finest, still the elegant professional continuing to play throughout a spirited alter-cation between a very drunk Scot sailor and a very aggres-sive local wharfie, that ends up with the wharfie flying into the piano and sending sheet music everywhere. Blood spurts, drinks fall, glass smashes, cries and screams abound. And Ruth just puts his English tailor-made cig-arette, flash filter and all, into the ash tray, admittedly with a shaky hand, pushes his red silk cravat back into its proper position beneath his Harris tweed jacket, and gives a crooked smile of thanks to one of the ladies who picks up the sheets of music from the floor and hastily rear-ranges them on the piano. Ruth dreamingly keeps right on playing, too far gone to recognise that he is now doing two songs simultaneously, playing the bottom half of 'I'm Gonna Sit Right Down And Write Myself A Letter' and the top half of 'Drinking Rum And Coca Cola'. Too snakes-hissed to notice the difference, or perhaps wrongly attributing it to what he regards as the corrupting and decadent influence of the new musical fashions, but not so far gone that he is unable to recognise his nephew. Ruth's jowly old face sparks with recognition. 'Hi-ho, Harry,' he says, his slurred voice somehow managing to syncopate with the unique melody emerging from the chest of the Wertheimer upright. 'Well, hi-ho. Long time no see.' Harry starts to tell Ruth his story, but their conversation is cut short by Ma, who storms up to the piano cranky as a cut snake and says, 'Jeezuz, Ruth! There won't be a single bloke left if you play any more of that Yankee bebop shit.' Ma starts humming 'The Kellys, Jo Byrne And Dan Hart'. Ruth looks back down at the sheet music and manages to focus long enough to recognise his grievous error. Without saying anything, he bursts into an Al Bowlly song. Ma smiles. 'You not too far gone not to remember a few of the good old tunes, eh Ruth? You remember, don't ya Ruth?' Ruth winks his assent to Ma, who for a moment looks forlornly into the distance, but only a moment, for she spots Harry and Reggie Ho.

'Who the hell are youse?' she asks.

Ruth introduces Harry to Ma and tells Ma of Harry's plight. Ma wanders off, then returns with a Dutchman who skippers a tramp steamer that carts apples to Europe. The skipper takes Harry into Ma's smoko room out the back of the pub and looks suspiciously at his right hand with its flap for a thumb. He says nothing. He turns his back, goes to the cupboard, opens it, searches around, then turns and without warning throws an egg at Harry. Harry catches it in the cup of the four fingers of his right hand.

'Okay,' says the Dutch skipper, whose name is Gerry and whose speech is idiosyncratic Euro-Hollywood.

'Okay. I owe a few of the greenbacks to the Ma for eating candy in the candy store, so okay. Hell, why nit, eh? Here to Naples. That's the racket. You cook and wash. Ja? Hell, let's do it, buddy. Okay? Why nit? Ain't this life one hell of a big crapshoot?'

Ain't it just, thinks Harry, ain't it just, whatever the bugger a crapshoot might be. No matter. Harry believes in fate, in somebody having his number up there and there not being a dam thing he can do about it. So even though he has never harboured any desire to travel, a job's a job, and he accepts with equanimity the prospect of steaming out of Hobart the following morning to a place that may as well be the moon for all it means to him.

Harry looks at the Dutchman dressed in his best suit of white cotton. A dapper man. A travelled man. Harry thought of travelling as something you did with the army if you were unlucky enough to be caught up in a war. But he had been without a job too long and any job was better than being on the dole. Now he was a little drunk and he wanted to wake up tomorrow and know that he was going somewhere, rather than drifting. Harry proffered his thumbless hand to shake his acceptance.

'What part of England is Naples in?' Harry asked as they shook hands.

A gambler is almost always a fatalist, because they accept both the good and bad throw of the dice as equally inevitable, and believe there is nothing they could have done to avoid that fall of the dice. If Auntie Ellie hadn't been such a powerful anti-gambler Harry could have ended up with a terrible problem with the dogs and the nags, because he would have lost and lost and simply thought that it was fate and that there wasn't a dam thing he could do about it. But Auntie Ellie had indoctrinated such a fear of gambling in his heart, he found even buying a lottery ticket mildly sinful. Harry, however, was a gambler with life. Which is, I suppose, why he ended up in Trieste.

Upon arriving at Naples some months later, after a hellish and gruelling trip, he is there abandoned by Gerry, who takes on a load of illegal refugees whom he can pay even less to crew the boat. Harry accepts the offer of an ex-GI called Hank. Hank looks like an emaciated Clark Gable and talks like Mickey Rooney. He has a burnt-out *pension* full of Japanese sewing machines he has got through a deal with a buddy, who is part of the occupation forces in Japan. Harry knows nothing about sewing machines, nor about Italy, nor can he speak Italian, but he does, according to Hank, have a winning smile. And winning, says Hank, is everything. 'I don't like losers,' says Hank. 'Are you a loser, Harry?' The expression 'loser' is as new to Harry as the concept. He pauses, a little unsure as to what to say. His entire world had shaped itself around the song of loss.

'I am not sure I've got anything left to lose,' he says after a time. Hank smiles and slaps him on the back.

Harry had never thought of being a salesman. He had seen the travellers who stayed overnight at Hamers with their cheap suits and soft hands. He had no desire of ever joining their ranks but he had no work, and this, after a fashion, was an offer of work. And whether it be good or bad, Harry believes that this is the job intended for him, and in the end there is for Harry no decison to make. The deal is simple. With his payout from the boat, Harry buys twenty sewing machines and secures an option on twenty more. 'Where do I start?' asks Harry.

'South of the city,' says Hank, eager to rid central Naples of any potential rival, even one as self-evidently witless as Harry.

I can't bear to watch this any more. If it were a movie on TV I'd hide behind the couch or go and make a coffee, because this fatalism is just so bloody irritating. Maybe because it reminds me so much of myself. I dunno. But how can someone be so resigned to whatever happens? This is my father I'm seeing, for crying out loud, not a frigging jellyfish. I should be able to do something, get him that job at the Empire Hotel, help him in some way. It just seems too unfair to watch people's lives like this and not be able to do anything. I try and summon another vision, but as I try and obliterate this helpless Harry from view I hear him say something entirely unexpected. He says one word. He says, 'Trieste.'

'Trieste?' says Hank, shocked. 'What the hell ya mean, Trieste?'

In the kitchen of the tramp steamer there had been a wall of postcards from around the world. One in particular had taken Harry's fancy. It looked somehow familiar. With its houses clustering on hills, and its harbour, it looked a bit like Hobart. 'What is this?' he asked Gerry one day. 'Trieste,' said Gerry. 'Full of weird guys and weirder dames. Slovenes and Croats and Krauts and wops. Nit a nice place. One hell of a jive-jointing dump for a continent but what the hell, eh?'

What the hell. Something was born in the mind of Harry Lewis as he looked at that curling postcard, something that went beyond his normal acquiescence to the river of events and was to lead him to my mother and to the matter – the no small matter, as far as I am concerned – of my conception.

'Trieste,' repeats Harry. 'That's where I'm going with my sewing machines.'

Hank pauses, then shrugs his shoulders. 'Have it your way, buddy,' he says. 'That's the wonderful freedom of capitalism.'

Harry smiles at Hank.

I remember the way he used smile. But this smile was somehow different, as though for once he had actually done something he wanted to do.

— Couta Ho, 1993 —

I am ready to absorb the details of Harry's trip north, to watch his adventures and seek to understand his responses – sometimes stunned, sometimes bemused, often delighted – to the strange land he found himself in. I want to observe how others saw this curious one-thumbed stranger. But I am not going with Harry. As much as I want to, try as I might, I am not going with him. I am already far, far away from Italy in that faraway time, dropping down into a city, into a street, over a laundromat, across the road and into an overgrown garden, the shapes of which are beginning to be lost in the dimming light of late afternoon. Facing the garden a sitting-room window illuminated by an unshaded electric light. Within the sitting-room, beneath the electric light, sit Couta Ho and Maria Magdalena Svevo.

I can see them, but they can't see me. Maybe that is why I suddenly flail my fists out at them both, like I sometimes used to throw a few punches out late at night in pubs here and there. Years ago now, let it be added. So that someone would notice me and say, Brother, you are part of this world and we do care about you and what you think and feel, and your thoughts and emotions do matter; you are not nothing. But of course no one ever said such things. They either snotted me or I snotted them, or more often than not we both succeeded only in snotting each other with no clear winner or loser. Whatever, the result was always the same. People laughed and jeered and drank on regardless. Because the people I was hitting were as invisible as me. Because we were all phantoms who had lost something central and we roamed the earth like haunted spirits trying to find that something, and we all ended up lying on the pavement outside, trying to staunch the blood running out of our mouths and eyes with our ragged sleeves. I brawled more when I was younger, when I thought it would somehow render me solid and whole. But I think it would be a good five years since I last blued, because I've lost even the hopeless ambition of forming a tunnel to the real world with my rolling fists. But at this moment something within me snaps, and I cannot help but throw a few blows at Maria Magdalena Svevo and Couta Ho. Of course nothing happens. Thankfully, nothing happens. My blows simply pass through their heads, my fists and arms only a violent intention without substance.

'I better be getting on,' I hear Maria Magdalena Svevo say as my body shrieks in agony from the sudden wild movement of my arms. Maria Magdalena Svevo stands up and walks over to a framed photo that hangs from the wall. It shows a small baby girl. 'She was a lovely little baby,' she says.

'Jemma was beautiful,' replies Couta Ho, 'but you know the funny thing is . . .' Couta Ho's voice begins to quaver. She goes to halt it, to stop it, to push it all back down, but then she stops, lowers her heads, pulls out a handkerchief, and when she looks back her eyes are streaming with tears and she just keeps on going as if they are normal, without embarrassment. I can see that Maria Magdalena Svevo thinks there is something beautiful about this, but she cannot name what it is. Perhaps she feels that it is a moment of honesty and trust and that perhaps there are not very many moments such as this in a person's life. She continues to stand.

Couta Ho keeps on talking.

'After a while after Jemma died, Aljaz came to think that I was too obsessed about it all. He said I needed to get my mind back on other things and stop being morbid. He meant well. I suppose that was how he coped with things. He trained harder, ran for miles and miles every night. He didn't think it did to dwell upon such things. "Why can't you be normal?" he'd ask. "Why can't you just be normal like everybody else?" "Because we're not normal," I'd say. "Because this thing has changed us and nothing is normal any more." "The baby's dead," he'd shout. "Dead, don't you understand." And I'd scream and cry and say, "Maybe Jemma is dead, but she's not gone, she'll never go, whether you want her to or not. She's part of us, whether you want her here or not." Silly things like that, I'd say. Silly things. But that's what I thought. It was then that Ali suggested I should take some classes of an evening to give me something other than the baby to think about. Ali always liked activity. "An active body is a healthy mind," he'd say. Jesus, can you believe it? He got into triathalons as well as his football, and he was always trying to do as many things as possible. Like his baby has just died, but it's as if – if he can just wear out enough Reebok rubber, if he can just make his knees hurt more than what he hurts inside, then it'll be okay. "There's just not enough hours in the day," he'd always say. But for me there were too many, hours that just had to be endured.'

Couta Ho looks up and realises that Maria Magdalena Svevo is still standing up. 'I'm sorry, Maria,' she says.

'Don't be sorry,' says Maria Magdalena Svevo. 'Nothing to be sorry about.'

Couta Ho apologises, says she will stop talking, and asks Maria Magdalena Svevo to sit down while she gathers herself.

'Don't stop talking,' says Maria Magdalena Svevo. 'Unless you want to.' So Couta Ho continues.

'Everyday I'd go to the cemetery to see Jemma's grave. She's buried down Kingston, in that modern cemetery down there where they don't have headstones, only plaques that sit in the lawn in neat rows, and everyone has to have the same size plaque. They bury all the babies together, in the same row. I don't know why, they just do. Some people try to make their plaque look a bit different from the others in the row by leaving some of their baby's favourite toys. It breaks you up to see that, you know, just these rows of babies' plaques, every second or third one with a little plastic doll or toy, just simple things like that, a Big Bird toy or a toy car or a teddy bear or that sort of thing, out there in the rain and cold and no one to pick them up and play with them and hold them . . .'

Couta Ho's voice trails off and she looks away, out of the window of her home, past her front garden to the laundromat across the road, the lights of which have just come on. She realises that it is almost entirely dark in the room and gets up and draws the curtains and switches on the light. As Couta Ho moves around her, Maria Magdalena Svevo speaks because she feels she ought, not because she wishes to.

'It must have been very hard,' she says, and immediately it is obvious that she hates herself for trying to put any gloss on what this woman feels.

'Hard?' asks Couta, sitting back down, feeling this small word in her throat. 'Yes,' she says, considering it, lending some dignity to Maria Magdalena Svevo's comment, as if one inadequate word is about as good as any other inadequate word. 'Yes, it was hard.' But the idea of hard is too small, the word 'hard' too insignificant to begin to approach what Couta carries within her. The closest approximation she can give to what she feels is her story, and Maria Magdalena Svevo realises she has interrupted that story and that she was wrong to do so. 'Hard,' says Couta, 'you could say that.' And then her gaze returns to the green laminex table top and she sees that their mugs are empty. 'Another cuppa?' asks Couta.

In the kitchen Maria Magdalena Svevo hears the tap running, hears the old chipped blue porcelain jug filling, the jug being plugged in, the snap of the power point being switched on. The electricity zaps and sparks in the loose fitting in the old jug, and then the fizzing gives way as the element begins to rumble deep down. And Couta resumes her story, her voice now tired and distant.

'Aljaz said I was to stop going to the cemetery except on the anniversary of her death. I thought, Maybe Ali is right. Maybe I do think about Jemma too much. Maybe I was sick. I didn't know. I didn't care. It didn't really matter to me what I did. If it made Ali feel better about things then I was happy enough to do it. I enrolled in a wool-spinning class. But the first night when I got in the car I just drove straight through the city and there I was, back at the cemetery. That's how it started. Each Tuesday night. Out I'd go and I would feel sort of happy, and Ali was happy that I was happy. And I was happy because I was going to see Jemma and Ali was smiling.'

'So you never went to any of the wool-spinning classes?' Maria Magdalena Svevo asks.

'No,' replies Couta over the sound of water being poured into mugs. 'It just gave me time to go down to the cemetery to see Jemma.'

And Couta Ho laughs at her small deception. She stands at the table holding a mug of instant coffee out to Maria Magdalena Svevo with her left hand, while she cradles her own close to her chest. She raises the mug to her lips – those small, soft undecorated lips – has a sip and continues a little smile at the memory of it all.

'Didn't you worry that Aljaz might twig to what was going on?' asks Maria Magdalena Svevo.

Couta places her coffee on the table, sits down, and entwines her hands in the mug's handle. They face one another across the table, but neither looks at the other, just at the table's surface, at the swirls in the coffee, at the stains and crumbs on the table.

'Well, I did,' says Couta after a time. 'Yes, I did.' She takes a sip of her coffee but as she does so she keeps her hands tightly clasped around the mug, as if she is in the midst of a blizzard and the hot mug is her only source of warmth. She puts the cup down but her hands stay tightly wrapped around it. 'I worried that if he found out he would be furious. The wool-spinning course went for twelve weeks and by the end of it I was getting worried that Ali would work out what was going on. So I went to a shop and brought two lovely hand-knitted jumpers made out of home-spun wool, one for Ali and one for Jemma. They cost a small fortune, but money hasn't really meant a lot since — since back *then*. Anyway, I got the right size for Jemma, because she would be two come the next month, and the lady in the shop said a two-year-old would get a good twelve months' wear out of it before it became too small. I got home that Tuesday night and gave Ali his jumper. He was thrilled. "I told you," he said. "See how it has helped to get things back in perspective?" '

Maria Magdalena Svevo laughs. 'He never realised?'

Couta begins to laugh too at the absurdity of it. 'I know,' she says. She laughs some more. 'It is funny. Now. Looking back on it, it is funny.' Couta seems mildly shocked at the thought of any humour coming out of that time, and the idea of any of it being funny amuses her as much as the joke itself. 'It is funny, isn't it? I mean, I'd forgotten — this is true, I swear it, you won't believe this — I'd forgotten to cut the tag off the inside of the neck. So there he is, pulling it on, and I saw it and I thought, Oh my god, what is going to happen now? But he never noticed a thing. I cut it out the next day, before he got home from work. He seemed so happy with his jumper and he told me about his plans for us to go on a holiday to Queensland the next summer. I said it all sounded wonderful and we sat up in bed for ages talking about what we would do on holiday. Then he started to kiss me on the back and wanted to make love. I didn't care because I couldn't feel anything, anything good or bad. I just lay there, still, and thought of the moon. That's how I felt, big and empty like the moon, like nothing could hurt me any more.' Couta looked up at Maria

Magdalena Svevo. 'Funny that I am telling you such private things. Because before, I would never have dreamt of talking to other people about such things. You remember what I was like. But now, what does it matter? If people know nothing or if they know everything, what does it matter? All I know is that Jemma was here and now she isn't.' Couta rested her cheek on one hand, looked down at her mug and swilled the remaining coffee around with her other hand. 'Anyway, I think Ali was a bit disappointed. He didn't say anything, but, well, you know how those things are.

'The next morning after he had gone to work, I drove down to the cemetery and put Jemma's jumper on her grave so that she would have it. I folded it neatly, the way it was in the shop when I bought it. I remember where I left it. It was on the top left-hand corner of the plaque. Funny, the things you remember. I remember the jumper, where I put it, how I folded it, but I don't remember Jemma. I mean, I do remember her, but not how she looked, how she moved, how she cried and smiled, how her hands moved, those sorts of little things. That was all gone. I'd look at our photos, but when I closed my eyes all I could see was the photos, not Jemma, not outside the photos. I'd try and try but it was like it was all gone. Except once. The night after I took the jumper to her grave.

'That night I slept real well, the first time I had slept properly since Jemma died, and I dreamt Jemma had grown into a little girl and she was this beautiful two-year-old running around the park in that jumper – and it did fit beautifully, like I knew it would. She ran into my arms and I could hear her laugh and I could feel her little body hot from running, and she said to me, 'I love you,

Mummy.' And I said, 'Now, make sure you don't get your new jumper dirty.' Couta laughs again and then her mouth draws up and her cheeks draw in and her mouth goes to open but no words come out; nothing comes out except some choked sobs.

Maria Magdalena Svevo takes Couta's hand. 'That's a good dream,' she says.

'Is it?' asks Couta and she withdraws her hand slowly. 'I don't know. I read this book once and in it − I've always remembered this, I don't know why − one character says how it's the dead people who won't let you go. That's true, isn't it? I've always remembered that. It's the dead who won't let you go. Anyway. I . . . I never went back after that.

'It was not long after that we broke up. There was no real reason, but it was like the thing that had held us together had snapped. Do you know what I mean? It was like it was broken and nothing could fix it.'

Couta looks Maria Magdalena Svevo in the eyes for the first time that day. Couta's face is confused. She is obviously at a loss to explain the final part of her story.

'But the funny thing was, he never knew it was broken until I told him. That *is* a funny thing.'

And she looks back down into her coffee cup, at the way the electric light above is reflected in its small blackness. 'Isn't it?'

Maria Magdalena Svevo looks on and says nothing. Then she reaches down into a plastic shopping bag she has brought with her. The plastic scriffles as she delves within to finally pull out a parcel wrapped in brown paper and baling twine. Maria Magdalena Svevo places the parcel upon the table.

Maria Magdalena Svevo unties the twine and spreads

out the brown paper. There, neatly folded and covered in a scattering of clove dust, is the tear-stained bedspread. Maria Magdalena Svevo puts her hands beneath the bedspread, lifts it up, and proffers it to Couta Ho.

Saying: 'If two lie together, then they have heat, but how can one be warm alone?'

— Seven —

Suddenly my eyes snap open and all sight of the ancient bedspread is immediately lost in the rushing river water. And returning with the water are the sensations of my agonised body, but I shall not dwell upon them. *I shall not.* To cut out the groping pain I concentrate on my outstretched arm. I can feel that whereas my arm was formerly covered in water to a point a little beyond my elbow, now only my hand and wrist seem to feel the chill of the air. Which means the river has risen a good twenty centimetres or so. Which means what little hope of rescue has further receded as the river grows more wild, the waterfall more ferocious.

Somewhere beyond the bubbling blackness a building begins to take shape: a house. More precisely, a home. A sky-blue shack made of tin. And now I see where that home sits: in the crabbed and cracked port town of Strahan, which in turn sits like a crusty skin cancer on the flesh of south-west Tasmanian wilderness. Nearby to the sky-blue shack, the railway station. I seem to have little immediate place in the happenings that boil up in front of this vision, but then it is perhaps those things most distant from our conscious mind that are most central to what we are. Least that's how some might put it. Harry would have said that if you want to follow a footy game, never watch the pack but the loose players at the edges.

— Auntie Ellie, 1940 —

The town had seen the smoke of the small mountain loco-motive, specially imported from Switzerland, for only forty years or so when, on an unusual day (unusual because the sun was shining) after a slow and long trip through the rainforest over mountain ranges and down the remote, wild King River Gorge, a scrawny dark child with a big nose got off at that railway station at the end of the line. He was greeted by a small, heavily powdered woman with a hairy chin and a somewhat old-fashioned dress, who bore a pram in front of her. In her mouth was a smoking clay pipe. Though the sun was shining, there was inevitably, this being the west coast of Tas-mania, this being the first piece of land that the roaring forties smash up against after thousands of miles of empty ocean, there was, inevitably, a sky of black clouds. But beneath the clouds a low winter sun shone from the west, and it lit the dark child and the powdered woman puffing her clay pipe, and the pram, as if they were a tableaux made by the elements purely for their own pleasure. Though the boy had only ever heard of her, this small, oddly attired woman seemed immediately familiar to him as he embraced her and then kissed the baby in the pram. She picked up the cardboard box bound with string which the boy carried, put it in one end of the pram, and, hand in hand, she pushing the pram with her free hand, they walked off toward the town's centre.

The town looked battered and tired, like a once corpulent man dying of cancer caused by good living; the skin, once taut with fat, now hanging limp in sad, loose folds. Large, formerly elegant houses where once a family with pretensions to a rising status had lived, were now decrepit and rundown, occupied by several struggling, spatting families.

I watch the recent past of this place like some crazy speeded-up film; watch how European progress arrives with the mineral boom of the 1880s and 1890s like a vast wave washing over the wilderness, transforming the west coast and leaving funny little towns like Strahan, the strange flotsam of deflated dreams and broken hopes. I watch the vast wild land of the west of Tasmania suddenly fill with people. Throughout its vast rainforests I watch them: prospecting, logging, laying waste to huge tracts of forests with massive fires. At the height of the great boom, in the year of federation, 1901, the mineral wealth of the west flows out through its ports, and flowing in like a king tide are the supplies and equipment and pimps and whores and speculators and sly-grog merchants and those desperate for anything, but chiefly a job, or failing that a dream, all bound for the land they briefly call Australia's El Dorado. In that year of self-congratulatory speech making, the town of Strahan boasted a population of two thousand. The film begins to slow further and further until it almost stops in the year 1940, when the town of Strahan has perhaps a quarter of its former population and is showing no sign of growing and every sign of shrinking further, perhaps ending up like so many other short-lived mining towns on the west coast, whose proud brass bands, Oddfellows Halls, Mechanics Institutes and footy teams had all proved as transitory as a westerly scud, whose grandiose hotels and smelting plants had disappeared into the peat of the rainforest that had already reclaimed the towns of Pillinger and Crotty and Lynchford and Teepookana.

Not that the myrtles and manferns were yet sprouting in the main street of Strahan. Not that a railway carriage yet stood suspended mid-air in the middle of the rainforest, as it did where once had been the town of Kelly Basin, in the heart of what once had been a busy railway yard. There a blackwood tree had grown up through the middle of an abandoned railway carriage, its broadening, rising trunk over the decades elevating the carriage a yard into the air, carrying the carriage with it in its exuberant journey toward the light above the forest canopy, so that the carriage now appeared to be flying in the midst of a steaming dank green profusion of tea-trees and vines and myrtles and celery top pines. No railway irons, no buildings, no material relics of the once muscular railway yard and the once bustling town remained. Nothing.

Save for a carriage that flew in the rainforest.

As yet, I can see only a few of the Strahan shops boarded up, and the boards are only a little green-slimed and rotted. The remaining shops boast window displays, however humble: half a dozen tins of IXL jam, stacked in a pyramid for so long that the labels have faded and started to peel; a few blowflies lying long dead at the base of a cardboard poster advertising 'Monkey Soap – It Won't Wash Clothes!' Those that remain have decided to wait on, but there is a feeling abroad in the town of people having taken on the natural world, and of people having been found wanting, of having learnt something in the process, and that something related to their own impermanence and their own insignificance. Outsiders mistake it for a feeling of doom. But they are wrong. It is a feeling of humility. I know, for I can smell that feeling. It is the scent of peat. The town has been there for fifty years. It might survive another fifty. Or even another hundred. Outside the town there are creeks with fallen Huon pine logs in them, as old and as sound as the day they fell forty thousand years ago. Not that the people of Strahan know this. But they feel it. And each day they feel it more strongly, and it has the scent of peat.

Half a mile before the town centre Auntie Ellie turned right up a small gravelled street. Near the top of the street they came to a dilapidated picket fence, through the gate of which Auntie Ellie turned. Harry followed, skipping occasionally to keep pace with her quick stride, along a gravel path, past a mass of tea-tree and button grass where once had been a vain attempt at a garden, and up a small bank to a cottage of tin, painted a bright sky-blue.

When they got close, Harry saw that the tin was a form of corrugated iron with much smaller corrugations than that found on roofing tin. Parts of it had been patched with flattened kerosene tins, also painted sky-blue. 'This is home, Harry,' said Auntie Ellie, smacking the corrugated iron with the flat of a big hand. 'Ripple iron, we calls it, best bloody building material this side of Gormanston. Don't rot, don't cost much, and always talks to you when it's raining.' And then she pointed an accusing finger down the road toward a house built of brick. 'Not like that rubbish, I can assure you, Harry.'

Auntie Ellie had never trusted brick houses, not from the time she had first seen one at the age of ten near the outskirts of the town of Deloraine. She had stopped and gawked for so long that her mum, Dolcie Dossitter, had to cuff her quick smart around her ears. 'Cut that out now.' Dolcie looked up at the brick cottage with its neat garden of cabbages and cauliflowers and pumpkins out the front, and saw the lace curtain on the window to the right of the front door sweep away slightly. Then a circle slightly darker than the rest of the interior gloom could be discerned. A face. Looking at them. 'Better bugger off quick,' said Dolcie to Ellie, 'otherwise they be thinking we're after somethin'.'

'But how does it stand up?' asked Ellie as Dolcie shoved her in the back with the palm of her hand.

'How the hell I know? Just get walking.' And she gave Ellie another shove. This time Ellie started walking, all the while turning and looking back at the brick cottage.

'But how does it?' asked Ellie.

'Them bloody whitefellas. I don't know. Just stop lookin' about and walk.'

'Houses have big wood beams to keep them up. And one bit of wood is nailed or pegged into the next. I know that because I saw the uncles build the birding shed. But if there ain't any beams, how does it hold up?'

'Unless them little square red stone houses have the spars and beams inside, hidden behind, maybe that's how it is done,' said Dolcie, trying her best to persuade Ellie to move on before trouble struck.

'Maybe that's it,' said Ellie.

'Maybe it don't matter,' said Dolcie, who had seen too many entirely new things and unbelievably fabulous things in her life to be shocked by anything any more. Dolcie's predominant attitude was one of acceptance.

'But how?'

'You let things be and that way you get on and you are allowed to live. But you want answers to things then you make trouble. You make trouble *and* –' She ran a finger across her throat like a knife and made a dreadful gurgling noise.

And then laughed. 'Who knows why them silly buggers do half the bloody silly things they do? I never understood 'em and never will.'

So it was in that small sky-blue cottage built of tin, elevated at one end by bricks and at the other by a Huon pine stump, in the small and declining port of Strahan in the winter of 1940, Auntie Ellie made up a roaring myrtle fire in her front room, which served as both parlour and kitchen, and made up a bath for Harry in front of the fireplace. The fireplace, also made of ripple iron, was almost as wide as the room, so large that Auntie Ellie sat Harry inside it while she fetched water in a kerosene tin from the tank outside. She hung the kerosene tin by its twined fencing-wire handle from the iron cooking rack that swung from the far side of the fireplace. As Harry and the kero tin warmed up close to the crack and spit of the bursting flames, Auntie Ellie bustled about. Harry looked at the blackened iron cooking rack, heavy with crusts and blisters of fatty soot. Auntie Ellie went back outside to fetch the old tin hip-bath from beneath the house. She put the bath close to the fire and took down the tin of hot water. Harry got up out of the fireplace and watched as a thick heavy tongue of water fell into a cloud of steam. His gaze switched to Auntie Ellie, who, he suddenly realised, was at once familiar and different. And the difference, Harry realised, was one he shared. He looked at her intently, hoping to see a physical manifestation of what this familiar difference was. She turned and laughed at his stare, and mistook it for interest in her pipe rather than in herself. 'You're a rum 'un, Harry. You want to try, eh?' And she passed the pipe to Harry, who looked up at her and, seeing the offer was serious and not an adult's joke, took the pipe and inhaled. As the soft smoke entered his mouth Harry looked above the fireplace to a plain mantelpiece, once painted cream, now wood-smoke darkened. Amidst the yellowing photographs and the wilting red geraniums in their vases full of urine-coloured water sat all that remained of Auntie Ellie's long-dead husband Reg: his dentures.

Reg had sold his teeth when things had begun to turn bad around Strahan following federation. He had previously bought a block of land with money he made from gold panning up the King River in the 1880s, and had got as far as framing up part of a house on that block some years later when the depression came. He had grand plans of finishing the house off with the cheap Oregon weatherboards that were flooding in from America, complete with a grand verandah painted in four different bright colours. The house was to have eight rooms, but Reg had only framed up four when his money and luck came to an end. Ellie was with child and Reg, unable to get work of any kind, sold his teeth to the local dentist, who anaesthetised Reg with a combination of laughing gas and laudanum before pulling out all his teeth. The dentist made more money pulling out healthy teeth than he did fixing decayed ones, and he had a lucrative trade going with his brother-in-law who lived in Bristol, England, and who sold the Tasmanian teeth to a firm in Pall Mall that made false dentures for the rich who had lost teeth through too much good living. The teeth emanating from Strahan were prized and fetched an often handsome sum, for although needing some polishing with an abrasive stone to rid them of their tobacco stains, they were generally the fine teeth of young men who had come to the west coast in the hope of striking it lucky on the diggings. When confronted with no work and no money, many chose to have their teeth pulled to buy a boat ticket back to Melbourne or Hobart. Reg and Ellie used part of the tooth money to buy the ripple iron to finish the house, and the rest simply to live on. Reg's mouth, which Ellie had found his most pleasing feature, collapsed into the puckered hollows of an old man's, and though he grew a large walrus moustache to cover the worst of the facial ravages inflicted on him by the dentist, he never got over the humiliation. Reg eventually found labouring work on the Strahan wharf and between the little he earnt and the little he stole they had enough to get by. The job had its own rewards, such as the tins of blue paint bound for the Mt Lyell Mining Company. Reg discovered that there was a discrepancy between the shipping docket and the actual amount of paint shipped, the latter exceeding the former by some two hundred gallons. Reg and the wharf clerk made sure that the amount on the shipping docket was trained up to Queenstown. The rest they sold surreptitiously, and over the following year, as people slowly got around to painting their houses, Strahan changed from an uneven hue to one in which sky-blue was predominant, as if an azure frost had settled permanently upon the town.

After he died of a stroke, Reg's cheap false teeth (not comparable in the least to the superb dentures into which his teeth had been fashioned) sat in the middle of the mantelpiece, for a time in a glass of water, but then without fluid company following a family party (the only kind of party Auntie Ellie permitted) in which they found use during a dance as a set of castanets. So they sat among the photographs and ashtrays and curling postcards and wilting geraniums, two yellowing crescents bound by a musk-coloured frame, a small memorial to one man's sacrifice.

Auntie Ellie had moved from the Mole Creek district to the west coast in 1891 via Melbourne, Victoria, following an incident on a farm where two of her brothers, Jack and Bert, laboured. The brothers worked for a farmer called Basil Moore who had a property out back of Mole Creek. At the time there had been an outbreak of cow plague and Basil had to slaughter much of his herd. He ordered the brothers to dig a large pit in which the animals were to be driven and slaughtered. While they dug, Basil, depressed at the ill fortune that had struck his farm, drank from a flagon of rum, pausing only long enough to gee them along, telling them to dig harder and deeper. When he had finished the flagon he threw the empty bottle at his feet, then wandered off. He reappeared about an hour and a half later. Evidently he had been back to the homestead, because he had another bottle of half-drunk rum as well as a shotgun. He leapt into the pit, which was by now seven feet deep, some three feet deeper than when he had last looked into it, falling face first in the clay at the bottom. He pulled himself onto his knees and looked up at the faces smiling down at him from the top of the pit. His rum-flamed eyes burnt with humiliation out of his muddied face.

'Throw me the shotgun!' he yelled at the brothers at the top. They looked at him, then at each other, then back at Basil. 'Throw down the shotgun, I said!' hollered Basil. He threw the empty rum bottle up at them. It rose up slowly, hit a wall of the pit near the surface and fell back down on Basil, who had to duck to avoid being struck. The brothers tied a piece of baling twine around the gun barrel and carefully lowered it down to Basil, who snatched it the moment his fingers could reach. He snapped the shotgun open, pulled two cartridges out of a coat pocket, loaded them into the barrel, then snapped the gun back together. He put the gun to his shoulder, raised the barrel to the sky, closed one eye, wobbled a little, regained his balance, then let his other eye roam the sky until he found one of the brothers in his sights. He put his finger on the trigger. And then he roared, 'Bury me, youse black bastards!'

The brothers looked down incredulously, perhaps even with a slight smirk on their faces. 'Bury me!' Then they realised that Basil was serious. 'I should never have left Devon,' said Basil, who, even when drunk in front of the brothers, persisted in the fiction he was a free settler from Devon rather than what all the district knew him to be, a convict from Salford, sentenced to death for bestiality, his sentence commuted to transportation to Van Diemen's Land for fourteen years. That had been when he was a young man. He was old now, and broken – by the System, by his own desire for a respectability he could never gain, by his inability to remake the land he had bought into his own image of himself.

'If you want to take your land back, bury me!' he cried.

The effort of standing erect and looking skywards without swaying proved too much at this point, and Basil lost his balance and fell over. Before the gun exploded the brothers were already well away from the hole. They ran off with Basil's curses chasing them.

'You pissweak black bastards. Get back here and bury me. That's what you want. That and my land. Well, come back and finish me off now. Bury me now,' and now he laboured every word, 'youse – filthy – black – *bastards*!'

But the brothers were not to return, not the next day, not the following week, not ever, for that night there was a knock on the family's shack door. Basil had been found dead from a shotgun wound in the bottom of a pit. The brothers had planned to return once the word went around the Mole Creek pub that Basil had been chastised by his wife for drinking and had resumed his normal God-fearing Gospel Hall ways, once Basil was back to threatening them only with the wrath of the Lord and not with a shotgun. But now there was no going back.

'They'll hang us for sure,' said Bert. 'Ain't no one going to believe the word of two blackfellas.'

Bert, Jack and Ellie fled across the water to Melbourne where they stayed for three years, until the fateful day that Bert met Reg Lewis in a Collingwood pub, the evening before the Melbourne Cup. Reg was over from Strahan for a holiday and had lost all his money in a two-up game. Bert took Reg home to the tenement he shared with Jack, Ellie, and two other families. They fed Reg up on silverside and spuds, and Bert lent him a pound – half his week's pay as a slaughterman at the local abattoir. Reg told them how the west coast of Tasmania was exploding with life, of how Nellie Melba had even sung in the mining town of Zeehan, a town about which there was talk of making the capital of Tasmania, so rapid and astonishing was its growth. The three of them were sickening for their home and people, and they told Reg why they had to leave and how much they wished to return. Reg began to sense something about the brothers' sister, a small dark attractive woman who smiled a lot as he told his stories of prospecting in the wild rainforest of the west. His tales grew wilder as her smiles grew bigger. He told them of how some lucky diggers who struck it rich lit their cigars with pound notes, and about how they told diggers from California that the Tassie tigers ate lone prospectors. Then at the end of it all he confessed that the greatest attribute a person on the west coast could have was to bullshit even more than the bloke next to him. They laughed a lot at that. 'Hell,' said Bert, 'I *knew* it was bullshit. I was just amazed how much bullshit one man could produce from a feed of silverside and spuds.' And they laughed all the more, till the tenement rocked with their laughing and Reg had to wipe the tears from his eyes.

Reg talked more of how they ought come to the west coast, which was awash with people from everywhere around the world and where they would never be found out and where there were plenty of jobs to be had. They nodded their heads and thought no more of it. The following day, in the race before the 1891 Melbourne Cup, Reg put the pound Bert had leant him on a thirty-six to one horse that ended up winning. Reg tracked Bert down at the abattoir the next morning, paid back the pound fivefold, and then handed over three one-way boat fares from Melbourne to Strahan. The family met and discussed the offer and in the end decided to go, feeling that it ought now be safe enough for them to return to Tasmania under aliases. Before the steamer had even got to the heads of Macquarie Harbour, Ellie had accepted Reg's proposal of marriage.

— Auntie Ellie, 1941 —

It was near the end of Harry's second year at Strahan that Auntie Ellie felled the white cow belonging to the manager of the Mt Lyell mine. Her granddaughter Daisy had fallen badly ill with a fever. At first Auntie Ellie had not worried unduly. But when night came and the fever became so pronounced that Daisy went into convulsions, Auntie Ellie decided to go out and fetch the doctor. She walked across to West Strahan to his house, only to discover that he was playing cards at the other end of the town at Lettes Bay. She walked along the long dark lonely road to Lettes Bay and felt all her old fears resurface. The darkness felt like a hole into which she might fall. She had, like the old people, always been frightened of the dark, but this time the fear grew and grew in her stomach until she could no longer hold it down. She screamed and began to run. And behind her she could feel a white face, chasing her. She held her dress up high and ran as hard as she could. Her clay pipe fell from her mouth as she began to pant and she had to leave it where it fell, scared to even pause to retrieve it. She ran until her guts ached and her throat burnt. Still she ran on, and as she ran she felt the stories of the old people coming back, stories she had forgotten since childhood, about how the whites had come for them in the dark, about how the mothers stuffed bark into the babies' mouths to stop them crying lest the noise give them away to their hunters, and how because of this the babies sometimes died. How there was not even the light of a fire to keep Werowa from stealing the dead babies' spirits away, for fear the smoke from the fire be sighted. She ran and her arms ached and her chest was afire, and still she felt the white face behind her. She remembered how they had told her their forebears had been snared and handled like wild beasts, how at Oyster Cove Dr Milligan gave them medicine to prevent them having babies. And the terrible stories that her mother had told her, how soldiers would keep a black girl tied up all night, then set her free and shoot her running in the morning. The story that Lallah had told her mother, of how some soldiers had roused them from a corroboree, and Lallah saw one of them stick an infant on his bayonet and put it on the fire.

And then she could run no more. She slowed her pace to a jog, then to a stagger, then halted altogether. At first the sound of her own panting, the pounding of her own heart, was so great it temporarily overwhelmed her fear. Then, as her breathing became more regular, she felt hot breath on her neck and knew the white face was behind her. And she knew it was Werowa's breath announcing a death. But whose death? She felt paralysed with total fear. She felt air surge through her flaring nostrils, felt her whole body tremble, felt the sweat on her nape grow cold as the breath of the white face that fell upon it.

Auntie Ellie suddenly swung around and threw as powerful a punch as she was capable of. She felt her fist strike something soft and velvety, then slide onto slobber and teeth, and then there was a tremendous bellow and a huge form slumped to the ground. Auntie Ellie looked down to see an unconscious white cow. She stood transfixed. Then she cried and cried.

Still weeping, she walked the remaining short distance to Lettes Bay, found the doctor, and together they drove back in his baby Austin to Auntie Ellie's home. But, as Auntie Ellie already knew, it was too late. They came into the house to find Harry sitting on the floor in front of the fire with Daisy's little limp body cradled in his arms. She had died some time before, of meningitis, the doctor said. Harry said she had gone into convulsions for a second time, then gone quiet. He had known, he said, the moment she had breathed her last. He didn't cry, though Auntie Ellie wished he would. He was a man, all right, she thought, even if he was only twelve. But when he looked up at her and asked why there was so much death, she could not help but seize his head and pull it into her own belly, black, damp and pungent smelling with the rain, heaving hard with heavy long sobs.

— Auntie Ellie, 1946 —

She sat on the floor in front of the fire and Harry knew from the amount of rouge on her face that she wasn't right, for the worse she felt, the more she powdered her face. She was proud of her skin, always talking of how lovely and light it was, though it never looked that light to Harry.

Not long after he first arrived in Strahan Harry looked at Auntie Ellie and asked, 'Is you an Abo, Auntie Ellie?' Ellie, for the first and only time that Harry ever remembered, laid into him.

'Don't you go talking about decent people in that sort of way. It does no good, you hear? We are good decent Catholic folk, good decent *white* Catholic folk, you understand?'

Harry didn't understand.

'I'm truly sorry, Auntie Ellie, I just thought you mighta been an Abo —' Harry got no further before Ellie cuffed him again and again, this time with a methodical violence that Harry recognised did not come from her, but was learnt, as she wanted him to learn it. For that reason it did not hurt him, but he took care to listen. She would slap him one side of the face and then say something, then slap him the other side and say something else. And as she slapped him the tears ran down her face, though her voice was fierce.

Slap.

'We ain't no Abos, we ain't no boongs, ya hear?'

Slap.

'Ya talk like that they'll take ya away, ya understand? They'll take ya back to the islands. I already told you what we are – decent white Catholic folk.

Slap.

'What are we?'

Slap.

'White Catholic folk.'

She stayed her hand at the side of her face. 'That's right.' Her head momentarily turned and she caught sight of her open palm, ready to strike again if necessary, and then her eyes quickly moved back to staring fiercely at Harry, as if she had glimpsed something alien and frightening which she had no wish to see. 'Decent white Catholic folk,' said Auntie Ellie, but her voice was now shaky and somehow less certain.

Though he did not understand, Harry knew not to say such things again, and neither of them ever referred to the incident. But Harry, with a child's unerring sense, proceeded to explore the area by subterfuge. He found that as long as he didn't specifically mention the word 'Abo' or 'Aborigine' there was much Auntie Ellie would tell him. Not that he consciously sought information to discover what it was that Auntie Ellie didn't want to talk about. He continued to push though he did not know he was pushing, or what purpose his questions and dissembling served.

Harry found the best time for his questions to be when they were out walking, a pastime of which Auntie Ellie was fond. They would walk many miles along Ocean Beach and they would eat the fleshy leaves of the plant they called pigface and she called dead men's fingers, would rub the bite of jack-jumpers and the inchmen with the pulpy flesh. They would walk in the bush up around Piccaninny Point on the King River and beyond the rainforested ruins of Teepookana. At such times she reminded Harry of a dark plum. She would pick the ripe kangaroo apples after they cracked open in the early morning sun and push them in his mouth, the taste sometimes like a boiled floury spud and sometimes like a banana. Auntie Ellie herself was particularly fond of mullas – large blueberries to be found on vines in the rainforest. And as they walked and Auntie Ellie fed him from the bush, she would start chattering away and tell him how they had to look after the land for the land was the spirit. When there was a mining disaster at Queenstown and many miners died, she said, as she always said in times of drought or flood or fire, that the land was soaked with blood and that such things happened 'because the spirit angry, because the spirit sad.' Sometimes, when she was ill or drunk or in the bush, she talked of her mother and her people, whom she only ever referred to as the old people, and sometimes, when she felt particularly happy or particularly sad, she would talk about the old people's ways. She was a stern and proud Catholic, though occasionally she called satan Werowa, which she said was the old people's name for the devil.

'Not that I know much about the old people,' she would say. 'A bit. Not much. A bit. You'd have to ask them professors at the museum, Harry, to get your answers. Now they know the lot.' She would tap her head and heart with her hand. 'I only know what I got in here and here and that's two parts of bugger all.' Then she'd look up in the trees, trying to find another possum run or batch of ripe mullas, and, never looking at him, say in a disinterested sort of way, 'Them poor buggers had it bad. Oh Lord, yes. Real bad, they had it.' But about herself she would only say, 'I am a good respectable white woman.' Much of being respected for Auntie Ellie was being part of the church, and her religion was, like her, a cranky combination of both the new and the old. She observed the church's great ceremonies – baptism, communion, confirmation, marriage, mass – wearing her other dress, her best dress, made of a dark serge material. But around her neck, in contrast to the prim drabness of her dress, she wore layers of beautiful meriner necklaces that she made from seashells she collected from Ocean Beach, that had all the colours of the sea upon a single thread of catgut. In anything that really mattered to her it was the old people's ways she stuck to, not the ways of the Church of Rome.

The following morning Harry knew for sure she wasn't well when she called him to scatter the ashes from the fire in the direction of the morning star, so as to warm it and ease its journey through the day. All that day, family from her mum's side gathered at home, a rough mob they were, but nice and decent and polite as could be. Late in the afternoon Harry's uncles Basil and George turned up. They all sat around with their dogs and chatted and laughed and hoyed their dogs to cut out this and that.

Auntie Ellie was dying.

It had begun after Daisy's death. Auntie Ellie began to shrivel up. She stopped doing everything. She stopped smoking all the time and took to smoking only of a mid-morning after she had chopped the firewood for the day, and then only rollies and not her pipe. She went to church only of a Sunday, not every day that the priest happened to be saying mass. She talked little and laughed less. She came to find walking very difficult. Each Sunday she would get in a tiny horse cart that she owned and, pos-sessing no horse, get Harry to pull it in a harness they had found on the tip and which she had converted for Harry's use. Harry would pull the cart to church and back. This practice went on for some months, till the Siddons took to calling in on their way to mass and giving Auntie Ellie and Harry a lift in their A-model Ford.

When the priest came to administer the last rites Auntie Ellie grew – for the first time anyone could remember – Auntie Ellie grew contemptuous, even abusive. 'Bugger off, Father Breen,' she said. 'I'm off to see the old people, and I ain't got no need of going to the Catholic heaven.' Father Breen was perplexed but determined to be forceful, until Harry's cousin, Big Mick Brennan, smelling strongly of muttonbirds, draped his arm, two threatening hairy joints of mutton, around the priest's shoulders and, smiling, repeated his aunt's injunc-tion. 'Be a good fella and bugger off, Father.' Father Breen took his hat and bade farewell.

After the door slammed Auntie Ellie had a cup of tea and started telling stories about the old people. She didn't tell any of the stories that she had remembered that night when she had been chased by the cow along the road to Lettes Bay, only the good stories and the funny stories about the past. Mostly stories about the family.

Then Auntie Ellie stopped telling her stories and lay back down on the floor. As Auntie Ellie lay on the floor dying, her brothers sat around in that old sky-blue tin house and told more stories. The stories got the men drinking, and then some of the men drank too much and the women grew angry and ordered them out of Auntie Ellie's house until they were prepared to give the bottle a rest. There was some screaming and shouting, then it all calmed down again, except for Noah, who just wouldn't shut up carrying on about how some people were saying he was drunk, just because he kept falling over, and how he knew plenty of sober people who fell over all the time, so how the hell did him falling over prove a thing, how did it prove he was drunk, when all it meant was that his balance wasn't perhaps as good as it might be? Then the women grew angry again and the men started to laugh and open bottles. In the end, even Auntie Ellie, sick as she was, had had enough and she rose up from her possie in front of the fire, where she had lain for some hours, and went outside to whistle up the wind in her anger. That was when everybody knew that it had all gone a bit too far. Normally Auntie Ellie only called up a wet westerly, but when she was really shitty she whistled up a northerly — she called it Werowa's breath — to give people headaches and bad chests. She'd make a high-pitched whistle, eerie really, and then the trees would begin to quiver and rustle, and before you knew it, there was a full bloody gale roaring.

As Auntie Ellie stood on her verandah in that soft mid-morning light, lips pursed and emitting a shrill strange sound, the wind rose like a slow-forming wave, at first just a small rustle, then, as it gathered power, beating at the windows and doors of her little tin home, making them rattle, and finally shaking the very house itself, so much so it frightened everybody inside. It was like a violent song, and every now and then, when it seemed to be beginning to wane a little, Auntie Ellie, with the door behind her slamming open and shut in the wild gusts, would whistle again, and the wind would immediately respond, even more ferocious, even more powerful. Everyone grew quiet, for Auntie Ellie had the powers of the old people. The men tipped their beer out and Auntie Ellie came back inside and resumed her possie and her impassive stare into the fire.

Harry had never met half of them, but they seemed to know all about him. Harry asked how they knew Auntie Ellie was so sick, because no word had been sent, and they just pointed to the tips of the trees moving in the wind and smiled. The wind seemed to make Auntie Ellie a lot happier, even though her normally immaculately tidy house was being turned upside down and she was, if nothing else, a fiercely proud housekeeper, but she continued to fade through that day and the following evening.

Near the end she lay down on the floor and asked for the fire in front of her to be built up. She curled up in front of the red heat and her dogs lay around her licking her hands and face and she seemed happy for this to be the way. The light of the fire played upon them and she stared past the dogs' panting tongues into the ever changing, dancing forms that seized and then fled from the red embers at the heart of the fire – mesmerised, as if seeing things in those flames that she had never seen before. When Harry arrived she became unusually talkative. 'A strange thing, Harry. Since they took the old people away, Harry, a strange thing. God has not filled this land with animals. The land used to be alive with wallaby and kangaroo, possums would come to your door to eat and you'd eat them. Now you have to hunt all day to find one. The emu gone, the tiger gone. The old people gone.'

Harry did not know what to say. 'We're still here, Auntie Ellie,' he said.

Auntie Ellie smiled. She looked up at Harry and said, 'Seems the whiter and whiter I get, the blacker you get,' and laughed and laughed. Then coughed, and the coughing became a sort of convulsion, then went quiet again.

'My people call,' she suddenly said and the dogs howled. 'No you cry for me, Harry,' she said. 'I go back to my people. Me going back. No you cry. My people take me away.' She took Harry's hand in hers, as if they were back in the bush and she was guiding him around. 'They rowing hard to get to me, Harry,' she said, pointing at the ceiling as if she had suddenly there spied a boat coming through the sky to take her away. 'Pull, you lousy buggers!' she shouted in an outburst uncharacteristically loud and vulgar for Auntie Ellie. 'Pull *hard*!' And she gripped Harry's hand so hard that it hurt and he could not believe that the old woman had so much strength left in her. Tears welled in Harry's eyes. Auntie Ellie cast her eyes downwards from the ceiling to look at Harry and spoke one last time.

Saying: 'No you cry for me, Harry. My people call.'

After Auntie Ellie died everyone howled, the family and the dogs, and even the rusty corro shook, for half an hour or more.

— Harry, 1946 —

I look into the fire, but be buggered if I can see what
Auntie Ellie saw there. I stare at the ceiling, but there's
nothing there save the painted Huon pine boards Reg
nailed there many years before. And even though I have
the power of my visions, the only boat I can summon
into my mind's eye is Harry's punt as he continues his
journey up the Franklin River and then up the Jane River.

It took Harry the rest of the day to get up to the
junction with the Jane River, and from there up the Jane
as far as the bottom of the first gorge. He camped the
night there, then the next morning pulled his boat high
up the riverbank, turned it upside down and tied it up.
He waited half a day before Norry and Joff Halsey turned
up, having walked around the first gorge. Together they
spent the next two days carrying the supplies Harry had
brought in the punt around the gorge to Norry's camp.
The camp was a roughie, a sheet of canvas pitched in an
A-frame, for there had been but little pine in the vicinity,
and Norry and Joff had cut and hauled most of what was
worth taking while waiting for Harry. Now they were to
move up above the second gorge, where word had it there
was plenty of good pine. The next day they began the
hard labour of carrying all their gear and supplies, as well
as Norry's punt, up over the part of the mountain range
known as Punt Hill. But before they went searching to
find the traces of the track that Barnes Abel and his boys
had cut back in 1936, they rowed up into the mouth of
the second gorge for a look-see. Harry had never seen
anything like it. The walls of the gorge cut up hundreds
of feet and a cold wild dank breath of wind ran down
this corridor of darkness. It seemed as if light hardly ever

reached inside the bottom of the gorge, so slimy and mossy were the rocks. The river now ran low, but the walls and rocks sweated moisture. Water seemed to drip from every opening, down every slope, over boulders the size of houses. The gorge glistened green and black in its splendid solitude, a world complete unto itself. Nobody spoke. Norry pointed to driftwood caught fifty feet up a cliff face, and the piners' blood ran cold with the thought of the gorge in flood, a wild demented cataract, an avalanche of white water sweeping before it everything unfortunate enough to be in this green and black world. They looked in excitement and in fear, in exhilaration and in terror, smelt the gorge's heaviness, felt its power turn their legs to jelly and make their heads reel with the vertigo of imagination.

'Bugger me dead,' said Norry. They turned and slowly rowed back to their camp at the base of the gorge.

They cut and hauled pine for the next six weeks from a stand above the second gorge that Norry had been told about by Barnes Abel. The stand was a few hundred yards back from a cliff that fronted the river. The logs of pine were branded with Norry's 'H' brand and, with the aid of block and tackles and a few long irons, the piners hauled them to the cliff, over which the logs were dropped into the deep water below. The pine trunks that had inched so slowly and with so much difficulty to the cliff would suddenly slither over the edge like seals, falling vertically into the deep pool below, briefly pogoing back out of the water to finally fall sideways and silent. They spent a few days freeing the logs from log jams that snared the river, and floated them down to the mouth of the gorge. There they left them to be carried out in the winter floods, and headed home.

At Flat Island they came upon Smeggsy and Old Bo, who told them how Old Jack had wanted a drink real bad and had decided to go out with another gang of piners they met heading home as Smeggsy, Old Bo and Jack were heading up the Franklin. Smeggsy was keen for a hand with hauling some logs, given that he was a man down, so Harry said he'd stay on with them, though as Norry and Joff disappeared around the corner he wasn't sure why.

It was early morning and the rain had been piss-dripping all night down onto the mossy King Billy pine slats that roofed their hut. Harry sat up in his sugarbag-lined bunk, rubbed a fist in each eye, and took a deep breath of the sweet smoke-heavy air. In the fireplace he found his boots, dusted with the fine light grey ash left by the burnt Huon pine, still a little damp, but warm. He pulled them on and they felt hot and comforting and he revelled in the good feeling they gave his feet, for he knew the rest of the day they would feel like murder. They ate some bread Old Bo had made on the previous Sunday and some bacon that Smeggsy fried, drank some tea, then they rowed the punt upriver to the track that led to the stand Smeggsy and Old Bo were working.

Old Bo had found the small stand of pine many years before, but then the trees had been a little too small to cut. Now they were of a good size. The stand lay about twenty chains back from the river. To get their logs through the rainforest they had a small kerosene-powered winch they had brought in pieces from Strahan in their punt and assembled in the rainforest.

Old Bo and Smeggsy took the wire rope up through the bush and hooked it up to a fallen log. When they were done Harry started the winch. It ran a little roughly, so as the log slowly inched toward him, Harry picked up the grease can and went to grease the winch. His damp boots skidded on a slimy sassafras sapling that had been felled along with the other scrub to make a clearing, and Harry fell, the thumb of his right hand going through the cog drive. Harry looked at the mangled stump that emerged and his legs felt weak and his head light. He called Smeggsy and Old Bo to come. They looked at Harry and Harry looked at them. Smeggsy went back up the gully and returned with his axe. Harry laid his injured hand on a fallen myrtle log. Old Bo clawed at the log and a big lump of brown mush came off the log like it was chocolate cake. The entire log was rotten to the core, a mass of decomposed peat held in shape only by the mosses and lichens that encircled it.

'Not there, Harry,' said Old Bo. 'It's too soft, mate.' It was the first word any of them had spoken since Harry had called them back. Smeggsy scarfed a flat surface from the top side of a pine log they had winched down the day before.

'Operating table, eh Harry?' said Old Bo and they laughed.

Then the laughter stopped.

Harry put the pulp, with its bone-flecked gore, upon the pine log. It looked to Harry like a blob of fatty silverside flecked with desiccated coconut. Smeggsy put a loose headlock upon Harry, swivelled Harry's face away from the sight of his hand, and tightened the headlock. Old Bo pinned Harry's right wrist firmly to the log with his left hand, and with his right, holding the axe halfway down the handle, raised the axe in the air.

'Hold the boy gentle, Smeggsy,' said Old Bo.

Then he let the axe fall.

Do I have to watch the rest?

Thank God for small mercies.

Instead of a toppling thumb I am seeing a watch, and looking down upon it is Aljaz. He realises with a shrug that the watch has stopped working. He looks back up at the valley upon which mist sits so low and heavy that the entire river seems shrouded in white. An extra-ordinary moment of peace, really – I can see that is what Aljaz is feeling. There is a silence about the river as the punters load the last of the gear on the rafts and do a final check of the campsite. Looking upon it now, it was a serene start for a day that was to prove anything but. And, as if respectful of the quiet, the rafts are untied in silence, kicked off from the riverbank by Aljaz and the Cockroach in silence, and they glide into the tea-black waters of the Franklin River with no sound. The paddling begins without talk. For once, all the punters manage to paddle in unison and the rafts follow each other as if held by some invisible thread. The current is far stronger than the punters have until then experienced. They feel the strength of the moving black sheet of river in their arms and are excited by it, excited by the way the rafts, formerly sluggish when the river was barely running, now seem to move at an almost excessive speed.

The reverie is broken by a scream. It is Ellen, on Aljaz's boat. 'A leech, a leech!' she cries. Aljaz clambers over the gear frame to the front of the boat where Ellen sits, and pulls a sleek black blister of blood off the back of her hand and throws it in the river, leaving Ellen shivering with a small free-flowing wound.

They paddle on. Noises strange and harsh crack the enshrouding mist, announcing the overhead flight of a flock of yellow-tailed black cockatoos. The punters briefly observe the birds through a hole in the mist before the flock has flown the length of the valley and left for elsewhere. For a time after the flock has disappeared the wild and rough cries can still be faintly heard, as if prophesying the imminent rain half humorously, half grimly. They paddle on. The mist rises to reveal clouds moving at a pace almost frantic across the narrowing slit of sky above. Nobody talks. The fear is upon the punters, though not yet their guides. They have been on the river for only an hour or so when the air turns suddenly and strangely chill. The Cockroach's raft is leading. The Cockroach slows his raft up and Aljaz's raft bumps into it. The Cockroach points up a side ridge further down the valley. It is covered in rain. They look at one another. Nothing is said. The weather has swung back to westerly. They paddle on.

They pass a small beach upon which a tiger cat strolls, watching their passing, too ignorant of who they are and what they are to flee. It is not afraid of them, but they are afraid of the small carrion-eating marsupial who observes the passing red rafts and their inhabitants as if they were nothing more than driftwood decorated with baubles being washed downriver by the flood, further strange flotsam of faraway worlds.

The day grows dark. An hour or more before midday, the sky looks as if night were about to fall. The patches of blue grow smaller and less frequently seen, until at length they can no more be found anywhere in the black sky, so strong and close and immediate that it makes the punters lean nervously into the centre of the raft. The hills grow steeper until the river is flowing not through a valley but into the beginning of a deep gorge. One of the punters on the Cockroach's boat begins to sing the old Willy Nelson song about seeing nothing but blue skies from now on. They laugh from relief at having been shown their depression without having to name it. The song ends. The laughter dies. Around them hangs an immense and still silence.

And they continue paddling into it, into the gorge, into the darkness.

– Eight –

I look into that darkness more now, far more than I did then, attempt to look into its heart. The darkness begins to fragment. It breaks into black pieces and each piece takes on the shape of an animal: a wombat, two ringtail possums, five pademelons, three potoroos, seven blue wrens, four bats, one rather handsome looking green tree frog, two companionable goannas, a serene-looking freshwater lobster, an angry reddening crayfish, and all sitting down one side of an old lino-topped table that has similarly manifested itself out of the darkness. On the other side of the table appears an equally bizarre menagerie: three Tasmanian devils, two tabby cats, a quoll, a Tasmanian tiger – jaw hugely distended, presumably waiting with anticipated appetite – a querulous mob of black cockatoos, a small whip snake all eager twists and turns, and next to it a rather disinterested coiled-up tiger snake seemingly oblivious to its reptilian cousin. An oak skink next to them, and next to that an owl and a pigmy possum, four mongrel dogs, two platypuses, five kangaroos and, right at the end, a shuffling echidina. And standing above this banquet of animals, smiling benignly, is an aged Harry.

The animals are slurping out of their plates and seem to be having rather a good time. Harry looks down upon them like the patriarch he never was. Of course, although Harry and Sonja only ever had me before Sonja died, they did dream of a large family and of all the things that they and their many kids would one day do together. After Sonja's death Harry continued to serve up a plate of food for her at his weekly barbeque. After a time he began to serve up an extra plate of salad and grilled meat and fish, additional to that he would normally serve for himself, me, Maria Magdalena Svevo and my dead mum. It was eighteen months or so after her death. He began to serve up a very small plate of diced meat and a few squashed vegetables, a baby's meal. After that, every eighteen months or so, he would add another plate to the number, as though he were feeding some growing family of phantoms. The servings grew over time, as if the ghost receiving them was growing from baby to child to adolescent to adult. Then he began to put out more food and drink for more invisible guests, whom he claimed were long-lost relatives come visiting, or friends of the phantom children. No one ever said anything. As if it were normal, which after a time it became, a curiosity only commented on by the occasional flesh-and-blood visitor to our weekly barbeque.

Toward the end, it must have become faintly ridiculous, though I never saw it, having long since left. Harry had the tables placed next to his barbeque, and he left them each Sunday afternoon heaped with rissoles and grilled fish. You might think that cats and stray dogs would have come and scoffed the lot, but it never happened. The food sat there on the long bench tables, under the grapevine that grew on the rickety old trellis above, until each Monday evening when Harry would whistle, a low eerie whistle, and a slight wind would blow. Animals would appear from everywhere: cats, dogs, possums, wombats and devils. Where, in the middle of a city the size of Hobart, they all came from, to this day I'm stumped. They seemed to materialise out of the earth. They would sit around and upon the tables and eat, sometimes spratting, sometimes sharing, while Harry stood above them puffing away on a hand-rolled cigarette, saying nothing, smiling a bit.

I watch as the Tasmanian tiger pulls itself with its fore-paws up to the table edge, observe how it leans across a plate of cold rissoles, picks up an old green-handled kitchen knife and brings the raucous gathering to attention by banging its handle upon the table top. And – I swear it's true, if I wasn't seeing and hearing this myself, I would never have believed it possible – she announces she is going to tell a story about loss. The announcement is not greeted with instant silence. A few go quiet, a few continue chatting, and a few howl derisively. The echidina yells out that he isn't going to listen to any animal that looks like a pedestrian crossing, and he and the quoll collapse into helpless giggles. The tiger tells them to piss off, says she couldn't care less what a dopey little ball of spikes thought. She has a fine, if somewhat high-pitched, voice, full and resonant, perhaps because of her splendidly large mouth. And so she begins.

– an ocean of wheat foretells a death –

The two men never exchanged a word, though they did pass the occasional cigarette. Once a year the small man would wait at the place where his farm was entered from an empty dirt road. This small man would wait, wearing a neat pair of purple Koratron trousers – the same pair of neat purple Koratron trousers that he had worn on this same day every year for the last twenty years – and an old faded green-checked flannelette shirt, worn and washed so much that it was now so thin it was pleasant to wear even in the worst heat. The dirt road ran through flat country that remained flat and, to those who did not understand its subtleties, featureless for many hundreds of miles, a land considered remote even to those in the remote town of Esperance, Western Australia, which this road had as its destination. The sleeves of the checked green flannelette shirt were neatly rolled up to the elbows, and below the flannelette folds the muscles of skin-cancer scored forearms twisted like old sisal rope as he rolled up a smoke and put it in his mouth. Once a year he would dawdle up to his farm's decrepit gate and there lean on a post, waiting for his mate to pick him up en route from Kambalda to Esperance for the annual races. This arrangement was never confirmed or acknowledged by either. It was part of the rhythm of their life which they neither questioned nor considered strange. Once a year a grubby grey-green EH utility kicking up a cloud of dust came to a halt alongside a small rundown farm and picked up a farmer and took him through to Esperance. It was a friendship that knew no doubt and hence required no conversation. It was as large as the country they drove through without talk hour after hour, and as irreducible to words.

Except this year.

This year was to be different. They picked up a hitch-hiker, a small stumpy man with a swarthy complexion and a big nose. He wore a pair of faded khaki work trousers, a pink singlet over which was draped a blue flannelette shirt, and on his head was a soiled yellow Caterpillar baseball cap, out of the back and sides of which protruded short red hair. The farmer got out of the EH on that hot dusty road and looked at the flat earth that rolled away forever. He wiped his brow and indicated to the hitchhiker that he was to sit in the middle. After an hour or so of driving, the driver asked where he was going.

'Home,' said the stumpy man in a voice that gave away nothing, flat, slow, burred.

'Home?' said the driver.

'Tasmania,' said the stumpy man.

'Further than we be goin',' said the driver. The farmer in the purple Koratron trousers and faded green flannelette shirt smiled. But only a little. Not so much that the stumpy man could see it. Not that it mattered. The stumpy man smiled too.

Nobody bothered to speak again for a few more hours until they pulled up at a road house that shimmered like a red brick mirage in the middle of the low blue-bush desert. They all got out and walked around a bit and the farmer looked up at the stumpy man and said, 'Go home much?'

'Not much,' said the stumpy man. 'Not for ten years.' The stumpy man looked at the farmer and decided to add, 'Family business.'

'O,' said the farmer, knowing full well that meant something bad. 'Ya mum or ya dad?'

'Me dad,' said the stumpy man.

If the farmer had then asked him when he knew his father was dying, Aljaz would not have been able to say it was when he first saw the wind swing round from east to west in an ocean of wheat in Western Australia. The wheat was bowing in its customary humility to the prevailing westerly wind. The wheat lay swept to the left of Aljaz, entombed within the dusty airconditioned dryness of a combine harvester that was heading relentlessly south. The wheat, which was one flat brown colour, suddenly lifted up then fell to the right of Aljaz, changing to a golden hue as it did so. Then, almost as soon as the colour had altered for as far as the horizon, the wind changed back, the wheat returned to its original position and resumed its dull brown. The ocean had changed colour. It was if the wheat were a Persian rug being flipped first this way then that by a salesman keen to reveal the magic of its perfect weave.

Nor would he have been able to say that it was during the course of the night following that day, when, as he lay in his motel room, airconditioner clunking through the long black evening, he dreamt of sea eagles flying far above a glittering river. But he would have said that after he rang home the next morning – the first time he had rung home in many months – and a neighbour had answered the phone and told him that his father was ill in hospital, he realised he had to go home. He went to the foreman and, asking for his pay, said he had to get home on urgent family business. The foreman said, 'Come back any time and I'll see you right.'

'Sure,' said Aljaz. The foreman was fair about his wages, paid out what Aljaz was owed, but it was nothing compared to what he would have got if he had worked the full hot summer. They both knew that.

'Shame,' said the foreman. 'You're good labour. And there's plenty of work for good labour,' said the foreman.

Aljaz said nothing. The foreman looked at him and wondered who the hell he was. Most of the drivers were local boys, and if he hadn't grown up with them he knew someone who had. Aljaz had blown into town, been told about the job in the pub, and applied to the foreman the following day. He had a New South Wales licence, but said he was from Tasmania. Beyond that he didn't say much at all. People liked Aljaz, for he was easy to get on with. He drank enough with the men that they were not suspicious of him, but not so much that anyone really got to know him. The whisper was that he had done time in Long Bay, but the foreman somehow doubted it. Still, there was something about Aljaz, about his easy straight-batting of personal questions, that made the foreman curious. The foreman kept talking, hoping to find out something more.

'Plenty work, plenty money,' said the foreman.

'Them's the breaks.'

'It's a long way from here to there,' said the foreman.

'Yeah,' said Aljaz. 'Spose. Spose always has been.'

'Well, that's how she goes, I reckon,' said the foreman.

'Reckon it is,' said Aljaz.

The farmer didn't bother talking any more. They went into the café, had a feed of steak and salad and chips, got back into the EH utility and did not speak again until they arrived at Esperance late that night, when they bade each other farewell under the huge southern night sky.

Aljaz had to wait until the next morning for a light plane to fly him up to Perth. That flight, via half a dozen bush airstrips, took half a day. He got into Perth to find there were no planes east for six hours due to a refuelling dispute. Then he was overcome with a great fear. He suddenly felt too frightened to return home, afraid of the people and the place. He did not know what to do. Having come so far it seemed ridiculous to halt his journey at this point. He felt paralysed and sick. He saw a phone booth and without consciously thinking walked up to it and rang the directory, asking for the number of a Couta Ho in Hobart. He was given a number which he then dialled.

The telephone sounded its pulsing signal twice, thrice, four times, and then Aljaz suddenly hung up.

He walked out of the terminal and looked at the taxi rank and looked at what remained in his wallet from his payout four days before in a faraway ocean of wheat, and made a calculation as to how much would remain after an airfare back east had been paid. He needed a drink, and not in an airport bar. He walked over to a taxi and asked the cost of a fare to town. The taxi driver was a thin middle-aged man with thick black hair that he wore swept back. He wore gold-rimmed sunglasses, of a type that had been voguish ten years previously and no doubt would be voguish again before the taxi driver was finished with them. He looked straight ahead all the time Aljaz talked to him.

'About thirty bucks, but don't hold me to it.'

'Well, I got forty,' said Aljaz, which wasn't quite true, but he wanted to impress upon the taxi driver that he didn't want to be messed about.

'Well, you'll be right, I reckon.'

Aljaz went round to the passenger door and got into the taxi. The metre started counting and the taxi pulled away.

'Mind if I . . . ?' The taxi driver waved a packet of cigarettes near Aljaz.

'It's your taxi,' said Aljaz.

The taxi driver lighted the cigarette, inhaled and relaxed considerably.

'Funny,' said Aljaz. 'Hardly any money left and I get a taxi. If I had plenty of money I'd be trying to save even more and catch the bus. But when you got nothing, well, it makes no difference.'

'Poor people are good customers, mate, that's what I say. People say, get the rich ones. I say, fuck 'em. The rich ones never give you cash, always run dodgy credit cards and always want a receipt. And if I want a smoke – no way. Bugger 'em, that's what I say. Why you reckon the rich are rich?'

The question is rhetorical. Aljaz looks out the window. The question does not interest him. He looks at the cars shuffling bumper to bumper along the freeway, looks at the endless expanse of housing, and wonders about the lives of all those who live in those houses and who drive those cars, what it must feel like to be *anchored*, even if it is only to a steering wheel for forty-five minutes every day getting to and from work. And then he wonders if perhaps they are maybe all like him. What if they were? What if nobody was anchored but everyone pretended to be? A panic arose within him and quickly reshaped itself as his old fear, this time scared of this new thought. What if nobody knew where they came from or where they were going? For the first time in many years he sensed that what was wrong with him might not be entirely his own fault, or capable of solution by him alone. But it was only a fleeting sensation that had passed almost as soon as he was aware of it.

'Why, you reckon?' asks the taxi driver, repeating his question, throwing his left arm about in a gesture of contempt. 'Why you reckon the rich are rich?'

'God knows,' says Aljaz finally.

'They're rich for the reason they're bad payers and mean as shit, that's why the rich are rich. Because they're arseholes.'

Aljaz turns and looks at the taxi driver, shrugs his shoulders and goes back to looking out the window. He wonders why he isn't rich if the only requirement is that he be an arsehole.

'I've had 'em all in this cab. All the big names. All mean as shit.' Aljaz continues looking at the houses and for no reason that he can name, bursts out laughing.

Maybe, thought Aljaz, just maybe everybody else was also on the road – from the beats through to the hippies to the yuppies to all the arsehole careerists of today, from me to the taxi driver, all of them and all of us seeking constant flight from our pasts, our families, and our places of birth. Even if we travelled in different standards of fashion and comfort. And maybe all the rest of them were as wrong as I was, thought Aljaz, and maybe it was time to walk off the road and head back into the bush whence we came.

At this point the Tasmanian tiger halted, her strange story complete. I feel dumbstruck. How could a bloody weird wolf know so much about me? About what I was thinking and feeling back then? But, as with everything else I have wanted to pursue since I first started having these visions, my mind is suddenly rushed off elsewhere before it is finished with the subject at hand. There is the sound of uproar, and the other animals, less enamoured of and interested in this story than me, are again becoming raucous, having broken into a supply of Harry's home-brewed stout that the oak skink has found. The black cockatoos are levering the bottle tops off with their big hooked beaks and it's on for one and all. With one of his powerful

225

purple-green pincers the freshwater lobster wrests the green-handled kitchen knife from the echidina, who had been hoping to speak, bangs it as if it were a gavel upon the table, and in spite of many of the animals paying not the slightest heed, proceeds to tell a second story.

Madonna santa! I don't believe this is happening – but I must stop thinking because the lobster is already into its story and I am no longer sure if it his story or my vision, and if I think any more I'll miss what he is telling the others.

— Harry, 1946 —

As they came down the river in the drizzle, Harry lay beneath the oilskins in the damp pungency of the Huon pine-planked bottom of the boat, the pain growing and growing until Harry had no existence beyond the pain. Anything else was just a small comma in his sentence of pain. With each pull of the oars the fire flared in the stump that had been his thumb and the flame consumed his hand and leapt up his arm. And every so often he would open his eyes and there would be the sea eagle, the same bird he had seen above Big Fall with the two tailfeathers missing. When Harry's eyes opened the bird would be staring down at them from a tree on the river-bank, and then it would fly off, only to be back when Harry next opened his eyes. Harry no longer knew if what he was seeing was real or a dream. He remembered Auntie Ellie telling him the story of a sea eagle plucking a baby out of a paddock up Port Sorell way, then flying out to sea with it, and how it had raised the baby in its nest on Three Hummock Island far out in the strait. She believed the story. Harry neither believed nor disbelieved, he simply listened. And remembered.

At Double Fall and Big Fall, they had to portage the punt around rapids, while Harry staggered alongside, wrapped in a shivering grey blanket. As they rounded into the Gordon River the rain began to bucket down and the river became curtained in low-lying mist that rose and fell and swept as if swirled by an invisible hand. The beginning of a fever gripped Harry, and the fire in his hand and arm sweetly warmed his entire body.

Harry drifted in and out of sleep. At one stage he pulled aside the blankets and oilskin that covered his head as well as his body and looked up at Old Bo and Smeggsy, each with an oar, Smeggsy on the right, Old Bo on the left. He looked at their legs, at their trousers, heavy with the wet, falling from their knees in folds, thickening out onto their boots. He looked at Smeggsy's thin hair, sitting wet and shiny black, flat upon his head. Old Bo wore a grubby green beanie that was covered with a white fur of water that looked like the mould upon an old lamb chop. He looked up at their stubbled, lined faces glistening with rain. The faces were unmoving, save for the occasional beads of water joining into a necklace of droplets that snaked down the grooves around their cheeks, and from there dripped onto their grey flannels. Their eyes were bright but empty, focused on some distant point to ensure they kept the correct line down the river. The rain spiked the river's surface. Harry fell back asleep and he dreamt that he was in a boat being rowed through the rainforest canopy by two ancient myrtle trees that bore the faces of Old Bo and Smeggsy.

They reached Sir John Falls late in the afternoon and went up to the old tourist hut where there was always kept a store of dry firewood. Old Bo lit a fire and made a billy of tea. They sat around and drank the tea in their chipped enamel mugs, drank it sweet and black, pondering whether to stop there the night. Harry said nothing. For one thing he was too much fevered; for another, in his few moments of lucidity, he felt it wrong to ask anything more of these men who would lose a week or so of work rowing to Strahan and then back up to their camp in the rainforest simply to help him. In the end he curled up like a dog in front of the fire in his blanket. He realised he was shaking bad, that his body was wildly convulsing and dripping sweat, while all the while his mind felt becalmed in the eye of the storm that had taken hold of him.

'The boy's buggered,' said Old Bo.

And that was that.

They walked back down to the punt, bailed out the rainwater, made Harry comfortable in the stern. The rain had for the time being ceased and the mist lifted. The sun sank before them as they rowed down the Gordon and Harry felt its final rays as a brief warm weight upon his eyes.

'Forty-five miles to go,' said Smeggsy.

'Piss it in before tea,' said Old Bo. They all laughed, even Harry, then no one spoke as the stillness of the night came upon them. Above him Harry watched the thin ribbon of stars shining, framed on either side by the rainforest. He fell asleep and again dreamt of being rowed by two myrtle trees, except this time they rowed through the stars to the moon, and it was quiet, and while everything went on forever the stars were as knowable and as safe and as comforting a world as that of the rainforested rivers.

They rowed past Butlers Island, past the Marble Cliffs, then for long silent hours down the long straights, past

Eagle Creek, past Limekiln Reach — where the barefooted starving convicts had once been stationed in the rainforest to burn lime — around Horseshoe Bend and out to the mouth of the river, where the river valley was swamped by the immensity of Macquarie Harbour. The moon had risen, a three-quarter moon that silvered the sky and sea, the flat sea, not a ripple upon it. They rowed to Sarah Island where the infamous convict settlement had been a century before, from where men had bolted only to have to resort to killing and eating each other in the bush, before they too died, their skeletons left to bleach and slime and entangle and entwine with the growing myrtle roots. They pulled into Sarah for a break. The moon was at its highest. The two men walked stiffly and awkwardly up to a small clearing in the blackberries used by local daytrippers. Harry slept on in the boat. Old Bo made the tea like a honeyed tar.

'Christ knows, I need something as bad as this to keep me going,' said the old man as he ladled the sugar into the billy.

'Twenty miles to go,' said Smeggsy, 'if we go direct.' Smeggsy wanted to cling to the shoreline lest a big sea blow up and swamp their small boat in the middle of the harbour, but it would extend their trip by another seven miles. Old Bo smelt the air and gazed at the stars.

'We go straight,' he said at last. 'No wind till mid-mornin'.' They drank the billy dry, then made another, and then another before their thirst was finally slaked. Smeggsy lay back on the earth and closed his eyes.

'I could sleep for a million years,' he said.

'Sleep as you row,' said Old Bo, kicking him in his side. 'For Chrissake, don't fall asleep here.' They stood up and pissed on the fire to put it out, and as their urine fell in a steaming arc they rubbed their hands in it, to make their hands tough yet supple for the rowing. Smeggsy's hands were pink with the loss of skin from the friction of the oar, and the urine smarted. He shivered. They walked without enthusiasm, with the gait of exhaustion, slow stumbly steps back to the punt.

Smeggsy closed his eyes now as he rowed and he wasn't sure if he was rowing, or whether he was simply dreaming he was rowing, so established had the dull pain of movement become to his body. Old Bo's eyes never closed. He kept the boat on its course across the inland sea to Strahan. Somewhere out in the middle of that sea, Old Bo began to tell stories, strange wonderful stories, and Smeggsy's eyes opened and as he listened he suddenly felt wide awake, so awake his mind left his body that rowed like a slow steam engine and entered the world of Old Bo's stories, a world where past, present and future seemed to collide and exist together.

– Harry, 1993 –

I can see Old Bo and I can see the freshwater lobster telling a new story, and at some point the two have merged so completely I am no longer sure whether a lobster is rowing the boat or Old Bo is telling the story. Then the punt they row disappears into the night light of Macquarie Harbour. All sight and sound of them is gone.

I thought I had a handle on this vision thing. At the beginning, watching myself being born – fine. Watching the early days of the river trip that led me to this mess – fine. Even watching what turns out to be my father losing his thumb whilst pining years before I was born – fine.

And I can understand seeing my childhood and all that business with Couta, but now I just feel myself getting more confused. Having drunk animals tell stories, personal stories, I ought add, about yourself and your family, then getting too drunk to continue – well, it's wrong. Visions ought be given you by some divine being, not bantered about by a mob of pissed marsupials and their mates. But these visions, they proceed as a series of abrupt images, being told to me by any number of people and animals, and the connection between one and the next is never stated or obvious, and now the visions all seem to be happening together, invading each other's worlds.

Which is perhaps why I am not surprised when Aljaz and the Cockroach and their party of punters fail to notice the hospital ward replete with heart monitors, drips, and stainless-steel tea trolleys that protrudes out of the rainforest and sits upon a beach, as though a modern hospital ward is as much a part of the river rainforest as a myrtle or a sassafras. Why nobody on either raft waves to Harry, who lies there upon the hospital bed. They just paddle on.

A nurse enters the ward from a copse of manferns.

'Your wrist, Mr Lewis?'

Harry looks up in surprise, his pleasure in watching and smelling and listening to the Franklin River in flood broken by the question.

'Your wrist,' she repeats. Harry looks up at her young face, upon which a smile briefly glimmers outward like the rings around a stone falling into water and then is lost, as she places a thermometer under his tongue. She finishes taking his pulse and wraps the blood pressure tourniquet around the slack, wrinkled skin of his arm. Harry feels embarrassment at the young nurse looking at such flaccid skin wrinkling over the withered waste of his arm, when once the arm had been strong, its strength evident in its taut suppleness, the forearm and bicep revealing individual muscles pulling up and down with the slightest move of his hand. Now – and the thought leaves him weary beyond despair – now it is the arm of an old man, soon to die. He feels the need to say something in explanation.

'Life is the cruellest of boxers,' he says.

Again the brief, glimmering smile. 'Yes, Mr Lewis.'

Harry continues to try and explain what it is that she ought know, almost a warning to her of her own mortality, of the fallibility of all flesh, even her most beautiful of flesh. While she knows from her work that all people are mortal, her youth prevents her from realising – beyond as an abstract, academic point – that this great truth also applies to her. 'Yes, it is,' he says. 'It gets you in a corner as you grow old, on the ropes, and there is no referee to call a halt. And it hits you and it hits you again and again. And when you slump there is no referee to say enough is enough. There is no referee to say you shouldn't kick a fella in the guts and in the head when he's down. But that's how it is. Life just keeps kicking you until there's nothing left to kick.' The nurse looks down at him as she unstraps the tourniquet, and pulls her mouth back in mild frustration.

Harry sees the great mountain ranges creasing around the river, wrapping around him, sees the rainforest, sees the river rising, feels the moist heaviness of the air upon his face, smells the scent of peat.

'Don't cry, Mr Lewis,' she says. 'Please don't cry.' She is about to say that it can't be as bad as all that, but her medical knowledge tells her that it is. She feels warm breath upon her back and turns to see Dr Elliot, the young registrar in whom she is more than passingly interested. Dr Elliot has overheard the conversation. He takes the nurse aside and whispers to her under a large myrtle tree.

'I think we might up Mr Lewis's morphine. He seems in a great deal of pain.' And then, 'Friday night – that new Thai restaurant in Barracouta Row.' She smiles her agreement.

Harry envies the young nurse and the young doctor their sexual communication, the way their flesh is so alive it has a life separate and independent of their minds, to the extent that small movements contain messages that are read by the other body in a rising excitement that can only be sated by their coupling. He might have even hated them for their sexual vibrancy, but he was as beyond hating for such reasons as he was now beyond loving.

Harry relapses into his solitary world of pain. He had never imagined old age would be like this, but then he had never really imagined what old age would be like. To the extent that he had talked about it in the past and had reflected upon the condition of those he knew who were old, he had presumed there would be some pleasures to be had, that he would feel satisfaction at having achieved some things of which he was proud. But on his deathbed he can only despair of so little achieved, of so many opportunities for friendship and love missed and dissolved in the minute trivia of daily living, and his final time approaches not as an autumn but with the sharp and fearful damp coldness of a mist rising on a winter's nightfall. He feels alone, terribly alone. Life seems to him to be the promise of pleasures unfulfilled. He looks upon what he knows of the world and finds it sad, sad, sad, and no longer has the confidence of youth to declare that the world can be remade better and kinder. There seems to be too little love and too much hate. He feels naked and the world and his life his own to wander through for a few short moments that stretch to infinity. In both he sees only desolation. There is nothing to look forward to, little to look back upon. He thinks what he would do if he had his life again, then thinks that he has no desire to have it again, that once was too hard and has worn him out so utterly that he wonders if he will even have the energy to die. He feels only an overbearing tiredness, which in the end eclipses even his capacity to think, and then, after that, his desire to dream.

And at that moment he sees his long-dead uncles Basil and George walking toward him. 'Get the load off your feet, Nugget,' says George. He sees his mother Rose coming toward him, a very powerful feeling it is, and she says, 'I love you.' He sees the river advance toward him. But it is no river he recognises. He sees two large old stringybark gums burst into flower in the middle of a blizzard, and as they do so, a miracle take place. The trees stretch and unravel toward the sky, unfolding into blossom, and as more of the cream-coloured flowers appear, the gum trees begin to float and then soar into the heavens. He sees Old Bo and Smeggsy, and Old Bo says, 'Carry the boy gentle, Smeggsy.' Harry opens his eyes.

But he is no longer in his hospital bed.

– Ned Quade, 1832 –

He is in a punt being rowed by a freshwater lobster talking with Old Bo's voice. They have just emerged from

234

a bank of gentle, fleecelike snowclouds when he spies far, far below the airborne punt a solitary figure upon a remote alpine moor. Old Bo the lobster is yakking away.

Saying: At the end only Ned Quade the stone man and Aaron Hersey remained. The others had passed on in the manner they had agreed upon before the escape, such desperate measures accepted as the corollary of the world they were fleeing. When it came to the moment of truth, only a badly fevered Jack Jenkins had not fought it, asking for half an hour alone to make his peace with the Lord. None quibbled that the alternative of returning was preferable. Aaron Hersey and the stone man sat around their campfire, gaunt-faced with exhaustion and terror, knowing whoever fell asleep first would only momentarily reawaken before being committed to that ultimate rest beneath the vast gorge of the southern night sky. In the event, it was the stone man whose eyes closed first. He rocked back and forth where he sat and his eyelids closed though the rocking continued. Aaron Hersey eyed him nervously, knowing this might be some trap. But after some minutes it was clear that the stone man was asleep, perhaps somehow thinking in the back of his mind that because he was still sitting upright and still rocking that therefore he must still be awake. He was not. But the moment that Aaron Hersey went to kill Ned Quade more or less as they had killed their three fellow escapees, cleaving his head open like a blighted turnip with the axe they carried, the stone man's eyes fluttered open. They eyed each other off, the stone man sitting, Aaron Hersey standing in front of him with the axe poised to fall.

'I seen some things,' said Aaron Hersey, not moving, axe held high.

The stone man said nothing.

'Seen barefoot men chained to a plough in place of

oxen. Seen a woman in Hobart made wear a spiked iron collar and her head shaved for lying with another woman, raped by redcoats and lags alike. Seen a native woman with child shot down like a bird from the tree in which she hid. I even seen a boy buggered by an entire chain gang, the constable holding him down.'

The stone man said nothing.

'Bad things mostly,' continued Aaron Hersey. 'Don't remember being bad myself before being sent out here. Maybe I was. Maybe it was always there and just needed this for it to come out. Don't remember exactly why I was transported any more. But they must have had their good reasons for doing it to me. Maybe not even a good reason but a bad reason. But there must have been a reason. There would have been. That I know for sure.'

The stone man's eyes were rheumy with tiredness.

'So many bad things,' said Aaron Hersey, 'that have been my punishment, and me a part of them bad things. Which is why it is right I have been punished and why it is right because there was this reason.'

'Reason,' said the stone man, 'is the evil fruit of the Tree of Knowledge.'

Then, with a movement both rapid and violent, the stone man lunged at the legs of Aaron Hersey and toppled him face first into the coals of the fire. Hersey screamed and rolled out of the fire, but not before the stone man had wrenched the axe from him and with it struck a fiercesome blow to the head.

The grey milky matter of Hersey's brain flowed forth and formed a gritty gruel with the dead coals at the edge of the fire. The stone man finished Aaron Hersey off by hacking through his neck. It takes a lot to kill a man though. Hersey did not fight, yet nor was it straight away

that he stopped breathing, and his breath and blood guttered through the rent in his neck for some moments,
steaming and hissing as it splashed the coals below. Then
Ned Quade stood up and looked into the speckled darkness and he felt beyond fear and beyond weariness, and
felt all the wretchedness of this earth arise within him and
he wished it he and not Hersey who had died so.

He stripped the corpse and hung it upside down from a
tree by its trousers to let it bleed. While it so hung, Ned
Quade cut it open and disembowelled the body. He built
the fire back up and upon it grilled the heart and the liver,
but such was his hunger that he ate them before they were
properly cooked. He travelled with renewed energy all that
following day and the day after that, carefully rationing out
Hersey's limbs to last him until he reached the New
Jerusalem. Upon a huge button-grass plain thick with black
wallaby turds he came across a mob of natives and he raised
the stick upon which he now hobbled and made as if it were
a musket and he about to fire upon them. He was not so
distant from his fellow countrymen that they did not understand the meaning of his gesture and they ran away, dropping
a possum carcass in their haste. This he took with him and
continued on, back into rainforest, in the reaches of which
he grew so dispirited that when he passed out of it, back
into the higher country, he stopped next to a King Billy pine
tree in which he prepared to hang himself by his leather belt.
The mood passed, and after two days he arose from where
he lay beneath the tree and staggered off. Ned Quade continued to hope that he would find the coast and there a boat
in which to get away from Van Diemen's Land to New South
Wales and from there make his way to the New Jerusalem.

Did he die? I wonder. Or did he, somewhere out there
in his delusion, in the middle of that river, did he find

the stockaded town of his dreams? Whether it was when an Aboriginal spear pierced his heart that he saw it rise up in front of him, or when he lay exhausted in the scrub, still alive but with the insects already eating him, his tongue as hard and dry and cracked as a convict's clog in his mouth, whether it was then that he heard the clamour of free voices making merry and saw Mother Lucky arrive and press water to his lips and take him to the New Jerusalem, I do not know and I have not yet been shown. But perhaps somewhere out there he saw freedom and its cost. Perhaps there is to be found somewhere between here and China the remnants of a stockaded town in which some records exist that show Ned Quade to have been, if not mayor of Parramatta, then at least an important underling to Mother Lucky. And I wonder, Who are these people, these poor people I see live and die, whose lives are so wretched that they feel death in this manner preferable to living, who see death in this manner redemption itself? And dreaming begins to reassert its power over thinking, and once more I see Ned Quade lying in a wilderness, his clothes rags, his ankles festering wounds, the iron collars enclosed in new and thicker collars of flies eating his suppurating flesh, their maggots being born in what is left of his emaciated body. And Ned Quade hears a drumming, a martial drumming, announcing an imminent and important arrival. The drumming grows louder and more insistent.

The stone man has lain for two days without movement. He knows now he is dying. For when he looks up from where he has lain on the bank of a rain-swollen river which is too deep and swift to ford, at the base of a ravine too great to scale back up, he sees a wooden punt being rowed through the evening sky by a ghost and a lobster, and a spectre peers out from the stern and stares down at him as if he knows him. The punt is coming toward him.

From far above Harry watches the stone man as he dies.

'Pay no heed,' says Old Bo, 'that's just the ghost of an old lag you're seeing.'

'A phantom,' says Smeggsy.

Harry looks back up and over to where I am floating in the night sky next to the punt. We go to talk but the clouds envelop us both and we are again, as always, lost to each other.

'A real deadflog,' I hear Smeggsy say.

'A right flogger,' I hear Old Bo reply.

'A rum 'un,' I hear Harry retort.

Harry shrugs his shoulders and looks back earthwards at the dying stone man.

— Aljaz, 1993 —

I hear a distant retching sound as the oak skink throws up. In the faraway apricot-coloured clouds of late afternoon I can just make out a punt disappearing over Mt Wellington, and behind it two tables of animals, now mostly sodden or singing or feuding, save for a few of the black cockatoos and the goanna who are playing cards.

And at the head of Barracouta Row, looking down the narrow street at its humble houses, I spy Aljaz. The street still smelt of the old wharf and its poverty, but it was changing. There was an antique shop at one end and a Thai restaurant at the other. But the family home looked much as it always had done – a dilapidated wooden house with a verandah that sat almost upon the street, so small was the front yard. Nevertheless there was still a front garden. Harry's front garden precisely outlined the contours of his heart. It was a wilderness of weeds and a few plants that had been there even before he and Sonja had moved in. And in the middle was the most beautiful and large rose bush, wild, overgrown, and sagging with heavy crimson roses.

Aljaz knocked on the weather-beaten front door, though he knew that with Harry in hospital there would be no answer. He wandered down the side lane to the little backyard, and there it stood, Harry's great creation, Harry's barbeque.

Where the house was humble, the barbeque was magnificent, a giant edifice of brick, broken glass and beer cans set in concrete and terracotta piping, with terrazzo slabs for meat and salads and drinks and whatever else needed somewhere to rest. It stood three metres high and at least as long. At its centre was a wood-fired grill, but the barbeque encompassed many more functions than that of simply grilling meat, encompassed functions of a diverse culinary, spiritual and historical nature. It drew upon the old Australia Harry had grown up in and the old Europe Sonja had grown up in, combining something of the elements of bush building with southern European shrines and gravestones. Sitting out to one side at head height was an old clothes dryer, repainted in sky-blue, gutted of its innards and now used as a dry-smoking cupboard, connected by galvanised piping to an old firebox at the base of the barbeque. Into the firebox would be placed she-oak or myrtle and a slow fire started, while in the smoker dryer would be placed kangaroo and trout and salmon and trevally and trumpeter and eels and wallaby and pork salamis, and out would emerge the most delectable smoked meats. Hanging from hooks screwed into the barbeque's rear wall at different levels were green and pink plastic Décor pots in which red flowering geraniums and pink flowering pelargoniums and cacti of all colours flourished and hung in festoons. At the heart of the barbeque, immediately below the grill, was an oven formed out of a kerosene tin set in adobe. Beneath the dry mud-insulated oven was an alcove, replete with ducting for the smoke, in which a fire would be built to heat the oven from which emerged Harry's bread, large round loaves broader than a man's chest, made in the same manner he had learnt from Boy all those years ago. Next to the oven was a smaller alcove lined with green cider bottles laid sideways, in which Harry put his dough to rise and Sonja left her pots of milk to sour into yoghurt. Set into the brickwork behind the grill were the purple pearly abalone shells gathered by Harry in his years as a fisherman's deckhand, the work which he had taken up upon returning to Australia. The shells were arranged in a circle, in the middle of which were two three-inch nails driven into the mortar. Hanging from one nail was a pair of barbeque tongs and from the other a sea eagle's skull that Harry had found many years before, small and delicately shaped. The various ducts rose to the top of the barbeque, where their smoky breath was released into broken terracotta pipes that ascended the rear wall at various heights, giving the barbeque the appearance of some crazed Baroque premonition of a Wurlitzer organ.

Aljaz smiled.

And there, sitting to the side of Harry's barbeque, in Harry's favourite chair, an ancient metal tractor seat mounted upon a ball joint on a steel pole, there she was. She had changed a little in the years they had not seen one another. Her hair had gone from grey to white, and she had exchanged the widow's weeds of old Europe – the black dress and black cardigan – for the widow's weeds of new Australia – a shiny green and purple tracksuit, complete with white lightning stripes and the words ACTION AEROBICS. While one hand rested upon her glossy tracksuit pants, the other placed a half-smoked cigar in her mouth.

'The last cigar?' asked Aljaz.

The tractor seat creaked as the ball joint swivelled slowly while she turned. She looked at Aljaz as though she had been expecting him for some time.

'No,' said Maria Magdalena Svevo. And then Aljaz knew for sure that he was too late.

At the funeral parlour they took Aljaz to see his father's body. 'We encourage people to look at the body of the loved one,' said the undertaker. 'It helps with the grieving process.' What grieving process? thought Aljaz. Is what I am feeling a process? It struck him as the most curious thought, that his feelings might be some sort of emotional locomotive, calling at all stops between the departure point of death and the destination of – well, whatever the destination was meant to be. Happiness, perhaps. Whatever that meant. Calling at all stops – guilt, anger, remorse, reconciliation. He looked at the vases of flowers on little stands, at the cheap prints of waves and sunsets that even department stores had stopped selling, the overall décor stuck somewhere in the early seventies, all yellow floral wallpaper and vinyl furniture. He looked at the burnished and stained wood walls of the coffin, at its elaborate shiny brass handles, at the studded plush velvet of its interior. It seemed a waste, all that work, all that elaboration and decoration, whose only destination was the wet earth. He wondered if they still made the coffins in the workshop out the back of this mock lounge room, or if the undertaker bought them in pre-made, perhaps imported from Asia. Probably pre-made, thought Aljaz, as he ran his fingers along the edges of the coffin. It ought be Huon pine, he thought. Now that would have been appropriate. But then he thought how Harry would have hated that, would have thought it a stupid waste of fine timber. Bury me in plywood, Harry would have said. He should have talked to Harry about such things, thought Aljaz. He should have come back and talked, full stop. There was so much unsaid, too much undone. Aljaz's eyes retreated to the handles, which he fingered, feeling their weight, watching the perspiration of his hands mark the immaculate brass. Then he took an involuntary and audible deep breath, a shudder of a breath, and raised his head and looked back into the coffin, at what lay between the stained and burnished wood, at what was cushioned by the studded plush velvet. What grieving process? thought Aljaz. Could that be him? Could that be him?

Aljaz looked up from his father's body.

'But I am not grieving,' he said in reply to the undertaker. Grief, as Aljaz knew it, bore no relation to this terrible vortex of emptiness into which his body and soul had collapsed. The undertaker, who was younger than Aljaz, smiled slightly, then remembered himself and stopped. No one had yet taught him the proper response to such a statement.

Back out on the street Aljaz felt without will or capacity to move. He lacked the sense to even decide which direction to walk. He saw a newsagent across the road and went into it, though why he did not know. Inside the newsagent he just stood, not moving, not picking up magazines or putting them down, just standing. He realised people were beginning to look at him. He stared down at the magazine rack but saw nothing. 'Excuse me, sir,' said a woman behind the counter, 'can I help you?'

'My father's dead,' said Aljaz before he knew he had spoken. The woman looked at him as if he were mad. 'He died. Last Friday, he died. Bowel cancer.' There seemed to be a need to verify what he had told her. 'They've got him in a box,' said Aljaz. The woman looked around for help. He pointed a finger in the direction of the rushing cars outside. 'Across the road. A box. A bloody box.' Aljaz knew he was crying and that everyone in the shop was staring at him. He stood as still as a statue, not because he was nervous or apprehensive but because he had no energy or will to do anything other. 'Is that a life?' He moved his head around and looked at everyone, their magazines and papers dropped to their waists, staring at him as if in a nightmare, this ring of staring, uncomprehending people, and all of a sudden he was frightened, so terribly frightened. 'Dad,' he said as he cried, and he raised his head up high and looked hither and thither for the familiar smell and sight of a giant parent, and then, in the manner of a child who has become separated from his parent and is fearful of ever seeing him or her again, he spoke again, his voice this time a cracking pant. 'Da-d?' and then, '*Dad?*' There was no answer. He dropped his face into his hands and shook his prayer of loss into his cupped splayed fingers, and now the word came out as a lament. He said the word five times and each time it came out of his mouth in a voice so thin and stretched and weak and aching it seemed to have travelled a million miles and a million years to be heard. Then he raised his face from his hands and, his face still shaking, he surveyed the newsagency and saw that everyone in the ring was quiet and watching him and his quivering head and crazed eyes. Then he turned and, still trembling, walked out.

Back home, Maria Magdalena Svevo looked tired and old. She seemed to have shrivelled in the years he had been away. Her wrinkled face reminded Aljaz of a dried apricot. Never tall, she now seemed tiny, most of her feisty bulk having disappeared along with something of her spirit. She had always been hard, and now the hardness was like flint. They sat inside the old family home, amidst its dust and smells so sweet and evocative that every draught brought a rush of memories to Aljaz. It was all much as he had remembered it, except even more beaten up and broken, the carpet even greyer.

Once the house had sparkled. All its humble accoutrements, second-hand, or the unwanted property of others given away, had glistened like well-fed cats and the house had looked as if it were loved. Most items in the house were patched, but patched and mended so thoroughly that they came to possess a quality that things merely purchased from a shop could only pretend to, qualities of authenticity, of age, and of character derived from having been remade first in the imagination of Sonja and Harry and then remade by them in the real world. There was the chair with new bracing, the saucepan with a carved wooden handle replacing its broken plastic handle, the old power hacksaw blade honed into a knife blade to replace the broken kitchen knife. Then Sonja died. Then Harry's heart broke.

Then when the arms of his favourite vinyl armchair began to split, Harry did not strip the vinyl off and reupholster it with some offcut material bought cheap from a warehouse as he formerly would have done. He did nothing until the splits were so bad that the stiff maroon vinyl, curling upright in sharp shards, began to irritate his resting foreams when he sat there drinking, too lost to even bother to turn on the TV. Then he went outside to the shed, found some electrical tape and taped the splits up. When the electrical tape in turn began to stretch and curl he simply ran more and more over the top of the old. And as it was for that armchair, so it was for the rest of the house. Repairs became unnecessarily destructive. He liquid nailed a rattling window so that it no longer opened; fixed the loose fridge door by putting two self-tapping screws into the fridge, one in its door, the other in its side wall, then making a rough hook latch with a piece of coathangar wire to connect the two. So it went. Apart from his weekly barbeques for phantoms, nothing could animate Harry.

Aljaz found some Turkish coffee in the freezer and made a pot of *turksa kava* for them both. He brought the pot and two demitasse cups into the lounge-room where Maria Magdalena Svevo sat slumped in the old maroon vinyl armchair, the arms of which were a tapestry of criss-crossing red and yellow and green electrical tape rising like humps on a camel's back. When Aljaz entered the dark lounge-room he was shocked because there seemed to be no person sitting in the armchair, only a lurid purple and green tracksuit that looked as if it had been tossed there. Not until an arm moved and a lighter flared was her face and its inevitable accompaniment, a cigar, illuminated. For a moment he thought some spectre was animating the tracksuit.

'What are you staring at, Ali?' she asked, the rasp of her voice emphasising the heavy accent she still carried.

'Sorry,' said Aljaz. 'Just getting used to the light.'

He poured the coffee and passed her a cup. She took the cigar out of her mouth and laughed. 'You know, it's a funny thing . . . ' and she paused and sat up and took a sip of the *turksa kava*, then put the cup down and took another draw on the cigar. 'Your father, he was a true-blue Aussie and he only ever drank *turksa kava*. He learned that from us. But your mama, she couldn't be bothered with it. She drank Nescafé.' She smiled. 'She learned that from Harry. She said the *turksa kava* was too much trouble. She said the Nescafé was easier.' Now it was Aljaz's turn to smile. But he didn't say anything. He sipped his *turksa kava*. He sensed that she wanted to say something more. Maria Magdalena Svevo continued. 'They were good people. Who else would sponsor me out as an immigrant, then let me live with them here all those years?' She suddenly yanked the cigar out of her mouth, brushed her tongue with the back of her hand, and stubbed the cigar out in an ashtray. 'Agh! Even the smoke tastes bad tonight.'

Aljaz looked across at the old woman and realised he could trust her, an emotion he experienced rarely. 'There are a lot of things I wished I had talked to him about,' said Aljaz.

'There always are,' said Maria Magdalena Svevo.

'If he could talk he might tell me what I should do now,' said Aljaz.

'There is no wisdom in the grave, Ali. None.' Maria Magdalena Svevo looked at him and wondered. And then spoke again. 'I wonder whether it is my place to tell you things that your father should have told you when he was still alive. And I think, If I don't, who will?' And so she told him, though only in the briefest way, the story of how Sonja had fled from Yugoslavia to Italy in the early 1950s, how she had met Harry in Trieste, and how Harry had shortly afterwards been imprisoned for smuggling by the Italian authorities after his partner turned informer. Harry did two years before being released. Aljaz, conceived in the short time between Harry and Sonja's initial meeting and Harry's imprisonment, took his mother's name of Cosini. What was initially a source of shame for Sonja – not being married, her child a bastard – later became her greatest pride. There was a perverse streak in her character, and though she permitted Harry to sponsor her as an immigrant to Australia in 1958 with the toddler Aljaz, and though she consented to live with Harry, she refused his entreaties to marry, saying that it was all too late, and now that she had borne the shame Aljaz could carry her old family name in the new world with pride.

And at this point in the story Maria Magdalena Svevo broke down.

Aljaz attempted to take the conversation into less troubled waters. 'See we've got new neighbours.'

'Ja, the Maloneys,' said Maria Magdalena Svevo, 'an Aboriginal family.'

'They were all out the front drunk when I came home,' said Aljaz with no particular rancour, then paused. Maria Magdalena Svevo looked up, then looked back down at her runners. Aljaz felt unbelievably tired. He continued talking for the sake of saying something. He felt angry, he didn't know why. He wanted to talk about his father, but something seemed to have come between them that wouldn't permit talk about Harry. He continued talking in the way that men on the farms and on the building sites had talked when they hadn't wanted to think, when they had talked enough about car engines and footy and cricket and had to talk about something without betraying what they felt or thought. He thought of Harry, how he wanted to see him just once more, wanted to talk to him once more. Wanted to ask him how had the world grown to be this way, so hard. He was angry that Harry had been unable to warn him. But he heard himself saying, for want of having anything to say, heard himself saying, 'Bloody Abos, eh.'

Maria Magdalena Svevo looked up again. 'You know what an Aborigine looks like?' she asked.

Aljaz realised he had upset the old woman. He backtracked. 'I'm sure they're all right.' He stopped. She said nothing and waited for him to finish. 'You know what I mean.'

Maria Magdalena Svevo's reply was some time in coming. 'No. I mean a real Aborigine. A dinky-di Aborigine.'

'Well, I spose . . . sure.'

'Harry never told you that either?'

'Told me what? What is there to tell? Everyone knows. You know, I know.'

'No. No, you don't know.' Her scrawny hands, so wasted and withered they looked like birds' talons, dug into the electrical-tape tapestry of the armchair's arms; her desperately thin arms tensed and she pulled herself into a standing position. She picked up her cigar and her stainless-steel Zippo lighter and relit the cigar, inhaled, then looked at Aljaz with a great, intense curiosity. 'Do you?'

'What are you talking about, Maria?'

But her back was to him and she was walking out of

249

the room. Aljaz was reading a K-Mart catalogue when she came back in. 'Here,' she said, 'look here.' Aljaz looked up from the catalogue. Clutched in her bird talons Maria Magdalena Svevo held before him Harry's shaving mirror, which had been cracked for as long as Aljaz could remember. In it, he saw his sallow face reflected, the hairline crack neatly bisecting his image. She held it for as long as he could bear to look into it, and then longer.

Saying: 'This is an Abo.'

— the fourth day —

Quiet.

Then the crash of scrub breaking and suddenly I see, half shoving, half falling out of the mirror into a mass of tea-tree, Aljaz and the Cockroach looking about for a route through the dense riverbank bush, scrub-bashing their way downriver to scout a rapid before shooting it in their rafts.

When they get near the rapid, the bank turns into a cliff and they have to swim down the side of the cliff hanging onto low-lying branches to avoid being swept downriver. Close to the rapids the cliff ends and they are able to climb back onto land and find a vantage point high enough to check the rapid. It is big, frighteningly big, nothing like the straightforward rapid it is at lower levels. They work out a line through the rapid to avoid the two major stoppers. Then they return by a long circuitous route behind the cliff to their punters who have waited in the rafts that are moored to the bank. Aljaz's body feels more comfortable, more in control, once he is back sitting on the rear pontoon of his raft.

'All right,' says the Cockroach, addressing the punters of both rafts, 'there is one line down this rapid, and if we mess it we're in big shit. So when Ali and I tell you to do something, do it, or we're all fucked. We're not playing around any more. This is serious.' The punters are uneasy. Up until today their river guides had seemed invincible, frightened of nothing, and it reassured the punters greatly. But this new river, these furious, confused waters that live in a wet and cold climate so dissimilar to their first balmy days on the river, this new river frightens the punters, and now, it is apparent, it also worries the guides.

Aljaz senses the unease. He tries to soften the Cockroach's message without lessening its import. 'Unfortunately we have hit the river in a bad way,' he says, 'and we just have to make sure we somehow get down and through this thing safely.'

When the rain comes no one comments, for it is expected and the depression at its arrival has already been met. At first the rain is light and occasional, then heavier and heavier, till it drums on the taut red hypalon of the rafts' inflated pontoons, till it runs in rills down all their faces, extinguishes what little conversation there is between the punters as it smashes down on the river. And beneath the rubber flooring of the raft both the Cockroach and Aljaz can feel the river halting its fall and beginning to rise. They feel the river rise in the way their rafts run, in the way they glide quicker on the flat, in the way little boils appear from nowhere, in the way the waves begin to crest over the top of the raft's pontoons, in the way eddies become more pronounced and powerful. They feel it in their arms, in the way their paddles grab harder onto stronger water and pull their forearms and shoulders. Aljaz feels it in his disrupted memories as they arrive at landmarks too quickly – first the Brook of Inverestra and then almost immediately Side Slip, and then they are in Inception Reach and they all feel it in their guts as a loosening unease. Once, not so long ago, none of the river's features had names, and Aljaz could not help but remember his early trips down the Franklin as a youth in the 1970s, when they experienced each day as a surprise, when people remembered the river as a whole, not as a collection of named sites that could be reduced to a series of photographs. But that was when the Franklin was unknown, when it was the province of only a handful who were interested in it for its own sake. Then the developers came to dam it and then the conservationists came to save it and word of this strange and beautiful river spread throughout the country. A great battle arose and ultimately the conservationists won. Part of their winning had been to name all the river's features, to render them citable and documentable by those who would never know them, and in that process of splitting the whole into little bits with silly names, Aljaz felt something of the river's soul had been stolen away. Aljaz hated all the hippie names – the Masterpiece, Ganymedes Pool, Serenity Sound. But most of all he hated that while they had done something, he had done nothing.

He could not help but remember how he had explored other rivers of the west, then watched them drown without helping them. He watched the Murchison River drown and he watched the Mackintosh River drown and he watched the Pieman River drown. He drove all the long way from Hobart by himself to watch the rivers begin to disappear on the first day the new hydro dams began to fill. Watched them begin to fill and their great gorges disappear and die and he cried and he drove all the long way back to Hobart and he did nothing. His was a memory of defeat only, and the most he felt capable of was bearing witness. So he watched, so he cried, so he tatooed all the blue and red feelings that arose within him upon his soul. I will remember, he thought as he drove all the long way home. But to what end?

Then there was the Blockade, the battle to save the Franklin. He had walked into the greenie camp at Strahan, intending to join the blockaders. A woman with a smile as wide as those once stitched onto the faces of rag clowns, a woman he did not know, came up and hugged him. He walked out of the camp. Thinking, These are not my people. These are not my people. He did nothing.

The rapids grow larger and run longer. What is a hundred-metre rapid in low water now runs three times that length. Too high, thinks Aljaz, too high.

And around them the hills begin to turn into mountains as the gorge begins to bank up around them, like a wave picking up height and power the closer it moves to shore.

Deception Gorge, thinks Aljaz. And he laughs. And then stops laughing.

Thinking: *Too high, too high.*

Aljaz walked the streets of Hobart aimlessly, wandering through the old town's streets, past its small stolid buildings of the state which were without ambition but retained a dour intent, past its dingy shops more akin in their emaciated displays to the shops of Eastern Europe before the wall came down than to those luxurious displays of the mainland. The whole town was poor, desperately poor, and he saw it in the eyes of the tracksuited hordes that walked by him and he smelt it rising from the gutters.

He tried not to look at his reflection in shop windows. It means nothing at all, he thought, remembering what Maria Magdalena Svevo had told him, because I'm nothing. It's just an *idea*.

It means nothing. And on he walked.

Aljaz walked and walked. Finally he stopped, looked up from the pavement and there it was. Without intending it, without even desiring it, his feet had finally brought him back to the home of Couta Ho for a second time since his return. He stood at the gate and stared up at the doorway. The paint – that he had painted one hot long-ago summer – was now peeling away in big blisters from the weatherboards. It had been a prosperous burgher's house once. It probably wasn't even so bad when old Reggie Ho had bought it. Now it was dilapidated. Would he go in or wouldn't he? For a second time he turned and walked away.

His guts felt bad again. He felt like a drink real bad and he had in his pocket a flask of rum that he had bought earlier in the day, after visiting the undertaker. But he did not open it. He did not. He walked on.

So I watch Aljaz continuing to roam the streets of Hobart, seemingly without purpose, yet his feet follow a path that his eyes and mind are blind to but that is known to his soul. So I can see that it was not coincidence, though it must have seemed entirely that way – indeed, I can truly say that it felt entirely that way – that after a great deal more walking, walking that took him through not only much of Hobart but also through that afternoon and much of that evening, Aljaz found himself standing outside a pub, wondering whether or not to go inside, nervously fingering a still unopened rum flask in his pocket.

Inside, he thinks, there will be the unavoidable problem of being recognised, of having to explain the last eight years. And he isn't drunk enough for that. He looks up at the colonial brickwork of the old pub, now painted Irish green, and remembers the story Harry had told him about William Lanne – King Billy Lanne – the so-called last of the so-called full-blood Tasmanian Aborigines, a whaling man who worked the southern seas upon the *Runnymede*, who had died on the top storey of the pub in 1869. When his body had been taken to the hospital, a local surgeon by the name of Crowther snuck in and cut Lanne's neck up its nape and pulled his skull out and placed a white pauper's skull in its place, then crudely stitched the mess back together. Later in the same evening another doctor, Stokell, turned up with the same aim, only to find to his dismay that he had been beaten, so he contented himself with chopping off and stealing Lanne's feet and hands for the Royal Society. The skull brought the surgeon scientific credibility, for there was much interest in Europe in the phrenology of supposed inferior and degenerate peoples. When very drunk, Harry would sometimes sing a song that swept the Hobart pubs at the time:

King Billy's dead, Crowther has his head,
Stokell his hands and feet.
My feet, my poor black feet,
That used to be so gritty,
They're not aboard the Runnymede
They're somewhere in this city.

Now Aljaz knew why Harry had sung it.
Will he go in or won't he? The pub is old and decrepit

and still witnessing knife fights and broken-bottle battles. Upon its walls had once been pasted Governor Denison's proclamation of 1848 forbidding fiddling and dancing because of their subversive nature. Will he go in or won't he?

And then before he could decide, before he could weigh up the pros and cons, he was stepping up through the narrow doorway, pushing past fat women in black mini-skirts and skinny men in large leather jackets. No one recognised him and Aljaz laughed at his own absurd vanity in thinking anyone any longer would. Through the shifting, steaming jackets, and past gloomy coats that leant to try and hear what they cared nothing to hear, past the eyes making all sort of motions but in which it was impossible to read anything, past the slack wet lips mouthing betrayals and the dancing dry lips, cigarette chapped, shaping inanities, beyond the smoking shuffling bar crowd jostling so close they rubbed shoulders and backs and buttocks but still managed to preserve their individual cell-hells of isolation – beyond all that, shattering the darkness, were shards of light in which a band could be discerned, sweating and playing, and no one seemed to care enough to listen. The lead singer was balding and had a paunch, the lead guitarist older and fatter with a mane of lank red hair. Behind them was draped a tatty Aboriginal flag. The lead singer introduced their next song. 'This is about Shag's sister who just left Tassie.' Shag, Aljaz surmised from the direction in which the lead singer waved a beer that rolled in small waves back and forth between the walls of its glass until it inevitably spilt upon his hand, was the lead guitarist. 'Why she leave, Shag?'

Shag stepped up to the microphone, looked over

towards the lead singer, smiled, coughed a ball of static, and said, 'Because she reckoned Tassie a shithole.' And as abruptly as the smile had appeared on his face, it departed. 'Because,' said Shag, 'she reckoned there was no hope here.' When Aljaz heard the sound that then screeched forth from Shag's guitar he knew what Shag was playing upon that guitar, knew that fat old man wanted to make those strings scream: *If you leave you can never be free.*

It was a dreadful noise, but there was something in it that even then I recognised. Now I know it was not a new song, but a song I had unknowingly carried within me for a long long time. But what was it? Once more I hear the lead singer, shouting, screaming, joining Shag's guitar. Even back there in the bar Aljaz felt compelled to watch the singer's hands, outstretched as if he were being electrocuted, watch the fat of his face wobble and his forehead sweat and the few thin streaks of hairs that crossed it grow wet with exertion. He screamed it out until he looked worse than some animal in agony. He was no longer singing for the crowd or for the lousy money those behind the ringing till would give the band at the end of the night. Nobody in that bar knew, but I know it now. That he was not even singing for himself. That he was singing out of himself and out of his soul and out of a memory of loss so big and so deep and so hurting that it could not be seen or described but only screamed about.

Away from the crowd, hearing his screams and shrieks here in my oppressive solitude, my mind fills with a vision of when the English first arrived and the land was fat and full of trees and game. Had the loss begun at this time? When the English first saw plains so thickly speckled with emu and wallaby dung that it looked as if the heavens must have hailed sleek black turds upon this land, when they first saw the sea and the vast blue Derwent River rainbowed with the vapoury spouts of pods of whales and schools of dolphins swimming beneath. From that time on, each succeeding generation found something new they could quarry to survive. First the emu disappeared, then the tigers, then the many different fishes and seals and whales and their rainbows became rare, then the rivers were stilled under dams, then the trees, and then the scallops and the abalone and the crayfish became few and were in consequence no longer the food of the poor but the waste of the rich.

I wonder whether the memory of loss was carried with those who had originally peopled this land. Had it begun with them fighting for the land because, although they knew they belonged to the land, the English had an idea that a single man could own land for his own advancement? Had it begun with this idea of the land not as a source of knowledge but as a source of wealth? Was it this: the white imagining, which grappled with and overwhelmed the black knowledge by claiming as its own the land that lay at the root of the black knowledge? Or was the memory of loss carried with those brought here in chains, ranked up like horses and sold out to the planters to plough the island they now called Van Diemen's Land? Or was it something the convicts and blackfellas shared, that divided them yet might one day bring them all together?

The singer picks up the microphone stand and slings it across his back, wearing it as if it were a crucifix. He sways dementedly, arches his head back and screams once more. His screaming comes from the heart of the loss and his scream pierces even this water around me now and fills it and fills me with the keening and lamenting and praying of all who filled the island prison as convicts, all those miserable bastards, all my poor forebears.

And then something rises up from these furious waters, and the singer's scream and the scream of the past and my own agony become one and the same. More than a vision, it is an all-encompassing madness which I cannot escape. The Van Diemen's Land that bubbles like boiling blood in my brain was not a world, nor even a society. It was a hell. Who would seek to change hell? I witness how the most ambitious only sought to escape it, by boat if possible, by death if desperate. I see how many convicts died, by their own hand, by the hands of others, by sickness. How many more felt something within them break that could not be fixed by conditional pardons nor healed by time, and they knew it could not be fixed or healed and they knew themselves to be somehow less. And after the English government stopped sending convicts and after they stopped sending the gold to pay for the upkeep of the convicts, the island entered a long winter of poverty and silence.

Nobody spoke. Unless it was to lie, nobody spoke.

The singer screeches now, and where his screech becomes so high pitched that it can no longer be heard, there is the most terrible silence. A silence that takes its form and its energy from a lie.

The lie that the blackfellas had died out. That the ex-convicts had left the island for gold rushes in other countries. That only pure free white settler stock remained. Like all great lies there was some truth in these assertions. A great many blackfellas had been killed, even more destroyed by the physical diseases and spiritual sickness of the Europeans. A great many ex-convicts availed themselves of any chance to leave the island prison, so many that the prudish people of the colony of Victoria passed a law forbidding them to emigrate to that land. But at the end of it all most blackfellas and convicts remained on the island, sick with syphilis and sadness and fear and madness and loss. And when the long night fell they slept together, some openly, some illicitly, but whether they slept together out of shame or pride or indifferent lust the consequence was the same: they begat children to one another. But the lies were told with sufficient force that for a good many years even the parents remained silent, and whispered their truths only occasionally, and then only in the wilds where no one could hear, or in the depths of drink when no one would remember.

It was a terrible and piteous time. They had remained and they had endured. But so had their fears. Children denied their parents and invented new lineages of respectable free settlers to replace the true genealogy of shame. The descendants of the convicts and the blackfellas became service-station attendants or shop assistants or lorry drivers or waitresses or clerks, if they were lucky. No one spoke. No one spoke. For a century nothing was heard. Even the writers and poets were mute to their own world. If possible they left, though with an insistent phrase sounding in their ears that would never depart.

If you leave you can never be free.

Ticket-of-leave men in their hearts, granted a pass permitting travel but never the freedom to leave, wherever their bodies ran their souls remained forever shackled to the strange mountainous island of horrors at the end of the world. And now Shag's guitar is back where it began, except now it is not merely a statement but a question and an accusation and a statement all bound together. Shag makes the strings shriek, because Shag wants so bad to be free, wants so bad for his sister to be free, and he can only free them both by playing this dim terrible memory.

If you leave you can never be free.

And he plays and plays that crappy old guitar, and the singer is crying and bellowing. As if all the island's weird agonies were their own. As if it all were more than flesh could bear, and yet flesh had borne the weight for a century. The drummer has come to life and is pounding out the beat and the bass guitarist is just keeping his line going as strong and hard a counterpoint as he can to Shag's riffs and the singer's screams. The smoke-swirled bar has gone strangely quiet and they are all listening and wondering why they weren't listening before and what it is that aches so much to listen to now.

Aljaz goes to leave. He feels a tug on his sleeve. He turns around. In the dim haze he is at first unable to distinguish who it is. Until he hears her voice.

Saying: 'Long time no see, Ali.'

And him grasping the rum flask in his pocket in surprise, searching for adequate words and only mumbling, 'Long time. For sure.'

And him then smiling.

Saying: 'Couta. *Couta* Ho.'

— Nine —

There was never any doubt in either of their minds that the baby was dead and, watching it all over again, it is perhaps this that lends the whole scene its particular melancholy. I see it pretty much as I saw it all then, as disconnected episodes which had the terrible misfortune to involve us, and me thinking, It is a mistake, a dream, a vision of horror from which I will awake – little knowing it was condemning me to thirteen years of a waking sleep. I see Couta shaking Jemma, Aljaz kissing Jemma all over her face as though there is some magic button that might so be activated, Couta dialling the ambulance and not remembering the number, he giving Jemma mouth to mouth, she dialling more wrong numbers, he saying, 'Jemma will not die, Jemma will not die,' and Jemma already dead, Couta running into the garden to get the neighbour to ring, but never reaching the neighbour's, just screaming in the backyard, 'Help, help, please help us,' he saying, 'Jemma will not die,' and holding her in his arms as he had done after she had first been born, and Jemma already dead, the two ambulance men, one for each month of her life, just watching; the older one trying not to cry, the younger one lost, and he, the younger one, finally taking the dead baby with an infinite gentleness and cradling her as if she were his own newly born and departing through the front door, Jemma's left foot dropping from its swaddling and leaving me with the most enduring memory I have of her: a puffy shin and yellow knitted woollen bootee, and us sitting in the ambulance with those who give life, and the nightmarish smells and the small yellow-light lit darkness of the hospital bay and Jemma already dead, and the people filling the house saying they were sorry for what had happened and those on the street, whom we knew, not saying anything but looking elsewhere as if life were forever and Jemma had somehow sullied their belief in their own immortality, and me wondering who had gone and why the world had changed and seeing only a puffy shin and yellow knitted bootee, and the funeral and the priest saying, 'Let us give thanks for Jemma's life,' and me standing up and yelling, 'Jemma will not die, she will not die,' and people crying and Jemma already dead.

Everything else of her – finding her in the cot, her baths, her lying on the bed gurgling, her birth – goes out of my mind as the mortuary door closes, not to return to me till now. I had not wanted Jemma: she was an accident, Couta during pregnancy not the woman I had spent the last three years with, Couta after the birth centred upon Jemma and me feeling some selfish shithead who failed to give her the space she now demanded. My resentment culminated in this terrible moment and I felt this death to be some punishment for having not wanted Jemma. Couta had grief. I had guilt and a memory of a puffy shin and yellow knitted woollen bootee.

I did not feel grief. I did not feel anguish. I felt as if some substantial part of me – my legs, my arms – had been cut from my body and thrown away. How could I grieve the loss of myself? I did not grieve. I began running as if in search of this missing limb, as if I might find it lying somewhere upon a roadside and then bring it home to Couta, and everything would once again be whole and in its home and as it should be and always had been, the circle unbroken. I did not grieve. I could not.

Madonna santa! Why do I feel this? Why do I feel as if I am being destroyed by history? As if the past is some snake venom that is paralysing me limb by limb, organ by organ, slowly tearing my mind apart piece by piece? I, who felt I had lived in a country beyond history! Who had no future and wanted no past! I never asked for these visions, was content to remain ignorant about who I was and where I came from. I might have been a confused mess, but at least I only had myself to hate for it. And now there is all this past welling up, cramming me from all sides, pushing me further down into the Cauldron, forcing more and more water into my lungs and into my mind, and I don't want any of it, because what good does any of it do? I should have ended up like Harry, an old pisshead slowly dying over many years, serving up banquets to animals that he never saw for the rest of the week. Not having my face endlessly washed and scrubbed by this tide of the past.

And yet why *did* he cook all those tons of rissoles and fish over the years for ghosts?

Maybe he did know something I never guessed he knew. But what does it matter if I know or if I don't know? The past is a nightmare and I want to wake up and I can't. I was happy in my way, running from all this – for now I can see *this* is what I quite rightly was running from. Who in their right mind wants to own up to all that? Why would you want to admit to all that? And what's the antidote to this snakebite of the past? Love. Of whom? Of what? My pain in my guts is back, but now it is the only pain, like my guts have blown up to become my entire body and it is all burning. Beneath the river I am being consumed by the most terrible fire. Am I being left to burn eternally?

Then, amidst these all-consuming flames, I see flags.

Burning flags!

And standing above the blaze is Couta Ho, and then, rushing in from her side is Aljaz, and he is grabbing the unburnt and partly burnt flags out of the fire and stopping her throwing any more upon the fire. And he is asking her are you crazy or what? She says nothing. Aljaz continues his rescue of the multi-coloured code flags, hosing the fire out, and saves almost all, save for seven of the numeral pendants with which Couta Ho began the fire. He tries to talk to her, but Couta Ho says nothing.

It is seven weeks after their chance meeting, seven weeks since he had gone with Couta to her home after that night in the pub, both falsely believing it arose out of a camaraderie that could be carried lightly, like an emblem of a past friendship, rather than from a true love. From an *enduring* love. She had not taken him into her bed, nor had their intimacy gone further than sharing a spoon to stir the sugar into their respective cups of coffee, and he too aware that even this was more than he had a right to ask for.

How could I have asked for more? As if I had any right to be beneath the sheets with her. But that evening I saw that thirteen years had not ended our love, that I loved her and she loved me, that our love had gone into another country beyond the borders of physical desire.

And this love so terrified Aljaz that with his coffee only half drunk he had abruptly got up, said his farewells and left.

Now is the first time since that evening Aljaz has been able to face visiting Couta. She still wears her black hair pulled back in a ponytail, but whereas it once made her look stylish, now it seems to accentuate her age. She has put on weight, more than he has even. Her face, though still little wrinkled, presages a severer, sadder middle age in its squarer form and floury skin. Her movements, once so definite and strong, have grown short and shaky. Her hands, he notices, those hands which once so resolutely pulled him toward her so many years before, now move with a quick diffidence. Her clothes are less individual, more mainstream department store, as though the youthful joy of using clothes to define her own small place in the world has passed, and she now dresses simply for comfort and modesty. She still wears large golden gypsy earrings, but they are tarnished and no longer glint when light plays upon them. He realises with a shock not that she is old, for he is prepared for that, but that he too is old. He wishes they could have shared this ageing together, wishes he could grow old and wrinkly and round and bone-sore with her.

'I'm sorry,' says Aljaz.

'I kept them till now,' says Couta Ho, pointing to the flags, 'then I thought, What was the point?'

'I should have come earlier,' says Aljaz.

'It's all past,' says Couta Ho.

It's pathetic to watch, really. More precisely: I'm pathetic to watch. 'I'm sorry,' he says. She says nothing.

He looks down at his feet. He recalls the various flags and their accompanying messages. He delves in the soggy steaming black mess to finally lift up a still-smoking flag showing a white cross upon a blue background. So he stands before her, a most ludicrous sight to behold, waving a flag above his head.

'My vessel is stopped and making no way through the water,' says Couta Ho, reading the flag's message. Aljaz nods. Couta Ho smiles. Couta Ho, for the first time, laughs.

She makes coffee and they sit down at the kitchen table, the same green laminex table that was there when he lived with her. The house's exterior belies its interior, which is, thinks Aljaz, so very Couta – pieces of ordinary suburban furniture and bric-à-brac which, anywhere else, would seem entirely ordinary, but in her juxtaposition of their laminex greens and vinyl reds takes on some special quality, at once homely and exotic. Aljaz, preoccupied with these and other thoughts, does not speak.

The nervous silence that had attracted Couta Ho so many years before was now almost unbearable. She filled the emptiness that lay between them with her halting words. She talked sketchily about her failed marriage to Phil, about her job cooking counter meals at a nearby pub, on these and other subjects about which he raised polite questions. Then the conversation stumbled. After a long time of looking and feeling awkward and neither saying anything, after a long time making clumsy smiles, with the sounds of coffee being drunk and the TV next door seeming too loud and then too silent, Couta Ho spoke further.

'Still drink?' she asked.

'Not for three months,' he lied, and she knew it. But it was not that bothering her.

Couta felt above all else an overwhelming feeling of falling into a void when she saw Aljaz. And she did not wish to fall. She felt as if she had walked a wire since he had left her so many years ago, and that she had learnt the art of walking that tightrope alone. It is too late for this, she wished to say. Don't you understand, she wished to say, too much has happened to me and you were not part of it. You were not here. She wished to say also that she hated him for taking her love, squeezing it all out of her like a lemon, living in her house and then leaving, running, when things got hard. But she said none of it. How could she tell him he had no right to come back into her life when she had been the one who, at the pub, had asked him to visit? She could cope – had coped – with him leaving. But him returning, that was so hard she wasn't sure if she were strong enough to bear the burden.

He was different, but the same. Still quiet, still bearing politeness as a shield to his shyness. And she unequal to it, vulnerable and opening up to it, without being able to tell what he was thinking or wanting. She remembered many years ago old Maria Magdalena Svevo, for whom Couta Ho would sometimes buy cigars, lighting one up, inhaling deeply, then asking how Aljaz was, and Couta Ho telling her how he had left and how she wondered if she would ever see him again. And Maria Magdalena Svevo responding by quoting from Ecclesiastes. Maria Magdalena Svevo had no truck with the church, saying that anybody who lived through the war in Italy couldn't have, and she had a generally low opinion of the Bible, which she described as a minestrone of opposing flavours. But of Ecclesiastes she had an altogether higher opinion, and she knew it by heart, and would sometimes quote from it, as she did this day. She took the cigar out of her mouth, coughed up some phlegm, let it slide back down her throat, and then leant forward.

Saying: '''All the rivers run into the sea; yet the sea *is* not full; unto the place from whence the rivers come, thither they return again.'''

'I'm sorry about Harry, Ali, I really am,' said Couta. 'He was a real nice old man.' She patted his hand with hers, once, twice, then moved it back to her side of the table.

Then they had some more coffee and Aljaz began telling Couta Ho his story. And once he began, which was hard, so hard, he could not stop, for he had to tell her it all, had to tell her everything, and all he had was this one story to tell everything with, and not until he stopped would he know whether it was possible to tell everything with only this one story. He detailed the endless casual jobs, the small towns and the big suburbs and the endless roads and the flushing airports, an inventory of despair. How he had ended up prawn trawling up the Cape – a small boat, an arsehole of a skipper and his wife, just the three of them in the long heat. Not that Aljaz minded. For three years he stuck with it. The skipper talked all the time and his wife and Aljaz just listened and worked. That was good, just trying to make his mind as empty as the edge between the sea and the sky. For a time. Then the skipper kept asking questions. More and more questions. So Aljaz went over to West Oz, down to Esperance to see an old friend. She had a new bloke, a surfboard shaper, but she was still nice to

Aljaz. She let him stay there for two months, and some-times they would talk a little, but when he stopped talking so did she. She was kind, Rhoda. Always was. Then he worked in the wheat. Then he came back here, but he thought he might head back north when summer was finished.

Then he told her what Maria Magdalena Svevo had told him.

'But you always were different,' said Couta, and then she pondered a moment before speaking again. 'Maybe it's just being able to name the difference.'

They sat on opposite sides of the laminex kitchen table. The lights of the laundromat across the road had gone out following its closure some time earlier and the room seemed dim. They sat formally, as if it were some form of interrogation, or, more precisely, a confession – she thinking of the years they had been apart and what might have come of staying together, he thinking of how his time without her seemed so desolate. He had fallen low, not to the bottom, he had seen enough to know it was possible to go down a lot farther, so desperate that you sold yourself to anybody and did anything, so needing that you would risk all busting into houses and nicking a telly or a video for which you might get a hundred dollars total. He had avoided that, and that was something, but it wasn't a lot and it didn't seem much to be proud of, just this *not* having done this and *not* having done that. There wasn't much he had done. There were few, if any, friends from those years. He had once thought that you went on making friends, but it hadn't turned out that way. Sure, he knew plenty of people, but he was wary of them and distant with them. They weren't friends. There was no money and no possessions, but he didn't care about that. It was the lack of being anything, of being part of anything, of belonging anywhere. He had fallen and, having fallen, he was fated to suffer ever greater indignities and adversities. And this is the essence of what I now see: Aljaz feeling himself doomed and Couta Ho knowing it beyond the the power of her love to redeem him.

Couta's hand came across the table and ruffled Aljaz's thin red spikes of hair. 'Not much of that mane left,' she laughed. He laughed a little too.

'Why did you cut it so short?' she asked, knowing it betrayed something of his self-loathing and wanting him to admit to it.

'Easier to wash,' he said, with the briefest flicker of a smile to warn her away from further such questions.

'Sure,' she said, and he momentarily and unintentionally fixed her with a stare that frightened her, such was the emptiness she saw in his blue eyes. 'Sure,' she continued, looking away, 'lot easier for sure.'

'Do you ever think it could have been different?' he asked in a voice so matter-of-fact it angered her, for he knew what the answer was.

'What do you reckon?' she said. 'Anyway, it wouldn't make it easier for me to think it,' she said, looking down, fiddling with her nails, 'so I don't.' And then Couta turned her head back up so that he would see her face, which was now serious and sad, so that he would understand her, and she said, 'In fact, I don't even want to talk about it.' And he realised that, long ago, without knowing it, like a child with something precious that it mistakes for a toy, he had broken what had held them together. And the shattered pieces could not be remade into a single item.

271

Aljaz remembered how he had once thought there would be plenty more women after he walked out on Couta, and that he would just take his time and pick the one he liked most when he was ready. There had been more women. But he felt about none of them the way he felt about Couta. And he never felt that any of them understood him the way Couta had understood him. Some had liked him for his front. But Couta had known his fear and his darkness and she had loved him in spite of them. That he never found again. And now it was too late.

'Do you ever think,' said Aljaz, 'that maybe you only get one or two chances in this life?' And before Couta even tried to reply Aljaz was talking again. 'And that if you throw them away, then that's it?' Now it was his turn to look downwards. 'You know what I mean? You get given a chance and you think there'll be plenty more of them. But there aren't, and if you just piss them up on the wall then life gives up on you.' Couta looked down at him, her expression unchanging. She knew what he meant and didn't want to acknowledge it. 'You know what I mean?' asked Aljaz for a second time. 'You don't get a second chance.' And he turned his head away, because he knew it. That it was too late. He wanted so bad to say he loved her, but he knew it would not be right, that it would somehow introduce an insincere force between them. It was too late, and all they had left was this moment of peace together.

His head jerked up. He looked at her and she saw what she had never before seen: that he was a frightened man. He looked up at her and he said the one word neither had said all that evening. He said, 'Jemma,' and halted.

Then he said, '*After* Jemma,' and halted a second time. And then he said, 'I woke up one morning after Jemma

272

and, I didn't mean it, believe me Couta, I never meant it, but I jumped up and ran and ran and I never could look back.'

At the end of that night they lay down in her bed to sleep. Not to make love but to sleep together one final time. That night was a conclusion for Couta, a moment of contrition for Aljaz. At Couta's invitation Aljaz was to stay on in her house; he preferred its living domesticity to the dusty memories that gathered at Harry's home. Perhaps in this new-found domestic order Aljaz sought some refuge from the fray of reality that so frightened him, though now I can see that the chaos of reality, beginning with Pig's Breath's phonecall a few days later, was only too soon to reassert itself and, like the river, carry Aljaz with it.

But I am not seeing that phonecall: I am seeing how at the end of that night they lay down in her bed and she pulled an old white bedspread over them. Even in the gloom Aljaz noticed how extraordinarily white the bedspread was, with the exception of a large yellowing blemish. And so I see them, both now asleep lying on their sides, two tarnished spoons. He clutching her, clutching her so tight, as if a gale were blowing around them threatening to uplift and part them forever if he did not hold on to her. The house and then the bedroom seemed to dissolve, and soon even the bed ceased to exist. He felt only they existed, that all around were the most wild and savage beasts with deformed faces and evil souls, which would destroy them both if they parted, which waited beyond reality for them and would consume everybody unless he could just hold on. When she moved he seized a new hold so tightly that she complained. But still he held on, and he saw them riding on clouds above an ocean of fiery torment, together safe from its waves of flames. As long as he held on, as long he felt the warmth of her flesh and the pulse of her body breathing in and out, as long as he could hold his nose into the flesh of her back and smell her, he was safe and free from the fear he knew would return when they inevitably parted. So he lay on his side shivering and she, with an arm behind her back, pulled the white bedspread up over his shoulders, and as she did so his eyes caught the ancient amber stain. He momentarily thought the stain contained some image, some revelation, some moment of truth, and he almost cried out at the horror and the beauty of it, but then the sensation passed as abruptly as it had arrived and he curled like the frightened animal he was into the back of Couta Ho. When she asked what was the matter, he was unable to say, but just spooned into her back, his body shaking, his nose smelling the sweat upon her flesh, his fear as total as it was unnameable.

So they slept, so they slept.

— the Churn —

I'll tell you something. It's not a vision. It's something I saw before I started having visions. Before I even started to drown. Watching Aljaz and Couta sleep together reminds me of it. Sometimes when I sleep, I am privy to a bad dream.

Sometimes in my sleep I see a terrible flower of death: its stamen stone, its petals water foam variegated with blood, one man disappearing into the foam, another, a different man, arising from the foam. And that different man is me.

Couta Ho says, 'It doesn't mean anything,' Couta Ho

says when I sit bolt upright in bed, cold and sweating and shivering and shitting myself.

And I turn and touch the warm skin of her cheeks with my cold fingers, and my teeth chatter and my head shakes.

'It don't mean a thing,' Couta Ho says, and after a time she makes me lie back down and I fall asleep under the flowing softness of the tear-stained bedspread.

But now my bad dream has possessed me and it will not leave and Couta Ho has gone. Everywhere I look, I see it. And what I now see with it is the worst, the very worst, of my bad dream made flesh and reality.

They are already in the heart of the gorge, at the Churn waterfall, the lead-in rapid too big to shoot. They rope the boats round the rapid's edge to an eddy immediately above the waterfall, and there organise the portage up and around the cliff face. The punters are shocked at the steep scrabble up the side of the cliff carrying gear. They are annoyed at having to undertake such arduous physical work, but relieved to be off the flooding river, back on dry land. So they set to without enthusiasm and without anger, following Aljaz and the Cockroach, who, in the manner of builders' labourers carrying loads of timber, sling the heavy food barrels diagonally across their shoulders.

A scream. Then cries. 'Help! Help!' Short, urgent, desperate. 'Aljaz! Cockroach!' Aljaz and the Cockroach drop their heavy barrels and start running, brushing aside scrub and confused punters with their gearbags as they force their bodies back up the steep gravel slide, as they climb up the small rock chimney, as they run along the track. The cries grow closer. 'It's Derek!' Then another voice. 'He can't hang on much longer!' Near where the track turns to head back down the mountainside they see him.

'O Jesus,' says the Cockroach. A third of the way down a near vertical rockface is Derek. He is hanging on to a lone tea-tree, whose spiny root, not even a wrist thick, long ago embedded the plant into the cliff face. Looking straight down, not much of Derek is visible. A tea-tree trunk, two hands grasping it, the top of a red whitewater helmet. A punter's helmet. Framing the red circle of his helmet is the waterfall that lies twenty metres below. 'Fucking idiot,' says the Cockroach. 'How could he manage to fall off this track?'

'He didn't,' says a nearby punter. 'His gearbag fell and he tried to fetch it and then he fell.'

'He's still a fucking idiot,' says the Cockroach. But even as the Cockroach curses he is getting ready to rescue. He reties his flip line as a climbing harness. 'Where's the longline?' he asks a punter. And before the punter can answer the Cockroach screams, *'Where's the fucking longline?'*

'In the raft down at the end of the portage trail,' says Aljaz.

'Rickie,' the Cockroach yells, 'go get it! And run, fucking run like you've never fucking run!' The Cockroach turns and yells reassurance to Derek far below. 'Don't worry, Derek. We'll get you out of this, mate. Just don't rock round down there.' Aljaz feels his breath hot and hard and fast racing out of his nostrils.

A protracted half-cry, half-yell climbs the cliff face and is just distinguishable from the roar of the waterfall. 'What's he saying?' asks the Cockroach.

'He's saying he can't hang on much longer,' says Sheena.

'Jeezuz,' says the Cockroach.

'You'll be right,' yells Aljaz. 'Don't look down. Look

at the rock, at the patterns in the rock, and think of that shithouse porridge you had for breakfast.'

The Cockroach pauses, looks along the track in the vain hope that the runner will have already returned with the rope. 'Are you going to go?' he asks. 'Or me?'

Aljaz feels fear rise within him like a fist pushing from his bowels up into his throat. As lead guide he ought to be the one who attempts the rescue. He is out of practice, unfit, and his old fear of heights is stronger than ever. But he knows there is no choice. He says yes, thinking the Cockroach means who will go down the rope. But the Cockroach doesn't mean this. He means who is going to climb down the cliff now, without the rope.

Aljaz goes to say that he is no climber, which he isn't, but stops, torn between his fear of climbing down the cliff and his greater fear of being seen by the Cockroach and the punters as a coward.

'Now?' says Aljaz. 'Without a rope, don't be bloody mad.'

'The fucking rope's five fucking minutes away,' says the Cockroach. He jerks a contemptuous thumb over his shoulder in the direction of the cliff. 'That silly prick isn't going to last that long. If he doesn't give up the ghost, that bloody tea-tree will anyway.' Aljaz looks around, hoping to see something that might help him. There is nothing. 'I'm going down,' says the Cockroach. 'Now.'

'No!' Aljaz suddenly shouts out of shame, surprising even himself. 'No, I'll go.' And before he has even finished speaking he has started to climb down the steep band of shrubbery that flanks the cliff.

God, what have I done to deserve this? It is interesting, watching now, how none of Aljaz's fear is apparent to the punters, who see him quickly and machinelike begin his descent of the cliff face. But Aljaz has no choice, and that, he thinks, is perhaps a mercy. For he knows he cannot act upon his fear and say, 'No, you go, I'll stay here where I feel safe.' If the punter dies it will be his fault. He looks sideways and sees the waterfall and feels ill. He looks back up at the half-circle of punters gawking at him and wonders why on earth any of them have any confidence or trust in him at all. He feels like saying, 'You fools, can't you see I'm as shit scared as you?' But instead he adopts his professional nonchalance, smiles and says, 'We'll have him back up here in no time.' Down he goes, trying to forget his vertigo, marvelling at how duty can overwhelm fear. Perhaps this is what soldiers ordered into battle feel, thinks Aljaz. Whatever will be will be.

But a short way down the cliff face he stops and can find no more footholds or handholds. As terror takes over he realises he is unable to go back up, and so he clings to the cliff only five metres below the crowd of punters gazing down, knowing he looks ludicrous and inept, terrified that he might at any moment fall to his death, and tormented by Derek's pleas from below for Aljaz to come down and rescue him.

The Cockroach also hears Derek, hears him cry out that the tea-tree trunk is fraying. He realises that they have lost valuable time and that Aljaz has frozen. So he turns and begins the descent down the rockface, slowly, cautiously. Aljaz watches him. He's good, thinks Aljaz, his shame rising in a hot flush. He's good. The Cockroach gets down next to Aljaz and quickly, with a measure of contempt he makes no attempt to disguise, shows him a route back up to the shrubbery.

'You should have told me you couldn't climb.' Aljaz

slowly climbs back up, his humiliation complete. About ten metres from Derek, the Cockroach, now visible only as the top of his head, runs out of rock to climb. He tries two different approaches to get to Derek, but fails and has to turn back. A third route gets him down to the same level as Derek but about six metres distant from him. The Cockroach talks to Derek, calms him down, gets him to hug the rock like it is his mother, to find tiny niches in which to rest his feet and take some of the stress off the fraying tea-tree trunk.

'Here.' Aljaz turns around. Rickie is back with the rope, his face bright red and flecked with foamy spittle. Aljaz ties the rope off to the firmest tree he can find and leans out on the rope, testing his weight against the tree and his knots. He climbs down the rope through the steep bank of shrubbery to the cliff edge, where he yells down to the Cockroach, then throws the rest of rope down in the Cockroach's direction. The rock is greasy with the rain and he wonders how the Cockroach can climb on it at all.

The Cockroach grabs the rope, wraps it around his body, then crabs it onto his emergency climbing harness. Then he kick-jumps himself off the cliff face, bouncing around to where Derek hangs onto his life by the fragile strength of a small tea-tree trunk. As he comes close to Derek he sees that the tea-tree is half pulled out of the rock crack it has spent a century or so extracting life from, and that its trunk is fraying badly under the strain. Two hands, one bloodied from the fall, hang onto the shrub, and from below the Cockroach hears the horrible rapid pant of a man who knows he may be about to die, smells the sharp ammoniac scent of true terror.

The bastard's going to die on me, thinks the Cockroach, and he panics. With this panic all his strength seems to abandon his body and he feels weak and unable to do anything. He is no longer sure if he will be able to rescue Derek. But he pushes the panic back down and just looks at the slimy rock, looks closely at its lichen-etched forms, looks at its small cracks the width of his lips in which tiny myrtle and pandanus seedlings, their leaves near waxen in their green rainwater-beaded perfection, flourish around miniature hardwater ferns, a small world, complete and wondrous unto itself, looks and marvels as he slowly works his way across to Derek.

The Cockroach hears Derek pray between panting breaths. 'Our-*eh*-father-*eh*-who-*eh*-art-*eh*-in-*eh*-heaven,' he hears.

'Derek,' says the Cockroach but Derek does not hear, for he is too intent on praying to God to deliver him from his peril. His panting prayer disintegrates into a rapid gobbling lament.

'Mygodmygodmygodmygod.' As if the repetition of His name will invoke His reality, will summon His omnipotent presence into existence to take Derek in His arms and rise with the warm updraught flowing from the rapid to the path above.

'Grab hold of the rope,' says the Cockroach over Derek's prayers, 'and we'll climb back up together.' Derek ignores the Cockroach, as if such a diversion might diminish the strength of his appeal for divine intercession. Now he simply calls for *Godgodgodgodgodgod*, like a hungry seagull desperate for a crust of bread.

'Grab hold of the rope,' says the Cockroach a second

time. He eases himself behind Derek and by placing his arms under Derek's shoulders takes some of the fat man's weight. 'Derek,' says the Cockroach, 'listen to me. Grab the rope. Please.' Derek slowly turns around and his eyes, those large locust eyes wet with tears, look into the Cockroach's as if he is looking at death. Derek's head shivers more than shakes Derek's refusal.

'I believe in God,' says Derek. 'I do. I believe in you, God.'

'Listen to me, Derek,' says the Cockroach. 'You've got to do it.'

Again the shivering head. 'No. I will do whatever you want of me, God, but spare me.'

'You've got to grab hold of the rope!' shouts the Cockroach.

'I believe in God the father, in Jesus Christ His son who on the third day rose from the dead to sit at the right hand of God the father almighty, and who on judgement day shall – '

The Cockroach interrupts Derek's prayer with a scream. *'Grab the fucking rope!'*

Derek begins to cry anew, and as his body heaves with his blubbering the tea-tree root gives way some more. The Cockroach gives up his bullying and tries desperately to calm Derek. 'All right mate, all right, she'll be okay, just stop crying, you'll be all right. God's with us, believe me, God's with us. If you just stop crying. *Please.*' Derek looks at the Cockroach with a new trust and confidence. *Jesus*, thinks the Cockroach. The Cockroach ties himself off, so that he can fall no farther.

'You understand?' says the Cockroach to Derek. 'I wrap this harness around your body. Then I connect that harness to the rope. Then I climb back up. Then we haul you up. Hang on tight, for Chrissake.' Derek looks blankly into the Cockroach's eyes. The Cockroach is not even sure Derek has understood what he has just been told. 'You ready?' asks the Cockroach. Derek nods. 'Just don't make any sudden movement, okay?' Derek has no fight left in him: life or death, he is equally ready to take the hand fate deals him. Unable to manoeuvre himself such that he can tie the flip line around Derek as a proper climbing harness, the Cockroach has to make do belting the flip line around Derek's fat waist, connecting the two ends with a carabiner.

Then, as a safety precaution, before he does anything else, the Cockroach connects Derek with himself by clipping their two harnesses together with a carabiner. Derek immediately lets go of the tea-tree. The Cockroach yells, *'Hang on to that root for Chrissake!'* But it is too late. The Cockroach screams, *'No!'* but Derek has let go. The Cockroach thinks, Jesus, now we're really going to die. They fall two metres, and the Cockroach shuts his eyes and his body goes loose and he thinks, This is how it ends. But it is only the rope sagging and the anchor tree loosening until the new weight is fully absorbed. The Cockroach comes to his senses and shivers with fear. And as they bob in space he looks down at the waterfall falling through the massive boulders below and wonders if you would feel anything at the moment of impact.

He feels the tree to which the rope is anchored move slightly with their combined weight. He realises Derek is hanging only by his harness. 'Put your arms around my neck,' the Cockroach says to Derek. And just as Derek starts to move, his body begins to topple. His forearms immediately lock around the Cockroach's neck and his legs wrap around the Cockroach's waist. The

Cockroach feels as if his neck is about to break with the strain. The Cockroach locks Derek in a bear hug. It hurts, it hurts like hell to take this fat man's weight with his neck and arms, but if he lets go the fat man might fall to his death. Locked in this curious, awkward embrace they swing in space above the waterfall, softly bouncing into the rock.

A human metronome slowly marking time against a cliff.

'Why me?' asks Derek. 'I'm only a tourist.'

Then, for no reason, Derek suddenly goes frantic. He pulls with all his might at the Cockroach's neck, trying to clamber up him as if he were a ladder. 'No!' yells the Cockroach, but Derek's wild scrambling overbalances the pair of them and their embracing bodies swing from a vertical to horizontal position. The Cockroach feels himself sliding out of his own harness as they topple. Instinctively he throws his hands up to grab the rope to stop them both falling. And for no reason, insanely, at the moment the Cockroach lets go of Derek, Derek, as if feeling he has been betrayed totally, also lets go. He throws his arms outwards, as if crucified, lets go of the Cockroach and topples backwards, slithers out of his harness, and falls.

Falls through the air. Falls fully ten metres. When Derek's body slams, back first, upon a round-topped boulder below, there is no sound discernible above the noise of the waterfall. The Cockroach watches Derek's body as if it were an insect shell, as if it were a clump of earth limply sliding off the boulder into the waterfall, at first slowly then quickly, leaving no trace in the foaming turbulence. The Cockroach is surprised at how little he feels at this precise moment, thinks how he will have the rest of his life to feel and at this moment he is glad to not feel.

– Eliza Quade, 1898 –

Let's get one thing straight. Now. Here and now. I have no desire to be here. Drowning, that is. You might think I am resigned to my fate – well, yes, perhaps I am, but that's not the point. Even if I accept that I am going to drown, that doesn't mean that I want to drown. Or that I won't struggle against drowning. I have never been one to accept what fate has dealt me, which has proven unfortunate, given that life has always been beyond my control, and I, limbs flailing in protest, have always, despite my protestations, been swept and bowled along by life until I got jammed at this point. A full stop at the end of the river.

You might think that I am rabbiting on too much when I should instead be concentrating on a way out of my plight, looking for some way I can physically lever myself out of this watery trap, trying, perhaps, to flex my body different ways to enable it to slip out. *Trying. Perhaps. Possibly.* All my life was *trying*, *perhaps*, *possibly*. And none of it made a jot of difference. For here I am where I was always intended, always fated to be. Put yourself in my shoes (so to speak – I can feel that mine were swept away by the river current some time ago) and recognise that the physical battle has long been lost. Perhaps these frantic, crazed meanderings of my mind, these visions, perhaps these represent the ultimate plane of conflict. Perhaps these visions are my precarious path back to existence.

If I am to die, and I am not saying that I will, believe

me I am not, but if I do, there will be at least one good consequence of my death. It will mean I will no longer age, no longer be confronted with the daily and ongoing disintegration of my body. In this death seems to share a purpose, as well as a sensation, with aerobics – to stop ageing. Except that where aerobics is ultimately doomed to fail, death will always succeed, as long as you are fortunate enough to have it come your way at a young age.

But then I am struck by the heretical thought: what if ageing were preferable to dying? What if growing old and the accompanying decline of the body were accepted with grace? Would it not be possible to see the growth in wisdom and in the heart as sufficient compensation for the slowing down of one's physical attributes? Could it be that I might even enjoy slowly wrinkling up next to the one I love more than jumping, almost trampolining, from the bed of one young girl to an even younger girl in the hope that their firmness of flesh and clear eyes be catching, like some socially transmitted disease? The question that obsesses me at this moment of mortal peril is perverse in the extreme, and one that goes against all the strictures and nostrums of our time. I feel silly even thinking such a question, for it is evidently only the product of a greatly distressed mind, but I must put it into words.

Is there life after youth?

I ponder this question for some time, then think, Yes, there is, and I want it, want to enjoy it for what it is, not despise it for what it isn't. It seems ridiculous, valuing old age, but why not?

I want to age.

I want to live.

And yet . . . and yet.

I am so very scared.

But it's getting harder to hang on to any thoughts. My mind pounds and wavers and feels so heavy, so very heavy, while my thoughts are so light and becoming lighter all the time. Just when I have nearly caught them, they swirl away with the bubbles above my face, away from me, upwards, towards life.

A woman's face, elderly, criss-crossed with lines that denote not only age but ongoing pain and incessant hardship, so deep and strongly defined that they look as if they have been gouged out of her flesh with a chisel, looks at a yellowed and brittle piece of paper upon which is scrawled the most curious message, the meaning of which still eludes her. Her husband, who is without teeth and without memory, comes into the poor kitchen in which she sits in front of the cooking fire with a rug over her legs. She folds the note. It has been folded and unfolded so many times that the creases have opened into tears, and only the infinite care with which she tenderly folds it back prevents it from falling into four separate pieces. She puts the note back into the book of prayers she is reading by the light of a kerosene lamp. Her husband apologises for interrupting and then asks her if she has seen his wife. She asks him to sit down and make himself comfortable, and he thanks her for the kindness she is showing to a stranger.

'We are all unknown to one another,' she says, but he does not hear, for he has started speaking again, this time of his brother.

'Successful bugger he is, mayor of Parramatta. You would like him, like him very much,' he says.

'Has he a wife?' she asks.

'O yes, my word. Has he a wife? Huh! O, yes. Beautiful woman. And a wonderful wife. Wonderful woman.'

A small red-headed girl runs into the kitchen. 'Rose,' says the old woman, 'what are you doing here?'

'Auntie Eileen sent me over with a loaf of bread for you and Grandad,' says Rose, and she goes and kisses the old man on the forehead.

'I am not your grandad,' says the old man. 'Your grandad is the mayor of Parramatta.'

'Pay no heed,' says the old woman to Rose, smiling, 'he is not too well today.' The old man looks hurt and confused. After the child has gone, she looks across at him and says to him, 'You remember none of it, do you?'

'Remember what?' he asks. 'Nothing wrong with my memory.'

'How Ned died escaping. And how you then married me and raised his children as your own.'

'But they are my own,' he says, perplexed.

'Of course,' she reassures him, 'of course.'

Within a few minutes he has fallen asleep, and starts snoring. The old woman takes the letter back out of the book of prayers and looks at it some more. Then looks into the fire and looks at the way the near-invisible red flames, as they so sensuously lick the coals, form into the image of her first husband, the father of all her children, Ned Quade, the brother of her second husband, Colum, who lies asleep in the chair opposite, an exclamation mark of dribble hanging from his slack lips.

Eliza looks at the letter and reads it yet one more time. Reads it for perhaps the thousandth time and still ponders its mystery.

My Esteemed and Most Noble Madame Elijah —

Well say You in th. New Jerusalem.
Your loving And humble Servant etc etc in Eyes of The lord
Ned Kwade His Mark

And below this message the outline of a Celtic cross, a cross enclosed within a circle. His mark, sure enough.

Well say You in th. New Jerusalem.

But where? And when?

— the Cockroach —

The Cockroach turns around to face the cliff and slowly climbs back up the rope to the top, his body finding the work a relief after hanging in one position so long. At the top Aljaz grabs the Cockroach's wrist in a strong grip for the final haul to the track. But he does not immediately heave the Cockroach up. Aljaz realises he is staring into the Cockroach's eyes.

The Cockroach cannot tell Aljaz that Derek is dead, because he cannot verify the fact of death. But he knows what he has witnessed. Further, he believes himself to be responsible for what happened because he acted and failed. Aljaz knows by the Cockroach's lack of speech what has happened. And Aljaz believes himself to be responsible because he didn't act. It eats at them both. Neither can bear the other carrying the burden of what they see as their own individual crime. With a sudden sharp burst of strength Aljaz heaves the Cockroach up past where Aljaz stands on the track, and I can see that Aljaz does not look around at his fellow river guide but is continuing to stare at the place where the Cockroach had been hanging from the rope. Or, more precisely, that he looks through and beyond that position into the vast roaring moiling maelstrom, and, beyond that, at the cliffs and at the base of the mountains and at the gorge itself. And sees his face and it looks no longer separate from the world around it: it looks as if it has been dead and petrified for millennia. As if it and he were part of the gorge and the mountains and the cliffs and the maelstrom. As if he were rock so hard that the furrows in his face down which the rainwater is channelled have taken an eternity to be so eroded by the wind and water. As if he were so hard, as if he were. As if he were alone. That is what he is thinking, yes, now it is all coming back to me.

I am so alone and alone.

So it is that Aljaz and the Cockroach stop talking to one another, except to coordinate their search around the base waters of the Churn, and later further below in Serenity Sound.

They drift the half-kilometre down toward the Coruscades, the towering walls of the gorge enclosing them on both sides as they examine every eddy and every backwater. Aljaz and the Cockroach notice the water line on the riverbanks, which shows how high the water is, and how it is continuing to rise. They pull in at the Coruscades campsite, which is still a little above the water line. Aljaz orders his punters to stay in the raft, while he and the Cockroach check the campsite. But they do not immediately go to the campsite. The pair, one small and stocky, the other long and straight, scramble up the bank, then head around to the boulders at the river's edge to survey the large rapid known as the Coruscades. Scanning the cataract for Derek's body. Standing on a boulder as large as a house they look up and down the river, two twigs jutting out upon part of the gorge's huge grim profile, the edges of which are softened by the heavy rain. They are numb, their emotions suspended, because they have not found the body, and the brief hope remains that somewhere down the river Derek may have been washed ashore alive. Neither believe it, but neither can dismiss it.

'So we camp there tonight?' asks the Cockroach, pointing at the riverbank campsite.

Aljaz nods his head.

'We won't get flooded out?'

Aljaz shakes his head, but they both look up at the cliffs and wonder how, if he is wrong and they are flooded out of the campsite, they will camp ten people up there.

'What does it matter?' says the Cockroach and turns to head back down to the rafts.

While the punters set up camp the two guilty men work their way back upriver to the Churn, scouring the waters and the rocks. They work like madmen, seeking to find where the body might be, pretending, as they must, that he might possibly be alive. They manage to climb back around to the boulders upon which Derek fell, and are able to identify the actual rock by the thin blood smear running down it to the water. They stand on a boulder directly opposite for some time, neither man talking. The boulder is round and smooth, and the rising river foam whipped up by the waterfall directly upriver banks up around the boulder's base. As the foam laps the edge of the rock the sticky blood loosens into drifting slags, then dissolves to stain the foam slightly pink, the whole like a bloom blushing at its centre then pale at its extremity, the rock the stamen. But there is no blood trail leading to the body, no body to be seen. Only a river made incarnate. They swim across to the boulder and they haul themselves up, their hair and faces covered in large tufts of pink and brown foam, like some malevolent creatures of the river. No body is to be felt in the water.

So they stand at the base of the roaring waterfall, deafened, foam-flecked faces slowly saturating and dissolving in the pounding mist thrown by the cascade above, the foam blown away by the wind gusts generated by the tons of falling water. Far below, Sheena looks up from the raft in which she and the other punters sit. What I notice looking at them now is how no one else looks back upriver except her. And what she sees at the base of the massive waterfall are two extensions of the boulder caught within the shadow of the gorge. She is no longer entirely sure who or what the figures are.

By the time it is dark they know that Derek's body must be somewhere in the river below the Churn. It is not visible in Serenity Sound, so it either has been washed by the flood waters further down the river, or it is snagged underwater, where it will remain till the waters fall and the gases of decay bloat the body and float it blimplike to the river's surface.

— Gaia Head —

The rain continues.

Heavy upon their tents, heavy upon the rainforest, heavy upon the surrounding mountains down which race the tributaries that fill the Franklin.

Just as night falls the despondent camp has a new and strange arrival: a tatty yellow rubber raft paddled by the bald dancer they met some days previous. He is very cold and has lost, in addition to his entire supply of food, something but not all of his previous arrogant distance.

He is given the warmest spot by the fire and he is given a bowl of vegetable curry, complete with sweet potato, which for all its aggressive energy he accepts with gratitude. He tells them his story and it is this.

On the day following their previous meeting, the woman with the nose-flute had declared her undying affection for both men and her physical desire to be with the man with dreadlocks. Enraged and embittered – for it had been the bald man who had organised the entire river trip in the first place, and who had funded their plane fare from Sydney – enraged and embittered and plain jealous, a fact he now freely admitted, he decided the party would be best split into two groups. He then announced that one group would be him, the other them. He set off immediately, but the following day met with bad luck when his raft was overturned in a rapid and swept off downriver. He spent a miserable night in the rainforest without food or clothes or fire, covered only in manfern fronds, cursing the river and the woman and his best friend. The following day he had to come to a decision as to whether to wait for his two ex-friends, which, as he now admits, would probably have been the most sensible option, or whether to attempt to find the raft and catch up with Aljaz's party. Pride in his own capacities and his desire to take his leave of the others prevailed, and he set off scrub-bashing his way down the river. At about mid-afternoon (here, having lost his watch, he was imprecise on detail) he discovered his ruck-sack with his clothes and his sleeping bag washed up in an eddy. Heartened, he continued his walk the next day in the heavy rain, to finally find his raft snagged on some sticks on his side of the river. He fashioned a new paddle out of a tea-tree trunk, string, and his enamel plate and plastic bowl which had been in the rucksack, and thus curiously equipped had continued downriver hoping to catch up with Aljaz's group.

The bigger rapids he has been forced to navigate that day have left him terrified and humbled. He asks Aljaz if he can henceforth travel with his party. Aljaz and the Cockroach agree. His name, he says, is George, but the Cockroach immediately announces that for the rest of the trip he will be called Gaia Head, because it seems to fit him much better than George as a name. At which Gaia Head looks away and shrugs his shoulders. Having decided to take their food and their shelter and their knowledge of the river, he now has no choice but to take their name.

Gaia Head wonders why they had been so grave and quiet when he told them his story. Until Sheena (Why her? I wonder now. Why was it she who had the courage that had abandoned the Cockroach and me?) tells him what she knows of what has passed that day at the Churn.

'Jeezus,' says Gaia Head. 'It was only meant to be a fucken holiday.' And shakes his head, now stubbled with circles of black hair, as if iron filings have been thrown upon it, his mind the determining magnet.

By the next morning the river is slapping within half a metre of their lowest tent. The mood of the punters is depressed and frightened. The Cockroach tells them, because he must, what he had not told them or Gaia Head the night before, tells them exactly what happened down the cliff, and bursts into tears in the middle of it. Aljaz, ashamed, guilty, says nothing. The punters stop asking him their insistent questions, which are now all directed to the Cockroach, who is seen as the real trip leader.

The rain continues.

They break camp quickly, partly because they must clear the gorge before the flood waters rise any higher, partly because of the forlorn hope of finding Derek, or at least his body. Down the slimy boulders of the Coruscades they work, carrying bags, paddles and ammo boxes, like ants carrying crumbs to the nest, they scurry up and over the boulders that dwarf them. Racing before them are the Cockroach and Aljaz dragging and lifting and pulling the rafts. Aljaz feels himself possessed. Of a madness made up of guilt and anger and shame about what has passed. And the madness makes him feel powerful and invulnerable, because he no longer has cares or fears about himself. And he knows that the Cockroach feels the same. Their work has become the expression of their madness. They feel no pain as their lungs sear with their efforts of racing with heavy loads over the uneven gorge boulders; or, rather, they feel the pain but they want to feel it more, wish it to hurt so much that the pain might extinguish all the guilt and shame and anger they feel about Derek. And their work is a fury, because they are mad and because they are caught in a frenzy, because they must get through the gorge quickly as the river is rising and they must keep ahead of the flood peak. For the portage to work quickly the guides must take the rafts, food barrels and their own gear through in the time most punters take to carry just their gearbags to the bottom of the rapid. The Cockroach and Aljaz race back for the next load, exhorting and praising the red-faced punters as they stumble and fall with their small waterproof gearbags and solitary paddles. And the punters look at them and their own fear is amplified by their guides' madness, for what they had only dimly felt as a titillating apprehension they now know as a truth: the river is not benign, the river is dangerous, the river kills. And their own fear is amplified by their guides' new lack of fear, by the inhuman loads they carry and the speed at which they labour and the way they seem to have become as unpredictable and as insane as the river itself. 'Good on ya, keep it up, let's keep her moving,' exhort the guides. But the punters only stare back in terror, at the guides and at the river. They move only because their fear of remaining is greater than their fear of moving.

Down the rapid they advance, then back into the rafts to shoot the bottom rapids of the Coruscades, Gaia Head's raft tied onto the gear frame, Gaia Head taking Derek's place in a big raft to shoot the big rapids, and although Aljaz partly wraps his raft on a rock, and takes in a lot of water, they keep moving on down the river. They take the easy chutes on the left-hand side of the next two rapids, paddle a few hundred metres then pull into the bank. Down the rocks on the left of the huge Thunderush rapid they advance, their teamwork now a sight to behold in the pouring rain, forming long human chains up and over the rain-darkened and slimy boulders, throwing bags and gear from one to the next. The podgy faces of the punters drip perspiration, though the gorge is chill, and they smack their tongues up beneath their noses, tasting their own moisture, still strong even though diluted by the rainwater running over them. They marvel at the fresh brine of their bodies, a taste unknown to them since childhood. Beneath their stinking wetsuits their pastry-coloured flesh bruises easily, like overripe fruit. Their feet hurt and their backs ache and the air rushes down their throats like a licking flame. Down the bank they race against the rising waters, and who knows who is going faster? Their wetsuits feel slippery with their sweat and though the day is cold the weather has long since ceased to worry them. They know only one thing: that they must get through the gorge before the flood peak reaches and overruns them. Their fear is all-encompassing. The gorge is death, and they want to put it behind them before it claims another one of their number. United in their fear and purpose they now talk little, and their exhilaration at their unity keeps their minds from falling off the tightrope into total fear. And racing back and forth between them, carrying ever greater loads, are their lifelines back to their real world: their gaudily clad guides. Exhorting, running, helping, running, praising, running. And searching, looking everywhere, in every eddy, around each partly submerged rock and every flooded bush, in the hope of finding Derek's body. And all the time it keeps on raining and the river continues to rise, its brown-foamed edges eating up the sides of the banks.

Occasionally the punters rest and look up from the rocks and see and hear and smell the massive moving force that is the river. In flood it is no longer the calm, serene, mild watercourse, little more than a creek, they had known until two days ago. It is an extraordinary physical presence that cannot be denied. The entire gorge seems to vibrate with the sound of its rapids. Its low hum is punctuated by the rumble of huge boulders being rolled along, clacking and cracking and groaning in their work of reshaping the riverbed, and by the clump of water-borne trees and logs colliding with low-lying riverbank trees, through which the flood waters now manoeuvre. The whole river is like a huge army on the march, over-running the countryside, taking all before it, collecting ever greater strength from every dripping moss-lined rock face, from every overexcited stream. And the rafting party are like refugees, seeking to avoid its power, seeking to avoid its wrath and its moments of terrible violence; and their momentum, like that of refugees, is inexorably linked to that of the martial movement of the river. They look down at their next footstep, trying to reorient this cracking, roaring world with their own human scale, back to something they can comprehend and control.

And Aljaz wonders was one day camped on the bank enough respect? It was his fault. It was he who had failed to listen to the shushing of the bending tea-trees, to read the swirls in the river properly, to read the way they had snaked toward the bank at the campsite, to understand the ebbs and flows of the little boils out in the current. They had all tried to warn Aljaz and he, who knew their language, had ignored them.

At the bottom of the Thunderush portage they come to a very big rapid which they must shoot. Aljaz and the Cockroach sense that there can be no time for contemplation, or doubts will set in with the punters. And the river guides, in their madness, have no fear of the rapid as they rightly ought. They shout instructions over the roar as they methodically load the portaged gear back into the boats. They get in the boats and Aljaz talks the rapid through with his customers, pointing out the line he wishes to take through the mêlée of huge waves and surging white water. He spins the raft into the current and suddenly feels terribly small. He feels the force of the rapid pick the raft up and start to rush it down toward the big fall. The boat spins around too far and Aljaz is heading into the drop with the raft in the suicide position – sideways to the drop. 'Hard left! Hard left!' he yells to his punters, but they are overwhelmed by the force of the water, by the sheer volume of noise, by the spray and waves confusing their senses. They no longer know where they are, whether or not they have shot the drop or are yet to go over it. Their strokes are out of time and ineffectual. Aljaz realises he has lost control of the raft. The punters realise that Aljaz has lost control and stop paddling, some screaming, all futilely turning their bodies sideways to the rapid, averting their faces from the huge waves as though this might save them. Aljaz puts in a massive reverse sweep with his paddle and manages to turn the boat a little around from its sideways position, just as they reach the lip of the fall. *'Fall into the centre!'* he screams. *'Fall in!'* he screams as he grabs Marco and throws him onto the floor of the raft and then throws himself over Marco and hangs on to the netting with his left hand. He feels the boat rear up near vertical as it falls over the drop, and looks up to see massive walls of white water crashing on every side, crashing down on their puny craft, to see one side of the raft again rear up almost vertical. His and Marco's bodies slide from one side of the raft to the other as the raft is rocked and buffeted and thrown hither and thither like a paper bag in a gale.

And then Aljaz realises that he is not flailing desperately in the rapid, not being sucked down deep into the river's entrails to then be suddenly tossed up to the surface just before his body is swept over another fall, realises they are through the drop and have not been flipped and that they are all still somehow, miraculously, in the raft and not swimming down the rapid. He sits back on the pontoon and sees that they are heading towards the rocks on the left. 'Paddle!' he yells and he scruffs and pulls the punters in the back of the boat with all his might into a sitting position. 'Paddle hard!' And then as they start to paddle he continues to shout just one word until they are all paddling in rhythm with his cry. 'Hard! Hard! Hard!' The boat flops sideways into a small stopper and temporarily stalls its downward descent. The stopper is not big enough to flip the raft. Aljaz uses the moment and the stopper to help him turn the boat to the right.

As the raft exits from the stopper it slowly, ponderously begins to turn and then they are heading right and they are safe. Aljaz jumps to his feet. He looks from the rear of the raft back up at the enormous rapid they have just descended and throws a defiant fist in the air. *'Yes!'* he screams. *'Yes!'* And as he punches the air again and again he feels the excitement, the old excitement back, the feeling of being one with the rapid's power and the gorge's passion, the feeling of belonging and living. For a few brief moments everything else is forgotten, even Derek's death, in the wonder of their achievement. He turns around to face the punters and grins. 'You dopey bastards – *look.*' And he waves his arm around behind his body to encompass the surging white immensity of the rapid that is their backdrop, against which their raft is a bobbing red speck. 'That was you.' The punters are unbelieving. Aljaz's body feels as if it has exploded into the gorge. He feels every slap of water and bead of rain as a caress, feels the warmth blowing down from the rainforest on the back of his neck and the cold rising from the river as a massage of the senses, sees every detail of the gorge as if it has all come into focus from a previous blur, sees every hue of every colour, sees every droplet of the mist rising from the waterfall, distinguishes every sound of the rapid and the boat. He feels as if he is the rainforest and the river and the rapid. It as though time has stopped and he has been given infinity with which to explore and know every aspect, every detail of this wondrous moment. The punters do not move. 'We are top of the wazza,' says Aljaz to them. 'I love you. I love you all.' Aljaz replaces his grin with a brief solemn glance and puts his hand upon Marco's shoulder. 'At this moment I even love Marco.' He knows he looks ridiculous, a soggy Napoleon thanking his troops. So he exaggerates his own absurdity by revelling in it, leaping about the raft, kissing them on their helmets in the manner of a possessed missionary anointing heads, laughing, screaming, 'Yes!' repeatedly and, 'Top of the bloody wazza!', occasionally throwing his fist in the air. 'Yes! Yes! Yes!' Then he looks down at the punters and he sees in their faces only terror, only the knowledge that they might follow Derek. There is no ecstasy on their part. They are too frightened of what is to come to acknowledge what has been achieved. And the moment of oneness vanishes. Aljaz feels the weight of Derek's death fall back upon him, feels his fear rise up to meet it, feels his own failure again and again and again.

'You're insane,' says Sheena from the front of the raft. Her voice is sullen. At this moment she speaks for all the punters.

'Yeah,' says Aljaz. In the face of their terror he feels the remnants of his excitement ebb away. 'Maybe,' he says coldly, 'maybe I am.' Nobody says anything in reply. He senses they will trust him in so far as they have to, but that he now frightens them. He feels distant, sad, cold, separate, like a moss-etched rock looking down upon the raft that bobs around at the base of the huge rapid. But he does not say it. He says words that he thinks may reassure them, that will join them together rather than pull them apart. 'One more easy portage around the final waterfall, an hour of easy paddling after that and we're out of Deception Gorge.' With buckets they bail out the water they have shipped. 'What I'm trying to say,' says Aljaz almost pleadingly, throwing a bucket of water into the river, 'is that you're nearly out of the bloody gorge.'

They watch the Cockroach's crew shoot the rapid. From so far away the Cockroach's raft looks like a bobbing toy boat and they fear for him and his crew almost as much as they just feared for themselves. The Cockroach takes his time. He carefully lines his raft up in the top eddy to avoid the mistake that Aljaz made of being swept sideways. Three times they go to break into the rapid then halt at the last moment as the Cockroach stops because the line is not quite correct. Then they disappear into the waves and reappear at the top of the drop in the correct position. They disappear into the fall and reemerge heading right, making it through the remainder of the rapid easily. Now through the big rapids, Gaia Head unties his small raft from the gear frame and flops it into the river. And jumps in. Although it is only a short distance to the next portage he seems keen to establish some small independence. Together the two big rafts with the small yellow raft drift the remaining few hundred metres downriver.

From above, it looks beautiful. Mist rises from the line at which the river abruptly ends and the waterfall they call the Cauldron begins. The two bright red rafts drift together toward the fall in the dimming afternoon light. Around the rafts are the slow-moving long trails of white froth produced by the big rapids upriver, intricate Paisley designs, all swirls within swirls.

Running down the right-hand side of the Cauldron is

a huge sloping rock slab. Only a few metres wide at the top of the waterfall, it is ten or more metres wide at its base, cutting a quarter of the way diagonally across the fall. It is down this slab that the rafts are portaged. Aljaz, knowing the way, goes first. A hundred metres out from the rapid he heads his raft river right, hugging the right-hand cliff face as he approaches the Cauldron. Aljaz only has to be a few metres out from the cliff face, out where the current runs stronger, and his boat will be swept down the waterfall. Rather than steer from the back of the raft as he normally does, Aljaz is steering from the front, holding the furled bow rope between his hand and the paddle shaft. There is a little notch in the rock slab, perhaps a third of the width of the front of the boat, into which Aljaz deftly places the raft. The moment the pontoon touches the rock slab, he is out of the raft scrambling up onto the rock slab with the bow rope. As he anchors the raft, he exhorts his punters to quickly get out. Once the raft is empty of people they drag it up onto the slab so that it cannot be washed down the waterfall, which begins its river-wide cascade less than two metres from where they stand. The punters look across the massive slab and at the huge gorge that seems to close in above and over them. 'Awesome,' says Marco, looking up. Aljaz looks down, using his eyes to find a secure foothold in the slimy rock.

The Cockroach follows Aljaz's line, choosing to stay in the rear of his raft. He notices a sea eagle sitting halfway up a dead myrtle stag on the opposite side of the river. They hit the rock slab and Aljaz's seizes their bow rope and heaves the front of the raft up onto the rocks. The punters scramble out like some military landing party.

And last comes Gaia Head, who, now fed and with the

knowledge that the worst is almost over, has regained some of his former ways. He kneels in his raft, surveying the vastness of the gorge around him, as if he is a mad being who has taken possession of this land and who, as property owner, is allowed to do as he pleases. Like a New Age squire he drifts the final distance toward the waterfall, acknowledging the waves of Aljaz and the Cockroach to come in closer to the dead water at the cliff edge with a slight ironic smile but with no action. He allows his raft to drift further into the main current, believing that because there is no rapid there is no power to the water, believing once again in his own capacity to be whatever he wants, to go wherever he wants. As the waves of the guides turn into yells, he nonchalantly dips the eating-bowl blade of his bush paddle into the river to turn the raft toward the river's edge, to take it toward the notch in the boulder. But the initial stroke has no effect, nor the second, nor even the third nor the more frantic fourth nor the entirely desperate fifth and sixth and seventh strokes. His scrawny arms are flailing the tea-tree connected bowl and enamel plate through the air, the only effect to spin the raft round so that he is being swept ever faster toward the waterfall in a backward rather than a forward position.

The Cockroach and Aljaz are now screaming and their screams awaken Gaia Head to his only recently forgotten terror. At which point Gaia Head remembers how the guides could not save Derek and, panicking, stands up in his raft and dives into the water. He swims away from the raft toward the rock slab, which, because it is only three metres away, he thinks he will reach easily, whatever the fate of the raft. He makes some progress, but a metre from the rock slab the current grabs Gaia Head's bobbing body, ungainly freestyling in its kapok life jacket, like a huge hand sweeping a table of crumbs. And drops it over the lip of the waterfall.

From above, on the rock slab, Aljaz and the punters watch the whole event unfold with a sickening sense of doom. As Gaia Head disappears over the drop, the Cockroach manages to get his raft back into the safe dead waters of the side of the river. Aljaz feels his fear creeping through his body, wanting to paralyse him. *Again*, thinks Aljaz with dread. *Again*. And then suddenly, before he has even decided what he will do or if he can do anything, he is shouting out, 'No,' and he is running, unclipping a throw-bag from his side as he does so, running down the edge of the wet slippery rock slab, and he knows that this time, whatever it takes, this time he will do it. This time he is terrified but he does not care; this time, for the first time ever, he has said no and will not do nothing and will do something. He is exhilarated and he feels free at last, at long long last, and at that precise moment he feels his left shoe lose its grip on the rock and he feels himself tumbling, falling over the edge, feels his body hit the water as a surprisingly gentle rushing softness, feels himself tumbled by the water, and then feels himself suddenly slam to a halt, feels rocks grip around his hips and his chest like tightening vices, feels the water that was for a few seconds benign, change its character immediately to that of a mad rushing sadist that forces his head and body forward and down and under.

And he knows this moment has been a long time coming.

— Ten —

And so I see them all now, standing on the rock slab above my body, below my vision, wondering what to do and what is to happen and whether or not this is the death of a man they are witnessing, and whether they would feel more attracted to the event if I died or if I lived, and feeling bad for thinking such things. The latter event is dramatic, but the former tastes of vicarious tragedy and has greater appeal for them. I can see them all, see their faces, see Otis and Marco, ever sensible, standing back from the edge of the rock slab; Rickie, ever foolish, standing too close to the edge; Gaia Head, lunar dome dripping and only a little chastened by his terrifying swim down the waterfall. And Sheena, sweet Sheena whom I thought crippled, looking at the Cockroach to make sure that what is happening is all right. Last, I see the Cockroach, and he is so scared, because only he knows the full enormity of what has happened and his powerlessness to alter any of it. He takes refuge in activity, ever more frantic activity, and refuses to acknowledge to the punters what he and I both know: that there is no

305

way out, that I cannot be rescued with the water so high and rising all the time. I want to hold the Cockroach like a child and tell him I love him and tell him not to be frightened, because I am not.

But although I can see them, they cannot see me. They stand on the vast rock slab that slopes down the side of the waterfall and stare into the violent, agitated torrent. And sticking up, not very far from the rock slab, is my hand. It is so close that they are able to grasp arms and legs and form a human chain out to my hand. The Cockroach is at the end of the chain, only a metre or so out from the side of the rock slab, dangling dangerously above the water's fury, his fingertips just touching mine. My hand throbs back and forth, in resonance with the violence of the falling cataract, like a jammed tree branch. My fingers and the Cockroach's outstretched fingers entwine. I feel his horror, and through my fingers try to reassure him.

But he cannot see me. I am hidden and being destroyed by this beautiful water, so clean and chill it feels as if someone has taken to my throat with a grinder that has a disc made of ice. This water, this water the colour of tea, this water so famed for its reflective qualities. When I open my eyes and stare into this wild brown turbulence of bubbles and water, I never see myself reflected, only others, only the faces of others, and I am strangely pleased to have their company.

For some time now my mind has felt oddly clear, its contents no longer a hurdy-gurdy of images and faces I cannot keep hold of, but, on the contrary, a bizarre, detached line of thoughts that seek to rationally understand where I am.

This line of thoughts begins in an exploration of my

306

physiological condition, which is clearly unusual and which forms a backdrop to all my other thoughts. From a first-aid course I remember that there are two types of drowning: wet drowning and dry drowning. In the former instance water pours into the lungs and floods them, rendering them useless and their possessor dead in a relatively short time. In the second, more interesting, and more common variant of drowning, a flap of the oesophagus flicks shut to prevent water entering the lungs. The body proceeds to shut down all but its most vital activities, rationing its most precious resource, oxygen, to its most precious organs. The heart can even cease to beat, but the brain remains alive, fed by tiny life-sustaining quantities of oxygen. In this instance it takes considerably longer to drown, and there are documented cases of people being pulled out of the water some hours after entering it, technically dead, yet who are brought back to life.

I can no longer see or feel the water which envelops me, am aware neither of its force, its patterns of movement around my body, nor its intense coldness. To the extent that I feel anything, I feel my body swaying and rocking, presumably from the water sweeping over and about it. But this is only presumption. I can no longer even be entirely sure that it is my body. Perhaps through some strange extra sense I have become aware of the movement of something else. Perhaps it is not a body after all, but the bough of a fallen tree, a myrtle perhaps, washed down by the rising waters. Part of the branch is thrashing around, and part of my mind tells me that this is my rescuers tugging away at my arm. But that also can now only be presumption. I can no longer know whether my arm is being cruelly wrenched this way or that in futile attempts to save me, can no longer know whether I am in agony or whether agony has become so all-encompassing that I no longer have anything to judge it against as my normal state of being. If I no longer feel any physical sensation yet can still think, then surely, I think to myself, surely I am still alive. Aware that I have been entombed in the water for what would seem to those above an infinity, and aware that I therefore should be dead, the notion of dry drowning appears no longer as a thought but as a solace. And it leads to a paradox: if I am only dying in this fashion, I reason, then there is a good chance I might live.

But immediately I think this, I am assailed by all sorts of doubts. The worst, the darkest question that insists upon me acknowledging it is this – who is this drowning?

There is no easy, quick answer. I wish to cry out that is surely me, Aljaz Cosini, river guide; wish to continue seeing in the river my life as evidence of who I am. But these thoughts, these images of childhood, of love and fear, of desire and loss, are weak.

And what is strong, what overrides all sense of progression and cohesion in my life, is the sensation of being nothing more than an outline.

I feel as if I am one of those figures that police chalk around twisted, bloodied corpses at car-accident sites. These chalk outlines remain on the bitumen for days, sometimes weeks, until the elements and countless car tyres eliminate them. People pass by and wonder who these chalk outlines were, with their strange distended limbs and empty faces, without ears to hear or eyes to see. I feel as if I am at once one of those curious passers-by and the chalk outline. Who is this? I ask of myself.

And, as if in reply, I realise I am floating above everything that has been my life, my time, my place. And yet, as I look beneath me it all seems so strange, for what should have cohesion, what should have progression and identity, has none of these things. All I can hear is confused and crazed babble. I feel myself nothing more than an outline without substance, without identity or individuality. Below I hear only gibberish. What does it mean, I wonder, all those crazed and contradictory words? How was it possible for me to once root myself in that nonsense and derive meaning and purpose from it? Maddening thoughts assail me. In an age when everything can mean anything, perhaps it is only possible to exist as a cipher, as a thin, fragile outline of a hope etched across an infinity of madness.

I see the figures crudely cut from steel plate by oxy-torch that lined the fence on Molle Street near where Couta lived in Hobart. The feet of the steel figures seek to escape the scorching steel flames that form the bottom of the fence, while their arms are extended toward the sky, toward the immense aqua presence of the mountain behind Hobart, lined at its summit by apricot clouds. Suspended between hell and heaven, simultaneously in agony and knowledge, unable to distinguish between either. Is that me? Is that me?

Before I have time to arrive at an answer, I feel a long skinny tube being pushed with some violence into my left eye.

What the Christ is going on!

I resent this action, not so much for the pain it creates, which is negligible compared to the burden of pain the rest of my body is carrying, but because it represents an unnatural indignity. Here I am getting on with the business of drowning – indeed, almost to the point of being resigned to it – when I get a piece of tube rammed into my face. Not only that, but they – whoever my unkind rescuer is, I can only presume it is the Cockroach – begin to blow through the tube, causing a furious bubbling around my face that tickles it.

Madonna santa!

Let me die in peace, I would shout, were it not that I only have water to mouth words with. The tube, after being temporarily rammed up my nose, finds my mouth and penetrates with some force my lips. Air is forced into my mouth, thereby forcing the water in my mouth and throat down into my stomach from which it rapidly returns accompanied by the burnt porridge I had for breakfast. The tube ejects from my mouth followed by a minor eruption of vomit. After a few similar, though smaller, eruptions, my rescuers finally succeed in keeping the tube in my mouth and getting air into my body.

Am I to live? Is my life to be saved? Am I finally to be made visible? Other people who nearly die go down a tunnel and see a great light at the end. But all I have seen are people, the whole lot of them, swirling, dirty, smelly, objectionable and ultimately lovable people, and, I think, if it is to be my misfortune to return into the lamentable physical vessel that has been my body, it is them – these people in the kitchens and office blocks and suburbs and pink leisure suits – that I must learn to make my peace with.

The clammy tube twists and turns and pulses air bubbles into my waterlogged body, bringing it literally back to its senses. This is not pleasant for me. I cease being a chalk outline seeking my world and return to being a mass of agonised, tortured flesh, whose sensations and impressions are only of the most immediately physical: the chill of the water, the fire in my chest, the jackhammer pounding in my head, the screams of my legs and torso, the pain like a red-hot poker across the shoulder of my upright arm. I am struck by the thought that death is nowhere as violent as life.

Suddenly the tube stops ferociously aerating my innards and goes strangely slack within me, then casually writhes out of my mouth like a tired tiger snake to wash away with the furious currents down the waterfall. I cannot see what has happened. I can only presume that someone – perhaps Rickie, perhaps Marco – has accidentally dropped the tube from the rock slab above. Dropped the tube and with it my chance of living.

– Black Pearl, 1828 –

My visions are growing shorter and more confused. I am unable to stay for long with those that appear, and before I am even sure what it is I am seeing, it is gone again. I see things, so many things, so many different worlds, though they come into focus but briefly and blur away again before I have time to make sense of them.

Now that my pain has dissolved into something beyond pain, there is not even the progress of my suffering to act as a timepiece to the onset and disappearance of my visions. I no longer know whether the vision I am seeing refers to another vision I've had, or whether my deranged mind with virtually no oxygen is constructing a complete and total world when there is no totality to know, only this bizarre series of fragments that seem so real and seem to somehow make sense. I feel dimly aware that I am seeing less and that I must fight this sensation.

I look through these murky waters, so turbulent on the surface yet here just pleasant swirls of bubbles, and I can see Harry standing beside his grandmother, the one everyone called Auntie Ellie. She looks like a shrivelled dark plum.

But the more I look at her, the more the wrinkles and lines dissolve, until a young girl is looking back at me. She looks at me for quite some time, examines my nose and eyes. She beckons me to come with her, turns and heads away, down through a sandy track around which the fleshy green pigface with its crimson flowers grows. She gives me some to eat. The track winds through dense boobialla bush and we walk for a long time, so long, in fact, that night falls and a near-full moon rises before our journey comes to an end. The track winds down to a beach, at the end of which there is dancing light.

We make our way towards the light and after a time it becomes possible to distinguish a white man and three black women sitting around a fire. The women look bedraggled and drunk. The man looks worse. All four are clad in strange combinations of seal and kangaroo skins crudely stitched together.

And I know, though I have no way of knowing, that this man is a sealer, the women slaves he has stolen from a Tasmanian tribe and brought to this remote island in Bass Strait to slay seals and dry their skins.

They are arguing about God. 'Is he a big fella?' asks one woman with a walleye.

'He like hunting kangaroo?' asks another. 'How he walk? Like an echidna walk, like a whitefella, or he walk good and quiet like black people?' They are goading the sealer, who until this point has been too drunk to bother responding. His immediate interest lies in his right arm, with which he has been stroking the woman wearing a red woollen stocking cap, rubbing her breast up and down.

'The Lord God Almighty walks on water,' he says to her.

'He's a bloody platypus then,' says the woman who wears the black beanie, and all three women cackle. Emboldened, the woman in the red woollen stocking cap pushes the sealer's arm away and asks, 'How come white-fellas nail platypuses onto crosses?' The women laugh even more. The sealer's temper immediately changes from one of lecherous intent to anger at the jibe at his religion.

'You blaspheming bitches!' shouts the sealer, whose patience with this conversation is now exhausted. His sharp blue eyes flash. *His* sharp blue eyes.

The sealer grabs the woman with the red woollen stocking cap. She says nothing, but stares into his face. Into those blue eyes. He cuffs her with a methodical violence that I recognise. He slaps her on one side of the face and says something, then slaps her on the other side and says something else. And his voice is fierce.

'Learn this and learn it well.'

Slap.

'I was made in the image of our Lord.'

Slap.

'White.'

Slap.

'White.'

Slap.

'And God gave me dominion over all his creatures.'

Slap.

'Including you.'

Slap.

'Including you.'

Slap.

Then he throws her onto her belly and takes her from behind, like he does with sheep, his right arm jamming her head back in a headlock, reducing her struggles to jerks and twists of her body. She feels a white face behind her and she knows that she will never forget the fear and humiliation of this moment, knows that she will never forget, nor will her children nor the children they beget nor their children, even long after they have forgotten from where their terrible fear comes, long after they cease to understand why they are afraid. She feels his breath upon the nape of her neck, hot, like the rainforest breath of Werowa announcing a death. And she wonders, But whose death?

Here I am, witnessing this strange and tragic event, feeling the greasy sand beneath my feet, so close that I can smell the seal blubber and cheap rum on the sealer's breath, yet unable to find adequate material evidence to prove that what is happening is a reality I share. I would pick up the sealer's fine sealskin jacket rimmed with wallaby fur which lies just to the left of me as material evidence, but the young girl beside me, Harry's grandmother, Auntie Ellie, my great-grandmother, has hold of my right hand, and I can feel through her palm and her fingers that I must not move, and when I so much as make a small bodily movement, my lungs immediately fill with fire.

And so I watch, mute, passive, horrified, as the other women start laying into the sealer, belting him in the guts and in the head, trying to wrench him away, and then backing off when he pulls a pistol out of his pocket and waves it wildly.

The woman being raped begins to sing a strange and forlorn song. Her song sounds the emptiness of the beach and the ocean, echoes the distant cry of the sea eagle, calls for the return screech of the black cockatoo. 'Shut up, Black Pearl,' warns the sealer as he thrusts in and out. 'Shut up.'

But Black Pearl continues to sing to her brother the blue-tongue lizard, her mother the river, her father the rocks, her sister the crayfish that smells of woman.

'Shut up,' he says again, punctuating his words with blows to her head.

Still Black Pearl sings to her family. His blows having no effect, he looks around, then laughs with enlightenment. He places the barrel of the pistol in her mouth and rests the stump of a long lost finger on the trigger.

'This'll fix you,' he says and laughs again.

But still Black Pearl sings and sighs the cold metal in her mouth, the fear in her guts, the searing pain between her thighs – none of it can smother her song. On and on the song goes, till the man, sated, hoists up his breeches, lets her fall upon her side into the sand, and staggers away to find his rum bottle.

On and on the song goes, and after the sealer pukes and then falls asleep in a stupor, the two other women come over and lie together with Black Pearl. They lie together on the land on which they once stood with pride. As they warm one another on the beach, they join in the low song that seems to cover all the sand. The song and the sound of the waves become as one and on and on it goes, and though the women are now asleep the black cockatoo and the sea eagle sing. The wind in the boobiallas passes the song on to the wind in the gums, who teaches it to the wind in the myrtles and celery top pines, who then sings it to the river and to the rocks.

We are now so close I can see that Black Pearl, though asleep, has not closed her eyes. Her pupils are black. There are no tear stains. I realise I am witness to the conception of Auntie Ellie's mother and to the genesis of all that I am. I feel afraid. The black eyes begin to fill with swirls and dancing bubbles. I realise I am entrapped, entombed in this all-encompassing water.

On a white quartz-sand beach the aqua-green waves pounding insistently. A woman's cry of pain, smothered partly by something in her mouth, a man's quickening groan and then cry of triumph, then stillness. Then nothing.

But everywhere the song.

On and on it goes, and here in this godforsaken water I cannot rid my mind of its infernal sound.

And now, joining the song, I feel a dull thrumming that vibrates the very rocks which grasp my body. At the same time as I feel these vibrations I am able to see the cause of them — a helicopter with the bright logo of a commercial TV station. Who knows how it came to be here? Perhaps it is a TV crew out shooting some stock footage of the south-west wilderness whom the Cockroach has managed to signal from the ground, and the crew, to their simultaneous horror and delight, have stumbled upon an actual news story in the middle of nowhere. Who cares? Least of all me, who can only watch as the helicopter hovers in mid-air, side on to the flow of the river, its side door open.

From the occasional glint of reflected sunlight in the dark open doorway, I know what it is they are doing.

They are filming my death, the sight of my forearm and hand rising from the furious surging waters to my helpless and hapless would-be rescuers above, whose efforts have now been redoubled by the knowledge that they will be on national TV news in a few short hours. Their arrival has created an audience, and hence my death moves in their minds from the plane of hopeless futility to the altogether higher plane of tragic drama. None of which brings any solace to me. Their new-found energies are transmitted to me only as greatly increased pain in my raised arm and shoulder as they wrench it this way and that. And the knowledge of the helicopter being there only to record my fate rather than to act against it fills my soul with despair. The helicopter should be dropping men and equipment here, should be bringing its technology so that I might live, should abet my hope instead of recording my terrible, terrible despair. But as long as it remains, as long as the rocks pulse around me, then some chance remains. Surely after finishing filming they will come to my aid. Perhaps they are in contact via radio with another chopper which is at this very moment rushing the appropriate gear and personnel to this remote wilderness to ensure that I live. Perhaps they are simply assessing the situation thoroughly before taking action. No doubt they have some very clever plan to rescue me, but a plan which must be totally checked out before being put into action. My rescue can only be a few short minutes away now, maybe less. But my mind is already begin to drift again. I must stop it wandering.

What is a minute? How long have I been here? Minutes? Hours? Days?

How long can I stay here?

Not much longer.

No! No! Minutes! Hours! Days! I can last. I can.
I must live.
They cannot leave me here to die.
Please! Please! I am here, a human being. Please don't go!
But as these words scream through my mind, I feel the pulsing of the rocks dying away. The helicopter has enough footage of my death and is returning to Hobart to file its report in time for the evening news.

All my hope and despair and pain seems to leave with the chopper. All that remains is an immense stillness.

For the first time the contours of my true country become clear in my mind as the clouds of life fall beneath me and the blueness of death beckons from above.

— Eliza, 1898 —

Eliza closes her eyes. For a moment she has the most child-ish notion that there is a dinghy coming through the clouds to take her away. She opens her eyes and her old watery eyelids blink away the foolery of such a vision. For a second time, Eliza closes her eyes. For the final time.

Thinking: *Well say You in th. New Jerusalem.*

— Aljaz —

As I float a little above the river I can see a group of men trying to pull something out of a flood-swollen waterfall. Their work is difficult and dangerous. They stand on the edge of a greasy rock with a furious torrent raging down beside them. They wear blue overalls marked POLICE SEARCH AND RESCUE in bold white capital letters across the yoke. I can see a stiffened hand and forearm rising out of the whitewater. The men try all sorts of things with the body that is apparently connected to the hand, and which is underwater, submerged in the monstrous deafening roar of the river. They attach ropes to the hidden body, and radio in a helicopter that lowers a winch cable which they connect to the rope. The helicopter pulls gently.

'If it pulls hard,' I hear one man say, 'it might just rip the body's arms off, or, alternatively, it might pull the helicopter down from the sky.'

'It don't take much to pull down a little chopper like that,' another says. The attempt with the helicopter fails and it is waved off. The men give up for a while and light cigarettes.

They talk about the difficulty of getting the body out, of other awful jobs where drowned bodies are so decomposed that the flesh parts like mush when they grasp them and they are left holding nothing but an arm or leg bone. They nervously joke about cutting the body out with knives, severing it in half at the waist, thereby freeing both halves. They walk back to the edge of the rock, and wave their cigarettes in the direction of the outstretched hand as they discuss the technical difficulties of freeing the body.

Their chief stands near the top of the rock, talking to the departing chopper on a walkie-talkie. He looks a troubled man. No doubt the job is anything but a straightforward one for him. Perhaps he has promised his wife he will be home early. Or perhaps he is worried about what he will say to the media when he gets back to Hobart, and what the media will say about his efforts. Maybe he is unsure how they can free the body without mangling it. He notices the men near the edge of the rock slab and shouts at them.

'For Christ's sake, watch your step near the edge of the rock slab. Already claimed one fucking life.' The men go sullen and quiet.

One fucking life?

Whose life? I don't recall that anyone has drowned at this rapid.

One generation passeth away, and another generation cometh. But what connects the two? What remains? What abideth in the earth forever?

I hear a half-horse, half-snort laugh.

Who am I talking to?

I see two tables of riotous drunken animals blow down through the gorge above all our heads, and as they tumble past way up high I feel the gale that is taking them begin to lift me, and I notice that the animals seem to be looking less and less like animals and more and more like people. Then they are gone. I see a piners' punt laden with lost souls descending from the stormy skies, all beckoning toward me.

Madonna santa!

These visions, these crazy crazy visions. As if I have seen them all before. As if they are eternal. As if they have all been written before and as if there is nothing new under the sun, neither the pleasure nor the misery nor the tears nor the laughter of man. As if there is only one story and it could be writ on a pinhead and within it every story of every man. They come to me faster and faster now. Perhaps I always held these visions within me. From the moment of birth when I looked up through the milky red orb that imprisoned me to see those muscatel eyes of Maria Magdalena Svevo staring back. Or even earlier. Perhaps my mind was never a blank slate upon which my solitary experience was to write its own small story, unaware that it was but part of so many other stories. Perhaps that is why these visions are not solely of me but of a whole world that leads to where I am. And beyond. To where we all are going.

I feel the water swirling and whorling about me and over me and now through me, and joining it is my head forming similar swirls and whorls, my life essence spilling out from my ears and nose and mouth and arse and tangling itself into untieable Celtic knots with the water, which is no longer destroying me but remaking me as something else, and I am no longer sure if I am me, or me the river or the river me.

And at this point there is one final sensation of physical pain, as total and unbearable as it is shortlived, that reminds me forever of what I have been. The rocks crack one final time at my shins, and for one last eternal moment the swirling water pushes my body downwards and buffets my face, and at the point the heaviness of my body becomes an overwhelming agony I feel as if I have abruptly lost my anchor and am flying ever higher above the waterfall, far above the departing helicopter, lighter than a kite whose string has been cut. The police far below give up on the sheath knife idea and go back to brooding as sheets of rain drench them. I would like to stay and watch them, see what they will ultimately do to get the body out. Yes, I would like to observe this, it is interesting, but I feel myself rising and drifting ever quicker away from the narrow wild gorge and I know I can no longer return.

And as I so rise I am filled with a single, dreadful question.

Am I alone?

— Eleven —

An immensity of blue.

Sky-blue. A fleck, a piece of flyshit at the centre of this vast emptiness. Moving.

A soul.

My soul?

— Twelve —

I continued travelling for what seemed a very long passage of time. In the course of my interrupted journey I saw many things along the banks of the Franklin and Gordon rivers and upon the shores and waters of Macquarie Harbour. Things both strange and wondrous. I saw the earth bulge up into mountains, saw plants flowering, some large and dramatic, and cover the earth. Saw ice and snow form over much of the land, and the rainforest retreat into the lowest and warmest valleys. Saw giant wombats bigger than a man, and huge kangaroos and monster emus arrive. Saw people and their truth of fire arrive. Saw them create a new land in the image of fire: mesmerising yet confrontational, old as time yet new as a flame, destructive yet fecund. Saw the huge animals disappear completely. Saw the ice and snow largely disappear and the rainforest reappear. Saw white man arrive and saw the world turned upside down. I saw all this and much more besides, saw it all and continued on.

I saw pods of slaughtered whales, huge somnolent presences, flying over Frenchmans Cap, casting small shadows upon me who watched in awe below, saw swirling through their ranks colonies of slaughtered seals similarly airborne. Saw an Aboriginal village of beehive huts whose women had been stolen and who had returned with terrible stories and strange haunting songs, shared their fire and danced with them, and out of their shimmering hands they cast meteorites and where each meteorite landed there grew a mountain or a valley or a hill or a river or a forest through which I travelled. Passed a colony set up on an island inhabited by ex-convicts and run upon the strictest communal principles, the first among these people being a large matriarch with a ring of moles around her neck; I did not share their fire but passed on. Saw hulks emptying convicts along the Milky Way, their coarse woollen magpie outfits transformed into the ethereal colours of the vast southern aurora, and they were all swirling and smiling and free at last. They all spin around me now. Whales, people, trees, animals, birds. A tunnel of grace through which I continue to travel. But to where? I am floating down the river. But it is no river I recognise.

— and sees the morning light —

'We're here.'

Smeggsy looks up and he feels an incoming tide of sensations wash over him as his mind races back to join with his body: a physical exhaustion so great that the oar suddenly feels as if it were weighed down by a locomotive and beyond his powers to ever move again, a tiredness so profound that it seems too much effort to even sleep; an arse that feels like it is made of two river rocks; a mouth parched, with a pebble for a tongue; a clammy coldness of the body that frightens him. He is no longer seeing Old Bo's stories, but the morning light smacking the scattering of weatherboard shops and pubs that compose the front street of Strahan and which face directly onto the wharf; sees three cars parked outside the pub, the doctor's baby Austin, a Studebaker he doesn't recognise and an old rusty wood truck, sees the old wood fishing boats stacked high with their wired willow-stick cray pots.

'We've done it, Smeggsy.'

And Smeggsy looks up to see Old Bo's face crack into the biggest, craggiest smile he has ever seen light across the old bastard's face.

'We've bloody well done it.'

And in the great fat yellow light of the new morning Aljaz opens his eyes to see his home and his people, sees the mighty snow-capped Triglav rising up the back of Strahan, sees the wharf heavy with blackfellas and a whole host of others happily eating mullas and crayfish together, sees Black Pearl climb out of the harbour wet and sleek and black and as naked as a seal with a big crayfish in her hands. She walks right through that whole mob, until she is at the hub of them all, and everyone radiates out like spokes on a bicycle wheel from where she stands, right smack bang in the middle of all those people, and there it is, smoking and spluttering, Harry's celebrated bar-beque, spitting and flaring, the griddle full of roo patties on one side and cevapcici on the other, and people crowding all around it eager for a feed of Harry's famous abalone patties which are yet to be grilled over the myrtle coals, and people around it shoving and laughing and yarning with each other. Aljaz sees them and he sees *him*,

Harry, and he is squatting, pulling a fresh loaf of bread out of the adobe oven beneath the grill, and behind him and around him, there on the Strahan wharf, sees Ned Quade embracing Eliza Quade holding a half-gnawed drumstick in one hand, sees Rose, sees Sonja, sees a man who is the dead spit for Harry and it's his twin brother Albert and he's smoking rollies and talking with George and Basil and Boy Lewis, sees Milton sitting on the ground picking up slaters and snails, kissing them, then throwing them on the barbeque plate, much to Harry's displeasure, sees Eileen and Tronce, and George — already drunk — and he's bent over backwards showing a wart on his bum to be read by cousin Dan Bevan, sees Willie Ho and Reggie Ho and he's already chatting up Auntie Ellie, sees Reg with sauce upon his walrus moustache and a glass of beer in one hand and the baby Daisy in the other arm, sees them all, his home and his people.

And he hears the peat crumbling and smells the colours of it growing and at last he knows the song and he knows.

How much he loves them!

And he sees Black Pearl is holding something to her chest. From below her forearm falls a puffy shin and a yellow woollen bootee, and the yellow woollen bootee is kicking up and down, and he sees cradled within Black Pearl's arms Jemma, all cooing and laughing. Black Pearl takes Jemma's hand and points at him, and he hears her tell the child that the sea eagle she can see high up in the myrtle tree carries the spirits of her ancestors.

But before Black Pearl has finished speaking he feels a warm updraught, and rising with it his body, wings outstretched, feathers feeling every sensation of the criss-crossing air currents, rising in a spiral, a circle growing ever outwards.